FOOLS' RIVER

Also by Timothy Hallinan

The Poke Rafferty Series
A Nail Through the Heart
The Fourth Watcher
Breathing Water
The Queen of Patpong
The Fear Artist
For the Dead
The Hot Countries

The Junior Bender Series
Crashed
Little Elvises
The Fame Thief
Herbie's Game
King Maybe
Fields Where They Lay

The Simeon Grist Series
The Four Last Things
Everything but the Squeal
Skin Deep
Incinerator
The Man with No Time
The Bone Polisher
Pulped

FOOLS' RIVER

Timothy Hallinan

Published by
Soho Press, Inc.
853 Broadway
New York, NY 10003

Library of Congress Cataloging-in-Publication Data

Hallinan, Timothy.
Fools' river / Timothy Hallinan.

ISBN 978-1-61695-750-6
eISBN 978-1-61695-751-3

1. Travel writers—Fiction. 2. Bangkok (Thailand)—Fiction. I. Title.
PS3558.A3923 F66 2017 813'.54—dc23 2017011761

Printed in the United States of America

10 9 8 7 6 5 4 3 2 1

To Munyin Choy . . .
. . . now and as close to forever
as we can get

Part One
THE CURRENT

1

French or Swiss

THE BLINDS ARE drawn the way they've been drawn forever, with the inside edges of the slats tilted upward to block his view of the sky and the fall of sunlight through the window, which means he has no idea what time it is. Not that knowing would do him any good.

He had a watch once, a gold one, French or Swiss or something like that, European, but he hasn't seen it since he got here.

Wherever here is.

Why are the blinds angled that way? The woman who pretends to be a nurse said it was to keep the sun from shining into his eyes and waking him up in the morning. When he asked her to open them so he could see the sky, she'd ducked her head and said, "Mmm-hmmm," the way she always does when she means no. Her uniform has an old stain, the color of tea and shaped like a flying bird, over her right breast, and the surgical mask she always wears is smeared with dark lipstick on both sides, as though she puts it on without looking at it. Usually the edges of the red imprint curve up in a kind of smile. It's the same mask and the same uniform day after day after day. She wears the nurse's cap at an angle he supposes is meant to be jaunty, so far to one side that it requires a glittering little fence of bobby pins to keep it in place.

He hasn't seen her face since he woke up in this bed, although he saw it several times before, even knew her name, or at any rate a name she used. But now it's the mask, the lipstick, the cap, the "Mmm-hmmm"s. So in addition to trying to track the time of day, he's been worrying about what the mask might mean.

She hasn't opened the blinds. Still, a few days ago—four? six?—he'd noticed that the room gets a little brighter during the day, and he's pretty sure that it would get *dimmer* if his room were on the sunrise side of the hospital. So there, his mind *is* still working. Despite all the shit they're pumping into him.

Except, he thinks, he might have realized it twice. Or even three times. It's hard to keep track. But the most recent time the thought had presented itself, he'd marked it mentally, the way he used to do when he was in business and drowning in information; he tied it to something everyday. The client with the pointed nose was Mr. Byrd; the office suite was 321, the *final countdown* in that awful, unforgettable song. It always worked. So this time he chose "Sunday," putting all the energy he could summon into chalking it on the wall in his mind. *Sunday. Sun day. The* sun *brightens as the* day *goes on: Sunday.*

So now he knows she lied to him about the blinds; if the sunlight ever reached his bed, it would be in the early evening, just before it set. And there's one *other* thing that she's not aware he knows. There's water outside. For a few hours every day, probably when the sun is highest, the ceiling just above the window *ripples.* It's got to be the sun, reflected off water and bouncing up through the angled blinds.

A *klong,* maybe? Bangkok is full of them, a fractal tangle of waterways, mostly brown and usually sluggish, with a thick skin of casual sewage despite recent cleanup campaigns, afloat on water from the Chao Phraya, the river that splits the city in two, like the center of a giant blighted butterfly: the river its spine, its wings the filthy city through which the *klongs* meander. So knowing that there's a *klong* out there—if there is—doesn't help much. Hell, it could be a swimming pool.

His nose itches. Now that he can't reach it, it always itches. The woman who's not a nurse cuffed both his hands to the frame of the hospital bed the day he tried to remove the IV drip. He'd guessed that whatever mixtures of dope they were giving him, they were in the drip. So he'd crimped the tube and then given it a yank, but it had set off some kind of alarm, and she'd come in with the doctor right behind her. The doctor, who was the size of a house, *enormous* for a Thai, had the cuffs in his hand. That was early on the day—he's *almost* certain it was the same day—that he woke up, maybe eight hours later, with a cast on his left leg. Hard as he tries, and he hasn't got much else to do, he can't remember breaking it.

She put in a new drip an hour or so ago, her mask upside down today so the corners of the red lip print angle down. The room seems to be changing size: bigger, smaller, bigger, smaller. His eyes close.

What was it about Sunday?

2

He's Prettier Than I Am

VIOLET IS HER *color*.

It's taken her years to learn that. To learn—she thinks with a little tingle that's not quite intense enough to call a thrill—that she even *has* a color. She never had a color before. When she was small, all her clothes had been worn to tatters in the process of being outgrown by half a dozen older kids and brutally washed hundreds of times. They'd had suds pummeled into them, they'd been pounded against the river's unyielding stones, they'd been wrung out and then hung to fade in the sun so many times that they had no recognizable color left. If they had any hue at all, it was a pale memory of having once been red, yellow, blue, or (her least favorite) brown. She hated brown. Brown gave her goosebumps, even in the hot season. Even faded. Even now, years later.

And, of course, the things she wore then hadn't been very colorful even when they were new, because they'd been *boys'* clothes. Boys don't have colors. What would they do with them?

But now she can wear pretty clothes, and in the colors she loves. Now she can wear violet.

And there it is, *her* color, two small circles of it, gleaming up at her from the top of a tiny box. Even the English word "violet."

"Those," she says. Pointing down through the glass top of the cabinet, she's suddenly aware that the brassy sheen of her "gold" bracelet wouldn't fool a twelve-year-old runaway from rural Myanmar.

She yanks her hand back and smooths the sleeve of her violet-colored dress over it. She already knows that the woman behind the counter disapproves of her. No reason to flaunt her hundred-baht jewelry.

"*Which* one?" the woman asks, her voice thickly frosted with patience. The saleswoman is middle-aged, not made any more attractive by a heavy layer of makeup that Lutanh mentally scrubbed off and redid the moment she came into the store. The saleswoman is obviously unhappy about many things—maybe being ugly, for one, and *certainly* having to wait on Lutanh. "I can't read your mind," the woman says.

"The violet ones," Miaow says, giving the woman's tone back to her, so pitch-perfect that Lutanh's head snaps around to stare at her friend. "The ones she's *pointing* at." Miaow can feel Lutanh's gaze and then her smile, but gratitude embarrasses her, so she swivels her stool to the window with its rows of dusty eyeglass frames and, beyond them, its view of the steamy Silom sidewalk. Behind her she hears the case slide open and Lutanh saying, "No, that one please," in her Lao-inflected Thai, and then one of the kids from Miaow's school goes by, talking animatedly into her phone.

Miaow looks at her new watch on its wide yellow patent-leather strap. "Bus just dropped everybody off," she says over her shoulder. "I should take a cab more often." She checks the time again, partly because she loves the watch, which Lutanh chose for her half an hour ago from the table of a sidewalk vendor—all of them identically uninteresting until Lutanh picked up this one—and partly because the two of them have only forty minutes to get to Dr. Srisai's acting class.

Behind her, Lutanh says, "How do I put them in?"

There's no reply, just a silence that grows ruder by the second. Miaow turns to see Lutanh hunched over the optometrist's counter, transfixed by the color on the box, her copper-dyed hair with its possibly natural curl falling around her shoulders to frame the profile Miaow desperately envies: the perfectly sculpted nose (Lutanh says the third try was the charm, after it was broken), the naturally full lips, the delicate curve of the chin. The saleswoman is leaning back in her cheap, ugly folding chair, her mouth pulled tight and her arms crossed as though to put as much distance between her and Lutanh as possible, and Miaow says, "She asked you how to put them in."

The saleswoman had been pleasant enough until, sitting on the other side of the counter from Lutanh, barely three feet away, she had realized that Lutanh was a ladyboy. To Miaow the woman says, "Are her hands clean?"

Miaow gets up. "Come on, Lutanh, get your stuff." She gestures at the knapsack with the shiny handmade wings sticking out of it. "You don't need this person in your life, and I'm sure no one else does either."

"I *want* these," Lutanh says, and beneath the wispy voice, insubstantial as steam, Miaow hears a note she's learned to recognize in the past months, the steely undertone of someone who has transformed herself through sheer will from an impoverished, scrawny, miserable teenage boy in a pig-filled village in Laos into a remarkably beautiful *katoey*—although Lutanh thinks of herself as a woman or, more accurately, a girl—earning good, if karmically damaging, money in Bangkok.

Switching to the rapid, almost unaccented American English she's mastered after seven years as the adopted daughter of an American and five years in an international school, Miaow says to the woman, "You have packages of wet wipes behind the counter. Give her one." It's a command.

The woman sits upright, blinking in confusion at the sound of English and the vehemence with which it's being spoken. A teenage ladyboy with an apparently normal friend is somewhat unusual, but for the normal one, the *real* girl—who, the woman now realizes, is wearing a crisp, clean school uniform, obviously from a private school—to go instantly from perfect Thai to rapid-fire English, considerably better than the version the woman behind the counter has laboriously acquired . . . *well*, that suggests that there's been a misreading, perhaps serious, of the relative status of the people in the room. Despite the darkness of the schoolgirl's skin. Despite the *katoey*.

So she's up in a shot, stammering that she'll get the wet wipes, of course, but she was afraid that the *other* . . . um, young lady might find the perfume offensive. "It's a very cheap-smelling scent," she says, getting the package of tissues, sniffing it ostentatiously, and pantomiming someone waving away a stink. Then, apologetically, she proffers it politely, with both hands, to Lutanh.

Lutanh takes the packet and pulls one out. She inhales, wrinkles the flawless little nose, shrugs, says, "Smell okay," and uses the tissue to wipe her hands and then, as an afterthought, her forehead. The woman actually rolls her eyes before she remembers that Miaow is looking at her, and to cover the reaction, she says to Lutanh, in a much more civil tone, "The ones in the case are just for display. I need your prescription before I can let you open a box."

Lutanh's eyes come up to her so fast the woman steps back, saying, "I mean, what I *mean* is that I need the prescription to make sure it's the *right* box." Her eyes dart to Miaow and then back to Lutanh.

Lutanh says, "What prescription? I not sick. Only I want blue eye."

"It's . . . it's just that these lenses, they're . . ."

In English, Miaow says, "I have *dozens* of friends who've bought these without a prescription."

"Not in here," the woman says, drawing a line in the sand.

Miaow was just four or five, living on the street, when she learned that the only way to deal with a line in the sand was to kick it into oblivion and cross it at top speed, pushing her aggression in front of her like a bulldozer pushing dirt. She says, "Do you have any *idea* who my father is?"

"Do I . . ." the woman stammers. "D-do I . . ."

"Where's the owner?" Miaow says, looking around the shop as though to conjure him up. "There's no point in talking to *you*. Where's the person who *matters*?"

"Not here." The woman has raised both hands as though she's facing a firing squad and hopes to stop the bullets with her palms. "He's in the . . . the other shop, the . . . the one on—"

"Call him."

"No, that's not . . . We can . . . I mean, we can . . ."

"Oh, for heaven's sake," Miaow says, turning away from her. In Thai she says, "Lutanh, do things look fuzzy to you up close?"

"Do you have trouble reading?" the woman interposes helpfully, but one look at Lutanh's face makes it clear that this is *exactly* the wrong way to ask the question, and she adds, "or are things . . . umm, fuzzy farther away?"

"Away," Lutanh says, obviously examining the question for a trap.

"Well," the woman says. She looks at the eye chart, with its characters that Lutanh almost certainly won't be able to read aloud, and begins to fidget. Miaow backs away across the store and holds up two fingers. "How many?"

Squinting so hard her eyes practically disappear, Lutanh says, "Three."

"Good," Miaow says, putting her hand behind her, taking several steps closer, and bringing the hand out again. "And now?"

"Two."

"She's nearsighted," Miaow announces. *"Obviously."* More politely she adds, "Would you agree?"

The woman pulls out a scented tissue and uses it to blot her upper lip. "Yes, yes, but . . ."

"Do you have a pencil and some paper? Please?"

"Surely, surely," the woman says, and puts the requested items on the counter in front of Miaow.

Miaow pushes them along to Lutanh and says, "See that big chart on the wall up there?"

"I'm not *blind*," Lutanh says.

The woman says, "You mean, she can . . . ahh, ahh, *yes*, I understand. Please ask her to move the chair back about a meter and a half."

"I can hear you," Lutanh says. "You're allowed to talk to me." She scoots the chair back, knocking over the knapsack with the wings protruding from it.

"Is that good?" Miaow asks the woman deferentially.

The woman takes a few steps back, folds her arms, assesses the distance, obviously establishing her expertise. "Just a little farther, please."

"Thank you," Miaow says, shooing Lutanh with the backs of her hands. She goes to the counter, gets the pad and the pencil, and hands them to Lutanh. "Draw the smallest character up there that you can see clearly and then draw the one next to it. *No squinting.*"

Lutanh widens her eyes, blinks twice, relaxes her face, yawns to stretch the muscles of her mouth, then scans the eye chart and starts to draw.

"There," Miaow says, tapping the pad and pointing at the chart. To the woman she says, "You *solved* it. Third line down."

"Yes," the woman says. She lets a quick sigh escape. "And

thank you for your help. Please, miss," she says to Lutanh, "bring your chair back up to the counter."

"THEY MORE BIGGER than *mangoes*." Lutanh is looking down at her lap, at her violet dress, and blinking fiercely. "I'll never be able to wear them."

"Everyone says that at first." The woman behind the counter has pulled her chair up close, instinctively joining the female circle as one of its members embarks on an adventure. "But in a day or two, you won't even notice them. When I got mine—"

"*You* have?" Lutanh looks up at the woman's face, still blinking rapidly. "I can't see . . ."

"Look," the woman says, leaning forward and touching her finger to the surface of her right eye, provoking a grimace from Lutanh. She slides her finger a tiny distance to the right, and beneath the perimeter of her hazel eyes, like the beginning of a tiny eclipse, the edge of a dark brown iris peeps out. Lutanh gasps.

"You're not *supposed* to know she's wearing them," Miaow says. She's on the stool beside Lutanh, craning her neck to see the new color of her friend's eyes. "Look at me," she says.

Lutanh closes her eyes and presses lightly on her lids, then lifts her face to Miaow.

Without knowing she's doing it, Miaow brings both hands, fingers interlaced, up to her heart. "They're beautiful," she says.

"Aren't they?" the woman says, as though they'd been her idea all along.

Sniffling because of the tears, Lutanh says, "Can I have a mirror?" She closes her eyes so hard that her nose wrinkles, and she then opens them, and when she does, the mirror is in front of her. "*Oh*," she says, and then she says, "Oh," again and starts to cry. "They're *perfect*."

The woman holds out a tissue and says, "Here. Don't ruin your makeup. And you haven't even looked at the world yet."

"At the, uhh . . ." Lutanh says, and, dabbing at her cheeks, she looks up at the far wall of the shop, and her jaw drops. "Is *this* how everything . . . I see *edge*," she says. "Everything *edge*. I never see . . . I see so much *little* thing, even from here."

The woman shares a quick smile with Miaow and says, "Look out the window."

Lutanh turns her head to look and then quickly gets up, her violet skirt sticking to the backs of her thighs, which are damp with nervous perspiration. She says, "Ohhhhh," and then again, "Ohhhhh." Her fingertips go up to her temples like she's afraid her head will explode. "Oh, my *God*," she says, in English, pronouncing it *Oh, my Gos*. "He's prettier than *I* am," and Miaow follows her gaze to see, looking in through the glass at her, a boy she recognizes instantly.

"It's Edward," she says. "What's he doing here?"

"You *know* him?" Grabbing at her knapsack, Lutanh says, "Whatever he doing, tell him wait for me."

3

The Triangle's Wayward Third Point

THERE'S AN AWKWARD, protracted silence when Lutanh joins them after fanning an uncounted, but obviously more than sufficient, wad of bills atop the counter and chasing Miaow out of the store. The three of them stand there in an extremely irregular triangle. Miaow and Edward—who'd been talking when Lutanh came out with her knapsack and a new bag bearing the optical shop's logo—are close enough to each other so that the people sweating their way down the sidewalk can't squeeze in between them, and Lutanh is quite a bit farther off, the triangle's wayward third point. She's hanging back, staring at Edward as though she expects him to shimmer and vanish in a cloud of white light and music, her weight on her left foot and the right foot raised and hooked behind the left ankle. One glance at the pose takes Miaow back to the time when she was much younger, freshly discarded on a sidewalk and only marginally welcome anywhere.

A bulky *farang* in a tight white T-shirt and shorts baring heavily tattooed calves cruises between Lutanh and Miaow, slowing as he comes, his eyes on Lutanh, and he turns to glance back at her when he's passed. When he's out of earshot, Miaow breaks the silence to say, "Lutanh, Edward. You guys can say hello to each other. You've already met."

Simultaneously but in different languages, Edward and Lutanh say, "No. I'd remember."

Miaow says, "You both said the same thing."

Lutanh says in English, "I know," and Edward says, "We did?"

"But that's right, you *wouldn't* remember each other." Miaow says to Edward, "Lutanh was in disguise, and you were in makeup. With your hair parted in the middle. For the play."

"The play?" Edward says, frowning, as Lutanh says, in Thai, "The play?"

Miaow says, "The *play*, Edward, the one and only—"

"I know *which* play," Edward says. He says to Lutanh, "I'm sorry if I don't remember. It was a very confusing night."

"Too much confuse," Lutanh says in English. She takes a couple of quick steps toward him. "That night, me . . . man, crazy man, boxing me *here*." She mimes several punches at her expensive little nose and then crosses her eyes and rolls her head back, her tongue in the corner of her mouth, absorbing the blow. When the pantomime is over, she takes a step toward Edward, gesturing at her nose to drive the point home. "Wery bad man."

"Yes, I'm . . . I'm sure he was." He looks up and then down the street. "Excuse me," he says to Lutanh. "I'm going to have to be rude. Miaow, I need to go home with you."

"Okeydoke," Lutanh says. "We go Miaow's—"

But Edward hasn't finished talking. "I need to talk to your father."

Miaow says, "To *Poke*?"

"Yes, Poke." He licks his lips, starts to say something, shakes his head, and says instead, "Your *father*, okay?"

"Well," Miaow says, thinking about acting class.

"It's important. I wouldn't be bothering you if it weren't . . ."

"You not bothering," Lutanh says. "Okay," she says to Miaow. "We go your house." She gives Edward her best smile, the one she practiced secretly for years in her mother's cracked and ever-dusty mirror, almost the only times she ever smiled when she was a boy. "Miaow papa, him wery brave."

"You have to go to Dr. Srisai's class," Miaow says to her. "This is your scene day."

"Oh." Lutanh's smile evaporates. *"Peetapan."*

"We take an acting class together," Miaow tells Edward. "She's very good."

"Today I Peetapan," Lutanh says. "When Tinkabel is dying, *na?* I want to play Tinkabel, but in this scene Peetapan number one. Tinkabel, she dying? And Peetapan say everybody need to believe in fairy." She fans her face with one hand. *"Woh.* Wery sad."

Edward says, "Isn't Peter Pan a boy?"

"No problem," Lutanh says. "I beautiful boy." She picks up her bag and pulls out one of the protruding objects, a piece of cane that's been bent into a teardrop shape and then covered tightly in plastic wrap. Delicate veins have been traced on the plastic with some kind of marker. "Wing," she says, presenting it one-handed as she struggles to free its mate. She holds them both up. "I make." She looks at them, and doubt creases her face. "Good, no good?"

"Uh, good," Edward says. "But Peter Pan doesn't have wings."

"My Peetapan have wing," Lutanh says with a bit of steel in her voice. "Him fly, him have *wing.*" She waves the wings in the air. They catch the sunlight nicely, and Lutanh nods satisfaction and then says to Miaow, in English, "You not come?"

"I can't," Miaow says. "Tell Dr. Srisai I'm sorry. A friend had an emergency." To Edward she says, "This *is* an emergency, right?"

"It is."

"Okeydoke," Lutanh says with a shrug. She starts to jam the wings into her bag. To Edward she says, "I show you Peetapan later."

"Good," Edward says. "Great."

"I helped her a little," Miaow says. "Just remember the *arms.*" She holds her arms above her head, slightly bent at the elbows, then slowly turns her palms and her elbows outward.

"I do," Lutanh says. "I do one hundred time. Make every-body cry."

"It might," Miaow says dubiously.

"No, in my *club*," Lutanh says. "Make everybody cry, my club. Girl cry everywhere, cry, cry, cry. Well," she adds, obviously in the interest of accuracy, "*half* girl cry. Half girl—" She tilts her head back and brushes the tip of her nose upward with her index finger, "snob" in any language. With a grunt she throws the pack over her shoulder, the optical bag dangling from one finger, and says to Edward, "My name Lutanh."

"Yeah, I . . . uh, I know," Edward says. "Miaow told me—"

"And you Edwudd. I say name okay? Edwudd?"

"Edwudd," Edward says, nodding.

"Okay. I see you after, Edwudd."

Edward says, "After what?"

"She means *later*," Miaow says. "See you later, Lutanh. And good luck."

"See you . . . later," Lutanh says. She turns and throws the bag over her shoulder. Looking back, she calls out, "Edwudd. You wery pretty."

"Bar girl," Edward says. Lutanh has threaded her way through the crowd like some exotic iridescent butterfly set loose in a cloud of cabbage moths, and Edward and Miaow have begun to walk. They're half an arm's length apart so they can hear each other, and Miaow occasionally finds herself drifting closer, even on such a hot day. "Right?" he says when she fails to answer. "Bar girl?"

"Not exactly," Miaow says, a little stung by his tone. Her adopted mother had been, after all, a bar girl, according to many the most beautiful of any of them. The sun has slipped below the tops of the buildings, and Silom is draped in the unconvincing urban dusk that announces to city dwellers the coming of the real thing. She glances over at him, taking in the fine, regular profile, the long eyelashes, and what she sees as his unreasonably beautiful, wavy light brown hair—wasted on a boy—that, taken in tandem with the profile, had inspired an almost audible buzz among the girls at school when he appeared on the fourth or fifth day of the previous semester, materializing in the hallways like a surprise delivery from another dimension, one where everybody always smells good. One of the things she likes about him is that he seems to be indifferent to his good looks. He's not, for example, a preener. She's never seen him check himself out in a shop window, and when he messes with the flop of hair on his forehead, it usually seems to be because it's irritating him. "But why do you say that? What makes you think she's a bar girl?"

"That makeup," he says. "The dyed hair, the dress, those ridiculous blue eyes."

"I *like* the eyes," Miaow says, as though her own taste is being criticized. "We just bought them for her."

"Okay, I take it back. Nice eyes."

"And they're not blue, they're violet. She's always *wanted* violet eyes. Why shouldn't she—"

He turns to look at her, apparently puzzled by her tone. "And I've always wanted to be tall enough to play basketball, but I'm not."

"Some people," Miaow says, "have the guts to become who they want to be."

"Yikes," he says. He looks forward again and slips his hands into his pockets. "I stepped in it, whatever it was. She's your friend, I guess."

They walk in silence for a few steps, and Miaow slows her pace so he gets ahead of her and has to wait. She says, "I *like* her. She's brave."

"Good. I mean, *good*. Friends are important."

"And I don't have a lot of friends."

He says, "That's your fault."

The response surprises her, and she thinks she'll let it pass but then hears herself asking, "What does that mean?"

"You hide in your cave," he says. "Every time someone even says hi, it's like you pull away into the dark, and by the time you say hi back, if you even do, whoever talked to you is a mile off."

"I do not."

He shrugs. "Up to you. So, if your friend—*what's* her name?"

"Lutanh."

"If Lutanh isn't a bar girl, what is she?"

"She . . . she works in a club. You heard her."

"What kind of club?"

"A horse riders' club," Miaow says irritably. "Guys who ride horses the whole day, after all that time in a saddle they need a place to sit on a regular chair and talk to girls."

He stops walking again. "Really. Are there a lot of these clubs?"

"They're everywhere."

"The things I don't know. Where are the horses? I haven't really seen a lot of . . ." When it becomes obvious she's not going to rise to the bait, he looks around to see how far they've come. "Aren't you going to call your father? How do you know where he is?"

"He's home. He's *always* home. Rose—my mom—is in her fourth month. I mean, she's pregnant, and he follows her around all day. Drives her crazy."

Edward says, "That's kind of nice."

"She says she married him for better or for worse, but not for lunch." Edward laughs, and Miaow says, "*Do* I?"

"Do you what?"

"What you *said*. What you said about the cave."

They've stopped at the turn to Soi Pipat, where Miaow's

apartment is. The sidewalk has gotten more crowded as people pour out of the office buildings, but Miaow is barely aware of them. Edward closes his eyes for a moment, and when he opens them, he's looking at a point just slightly above her head, as though her gaze would break his concentration.

"It's like I said, you hide." He's choosing his words. "As though you think you can make yourself . . . invisible, like no one can see you, when you're just . . . I don't know, walking in the hall, as solid as everybody else. And when someone says hello? You look surprised and you retreat, sort of go all octopus, like you want to change color and disappear."

"But I *act*," she says. "I get up on the stage in front of the whole world. How could I do that if—"

"When you act," he says, "you're not Miaow."

She glances at him, startled, but he's still focused on a point somewhere above her. "So," she says, unable to think of any other subject, "why do you need to talk to Poke?"

4

Where I Am When I'm Seventeen

"IT'S BEEN TWELVE days, I think," Edward says. He's on the white hassock where Poke usually sits, and Poke is beside Rose on the couch, a little closer than she looks like she wants him to be. Miaow is sitting on the floor, midway between Rose's bare feet and Edward's running shoes, so immaculate it's as though they never touch the sidewalk. The four of them are dead center in a cloud of citrus fragrance, courtesy of a half-eaten tangerine, a fruit Miaow learned to like when the family spent some time hiding in a hotel that ran out of her usual favorite, oranges. Rose is dredging tangerine sections through an open container of unflavored yogurt—a pregnancy enthusiasm—and Edward has glanced at the ritual a couple of times.

"Has he disappeared before?" Poke asks.

"Not this long. I mean, he's gone all the time, but not for more than a couple of—" He stops, considering the question in Poke's expression, and says, "You know about my—his—*our* living situation, right?"

"I do?" Rafferty asks.

Edward glances over at Miaow. "Miaow hasn't told you?"

"Why would I?" Miaow says, blushing. "It was your business."

"You were embarrassed," Edward says, looking at her. "For me."

"She's much more sensitive than she seems," Rafferty says, earning a glare from Miaow and a smile, quickly hidden, from Rose.

"I know how sensitive she is," Edward says. "We were just talking about it."

Sitting forward attentively, Poke says, *"Really."*

Miaow says, "And let's *stop* talking about it."

"At the play," Edward says to Rose, "you met my Auntie Pancake. She talked about you later."

"I remember her," Rose says in English, her tone careful. Waiting in the lobby for Miaow's school play, *Small Town*, to begin, she had tried to talk with the woman, but Edward's father had bristled and shoved his way into the conversation whenever the two of them spoke Thai. At one point he'd stiffened a blunt index finger and poked Auntie Pancake, who was in her well-upholstered mid-forties, on her upper arm, hard enough to make her take a step to the side. At that point Rose had said, in Thai, "You can do better than this," but Auntie Pancake had laughed as though it had been a joke and looped her arm through Edward's father's, her eyes not merry at all.

"So," Rafferty says, sidestepping one awkward topic and bumping into another one, "has your father been . . . well, fighting with Auntie . . . Auntie . . ."

"Pancake," Rose says. She puts a possessive hand on her belly, just perceptibly fuller than it was four months ago, and arches her back slightly. "It was a popular nickname when I was younger. There was an older woman named Pancake in my village. She had worked in Bangkok, in the bars, I think, and she brought the name back with her."

"So did Auntie Pancake," Edward says. "Work in the bars, I mean. So did all my aunties. No, they haven't been fighting. Nobody fights with my father. They either do what he says or they go away."

Rafferty says, "*All* your aunties?"

"Four," Edward says. He's not looking at anybody. He begins to straighten one finger at a time to accompany the names he ticks off. "Auntie Pancake, Auntie Bai, Auntie Baby, and Auntie Aspirin." He looks at his hand and puts it between his thighs.

Miaow opens her mouth to ask a question and closes it again.

"All in the . . . uh, the same house?" Poke asks.

"No, three houses. And miles apart. I live in the main house, where my father lives most of the time, with Auntie Pancake. Auntie Bai and Auntie Baby live together. I think they're . . . you know, girlfriends. My father likes that kind of thing. Auntie Aspirin hates all the other aunties and everyone else in the world, so she lives alone."

"I see," Rafferty says.

"He, like, rotates. He's with us—Auntie Pancake and me—Monday through Wednesday, and then he's at the other houses Thursday through Sunday, two days each. Usually. And then some nights he's not in any of those places, he's in some hotel with somebody else, so he's gone a lot. Two weeks ago Friday was the last time I saw him. He came back for some money." He counts on his fingers. "This is Wednesday, so yeah, he's been gone twelve days."

"Have you checked with all the aunties?"

"Sure. I called Auntie Bai and Auntie Baby when he'd been gone five days, and they hadn't seen him that weekend. Auntie Aspirin didn't answer, so I figured, okay, he's with her, and she's probably thrown both their phones in the toilet. She does stuff like that. But then, the day before yesterday, she called me back and said she'd been up north where her phone didn't work, and she hadn't heard from him in days and days."

"What about his phone?"

"No answer, but there never is. He says he won't jump every time a cheap circuit calls his name. That's a quote, or almost a quote, and his phone *does* call him—it says his name in a kind of cheesy female voice, 'Oh, *Buuuddeee*.'" He rubs his eyes and the bridge of his nose, as though the thought of his father's ringtone exhausts him. "It doesn't occur to him that the person who *makes* the call might actually need something." Edward regards Poke and Rose, as though trying to gauge their reactions. "You know, maybe I should just tell you about my father. It might make things easier."

"Great idea," Rafferty says. To Rose he says, "Could I have one of those? With the yogurt on it?"

Rose says, "No."

"Got it," Rafferty says. "I don't know what I was thinking."

"Yogurt for two," Rose says. "And neither of them is you." She softens it with a smile and then softens it further by giving him one dripping tangerine section.

"Okay," Edward says. He brushes the flop of hair aside as though he's just become aware of it and then uses his index and second fingers to reposition it. "He's not what you'd call responsible. He doesn't really do anything except what he wants."

"Lucky him," Rafferty says.

Miaow says, "Like *you* slave all day."

"It doesn't make him happy," Edward says. "Nothing does. He's always pissed off—sorry," he says to Rose. "He's a big spoiled brat. He's had a trust fund his whole life, and he's used to everything he wants sort of falling into his hand. He thinks it's a hardship to have to go on tiptoe to reach anything." Edward stops and looks down at the glass surface of the coffee table, like someone who's waiting for the text to scroll up on his teleprompter.

Rafferty says, "Where does the money come from?"

Edward shrugs. "*His* father figured out something about carbonation that makes soft drinks fizz better, so the family got rich on the kind of junk he doesn't want me to drink. He went to law school because his father made him, but then his father did him a favor and died while Dad was in his senior year, and as he puts it, he was 'out of Harvard in a shot.' Like that was something to be proud of. And he, you know, started a couple of businesses, but it was just a way not to get bored."

Rose's eyebrows are raised. Her own father had tried to sell her into the sex trade, but she's never spoken about him as Edward is talking about his father. She says, "You should respect him anyway."

"He doesn't make it easy. He doesn't care about anybody. I mean, he campaigns for . . . you know, the Indians in the Amazon and some species of bird that's got problems, or regular old corn instead of whatever kind of corn, *modified* or whatever, they're making now, but he's not interested in people."

"What about your mother?" Rose asks.

"Oh, her." He has both hands clasped between his thighs now, and he's rocking back and forth a little. "She doesn't do much either. She was a banker for a while, or she said she was—in one of the banks my father kept his money in, so it probably wasn't a real job. She almost never went to work. After a while she didn't go at all. Anyway, she's not here."

Rafferty says, "I'm sorry to hear—"

"It's not like she's dead or anything." Edward stops rocking and sits back carefully on the hassock, which can tip over with very little provocation and has already deposited him on the carpet once. "I just mean she's not *here*. She's in California. With my sister."

"How old is your sister?" Rose asks.

"Twelve," Edward says. He reaches for the flop again and thinks better of it. "Her name is Bessie. I mean, Elizabeth."

Rafferty says, "And *you're* how old?"

"Seventeen. For a month."

Rose says, "Happy birthday."

Edward looks confused for a moment and then says, "Thanks."

"How long since you've seen her?" Rose asks.

"My sister or my mother?"

"Either one."

"Almost a year."

"Eleven months ago. That's when you came to my school," Miaow says, and looks like she just bit her tongue.

"You have a better memory than I do," Edward says. "I guess it was eleven months. If you say so."

"That's how long it's been," Miaow says to the top of the table.

"You remind me of her," Edward says. "My sister."

"Oh," Miaow says. The syllable seems to Rafferty to contain eight or nine meanings. "That's . . . that's nice."

"You're smart like her. And sort of shy. I mean, she's shy, too."

Rose says, "Has she been here? Your sister, has she been in Bangkok?"

"No."

"You must be lonely."

"I . . . uh. I get along."

"Why are you *here*," Rose asks, "when your sister and your mother are . . . where? In America?"

"In California. And they'll stay there." He looks up to find every eye in the room on him, and he sighs. "My father took a couple of vacations here in Thailand, and then, two years ago, he moved here and divorced my mother. The next year my mother sent me to live with him." He smiles to lighten what he's saying. "Just packed me up, like in the mail. Put my stuff in a suitcase, all the clothes I didn't like, as it turned out, pushed me into a plane, and then emailed him to go to the airport and get me. Said she didn't want males in the house anymore." He reaches for the flop of hair but lets his hand fall back into his lap, then fills his cheeks with air and blows it out. "As my father says, when he's losing an argument, we *have* wandered far afield, haven't we?"

"I didn't know any of that part," Miaow says. "About how your mother—"

"No reason you should," Edward says. "It's not like this is my *fate* or anything. It's just where I am when I'm seventeen. I even like it. Some." When Miaow looks up at him, he says, "I like knowing you."

Rafferty can hear Miaow's swallow.

Like someone making a long-overdue announcement, Rose says, "You need to stay for dinner. Poke is very good at getting takeout."

"So is Auntie Pancake. We live on takeout."

"Is she good to you?" Rose asks.

"She's okay," Edward says. He shrugs again, and Rafferty sees a lot of practice in the gesture. "No, better than that. She's nice most of the time. She doesn't *have* to be—she knows my father doesn't want me here in Bangkok, I interfere with his *lifestyle*— but she is. Nice. I don't think I'd be so nice in her position. And it's not like she's got it easy. It's not like she doesn't know that my father is . . . you know, a hound, and she stopped working—I guess that's what you'd call it, working—"

"That's what you'd call it," Rose says.

"So she stopped because of him, to please him, you know? And she'd be totally stranded if my father dumped her," Edward says. "And we both know, her and me, that he will when he gets bored or somebody hotter or more . . . cooperative comes along. So yeah, I like her." He straightens his legs and looks down at them through the glass table. "My mother won't let my sister come here because she says the whole place is—" He stops, and his right foot begins to jiggle up and down.

"Is what?" Rafferty says.

"A whorehouse," Edward says with his eyes still on his nervous foot. He raises his fingers to his mouth and starts to chew on his thumbnail but then lowers it again.

"Some men use it as one." Rose says. To Rafferty she says, "I want larb kai and oranges and unflavored yogurt. And some maraschino cherries."

Edward says doubtfully, "Is that good?"

"It's awful," Rose says. "But it's what the baby seems to want."

AFTER ROSE ESSENTIALLY pushes them out of the apartment, saying she has a backache and wants a nap before dinner, they hit the sidewalk. Edward, who's still relatively new to Bangkok, puts his hand over his mouth and nose as though to defend against the city's distinctive perfume of heat and carbon monoxide. Glancing over at him, Miaow stifles a smile. Rafferty is in the middle, but when Miaow says something and Edward leans forward and says, "Sorry?" he moves over so the kids can chat side by side and he's flanking Miaow on her left. They've gone half a block when he feels Edward's eyes on him.

"What?" he says.

"Just . . . you know, watching you."

"Why?"

"You really look at things. I bet you could describe the last five people who went by."

Rafferty looks surprised. "I didn't know it showed. I've been working on it for a while. A few years ago, Rose said I had the 'American disease.' When I looked at something, I compared it to something I had or something I *used* to have or something I wanted. But none of those things, she said, were—are—*here*, on this street, at this moment, and her point was that the things that *are* here should get my attention. She told me to think of it as the walking-and-looking meditation, just paying attention to what's going on."

"Does it work?"

"I don't know. I guess it does. I don't get lost anymore." Miaow laughs, and he grins at her and says, "She'll tell you. Four or five years ago, we'd turn two corners and I'd have to flag a cab to get back home. I carried my address everywhere, written on my palm in Thai so I wouldn't just disappear." They come to the Silom intersection, and he says, "Foodland is down there, with the oranges and the yogurt, and the good food stands—good for this neighborhood anyway—are up here. We could split up, get back faster."

Miaow says, "She doesn't want us to get back faster."

"No," Rafferty says. "Probably not."

"She told me yesterday she feels like she hasn't been alone for months."

Rafferty says, "Well."

"Yeah, well."

"I *worry* about her." He pats the pockets of his pants, not knowing he's doing it. "So," he says, "we stick together? Take our time?"

"I'd go for that," Edward says. "Foodland first?"

"Sure," Rafferty says. "Why?"

"You'll get used to this if you hang around," Miaow says to Edward. "He always thinks everyone else is wrong."

"Okay," Rafferty says. "Foodland it is. Look how reasonable I am." He heads off down the sidewalk, and Miaow and Edward hurry to catch up.

"Edward," he says, "why me? Your father doesn't show up, why'd you think of me?"

"You know why. The police are no good. And everybody at school knows what happened that night after the play. You got that guy who murdered those people."

"I got someone else killed, too, someone who should still be alive. I'm not proud of myself."

"With all due respect, Mr. Rafferty, all the people who were with you knew it was dangerous. You set it all up, and it worked."

"That's what I tell him," Miaow says.

They walk in silence for a few yards. Then Rafferty says, "Okay, then, what else is there? We kind of sidetracked you back at the apartment, and I don't think you were finished. You're not worried just because your father hasn't come back. What else happened?"

Edward shoves both hands into his pockets and nods. "Two or three days after he split, someone broke into our house. I was at school, and Auntie Pancake was out with her friends, like she is every day when my father's not there. When I got home, the window in the back door, the door to the kitchen, was broken, and someone had gone in through it. There are two locks, one in the knob, which they could turn by reaching in through the window, and a dead bolt, which could be opened from inside but had to be manually locked again when they left. They left the dead bolt unlatched, so I know they opened the door."

"*How* long ago?"

"Let me see." An oncoming sidewalk-wide group of Japanese men, undoubtedly on their way to the Japanese-only bars on Soi Thaniya, politely separates to let Rafferty and the kids get through. "He's been gone twelve days. The last time we saw him was Friday before last. The break-in happened on Monday, my first day at school that week, so it was the third day he was gone. Nine days, that would make it, nine days ago."

"Did you call the cops?"

"Yeah, sure, although Auntie Pancake said I shouldn't have. She really hates them. Anyway, they showed up, looked at the door, and asked what was missing. I said I hadn't noticed anything that wasn't . . . you know, where it was supposed to be, and they went through the house, sort of picking things up and putting them down, and they asked where my father was and told me to have him call them when he came back. Then they went away."

"*Nothing* was taken?"

"Not that I saw then. I went through the house before the cops got there and didn't notice anything. And I looked around a little later, too. But the day before yesterday, the rent was due, so I went into my father's office to open his safe and get his business check-book, and it was gone. He had three checkbooks, and they were all gone, and so were a bunch of credit cards. And whoever broke in had opened the safe to get them and then closed it again. Only my father and I know the combination."

"Maybe it *was* your father. Maybe he lost his house key. Maybe he just needed—"

"My father never uses checks except to pay bills. He lives on credit cards. He's got three or four cards he uses all the time. And even if he did come back for a check, like if he needed some cash and didn't want it on his credit-card record for some reason, he'd just write one and tear it out. No reason to take the whole book. Much less three books."

"Okay," Rafferty says.

"And he never would have broken that window. There's a key hidden outside. He's the one who hid it."

Miaow puts a hand on Edward's arm. "Maybe you're not safe there."

"I'm pretty sure they got what they wanted," Edward says. "I don't think they were after phony antiques. Shouldn't we cross here?"

Rafferty has been so focused on Edward that he hasn't regis-tered the permanent snarl of Patpong across the way. Miaow leads them into the traffic with the Bangkok native's assurance that what seem to be hurtling projectiles of steel and glass are actually spirit images devoid of mass, and despite a few doomed gasps from Edward, they make it to the center island unscathed. Both she and Rafferty know where to part some shrubbery to reveal an opening in the railing that runs down the center of the island that separates the boulevard into two theoretically one-way thorough-fares. Once they're on the other side of the street and they've dodged their way through the crowd and the booths of the night bazaar to the relative emptiness of Patpong 2, Rafferty says, "Why are you so positive they won't come back?"

"I got to thinking about those checkbooks," Edward says. "Yesterday I went to all three banks. Every one of them had cashed a big check on my father's account in the past week. One of them had cashed two."

Miaow says, "For how much?"

"Altogether," Edward says, "all four checks, a little more than thirty-six thousand dollars."

Rafferty says, "In twelve days."

"Yeah," Edward says. "Moving fast."

5

If She Likes You, You Can Hurt Her

IT'S DARK AND still hot—it'll be hot all night—and she should be hurrying to make it to This or That Bar in time to put on her stage makeup with the other girls, but Lutanh is dawdling, hugging to her the moment when Dr. Srisai had said she was "excellent," trying to rekindle the feeling that had blossomed in her chest when he said, "Very *good*, Lutanh, excellent." He'd said her approach was "fresh" and "believable." And he doesn't usually like anything. The last scene she'd done, a couple of weeks ago, he said it looked like she was trying to imitate a robot. "If you must imitate rather than *invent*," he'd finished as she sank even lower into her chair, "at least imitate a human being." She'd stayed out of class for two days until Miaow dragged her back in.

But he liked her Peetapan. Her Peetapan was "excel—"

She stops walking, struck by a horrifying thought. Peetapan is a *boy*. Is she only any good when she plays a—

No, it can't be. Not true. Not worth considering. Impossible. How can she play the Little Mermaid? How can she play her new dream role, Mulan? Her friend Betty, who dances at the Queen's Corner bar, had given her a DVD of *Mulan*, the story of a beautiful Chinese girl who disguises herself as a boy so she can fight in a war. "You'll be a girl who used to be a boy playing a girl who's pretending to be a boy," Betty had said, adding in English, "*That'll* fuck them up."

But that wasn't what Dr. Srisai had meant, that she should play boys. It couldn't have been. For a moment she thinks she'll go back and ask him to clarify, but as soon as she's turned around, she realizes he'll be gone by the time she gets back to the classroom; she's been walking for more than ten minutes. She turns forward again, irresolute, and then wheels around, struck by the sense that someone might have been back there, someone who moved quickly when she changed direction. It's a narrow street, badly lit, but she stands still, surveying the gloom with a kind of bristling of the tiny hairs at the top of her spine. Nothing she sees stands out in this dark, angular cityscape. No curved lines, no pale patches, no movement.

Nothing. It was the lenses, she decides. She's still being distracted by small details she'd never been able to see before. Or maybe a reflection, it could have been . . .

"Not what he meant," she says aloud in Lao. It sounds good, so she says it again. Peetapan was *always* played by girls. She/he had been played by a girl the first time Lutanh had seen her, in the very silly musical version that had been on the television in some customer's hotel room, Lutanh fighting to stay near the screen as her customer wrestled her repeatedly to the bed. The fifth or sixth time she'd wriggled free, she'd improvised an imitation of Tinkabel, using the bed as a launch pad for flying, a diversion that got him laughing for a few minutes but then ended when he stopped laughing and started looking at her very differently. She knew that the look meant it was time to go to work, and by then everyone on the TV screen was back in the boring place where the children originally came from and they were all singing at one another, with nobody flying. So she gave her customer Tinkabel. He came back the next night and the night after.

Customers.

She waves the thought away. So even if Peetapan *is* supposed to be a boy, he's always played by girls, and Dr. Srisai, who knows *everything*, certainly knows that. If he said she was a good Peetapan, that's what he meant. He meant she was good in a part that girls always play.

Maybe.

But wouldn't it be awful if she had to play boys?

In a moment of panic, she checks her backpack to make sure she remembered her wings and her violet dress, packed up when she put on the denim shorts and the green T-shirt she wore as Peetapan; she was elated enough to have forgotten anything. The wings had been perfect. The only thing Dr. Srisai hadn't liked was the gesture with the arms that Miaow thought up for her. He'd said it felt "external," whatever that meant. Lutanh would like to ask Miaow about it, but she knows she can't tell her friend that Dr. Srisai criticized her idea. Miaow is so much easier to hurt than she pretends to be. If she likes you, you can hurt her.

She looks around quickly, seeing movement again at the edge of her vision, but then it's gone. Making sure that no one is looking at her, she spreads her arms and does the three long leaps, her legs free and unencumbered in the shorts. She concludes the movement with the half-airborne twirl she'd used to get onto the stage. It really feels like she's flying.

She's *acting*.

What a shame Edwudd didn't see her.

When she first decided, back in the village, that ultimately she would live as a girl, she'd had a dream of what her life would be. She'd seen newspaper pictures of the glittering *katoey* pageants at Thailand's Alcazar Theatre, each girl ravishing from the top of her jewel-covered headdress to the hem of her trailing, spangled gown. It had been so easy to imagine herself gliding across the stage as the spotlight followed her helplessly, enslaved by her charm, and a thousand people in the audience craned their necks to see her every move.

It took about two minutes during her first and only visit to the Alcazar, soon after she ran away, for the truth to rear itself up like a cobra and spit in her face. The girls were all so much taller than she was, and more beautiful in a formal, shiny-page-magazine way. They had a kind of gorgeousness that was grown up and at its peak, while hers was still changing, still a young girl's beauty and a *short* young girl's beauty at that. And maybe, although she hates the idea, less beautiful than *cute*. So no more Alcazar. The vision of the brightly lit stage, the intake of breath from the audience, the adoration from a safe distance across the footlights, was replaced by the cramped confines and stinking bathroom of This or That Bar, with *farang* men pissing on the ice cubes in the urinals or pooping in the cubicles, the same cubicles where she sometimes holds the broken door closed so she can use the toilet or, once in a while, cry for a couple of minutes, then fix her makeup and go back out, smiling, into the light. Where the customers were waiting.

But now she's acting. Now Dr. Srisai has said she was "excellent." And she can't help glimpsing a new dream, a universe away from This or That Bar and its poop stench and its customers pawing at her.

All because her favorite *farang*, Leon Hofstedler, had introduced her to Rafferty, and when Rafferty wanted her to pretend to be someone else for a few hours, Miaow had come to her tiny room to show her how to do it—how to change her walk and the way she held herself, and to explain why the person she was imitating behaved that way. Lutanh had a lot of experience with pretending—trying to stop being the sissy the bigger kids tripped and tormented whenever they felt like it, trying to make customers believe that she enjoyed her time with them—so the pose had come easily and the deception had worked, even though the man she was fooling that night punched her before he was killed. And then Miaow had taken her to Dr. Srisai's class, and Rafferty's policeman friend and his wife had offered to pay for the lessons, and the Alcazar had dried up in her imagination and blown away. In its place is the famous Lutanh, Asia's first *katoey* movie star, just fabulous costumes and big close-ups with tears gleaming in her eyes, one heartbreaking story after another, boys like the one she used to be, the one who beat her up, packing the theaters and crying their eyes out all over Thailand. No more customers hauling her into cheap hotels. She won't even have to be in the same *room* as the customers. No more scorn from her older brother. She'll be able to lend him money, and *nothing* establishes relative status like that does.

Feeling almost as though she really can fly, she makes the turn onto a main street, glancing at the time on her phone, scanning the traffic for a moto, and thinking again about Edwudd. She doesn't see the heavily tattooed *farang* in the tight white T-shirt who comes out of the side street half a minute behind her and watches, hands on hips, as the moto slows and she jumps on.

As the moto pulls away, he lights a cigarette. He'll get something to eat now. He knows where she'll be later.

6

Scraping a Little Skin Off You

THE AIR CONDITIONER *whumps* into action, and Rose says into the phone, "He's gone." She's lying down flat in bed with her knees up to ease the ache in her lower back, an ache that's come and gone for days now. The lights of the city gleam with all the reassurance of a badly told lie in the top half of the window, the half the air-con doesn't block. "I can't believe it, but he's gone."

"You're awful," her friend Fon says. "You have a rich, handsome husband who loves you and never hits you and treats you like you're made out of glass because he thinks you're the only woman who ever got pregnant, and you—"

"He's not rich." She feels the tug in her back as she reaches over to replace the remote for the air-con on the table. "When you were carrying Oy, didn't you have times when absolutely everything seemed to scratch?"

"Scratch?"

"Like . . . like everything was scraping a little skin off you." What's *not* on the table, she sees for what feels like the thousandth time since she became pregnant, is her giant ashtray, the ashtray that had been beside all her beds in the years since she ran south to Bangkok. And she smells the stale smoke from the carpet, and the desire for a cigarette raises its black serpent's head somewhere inside her and looks around, its tongue flicking the air.

"No," Fon says. "I loved being pregnant. I wish I were pregnant now. I wish I could be pregnant for a living."

Rose rolls a little to her right, looking for a better position and trying not to think about a cigarette. She rolls back again. "You're no fun. I want someone to tell me I'm right."

"About what?"

"Everything. Can't I ever be right about everything?"

"No. Tell me something you specifically want to be right about."

"It's okay for me to want to be alone sometimes."

"Absolutely. You're completely right. It's okay for you—"

"Then why do I feel guilty all the time?"

Fon doesn't say anything.

"Fon?"

Fon clears her throat. They've been friends long enough for Rose to know that throat-clearing means Fon is about to tell a lie. "How would I know?"

Maybe, she thinks, if she brings her knees up a little more, it'll ease the pangs from her back. "Well," Rose says, "I *do* feel guilty all the time."

Fon finds a way to approach it. "So why do you *think* you feel guilty?"

Rose says, "You know why."

"It was a long time ago," Fon says, so promptly that she's obviously been waiting for it. "It didn't have anything to do with him. You didn't even know him."

"It's not *exactly* that," Rose says. "We've been together almost eight years now. He knows who I was and what I did. He even knows some of the men I went with."

"Who?"

"Why do you want to—"

"Oh, come on. Who?"

"This is embarrassing." Rose says. "Do you remember Bob Campeau?"

"Old Power Man or Juice Man or whatever he called himself? Old Triple-Pop?" Fon laughs. "You mean to tell me you went with—"

"So did you. So did everyone who could move one foot at a time on the stage and didn't have a bunch of missing teeth and weigh four hundred pounds. He went through the bars like a bus. He would have fucked the crack of dawn if it had held still."

"Poke knows about *him?*"

"He does."

"You told him you went with—"

"*I* didn't tell him." Without knowing she's doing it, she begins to rub her abdomen in small, light circles. "Old Triple-Pop did."

"He's still alive?"

"If that's what you want to call it. He's combing his hair forward—"

"Probably from the middle of his back," Fon says, and then she laughs. "Do you remember how much hair he had on his—"

"And he's old and wrinkly and dried up."

"If *anybody* should be dried up, it's him. For years he was like a soap dispenser, just squirt, squirt, squirt."

"But anyway, that's not the problem."

There's a pause, and then Fon says, "No. Of course not."

"I'm all alone when I most need someone with me," Rose says, "and it's my fault."

"You mean you're alone with—"

"Being frightened."

This time Fon is silent for so long that Rose says, "Hello?"

"I'm here. I know what you mean. I'm not going to say I know how it feels, but I know what you mean."

Rose is getting cold, and she thinks, *I deserve it.* "I should have told him the night I knew I was pregnant."

"But you didn't," Fon says, "so forget that. You can't go back there and make it right. Whatever you can do to fix things, you have to do it now."

Rose lets her eyes roam the room. This was their bedroom even before they formally adopted Miaow. When they talk about moving—for the baby, for the *baby*—this is the room she wishes she could take with her, dreary and cramped and cold as it is, with that damned air-con. "I get cranky with him, I snap at him. And he *knows*. He can . . . he can see when I feel something that isn't right—"

"When you feel something you *think* isn't right."

"He can feel it the second I get frightened, and all I can do is tell him there's no problem, just go away. I can't tell him now. I can't tell him why I'm frightened."

"Maybe you can. Maybe you should."

"Right now," Rose says, as though Fon hasn't spoken, "I have a backache, and it's scaring me to death."

"Everybody has backaches. I had a backache the whole time I was carrying Oy. I spent the last two months lying down with my knees up."

"I *know* that. But it's early. It's *too* early. I'm only in the fourth month." Rose feels something blocking her throat, and she swallows it down. "*Last* time it was in the fourth month."

"You're fine."

"It's the only secret I've kept from him," Rose says. She shivers against the cold, looks down at her arm, at the goose-bumps, the tiny hairs tugged upward. "The only one that matters anyway."

"Kwan," Fon says, using Rose's real name, her Thai name. "Just because you lost one baby, that doesn't mean you're going to lose another one."

"Two," Rose says.

Silence clogs the line for a moment. Fon says, "Two?"

"I . . . I think so. When I had only been working a few months, I missed a month and then another month, and then, a week after it was supposed to have come, I had a heavy—"

"But that doesn't mean . . ." Fon says, and she trails off.

"I don't *want to lose the baby*," Rose says. She gets her voice under control. "I don't want to . . . to lose the . . . all of it. Him, Miaow, the baby. All of it."

"That won't happen."

"I lied to him. I never told him I'd lost a baby. He was so happy when I said I was pregnant. His *eyes* got all watery. I thought if I told him about . . . about *those times*, he'd . . . I don't know, keep me in bed for nine months. *Worry* at me, stand over me when I eat, make me drink milk."

She breaks off because Fon is laughing.

"He would have," Rose says. "He's never bossed me around before, but you should hear him about the baby." She blinks a couple of times, surprised to find her eyes full of tears. "I won't let him talk about names," she says. "I tell him it's bad luck. Miaow named the baby Angelina as a joke months ago, and he's dying to change it, and I . . . I can't . . ." She rolls over and pushes her face into her pillow to blot her eyes and, still lying on her stomach, says, "He wants this baby so much."

"And you'll give it to him," Fon says.

Rose just closes her eyes.

"*I* know," Fon says. "Tomorrow I'll take you out to lunch. Anywhere you want to go that won't cost more than three thousand baht. For both of us, I mean. And you can eat anything, as long as it's not expensive and you don't drink or smoke."

"You're no fun."

"Tomorrow. I'll come get you at noon."

"Choose someplace in between us and I'll come to you. If you

come here, he'll want to go with us," Rose says, and she laughs and
then blots her eyes again.

"Well, he can't. It'll be good for him. Americans always think
they can have anything they want. This will give him a chance to
grow emotionally."

"Fine," Rose says. "And thanks."

"We both survived Old Triple-Pop," Fon says. "We can get
through anything."

"Fon?" she says.

"What, honey? What is it?"

"I lied to you, too. It's not because I knew how he'd fuss over
me, that's not why I haven't told him."

"I know," Fon says.

"It's because, when he . . . when I said I was pregnant and he
acted the way he did, like something had just happened that had
never happened before to anyone before, just to him and me . . ."

"I *know*," Fon says again.

"I couldn't tell him—I mean, even after he knew about
Campeau, I couldn't tell him I'd had another man's child inside
me. *Two* other men's children. Before his."

"Kwan," Fon says. "He has the best, the most beautiful woman
I know. And he has Miaow."

"He loves Miaow so much."

"He loves both of you. And now he'll have a baby. Your baby,
his baby. He's not a terrible-looking man," Fon says, laughing,
"and you're you. *Imagine* what the baby will look like. You're going
to make him so happy."

"I hope," Rose says, thinking, *I don't like the way my back hurts.*

"You will," Fon says. "Just don't *worry.* See you tomorrow." She
hangs up, and instantly Rose is lonely again.

She rolls onto her side and grabs Poke's pillow, the lumpy one,
hugs it to her belly, then rolls onto her back again. Out of nowhere

comes a fragment of a thought: *If this was the last time I could look at this place* . . . And she pulls the cord that turns on the little light on her bedside table, right where her ashtray used to be. *What did Poke do with my ashtray?*

The lampshade is a powdery blue she loved in the store but hated the moment she got it home, and the light that filters through it is both dim and cold. It's cold enough, in fact, to make her pick up the remote and turn off the air conditioner. She settles back against her pillow, the good one without the lumps because Poke forced it on her when he learned about the baby, and she closes her eyes. From the center of her body, she can feel every square foot of the apartment, each of its four rooms: the kitchen with its dining counter and stools; the long, awkwardly shaped living room now bisected by the huge flat-screen that Poke bought her the night she told him she was pregnant and that he now hates because it blocks their view of the city through the sliding glass door to the balcony they're all afraid to sit on; and Miaow's room, dark and windowless, across the short hall with the bathroom at the end of it. She and Poke have made love in every room except Miaow's. Poke proposed to her, back when she was saying no, in every room except Miaow's, *including* the bathroom. She was in the kitchen when she accepted the ninth or tenth proposal, after hours of seeing the ring box bulging in the pocket of his robe and saying silently *yes*, finally *yes*, until he took the little box out at last and asked her.

She opens her eyes. The room's corners are pools of gloom, but she doesn't need to see them to know what's there. Poke's four pairs of shoes live in a straggling, constantly changing formation in the far right corner. Across the room stands the chest of drawers she shares with him, two drawers for each of them, and in the top drawer are the smelly Singha beer cans he dumps his change into every night so that he can count it all up once a year and pour it

into a lopsided tin bucket for Miaow's birthday, a date they estab-
lished in committee, since no one has any idea when she was
actually born.

Poke had guessed that Miaow, who had spent five of her first
six or seven years begging for, and sometimes stealing, money in
very small denominations, would be more thrilled by a big bucket
of small money than by a thin wad of bills. The first year they'd
given it to her, she'd let out a shrill yip they'd never heard before
and then covered her face with her hands, instinctively hiding her
joy, something she did for almost a year until she understood that
where she was now, no one would steal whatever it was that made
her happy. Poke had looked helplessly over at Rose when Miaow's
hands went to her face, and Rose sometimes thought that she'd
have fallen in love with him at that moment if she hadn't already
loved him.

Poke loves being a father. Poke was born to be a . . .

She shoulders the thought aside and takes refuge in considering the closet. Miaow's bucket, brought into view only on her
birthday, is empty now, jammed into a corner of the high second
shelf, where Poke always stashes Rose's Christmas presents,
behind a couple of old boxes. His choice of a hiding place forces
her to drag the hassock from the living room when he's not home
so she can peek. She felt guilty about peeking until the third year,
when he bought her a dress so ugly that she spent weeks trying to
make it clear that what she wanted was a pair of boots that were
so expensive he couldn't even think about getting her anything
else. It took *forever* for him to hear what she was saying, but one
day the dress wasn't there anymore and the boots replaced them.
After that she felt virtuous about peeking. It was her contribution
to Christmas, making sure he didn't waste money on her.

She hadn't celebrated Christmas until she moved in with him.
She'd heard the unending carols in the stores and worn a blinking

Santa Claus hat, like almost everyone else in Bangkok, and, once or twice, a white cotton beard. One Christmas Eve in the bar, the customers had voted *her* the present they wanted most, and they had wrapped a ribbon around her and held a drawing of slips of paper from a giant cognac snifter, with the winner getting to take her to the hotel for the whole night, free. Not *actually* free, of course; the bar paid her the following night, subtracting a small fine for the time she wasn't squeezing the customers for colas because she'd been in the winner's hotel room, being unwrapped.

Merry Christmas.

Now she loves Christmas.

Below the closet's two shelves stretches the single, long wooden rod from which their clothes hang, hers neatly spaced half an inch apart and taking up eighty percent of the space and his wedged into a dense mass at the right end, so close together that he once said that someday they would all fuse into a single six-pound T-shirt, eight inches thick. When it did, she promised him, she'd iron it for him.

She gets up and goes to the closet. For an unfocused moment, she stands in the open door, and then she tugs the bottom of that hanging row of compressed shirts to her, buries her face in the cloth, and inhales.

The breath she draws is so deep it makes her light-headed, and she opens her eyes wide, puts a hand on the doorjamb, and focuses on the dark outline of the dresser to make the room stop spinning. When it does, she goes to the bed, picks up the phone, and holds down the *1* key.

"Hey," Rafferty says.

She clears her throat. "Have you gotten the takeout yet?"

"No, we're following each other around in Foodland trying to find the yogurt. They've moved everything again . . . I *know*, Miaow, I know."

"You know what?"

"That they move stuff around to make you buy more. It's a basic supermarket principle. So what's up? Everything okay?"

"*Yes*, everything's—" She stops and strokes the front of her throat with her fingertips. "Why don't you take Miaow and the boy out to dinner?"

"Edward," Rafferty says, "his name is Edward." There's a moment of silence except for the store's tinny Muzak, a little cricket orchestra that's had too much coffee. "You don't want your horrible yogurt or your awful, poisonous cherries?"

"I'm not hungry yet." She turns around, going nowhere. "Since you haven't bought it, why not get yourselves something to eat there and then pick up the yogurt and the other things on your way home? I can wait. Miaow likes to eat out."

"I don't want to leave you alone that long."

"I know, Poke. I *know* you don't want to leave me alone, but right now I *want* to be alone. Is that okay?" She sits on the edge of the bed and lets her head fall all the way forward onto her chest.

"Sure," he says, probably thinking he sounds heartier than he does. "Tell you what. I'll take them to Patpong. I've got a reason to go anyway."

"Good," she says, barely registering his words. "They'll like that. All children should go to Patpong." And she disconnects and listens to the silence and feels the fear slip its fingers around the edge of the door to her heart.

7

Depends

THEY ESCAPE FROM the chill and the bright fluorescents of the supermarket, Edward teasing Miaow for shivering, and into the rank swamp of Patpong 2, mostly abandoned bars at this end, plus a couple of restaurants open and throwing light through their windows in a doomed effort to cheer up the neighborhood. To Rafferty the Silom end of Patpong 2 has always looked like a zip code for rats. Several of the women stationed at the table in front of the immemorial oral emporium called the Star of Light give Rafferty a quick business appraisal and, seeing Miaow and Edward, return to their conversation. Their cigarette smoke puts a sharp edge on the air.

Rafferty leads Miaow and Edward across the narrow street and into what the old-timers still occasionally call Soi Bookshop, a little stub of road that connects the two Patpongs like the crossbar in an *H*. The name is all that's left of a business that disappeared long before Rafferty's arrival, replaced, no doubt, by an enterprise that targeted a lower chakra.

Soi Bookshop gets brighter and louder as they approach Patpong 1 and the milling herd of punters and shoppers drawn by the bars on either side and the night market that runs down the center of the road. The crowd is mostly Western and mostly men, either alone or in small packs. Some of them appear to be defiantly guilt-free, shopping for flesh as cheerfully as they might for doughnuts, but there's also a scattering of solitaries, some of them the type of guys who are often depicted in ratty raincoats. Set in bright relief against this backdrop of anticipatory testosterone are sunburned families whose adults have come to paw the overpriced merchandise in the night market while their staring children store up memories they'll probably ponder for years until the penny drops.

It's a little after eight. Miaow, who was selling gum on this very street when Rafferty met her, plunges into the flow without so much as a look left or right, but Edward has slowed to take it all in. Rafferty is mother-henning the two young people when he hears what can only be a bar-girl shriek, high enough to etch glass and audible from an extraordinary distance. He looks to his right to see a small girl in satin hot pants and an abbreviated cowboy vest waving happily at him from the doorway of a bar, and as he locates her, she recognizes his companions. Her jaw drops, and she yanks her arm down, clamps both hands over her face, and ducks sideways through the door. THIS OR THAT BAR, the sign reads, and he realizes it was Lutanh.

He grabs Edward, who's turned instinctively toward the sound, and says, "We're going this way." There's amusement in Miaow's eyes; she recognized Lutanh, too. The three of them, in a tight triangle with Poke in the lead, push through the crowd to a passageway between two night-market booths. When they reach the other side of the street, he leads them to his left.

"Where are we going?" Miaow says. She doesn't hate Patpong the way Rose does, but it holds no interest value for her.

"To ask some questions about Edward's father."

Miaow looks around. "Sure," she says. "I should have known. The old guys." But then she stops, looking up, and the others stop with her. "That's a new sign, isn't it?" she says. "And what's that *apostrophe* doing there?"

"I'm raising a grammar snob," Rafferty says. "And I couldn't be prouder." Ahead of them is a very small bar with a single, streaked window. In contrast to all the wattage blazing away to proclaim the bigger bars, this window's only lure is a short, depressed-looking loop of red and green Christmas-tree lights, two of which have burned out. Above the door is an inexpensive wooden sign, sloppily cut and badly painted, that says LEON AND TOOT'S.

"Well," Miaow says, "her name isn't *Toot*. No one's is. *What* did it used to be called?"

"The Expat Bar," Rafferty says. There's a sudden cramping in his stomach—he's only been here twice since the terrible night at Miaow's school. He displaces his discomfort by glancing over at Edward, who's wide-eyed and clearly unsure where to look next. "This all new to you, Edward?"

"Yes," Edward says. "My father came here a few times, but he liked . . . I mean, he *likes* Soi Cowboy. Likes it better, I mean. That's what he said at any . . ." A girl half wrapped in the spar-kling curtain hanging in the doorway of a bar to their right calls something cheerfully rude to Edward and wiggles her tongue at him, and his eyes bounce off her as fast as a finger yanked from a hot stove. Looking everywhere else, he says, "He said, I mean, that he liked Soi Cowboy—"

"You're getting a lot of attention tonight," Rafferty says, and in fact a couple of women in the next bar up are trying to hail him, too. "But your father's not alone. *Everyone* likes Soi Cowboy better. Soi Cowboy is the future, or at least one melancholy ver-sion of the future. It's the current hot spot in the city of bliss and burnout. The trophy is a drinking cup with a hole in it."

"Dad's town," Edward says.

"And this, *this* is an ancient shipwreck, pressed beneath a magic spell at the bottom of the sea. The women here are the spirits of sirens, and the men are the ghosts of dead sailors."

"A sea change," Miaow says. "Wooo-wooo."

"My little Shakespearean," Rafferty says. To Edward he says, "Ariel, in *The Tempest*, was Miaow's first part."

"I know," Edward says. "I saw it."

"How was I?" Miaow asks with absolutely no self-consciousness.

"You were the best one," he says. She starts to smile, and he adds, "Your boyfriend was in it, too, wasn't he?"

"Andrew," Miaow says. She looks down at her feet. "He's in Vietnam now."

"I wondered," Edward says, but he doesn't put much into it, and Miaow's eyes come up for a moment and drop down again.

"Come on, let's go," Rafferty says. "No matter how much your mother wants to be alone, Miaow, I'm still anxious to get back."

Miaow says, "Breaking news."

The bell over the door rings as he pushes his way into a room that never changes. It looks like it might have been made of some elastic material that's been forcibly stretched lengthwise to create a narrow, cramped space the width of a couple of bowling lanes with a bar on the right, in front of the usual mirrored selection of brand-name intoxicants. Stools are drawn up to the bar, which has been painted in several colors over the years and then chipped to create patches that look like cut-rate camouflage. A couple of deteriorating booths in an unpleasant salmon-colored plastic sag in an exhausted fashion against the left wall in a way that suggests they wish the party had ended a decade ago.

As Rafferty enters with the kids in tow, everyone in the place looks at them with an intensity of expectation that says it must be a very boring evening indeed. Leon and Toot's, as it was renamed by Toots, the ageless Thai bartender who now owns the place, is a tiny lost continent of the almost-extinct, the dwindling members of Bangkok's first male *farang* generation, mostly guys who came here in the late 1960s for R&R from Vietnam and never left. For more than fifty years, they've taken refuge in this bar, where they've told and retold lies to each other until they've mostly come to believe their own rewrites of the lives they led, decades ago, in a city that's changed beyond their recognition.

"Hey," Rafferty says, uncertain of his welcome. But the look on their faces tells him they'd buy a drink for a resurrected Saddam Hussein if he offered relief from the others' company.

"It's our little movie star," Bob Campeau says, making a genuine social effort from the stool he always occupies at the far end of the bar, a stool Rafferty fully expects Toots to bronze once Campeau is no longer with them. Miaow nods, blushes, and says something inaudible. Pinky Holland, his bald, tanned head gleaming, is in his solitary booth, and the Growing Younger Man sits about half of the way to Campeau, working on a drink, the profound greenness of which announces an infusion of powdered algae to redeem the vodka. He plans to live forever, and his main topic is how he's going to do it. The fourth customer is a man who might be named Ron but whom Leon Hofstedler, once Poke's best friend in the bar, always called "the guy with the hair," since neither Leon nor Rafferty could get the name Ron or any other to stick to him. He sports a steely seascape of well-combed waves sweeping back dramatically from a low forehead that seems remarkably unmarred by thought, a characteristic that led Hofstedler to claimed that the man's hair was so profuse because the roots had a lot of room to move around in.

"You all already know Miaow," Rafferty says, "and this is Edward." Realizing he's still not sure whether the guy with the hair is really named Ron, he says, "Why don't you all introduce yourselves?"

He sees the bright sharpening of interest in Miaow's face when Bob Campeau says his name. She's seen him before, in this very room, but without an introduction, and she had been present at an argument a few months back when Rose told Poke about Campeau's insistence that his girl of the night should allow him to give multiple demonstrations of his potency. The others mumble their names as though they might have expired. They're so self-conscious that it brings home to Poke how seldom they meet new people. The Growing Younger Man calls himself Louis, and the moment he says it, Poke remembers Leon calling him that once. The guy with the hair introduces himself as Ron. Pinky is the only one who seems comfortable with the ritual of self-introduction, but then Pinky's only been coming to the bar for maybe ten years, so his conscience is relatively clear.

Toots briskly brushes her hands together, a habit she has when customers come in, a ceremonial clearing of the deck to make way for a new chore, and says, "Children want what?"

Edward says, "*Children*," but Rafferty speaks over him. "Toots has Coke, Diet Coke, soda water, and—what was the name of that orange drink Leon used to keep here for his ladyboy friend?"

"Lut—" Miaow begins, and then bites it off, her tongue literally grasped between her teeth.

"Orangina," Toots says. "Have. You want beer Sing?"

"How did you guess?"

"Ho-ho," Toots says. "Every night same same. Sit, sit. Move Leon chair over so you have one-two-three."

Miaow is still staring at Campeau, whose comb-over is unusually off center tonight, and Rafferty can almost hear the *eeeewwww* in her mind.

Sensing her attention, Campeau says to her, "You were great in the play," and her eyebrows climb a little. To Edward, Campeau says, "You were the kid, right? Her boyfriend?"

"I was," Edward says a bit stiffly, and Rafferty sees the money and exclusivity in the boy's background and then immediately wonders whether he's wrong, whether what he's seeing is Edward looking at Campeau and getting a glimpse of his own father in a few years.

"You were good, too," Campeau says, a bit grudgingly. He isn't one to throw praise around. "Couldn't hear you all the time."

"I know," Edward says. "Miaow was always on me about that."

"How's Rose?" Campeau asks.

Rafferty can feel Miaow's eyes on him. "Same as always," he says. "Better than I deserve."

"No kidding," Campeau says.

"And the baby?" Toots says to Poke. She plops a big bottle of Orangina on the counter. "For you?" she asks Miaow, who wrinkles her nose and asks for a Coke.

"Babying away," Rafferty says. "You'd have to ask Rose to get anything more specific."

"You *should* know," Toots says, pouring, and even though she's too polite not to mute her tone, it's clearly a reproach.

"I'd love to. But Rose . . . as far as *Rose* is concerned, pregnancy is something that happens in the other room."

"What other room?" Miaow asks, rising to her mother's defense.

"The one I'm not in," Rafferty says.

Miaow says, "That's not fair," and then thanks Toots as her Coke is put in front of her.

Rafferty is wrestling with his reluctance to move Leon's stool, with its burnished nameplate and the red ribbon knotted tautly between the arms to keep people from sitting on it. The chair and a cheap, dented urn full of ashes on Toots's side of the bar are all that's left of Leon—once such a dominant presence here in this dive that's suddenly been named after him and that was, in so many ways, his true home in Bangkok. Rafferty has just decided to leave the stool where it is and sit on the far side of it, leaving it between him and Miaow, when Campeau, who's on his best behavior, says with a kind of microwaved geniality, "So what's the next play?"

"Something old," Miaow says dismissively. "Maybe Ancient Greek old. Pig-something."

"*Pygma*—" Rafferty says, but he's cut off by the Growing Younger Man.

"That's not Greek," he says, "although it's based on a Greek story about a king who didn't like women very much, so he carved one out of stone that was perfect, for him anyway, and then he fell in love with it."

"Serves him right," Miaow says.

"She couldn't talk," Pinky Holland says, sounding wistful.

As though no one had spoken, the Growing Younger man says, "The goddess of love brought her to life, and the king married her, and they lived blissfully ever after."

"Does the statue *learn* to talk?" Miaow asks. "I mean, after it comes to—"

"The play is all *about* talk, how people talk," the Growing Younger Man says. "It's called *Pygmalion*, by an Irish playwright." He squints at the wall of bottles. "George Bernard Shaw? He turned the legend into the story of an upper-class English guy who finds a sort of street girl and teaches her how to be a lady."

"Wait," Miaow says.

Pinky says, "Yeah, Shaw."

"Well," the Growing Younger Man says, "I haven't completely lost it. So he gives her, the upper-class English guy does, a bunch of lessons about, you know, talking right and which fork and all that, and then he takes her to a big fancy ball, and everyone thinks she's noble, royalty or something. A prince dances with her. A young nobleman falls in love with her."

Campeau says, "That sounds like My *Fair*—"

Miaow says, over him, "He turns her into a . . . a high-class girl?" Her face is as intent as Rafferty has ever seen it. "How?"

The Growing Younger Man, who has raised his green glass,

lowers it again. "I told you. He teaches her how to talk. How to behave."

"Oh," Miaow says. She's so focused on the thought that she leaves her lips in the circle she made for the O sound.

"I'm going to try out for Freddie," Edward says to Poke, sounding doubtful. "You know, the noble guy who falls in love with her?"

Miaow doesn't even seem to hear him. To Poke she says, "Would that *work*?"

"In a play," he says.

"But what about . . . ?" Her fists are clenched. "Do you know *anything* about this play?"

"I know something about everything," he says. But then he reads the look in her eyes and says, "Some. I know about it some."

"Would you . . . would you *help* me?"

"We'll download the script tonight. We'll read it together and talk about it."

She closes her eyes for a moment and then nods. "Fine," she says.

Edward says, "We could rehearse together."

"Fine," she says again. Then she says, "I mean, *fine*, that would be great."

"Maybe we'll all go again," Campeau says without thinking, and Toots freezes in mid-pour behind the bar, and Campeau shuts his mouth and sits frozen, the room held hostage by a profound silence, broken only by a sudden sniffle from Toots. The pressure in the room rises until Rafferty's ears almost pop.

Edward surveys the bar's customers, looking puzzled, and says to Toots, "I'd like some of that orange stuff."

"This is Bangkok," Campeau says, with the authority of someone who knows he's right. "People disappear all the time. And then they pop up again."

"Not always," the guy with the hair says, prompting a second awkward silence as the bar's patrons, who have been trying to reassure Edward that his father was probably off fishing somewhere and is already on his way home, glare at the guy with the hair. He senses it and looks up and says, "But I . . . I mean, your father, I'm sure he's—"

"There's disappearing," Campeau says with lethal authority, "and there's *disappearing*."

"Really," Rafferty says. Edward has his Orangina in his hand and his straw, forgotten, in his mouth, and he's looking at Campeau as though Campeau is an oracle, which, Rafferty thinks, he almost is. No one he knows can match the breadth of Campeau's knowledge of the Bangkok bar scene. He's the Neil deGrasse Tyson of pay-for-play. In a different, and slightly worse, world, he'd probably have a television show.

"There's *selective* disappearing," Campeau says, clearly enjoying the attention. "You know, where your friends know where you are and they've got a list of people who aren't allowed to find out."

"Like who?" Miaow says. It's the first remark that's snagged her interest since the group stopped talking about *Pygmalion*.

"The little woman," Campeau says. "The other little woman. A bunch of other little women. The insane girlfriend with the gun. The cops. Collection agencies. Immigration. *Yaa baa* dealers. The American IRS. Lawyers." He shrugs. "Those people."

"If a woman asked you where her husband was and you knew, you'd lie to her?" Miaow asks.

"Sure," Campeau says, sounding surprised at the question.

"Even if she thinks he's dead?"

"She knows he's not *dead*," Campeau says, shaking his head at the obviousness of it all. "People like this, she knows he's not dead. Women," he says, "whatever other problems they've got, they're not *stupid*."

Pinky Holland says to Edward, "How long has he been gone?" and Edward tells him. Campeau shrugs and says, "That's no time. He could be around the fucking—Excuse me," he says to Miaow. "Around the corner, I mean, he could be . . ."

"We have other reasons for being worried," Poke says. "So let's just say, for the sake of getting me home to my wife before the baby is born, that our reasons are worth taking seriously. You guys have been here forever, you've known thousands of men who came through here. None of you can think of anyone who disappeared like this in the last five, ten years?"

"Sure we can," Pinky says. "Up to the northeast, into Cambodia or Vietnam, down to Bali or anywhere. But most of them came back."

"No horror stories?" Poke says. "No one got robbed or beaten up or anything?"

"Hold it, hold it," Campeau says. He closes his eyes, looking momentarily like the centuries-old death mask of someone with a bad reputation. "Larry Finch," he says, opening his eyes. "Larry got waylaid somewhere four, five years ago. Got beat up so bad he was in the hospital. We didn't know anything for a couple weeks, and then he walked through that door, all wrapped up like a Christmas problem. I mean, present."

"My auntie has called the hospitals," Edward says. "He's not in any of them."

"Auntie?" Pinky says, looking interested.

"Never mind," Rafferty says, but Edward says, over him, "One of my father's girls. *Women*, one of his women."

Sounding like a lepidopterist who's just heard a description of a possibly unknown butterfly, Campeau says, "*What's* your father's name?"

"Herbert Dell." Edward glances down into his drink. "But he likes people to call him Buddy."

"I'll bet he does," Pinky says, and then realizes he's said it out loud and looks up, startled, negating the words with a side-to-side movement of his upraised hand.

"I *know* my father's an asshole," Edward says. The cool he usually affects has been dropped like a jacket. "I don't need input from—"

"Sorry, sorry," Pinky says. "I'm sure he's actually—"

"He's not," Edward says.

"Buddy Dell," Campeau says, his eyes half closed and apparently trained on something on the other side of the bar's front wall. Everyone falls silent in deference to the oracle. He reaches up and scratches his head, a clichéd mannerism Westerners may have relearned from Thais, who probably picked it up from old American movies; Southeast Asia is full of people who scratch their heads when they're stumped. "Buddy," he says. "Buddy, Buddy, Buddy." He swivels his stool back and forth, making it squeal, until Toots's flat hand lands on the bar with a *crack*. Campeau jumps and says, "Sorry." He picks up his drink and puts it down again, squints at something only he can see, and says, "Soi Cowboy?"

"Wow," Edward says, and it sounds sincere.

"White shoes?"

"That's him."

"Reason I remember," Campeau says. "It was raining like shit. His shoes were muddy as hell, and some of it wasn't exactly mud, you know what I mean? *Buddy*," he says. A grin escapes, but he shuts it off.

"He had to throw those shoes away," Edward says.

"Shoulda thrown them all away. I saw him again later, he had on another pair. Tell you something, sonny. Your dad drinks too much."

"I know," Edward says, tight-lipped.

"I mean for Bangkok. You can't get shitfaced night after night wearing white shoes and stumble around in Bangkok without something . . ." He looks down into his drink and clears his throat. "Right," he says.

"So . . . old Larry," Rafferty says over Campeau. "What *did* happen to Larry—what was his name?"

"Finch," Campeau says. "He never told us. Wouldn't talk about it at all. Just disappeared for a week or two and then showed up knocked half to pieces with nothing to say. Couple months later he went to Phnom Penh. Or someplace."

"Phnom Penh," the Growing Younger Man says. "I saw him there once. At Martini."

"Used to be a great bar," Pinky Holland says, gazing into a better past.

"Well, you guys are no help," Rafferty says.

Campeau hits his drink and puts it down. "Hang on. Takes a while to get the old motor running." To the Growing Younger Man, he says, "What about that clown Bruce?"

"Bruce Wayne," the Growing Younger Man says to Rafferty. "Not his real name, not Batman, just what he called himself. Acted like Interpol was on his trail all the time. International man of mystery, that kinda nonsense. Wore sunglasses at night, walked into things, never told anybody where he was staying. Yeah, he went missing for eight, ten days, but . . ."

"But what?"

"But they found him facedown in a canal."

"With a cast on his leg," Campeau supplies. He snaps his fingers. "Jeez, it was even in the papers."

"I forgot about that," the Growing Younger Man says. "Getting old. Still, if anyone deserved to end up in a canal—"

"Let me get this straight," Rafferty says. "He goes away with two good legs and winds up dead a week or so later in a canal with a broken one?"

"Somebody, I can't remember who, said the leg wasn't even broken, cast or no cast." Campeau shrugs. "But, you know, there's people here who think that whole thing with the moon was in Arizona."

Edward says, "What whole thing with the—"

"Apollo. Think it was just some guys running around in slo-mo in the desert."

Edward says, "My dad thinks—"

"Depends," says the guy with the hair, only his second sign of life since saying his name, which Rafferty has already forgotten.

"On *what?*" Campeau snaps. "You mean you think Neil Armstrong was in Phoenix or something? Maybe at the Hilton? 'One small step for a man, one great leap over a cactus'?"

"No, I mean old *Depends*," the guy with the hair says. "You remember."

"You mean he wore those . . . you mean he was incontinent?" Rafferty says.

Miaow says, "What does 'incontinent' mean?"

"Later," Rafferty says.

"It was just a nickname," the guy with the hair says, sounding defensive. "He had some name that *sounded* like that, you know, like Nelson sounds like Wilson."

"Nelson doesn't sound like Wilson," Pinky says. "Jeez, don't go into writing valentines, okay?"

"I know who you mean," Campeau says. He reaches up to check his comb-over and adjusts it so that it's off center in the other direction. "Name was Stu, Stuart. Stuart Depend . . . Depend-something."

"That's what I *said*," the guy with the hair says, sounding aggrieved.

"Dependahl," Campeau says. He snaps his fingers. "Damn, I

still got it. Stuart Dependahl. Hey, you know what? They found him in a canal, too. And jeez, he had casts on *both* legs."

"Dead?" Rafferty says.

"As good as."

"What does that mean?"

"Brain stopped working," Campeau says. "Like he went too long without oxygen. Only reason we knew he even turned up was it was in the papers. Because of a tattoo he had, somebody recognized it from the story in the papers."

"Tattoo of what?" Pinky says.

"That caterpillar from whatsit, *Alice in Wonderland*. Sitting under a mushroom and doing hits on a water pipe. Old Stu never got over the sixties."

"He was the one, his wife came by," the Growing Younger Man says. "Wanted to ask about him, right?"

Edward says, "His Thai wife?"

"Naw," Campeau says, reclaiming the floor. "American wife. Came all the way here from someplace to see what she could do for him. Long as she was in Bangkok, she dropped by to talk to us about him."

"And what *could* she do?" Rafferty says.

"Nothing," Campeau says. "Stand the old vegetable watch, you know? Guy never opened his eyes."

"Okay." Rafferty finishes his beer and looks at his wristwatch. "So what you're telling me is that there's a minor epidemic of Western punters dropping out of sight and then falling into canals, is that it?"

"Hey," Campeau says, "we just report the news, we don't make it up."

"I've got to get these kids some food before we go home," Rafferty says. He puts his glass on the counter, says, "Toots?" and mimes signing a check.

"Where you gonna take them?" Campeau says.

"I don't know." To Miaow he says, "Want to go to RiffRaff?"

Miaow sticks out her tongue.

"Okay, but that's where we met each other."

"I remember," she says. "How about the Sizzler?'"

"Okay with you, Edward?"

Edward seems startled at the sound of his name. He's clearly been following his own train of thought. "Sure," he says. "I don't care."

"Okay. Drink up and let's go."

From behind the bar, Toots clears her throat and says softly, "Have more."

"More?" Rafferty says.

"More man in water. Two, maybe three. You talk bar girl, *old* bar girl. Maybe bad bar, upstair bar. Some old girl work there now." She shrugs. "*Leon* know. Before, him talk about."

Edward starts to say something, but over him Campeau says impatiently, "Do you want to talk to her?"

Rafferty says, "Who?"

"The *wife*. Mrs. Dependahl." Campeau pulls a creased and battered spiral notebook from his jeans, licks a finger, and begins to flip through it. "She's still here," he says. "In Bangkok. You want a phone number?"

8

You Did That?

THE CUSTOMER HAS apparently never heard of dental floss. His breath smells like he has an entire herd of tiny, long-dead animals stuck between his teeth.

Dental floss. Her second life, in a way, had begun with dental floss.

But the customer she's with at the moment doesn't use it, so she looks down demurely when he talks to her, holding her breath until he's done. Then, whatever he's said, she puts an appreciative hand on his arm, turns to show him her left profile, and inhales through the right corner of her mouth.

This is *not* how it was supposed to be.

Being a girl, Lutanh thinks for the hundredth time, *doesn't solve everything.*

After the scrawny, unloved Lao village boy named Keo had been told the great secret, he'd occasionally glimpsed his future female self as a beautiful, possibly semitransparent entity wrapped in a golden haze who would inspire appreciation—and maybe a little awe—from all. He, or rather she, would be a remote flower that people would appreciate from a distance or, at least (if they got too close), gently. The way beauty *should* be treated. Not—not this. Half naked, half freezing, covered in goosebumps, and stuck next to a man whose breath would smell better if he set his tongue on fire. And who keeps putting his hand in her lap to see whether she's still got what she was born with. If she knew which he wanted, pre- or post-, she'd just *tell* him, but that would deprive him of his fun, fondling her like a *thing*. A thing he hasn't even paid for yet. *I'm fun*, she thinks.

And the place smells like piss.

This is the future. It already seems to have lasted a long time.

Keo had sealed his fate in his Lao village at the age of eight, when he'd gone outside twice, dressed happily in his sisters' best clothes, thinking only how pretty he looked. He'd been laughed at the first time and beaten up the second. As he grew older and his identity became more unmistakable, a few of the other boys flounced around him, pitching their unchanged voices into soprano squeaks, miming the way he walked, the way he washed his hands, the way he touched his hair. Although most of the village was either sympathetic or neutral, Keo became the secret plaything of three older, bigger boys. They waited for him on his walk home from school, yanked his pants off and threw them up into a tree, rubbed dirt in his face, in his hair. Blew him kisses.

Broke his arm.

Lutanh runs her fingertips over the arm, almost surprised at the smoothness of her own skin, feeling the irregularity where the bones were imprecisely joined. The man misreads the gesture and puts an arm around her, squeezing her close, saying, "Baby's cold, huh?" and giving her a generous whiff of the open grave.

She turns away, grabs a breath openmouthed, nods toward the girls on the stage, and says, "Very pretty, yes?" The shift onstage is the group of girls she dislikes. She and her friends are due up in two more songs.

"Not as pretty as you. Hey, you want a drink?"

"Oh, *thank* you," she says. It's a few baht in her purse. She unwinds his arm from around her shoulders and says, "I get."

"No, wait—" he says, but she's already gone.

One of the girls onstage makes loud kissing noise. When Lutanh turns to glare at her, the dancer fans her hand in front of her face and laughs. She knows about the customer. Lutanh gives her a sharp, rude tilt of her chin and goes to the bartender to request a cola, asking him to pour it slowly.

WHEN KEO WAS very small, his mother had told him and his sisters of the young girl in the ancient tale whose stepmother sent her into the forest to get water from the river. On her way back, carrying two heavy, brimming buckets, she met a filthy, ragged old woman who put a spidery hand on her arm, fixed her with oddly bright eyes, and asked for a drink. The girl told her to drink all she wanted and, since Thais and Laos value cleanliness so highly, to wash her hands and face if she wished. "Please," the girl said, "I can go back for more."

"You are kind and good-hearted," said the old woman, who was actually an angel. "I will bless you." And from that moment, whenever the girl's words were truthful and compassionate, the beautiful, prized flowers called *phikul* would fall from her mouth to show the world that the girl's goodness and beauty came from the center of her heart. Her evil stepmother sold the flowers and became rich, but ultimately the girl, who by then was also called Phikul, met a young man and married him and lived the fairy-tale life of a beloved wife: a beautiful woman, treasured and safe. The story pierced Keo's chest like an arrow and lodged in his heart.

Oh, to meet the angel who could turn him into Phikul.

THE COLA IS icy in her already-cold hand. She tucks the tag for the drink into her shorts, to be redeemed later that evening, since this is payday, and shivers, exaggerating it as comedy for her friend Fai, who's sitting across the room. Then she forces a smile and turns back toward her customer, only to see him disappearing toward the malodorous toilet at the far end of the room.

Like most Patpong clubs, This or That Bar is a long rectangle, squeezed for width by the developers' goal of jamming the largest possible number of profit centers into a single block. The stage claims the rear third of the room, in front of the toilets and the cramped changing room for the girls, the doorway to both of which is screened by a heavy, damp-smelling length of fabric through which the dancers make their first entrance of the evening. Later, whenever it's her turn again, she will jump off her customer's lap or shimmy out from under his arm and just clamber onto the stage at the point nearest to where they've been sitting.

Poles are set into the stage every six feet or so, giving the girls a center for the stage space they claim during their sets and also something to hang on to later in the evening, when the stimulants are wearing off and the more serious stuff coming on. Down the walls on the room's long sides runs a raised platform with a padded bench for customers extending its entire length. In front of the benches are small, square tables, anchored to the floor every two meters. The place is only half full, but Lutanh has no trouble identifying the empty stretch of bench and the table where Mr. Breath of Death has been pawing at her.

Occupying the center of the room is the bar, an extended ellipse with a counter surrounding it and swivel stools packed densely all the way around. The bartenders work at the center of the ellipse, so Lutanh only has to go ten or twelve feet from where the cola was handed to her to be at the table where her customer would be waiting if he hadn't had to pee. She sighs, offering a small prayer of gratitude for his brief absence, and almost trips over an outstretched pair of legs, covered in Japanese-style tattoos. Dragons and serpents wind their way up toward the dubious paradise of his shorts.

The legs weren't there a moment ago. He stuck them out on purpose.

But he's not looking at her. He's watching the stage, even though it's clear he knows she's there. He's a sunburned *farang*, stocky in a way that says strong beneath the fat, with a peculiar haircut; his hair is only about half an inch long, but he's got wide sideburns stretching almost all the way to his jawbone. The whole thing looks like a fuzz helmet he pulls on in the morning, except that there's nothing amusing about it.

He pretends to feel her gaze and turns to face her, painstakingly assembling a surprised expression. It seems to go on for a little more time than it should; either he's intentionally letting her see it take shape or his internal clock runs more slowly than hers. Looks up at her, then down at his legs. "Oh," he says, pulling them back at that same deliberate speed. "Sorry. Where's your boyfriend?"

"He go brush teeth," she says. "Where your girlfriend?"

"Just sitting here, waiting for you." The smile is also put together a piece at a time: the corners of the mouth, the slight tilt of the head, the crinkling of the eyes.

"Your girlfriend waiting for me?" Lutanh says. "She no like you?"

She watches it sail past him and then, slowly, hit home. The smile broadens a little, but there's also a flush on his cheeks that wasn't there before. He starts to speak, but Lutanh says, "No problem. Maybe she come back," and turns away to cross the room. She can feel his eyes on her back like a spot of warmth, like the red light from rifle sights she's seen in movies, flashing in someone's eyes just before his head explodes.

She sighs again. Her customer won't be in the bathroom forever.

Keo's angel had taken the form of an older woman, maybe sixty, who came from nowhere to buy the best house in the village when Keo was twelve. Straight-backed and slender, Than Taeng moved through the dusty, ramshackle village with its filthy, snot-streaked children, as though she were in an immaculate, orderly city, full of people like her. The villagers joked about her behind her back—Keo's mother sometimes referred to her as "Her Highness"—but to her face everyone gave her a respectful salute and treated her as though she might secretly be someone important, some slumming millionairess or the former favorite minor wife of an unknown person with the power to change their lives.

From the time she arrived, Keo occasionally felt her gazing at him, but she never met his eyes. Unlike that of some in the village, her gaze was not disapproving, although he knew it would be untrue to call it warm. Still, he sometimes imagined that she took a special interest in him, that she was watching over him, like the spirit in the story of Phikul. That feeling was strongest on the nights when his brothers and sister were asleep and his parents' single light was still burning, creating a sharp-outlined shadow theater on the wall. Keo would turn his head just so, until the contours of his face were thrown in three-quarter view on the wall, and he would study the shape of his long, delicate eyelashes and his high cheekbones and slender neck and imagine that he was the beautiful, good-hearted girl and that Than Taeng was the angel and that she could transform him into the person he so desperately wanted to be.

THE CONDENSATION FROM the cola glass is dripping from the tabletop and onto her bare thigh. She goes back to the bar, grabs a paper napkin, and scrubs her thigh dry, then wraps the napkin around the base of the glass. The goosebumps on her arms stand up like a tiny mountainscape, and suddenly all she wants to do is go into the bathroom, hold the door closed, and weep. But the next-to-last song of the current shift of dancers is coming to an end, maybe half a minute to go, and that means that in four min-utes or so she'll be up there moving around, getting warm. She glances back at the man with the tattooed legs, sees him avert his eyes, and then the curtain at the left of the stage is shoved aside and her customer comes out, drying his hands on his pants.

Well, at least he rinsed them.

She pastes on a smile and climbs up onto the padded bench to wait for him, hyperventilating a little so she'll be able to hold her breath longer when he's talking. He goes past her, around the table in front of her, and sits. She shifts to face him, which puts her back to the stage.

"I missed you," he says, his hand searching her lap. She crosses her legs to make it difficult and starts to say something, anything, but the onstage shift's next-to-last song ends, the last one comes on, and he looks past her, laughs, and says, "For Christ's sake, look at that."

And she does. And her heart almost stops.

THE THREE OLDER boys had been gaining on him, toying with him because they knew that they could catch him anytime. They were playing their newest game, in which they spiraled him out into the forest, where they could catch him and rip his clothes off—just to make sure, they said, that he was really a boy. Then they'd tie his clothes into knots and throw them back into the village so he had to run in naked and get them.

He'd been circling the village in panic, trying to avoid being forced into the woods, but when they'd come, for the third time, to Than Taeng's house, they saw her standing outside her door, her hands raised, palms facing toward them, in a gesture with a surprising amount of strength behind it. The gesture said *stop*, and it turned the pursuing boys into a loose knot of confused children.

Keo found himself standing very close to her, his knees shaking violently. He could smell something, perhaps not perfume, perhaps soap, and it was the most beautiful scent he'd ever breathed. He learned much later, in Bangkok, that it was a graceful white flower the Thais call *sôn glìn*—in English, tuberose. It *was* in fact her soap, and later, when he was Lutanh, he bought it by the boxful.

She said to the boys, "Go away." She hadn't raised her voice, but its authority scattered them like leaves. When they were out of sight, she said, "Come in," and stepped back so he could precede her through the open door. As he passed, she rested her hand on his shoulder for a moment. The gesture's warmth made his legs go weak.

The house, Keo could see as Than Taeng closed the door behind him, had once been much like his parents', but care and money had been lavished on it. A floor of concrete, somehow dyed a leathery tan, had been poured over the dirt, smoothed until it was almost polished, and covered here and there with thick rugs of deep red. Against the walls stood the furniture he had seen in movies, big, soft-looking chairs with thick cushions. One of them—behind a smooth, shining wooden table—was long enough to hold four people, side by side: the first couch he would ever sit on. The vertical blinds had been adjusted against the glare of the afternoon sun so that the room was a series of angled stripes of light, tracing their way across the floor and partway up the opposite walls.

To Keo it was a palace.

"Over there," Than Taeng said, pointing to the long chair. "On the couch."

When he was sitting, as lightly as he could, on the soft leather, jamming himself into one end to take up as little space as possible, he felt something brushing his chest and looked down to see the fabric of his T-shirt vibrating in time to the pounding of his heart. He was still panting from the run.

"Stay there," she said. "Keep your feet on the floor. Don't put them on the furniture." Moving noiselessly, her back absolutely straight, she went to the wall to the left of the door, which she closed. The open door had partially hidden a sink and a small, two-burner gas hot plate. Glass-faced cabinets held plates and cups and saucers that all looked alike. In his heart Keo seized on that detail: Someday all his plates and cups and saucers would look alike, and so would his drinking glasses.

"Water?" she said. "Grass jelly drink? Coca?"

"Do you—" He had to stop and clear his throat. "Do you have Orangina?"

"Water, grass jelly drink, Coca," she repeated, but this time it wasn't a question.

"Coca, please."

"Not good for your teeth," she said, stooping toward a small refrigerator that came up to her waist.

"What is," he began, and then he swallowed and finished the question, "good for my teeth?"

"Water," she said. "Also, brushing them every morning and every evening."

"I do," Keo said, almost truthfully.

"Smile at me."

He pulled his lips back, feeling like a monkey.

"Not bad. But you should straighten them."

"How?"

She made a clucking sound with her tongue, mild reproof at the stupidity of his question, but there was something so harmless in it that he felt his smile broaden. She returned the smile and came up with a plastic bottle of water, took down one of the very thin, gracefully curved glasses, and filled it. "Better for you," she said.

He said, "I'll break it."

"Right now is when you begin learning not to." She picked up something circular and green and glassy from the top of the refrigerator and brought it and the goblet of water across the room to him. She put the green circle on the table and placed the goblet on top of it. "This is a *coaster*. When you drink, put the glass back on the coaster. It protects the table. When you're around people who have nice things, you need to know how to use them, how to protect them."

He nodded, feeling the awkwardness of the gesture.

"Now, drink your water, make yourself comfortable, and *keep your feet on the floor*." She bent down and pulled a thick, black, leather-bound book from the table's lower shelf. "Look at this," she said, "and I'll be right back."

She straightened and disappeared through a door in the wall to Keo's left. Keo's house didn't have a door in that wall. He took another look at the room he was in, revised his first guess that Than Taeng slept on the couch, and wondered what the bedroom looked like.

Beside the door to the bedroom hung a large photograph, perhaps a meter long, covered with glass. The glass reflected the stripes of sunlight, making it difficult for him to see the picture properly, but he slid as quietly as possible down the length of the couch, and the reflections on the glass moved far enough for him to confirm that it was a black-and-white image of a beautiful woman dressed all in black, or a color that photographed black, looking at the camera with such intensity that he wouldn't have been surprised to see her blink.

"Me," she said, coming out of the bedroom with a small greenish something in her hands. "In Bangkok, thirty years ago. When your mother was just a girl. Move back down, I want to sit."

He slid over to the black album she'd put on the table, and she sat beside him and held out her hand. It held what looked to him like a spool of thread inside a transparent box. "This is dental floss," she said. "You pull some out, knot it around your index fingers, and slide it back and forth between your teeth. Every space between your teeth. In the morning, at night. And you *do not* let anyone see you doing it. Here."

She offered him the small, neat-looking box and coached him through the process, and when she was satisfied with his technique and he was sitting there with a wad of floss in his hand, his gums bleeding a little, she said, "Moment," and got up again. When she returned, she had a paper towel in her hand. "On this," she said, and he carefully placed the used floss on the center of the towel, and she wadded it up, took it back to the kitchen, and dropped it into a can with a top that popped open when she stepped on a pedal.

"Every day," she said. "Keep the floss hidden. *Hidden.* Listen to me." She stopped in the center of the room, brilliant stripes of sunlight angling over her from head to foot. "*Anything you do that other people don't do* will be a weapon for them. Do you understand that?"

"Yes."

"The way you walk, the way you talk, the clothes you wear. If you floss your teeth and they don't. They can all be weapons that some people will use against you. Even the way you *think* about yourself."

"The way I think . . ." He looked up at her.

She leaned toward him slightly, just sending the words home. "As a girl," she said.

His eyes dropped to his lap, to his bare legs, dirty from the chase, with their ugly, knobby knees. Around the obstruction of his heartbeat, he said, without bringing his gaze up to meet hers, "I'm a boy."

"Open the album," she said.

It seemed like the safest thing to do. He lifted the cover and saw a smaller version of the photo on the wall, the black dress, the confidence in her eyes, eyes that said, *I'm beautiful and I know it.* He passed his fingers over the face.

"Turn the page," she said.

He did, and there she was again. There were pages of pictures, some big, some small. In some of them, she looked like she knew they were being taken and there was some kind of private joke between her and the camera. In some she seemed to be gazing straight through the camera at Keo—at, he thought, whoever might look at the picture.

He said, "You're beautiful." It felt strange to say it. He'd never said it to anyone, although he had imagined hearing it said to him.

"I was," she said. "For a while. Keep turning the pages."

As the pictures got older, they became less formal, and there were three or four on a page. In some of them, she was talking or laughing or smoking, unaware of the camera, but in most of them she had turned her head or raised her eyes to meet it. Usually she was with other women, but then, after a certain number of pages, they were *girls*, in their late teens and early twenties, and so was she. In many of these photos, the girls were heavily made up, and in a few the groups included *farang* men, usually older and bulkier, not laughing as loudly or smiling as broadly as the girls were. And then, toward the end of the book, she was a teenager, five or six years older than Keo, without makeup and wearing plain, simple clothes. Her eyes in these pictures weren't so confident.

Every now and then as he turned a page, she murmured a number, her age when the picture was taken, and then he turned to the last page and found himself looking at a village family, not much different from his family. There was a hut in the back-ground. The four children were standing stiffly, the mother shading her eyes against the sunlight, and the father's expression made it clear that he was putting up with being photographed, but not for much longer.

"Your mother and father?" Keo asked.

"Yes," she said, and then she put a finger on the girl on the left. "My sister Yim," she said, moving the finger. "My brother, Nong, my sister Kan." The last child in the row was a boy, standing slightly apart, with a sullen expression. She said, "Me."

Keo heard the word, but he couldn't make it mean anything until he squinted for a long, frozen moment at the child in the photo, definitely a boy, an *unhappy* boy, and then it seemed to him that he heard a buzzing noise and the room began to spin. He pulled his head back to take in a larger vista, to stop the whirling sensation, and she reached down and tapped a vermilion nail against the plastic over the boy's face. She said again, "Me."

He said, "*You? You did that?*"

"I did," she said. "And so can you." And then she told him what he was going to do to stay alive for the next few years.

L u t a n h   i s   s t a n d i n g, although she has no memory of having gotten up. Like her customer, all the girls on the stage are laughing. And she sees what they're laughing at.

The girl who's just pushed her way though the hanging cloth at the back of the stage, the one who calls herself Ying, or "woman," even though anyone whose eyes work can tell she began life as a big, ugly male, is waving her arms around like a drunken bird, making high, trilling sounds, and on her arms are Lutanh's wings.

Seeing them up there freezes Lutanh where she stands. When she wore them onstage as Peetapan, they felt transparent, airy, light enough to lift her from the ground. On Ying's big, loose-fleshed arms, under these horrible pink lights, they look cheap and childish. They're not even the same size.

But Dr. Srisai . . . He'd said . . .

Lutanh feels the foulest insults she knows rise inside her and rip at her throat, and as the other girls on the stage look at her wide-eyed, Ying turns her back, the wings catching the light, and yanks her pants down, giving Lutanh a deeply unwanted look at her big, fat ass.

Lutanh is on the stage in a blink, pushing girls right and left. Ying is at least a foot taller than she is, but Lutanh grabs her hair and yanks her around so they're face-to-face, and then reaches back as far as she can, balls up her fist, screams, and with Than Taeng's careful instructions in her ears, hits Ying's upper lip squarely on a slight downward angle, feeling it split like a grape beneath her knuckles. As Ying's blood, brilliant in the pink light, cascades down over her costume, Lutanh's friends swarm the stage behind her, and she's in a world of fists and elbows and screams and sweat and perfume and high-heeled shoes brought down on insteps.

Twenty minutes later she's shoved onto the sidewalk, still buttoning her denim shorts, four deep scratches making parallel tracks down her left cheek and her stage eye makeup smeared all the way to her chin. Her backpack hangs from her left shoulder—they didn't even give her time to work her arms through the straps—containing her violet dress, her stage shoes and costume, and her club makeup. Her shredded wings stick out at odd angles from the top of the pack. Behind her, seven or eight of Ying's friends shout curses from the doorway, and the fire kicks up inside her again. She whirls around and finds herself facing one of the street's "peacekeepers," mostly cops and former cops who are trained to apply just the right amount of violence to prevent *worse* violence on a street where hormones, rivalries, jealousy, and blood-alcohol levels run high. This one, who wears an amulet that looks like it weighs half a kilo hanging outside his striped polo shirt, gives her a flat stare that, she understands immediately, is the only alternative to *punch in the face* she'll be offered. He says, "Keep going."

She keeps going, her heart pounding in her ears, heading toward Silom and who knows what. She's been fired and cheated of the money she was owed for the week: her tiny salary, her cut of the drinks she's cadged, and a token piece of the bar fines customers shelled out for an hour or two of her time. She's been told it will be difficult, if not impossible, for her to get hired anywhere else. Her wings are destroyed, the plastic wrap sliced into a tangle of glistening ribbons by vengeful fingernails. The joy she'd felt after Dr. Srisai's class feels like a cruel joke played by malign spirits: first make her float on air, then bring her down and pull the floor out from under her at the same time.

She has no job, she's spent most of her money on Miaow's watch and her new violet eyes—only *this morning?*—her rent is weeks overdue and promised, against the threat of eviction, for this very night. *And* she knows the guy with the weird hair helmet and tattooed legs is following her. As she reaches Silom, she stops, turns, and gives him a glare that drives him back a full stride.

She steps down from the curb and holds out a hand to flag a motorcycle taxi, thinking that she'll get home, slip past the landlady somehow, and wash her face, and tomorrow she'll call Miaow and try to borrow some money. And get her to talk about Edwudd. A moto swerves toward her and she's moving aside for it when—like magic, because she's just thought about him—Edwudd comes up the stairs from one of the basement-level restaurants across the street, with Poke and Miaow flanking him. She turns quickly and bumps into the man with the tattooed legs.

Who puts his arms around her. Who says, "Where do you think you're going?"

9

Tomcatting

"ONE MORE STOP," Rafferty says, pocketing his cell phone and settling into the cab's backseat. "You have to be home at any special time, Edward?"

"I don't have to be home at all," Edward says from the front. "Auntie Pancake won't be back until we learn my father's coming. Then I'm supposed to phone her."

"Phone her where?" Miaow asks. She's beside Rafferty in the backseat.

"She *says* it's her sister's place," Edward says, "but a man answers the phone."

"Sister's husband," Rafferty suggests tactfully.

"Auntie's Thai boyfriend," Edward says. "I've heard her and my father yelling at each other about it."

"So you're alone in the house."

"I'm used to it." His tone closes the topic.

Miaow barges in anyway. "But what about the burglars?"

"Nothing left to take," he says. "Bunch of crap, fake antiques, cheap furniture. My dad has money, but he doesn't care where he lives. Anyway, they'd be dumb to come back. They got everything that's worth anything."

"Uh-uh," Miaow says. "They didn't get you."

Edward turns to look at her, and she settles into the seat, blushing furiously, eyes wide at her own courage.

* * *

ARTHIT HAS TRADED his police lieutenant colonel's uniform for a Boston Red Sox T-shirt, loose shorts, and gray workout socks, not a style Rafferty would suggest to anyone he liked, but it's Arthit's house. Arthit crosses a hairy calf over his knee, the sole of his foot pointed politely away from everyone in the room, and leans back, a short, dark, heavyset man in an unflattering yellow circle of light from the table lamp beside the sofa. He's got a beer in his hand. "First," he says, focusing on Edward, "just to give you an overview, here's what we're doing in the way of routine."

Edward says, as though the word hurts, "Routine?" He and Miaow occupy the pair of easy chairs that face the coffee table and the couch behind it. Rafferty and Arthit share the couch as though they've done it for years, which they have. Edward is leaning forward in his chair, hands clasped between his thighs. For all his bravado up until now, it's a vulnerable-looking position. The three of them had declined a drink when Arthit popped his beer.

Arthit lifts a hand. "I know, I know. There's nothing routine about this for you. To a cop, 'routine' refers to a checklist of things, important things, that have to be done because they often produce results. So here's the routine. We're checking immigration to make sure your father hasn't left the country. We're talking to immigration in the *other* countries in the region to rule out his having entered any of those. Thailand has some very porous river and mountain borders, so he could have left . . . umm, unofficially. I don't know why he would, but we're not making assumptions. His photograph and personal details have been sent as part of a priority be-on-the-lookout list to every police station in the country. We'll be showing his picture to bar employees in Nana Plaza, Soi Cowboy, and Patpong to see who might remember him and who might have seen him leave with anyone. Same routine with massage parlors in those areas. Cops on foot patrol here in Bangkok have his photograph. And there are other things we're doing and *will* be doing as we develop information. *Hundreds* of us, all over the country."

He hoists his beer, which is sheathed in a thick, clumsy-looking plastic sleeve that keeps the beer cold and prevents rings on the highly polished coffee table by filling up with condensation that spills out onto his shirt every time he drinks. The table is one of several new pieces in the room, brought in by his current partner, Anna, to replace the furniture that had stood there all the years Arthit had shared the place with his late wife, Noi. Since Noi died and Anna moved in, she's been claiming the house for herself, a few square meters at a time.

Arthit swallows, blots his wet shirt with his free hand, looks over at Poke and then at Edward. "I'm telling you all this just so you know we're not missing any bets. But we, by which I mean mainly Poke and I and a few others, are also going to pay a lot of attention to the men found in the canals."

Edward says, "Why?"

"I've been on the phone nonstop since Poke called from his apartment . . . what? Three hours ago? I put a couple of people I trust onto finding out what they could about the canal cases. What sticks out are, first, the robbery at your house and, second, the credit-card use. Two of the canal victims had apartments here, and both were burglarized immediately after they disappeared. Two more, who lived in hotels, had their rooms ransacked. And every one of them—at least all the ones we could identify and whose survivors we could locate—well, the survivors said that the victims' credit cards had been maxed. And finally there's been some work done on these cases, although not much, and we may find information we can use locked up in various files and in the boxes of the victims' effects." He sits back and exhales heavily. "So that's why."

Rafferty says, "You said two lived in hotels and two lived in apartments. How many have there been?"

"Twelve," Arthit says. "That I know of. Could be more."

Miaow says, "Twelve what, exactly?"

"Sorry," Arthit says. "Twelve dead men with casts, found in *klongs*. The brain-dead man you described to me, Poke, and the one your friend read about in the newspaper, plus ten whose files I've had people dig up since you called. And, who knows, maybe the man who left the country—"

"The guys I talked to only knew about two," Rafferty says. "Plus, as you say, maybe the one who ran away. And the bartender at the Expat—well, what used to be the Expat—said there were more."

"There are," Arthit says. "And the most recent was only a few months ago, so there's no reason to think the people behind it have folded their tents and moved up-country." He sits forward and uses the bottom of his T-shirt to mop a minuscule drop of water or beer from the table's surface. Anna, Rafferty knows, is particular about things like that. To Edward, Arthit says, "Sorry to have to tell you this."

Rafferty says, "Wait a minute. I live here. I'm not a hermit. I get out once in a while, and I even read the newspaper occasionally. If there were an army of men drowned in canals with casts on their legs, wouldn't I have heard about it?"

Arthit sighs. "There hasn't actually been much publicity."

Knowing he's just accidentally opened up a sore subject, Rafferty says, "Shit."

"So maybe thirteen in all, counting your one who got away. Ten Caucasians, if the one who escaped was."

"He was."

"And three Asians. And I have to ask you, the one who got away, had he been wearing a cast?"

"I didn't ask." Rafferty says. "I'm not sure the guys who told me about him would know."

"Well, then either he has nothing to do with this or else he's uniquely fortunate. And there might be a few more that the cops I talked to just haven't heard about yet."

Rafferty says, "Over what period of time?"

"A little less than eight years," Arthit says, looking uneasy.

"Excuse me," Edward says, moving through the opening Rafferty inadvertently created, "why *hasn't* there been much publicity?"

Arthit shifts as though his seat is uneven and lumpy. He says, "This is awkward." He clears his throat, probably just to get a moment to organize his thoughts. "The least venal reason is that the media are under a certain amount of pressure not to focus on events that would dampen tourist enthusiasm. Bad for the economy." He's using the impersonal, official voice the police use to explain why yet another rich drunk driver has been set free, but then he looks down at his lap, and when he looks back up, his expression has changed. "One of the *more* venal reasons is that my colleagues—by which I mean the Royal Thai Police— haven't done much, if anything, to solve the crimes. In fact, there's been an ongoing effort to deny that crimes were committed at all. In six of the cases I've learned about since Poke's phone call, details like the canals and the casts were omitted from the official reports and the cause of death was listed as 'heart stopped.'"

"That's pretty generic," Edward says.

"Yes, it covers what the New Testament describes as 'a multitude of sins.' In a world where so many murders go unsolved, it's a very useful phrase."

"Why?" Edward's face has tightened in a way that makes him look older. "Why do so many murders go unsolved?"

"Good question," Arthit says. He takes a deep, resigned-sounding breath, uncrosses his legs, and leans forward, giving Edward all his attention. "I'm sorry if I sounded flip. I know, this might be your father we're talking about—let's hope not—but I forget how strange this appears to people who don't live here. Cases go unsolved for several reasons. The main one is money, or the lack of it. Police at the bottom of the pyramid make less than minimum wage, not even ten dollars a day, nowhere near enough to feed a family and pay rent, and they have to pay for things like their uniforms and their guns, so they devote quite a lot of energy to supplementing their income. It's hard to do that if you're spending too much time on cases that don't pay off, and there doesn't seem to be any money in this one."

"Why aren't they paid better?"

Arthit's glance at Poke says he holds his friend responsible for the conversation. "I'm not big on conspiracy theories," he says, "so I'll deny ever having said this. Looked at in one way, putting thousands of underpaid, overarmed cops on the street, with all the authority of uniforms everywhere, might satisfy two objectives. First, it reduces the budget of the police force, makes it look 'cost-effective,' a phrase politicians love. Second, with thousands of them out there, soliciting and taking small bribes all day, you create a substantial flow of money. Some of that money goes upstairs, and some of what goes upstairs goes farther upstairs, and you wind up with high-ranking cops retiring with tens of millions of baht when their salary would barely keep a large American family in shoes. I am not, of course, suggesting that such a scheme actually exists." He looks around the living room. "But this house? I could never afford it on my salary. My wife's family had the money."

Edward is rubbing his face with both hands.

"So if you're going to operate like that," Arthit continues, "sitting on some cases and perhaps even *profiting* from others, you don't want a bunch of unsolved murders cluttering up the records."

"Profiting?" Edward says.

"It's not unknown, it's not even uncommon, for a cop who stumbles over a particularly juicy scheme to make himself a kind of partner. He'll deflect inquiries, and if other cops seem to be getting close, he'll hold up a warning sign and give the crooks a chance to disappear. All, naturally, in exchange for a cut. This kind of thing is, of course, solid gold for crusading journalists and ambitions politicians. The official cause of death 'heart stopped' keeps the record looking respectable, makes it harder for some would-be hero with his own agenda to characterize the police as venal and fumbling."

"But they *are*," Miaow says, and Edward, who has opened his mouth to reply, sits back an inch or two.

Arthit nods. "I know dozens of cops who hold a second full-time job, working sixteen or more hours a day, just to stay afloat, and many of them do the best they can. But that's not true of all of them." He lifts the beer and then puts if down again. "Obviously. What I'm telling you, I suppose, is that it's more complex than you might think." Poke can hear the clipped edges of Arthit's old British accent, earned decades ago during his years at an English university. It's a sign that his friend dislikes the direction the conversation has taken.

"I still don't know how you can work in a . . . in an outfit like that," Edward says.

Arthit regards the boy for a moment before he says, "By not *doing* any of that." Rafferty starts to say something, but Arthit, with a barely visible gesture, waves him off. "And by listening to people like you here, rather than at the station."

Edward nods and then lowers his head further, a gesture that looks something like an apology.

Rafferty lets the silence stretch out.

* * *

THE DINING ROOM is rich with the fragrance of coffee. "I'm not widely seen as a team player," Arthit says, "so I'm intention-ally kept out of the flow of information on things that don't concern me. That means all this is new to me and all I really know is what I learned from my friends on the force after Poke called me." He puts his cup down, empty, after two gulps. He's brewed two cups of a dark Vietnamese roast for himself and Poke and poured some kind of juice for Miaow, but at the last moment Edward said he wanted coffee, too, so Arthit divided two cups' worth into three smaller cups and put another pot on to brew. With the cups and glasses in hand, they're more comfortable at the dining-room table, so highly polished that they can look down, if they want to, at rippled, oddly colored versions of their own faces.

Arthit opens a small black notebook covered in imitation leather that's already split in several places to reveal the cardboard beneath. "Okay, this isn't encouraging stuff. As I said, twelve or thirteen victims so far, and probably more that we don't know about. Here's what they have in common: They're all older men, non-Thai, who arrived alone in Bangkok and, to some extent or another, participated in the commercial sex scene, usually the gaudier, more public variety, where anyone who's looking could spot a good prospect."

"What does 'good prospect' mean?" Edward says.

"That they frequent places like Soi Cowboy or Nana, where an observer could hide in a crowd. That they come back often to give the watcher a look at their routines, that they flash money around and wear nice clothes. And that most nights they get drunk enough to be—by normal standards anyway—impaired." He looks up. "That doesn't mean the killers couldn't also have recruited the

victims through escort services, massage parlors, the Internet—
you name it. That's why we're checking those. The length of time
between the date the missing men disappeared and the date on
which they were found suggests to me that the casts on the perfectly good legs are primarily a means of immobilizing the victims.
Also, they all had enormous amounts of dope in their systems."

"What kind?" Rafferty says.

"Pain medication, by which I mean opioids, muscle relaxants,
tranquilizers, sleepers—pretty much anything on the downer end
of the spectrum." He glances over at Edward. "If it helps at all,
they were probably barely aware of what was happening to them."

"The people doing this are *doctors?*" Edward sounds incredu-
lous.

"I doubt it. Doctors make a good living, and they've probably
got too much to lose. I suppose one of them could be a doctor who
was driven out of practice. But whoever they are, they seem to
have some medical experience. The casts are apparently professionally done, and as much dope as the victims had in their
systems, they also had water in their lungs, which means they
were alive when they were thrown in. A male nurse, maybe, some
kind of orderly, someone who's done these things professionally."

Rafferty says, "You said that the places some of the victims
lived in were broken into later, like Edward's house was. Only
some of them?"

Arthit flips through his notes for a moment. "It might have
been all of them, but we don't know. The two who lived in apartments, yes. The ones who stayed in hotels—most of them, in
other words—well, after a few days the hotels figured they'd
ducked out or had a heart attack or something, so the rooms got
cleared out and other people moved in. They might *all* have been
searched, rather than just the two we know about, but neatly
enough that the maids didn't realize it. If the stuff the killers

wanted was clearly visible or in the room safe . . . well, most of those are just the little tin cans where you can enter a four-digit code. About half the people who use those enter numbers based on their birthday or address, so if these guys were walking around with, say, a driver's license, their kidnappers would have that information. Eventually the hotels just bagged up the victims' stuff and put it in storage. There was no way later for us to know what was missing and what had been pocketed by the staff."

"Auntie Pancake," Edward says, "my father's live-in girlfriend, said it wouldn't do any good to talk to the cops. And from what you've said about them—"

"Your auntie was probably right. But I'm not just 'the cops,' and *Poke*, who's not a cop at all, doesn't need approval from anyone in the department. And through me he can access some of the information we—the police—have."

"You'd do that?" Edward says to Arthit. "You'd break the rules like that?"

"That's why we're here, isn't it?" Arthit says. Edward looks down at the table, as though he's checking his reflection, but Rafferty can see how fast he's blinking.

Arthit stands, saying, "How about a full cup of coffee, Edward?"

RAFFERTY STIRS WHAT'S left in his cup, which has gone cold, with his index finger and then licks his finger, trying to think of a new question, but Arthit speaks up first.

"Several of the victims, all *farang*, left in their rooms cards and handwritten notes that suggest they might have used massage parlors and outcall services in addition to hitting the bars. If that's true, and if we can establish that there's one or more services they all used, then there's probably a source there somewhere, someone who tipped off the killers. Or maybe even lured them in in the first place."

"What about laptops?" Miaow asks.

"I'll check," Arthit says, making a note in the scruffy book. "You'd think they'd be taken, but who knows? Maybe they were ratty and old."

"Or ran Windows," Miaow says.

"Edward," Rafferty says, "do you know whether your father used outcall services, massage parlors, places like that?"

"I don't think he missed a bet," Edward says. "I think he'd check out skywriting."

There's an awkward pause. It's Miaow who takes the leap. "Did women come home with him? I mean, women who weren't your aunties?

"All the time. Whenever Auntie Pancake was gone."

"So," Arthit says, "can I send someone over to look through his things?"

"Sure," Edward says. "Just call me so I'll be there. After school."

Rafferty says, "I'll do it."

"You can't do them all," Arthit says. "There are apparently some boxes of stuff at various stations that belonged to some of the victims. I'll put someone on those, either Anand or Clemente."

"Clemente? That's the half-Filipina with the amazing eyes?"

"It is."

"Are she and Anand . . . well, are they?"

"Far as I know."

"Young love," Rafferty says. "I remember it distantly."

"You're not *that* old," Miaow says.

"Yes he is," Arthit says. "But to get back to the topic, I'll put Clemente on going through all the effects of the other victims. If she can find an overlap, a possible connection at an outcall service or a massage parlor or even a bar, it might move things along. But, Edward, remember that while Poke and my handpicked people will be working on this, we've got hundreds of cops doing the routine. Among the lot of us, we'll work it out. We'll find the killers."

Rafferty says, "You keep saying 'killers.'"

"At least two, probably more," Arthit says. "If we're talking about the canal deaths, I mean. The victims couldn't have walked down to those canals even if their legs hadn't been in casts. The ones who were subjected to tissue samples, including the one who's brain-dead, had so much dope in them you could have nailed them to a tree and they wouldn't have noticed. So they were all both heavy *and* limp, essentially deadweight. And awkward with those rigid legs. Probably took two people, at a minimum, to get them down to the *klong* and toss them in and a third to drive, since this isn't the kind of thing you flag a cab for. My guess is the driver got them to the drop-off point and then took a couple of runs around the block so the car, just idling by the canal, wouldn't attract attention. And there's a certainty, as far as I'm concerned, that one of them, probably the driver, is a black widow, the woman who gets them to go with her in the first place, probably gives them the mickey that lets the others come in and get him, take him wherever they take them and dope them while they siphon off their lines of credit."

Rafferty says, "Jesus."

"And what I started to say about the casts. They're weighted, to make sure the victims sink. Later, of course, as the gases build up, they float, but."

He stops talking. Edward is rocking back and forth in his chair, his eyes on the table. It's cool in the house, but there's perspiration on his upper lip.

Miaow says, "Hey," and leans over to put her left hand over Edward's right. He stops suddenly and looks up at them, then shakes his head.

"Sorry," he says. "I don't . . . I don't like my father very much, but . . . but ummm . . ." He closes his eyes.

"Nobody deserves this," Miaow says.

"No," Arthit says briskly. "Nobody. And they might not have your father at all."

"The burglaries," Edward says.

"Could be coincidence," Arthit says. "Poke, why don't you and I finish—"

"Please," Edward says. "I need to know all this." He eases his hand out from under Miaow's gently, and she snatches hers back as though unaware she's touched him. He uses both palms to wipe his face, and then he dries his hands on his shirt and puts his right hand back where it was when Miaow covered it with hers. Then he moves it a little closer to her, and after a moment she touches him again.

"So," Edward says, "if this is what happened, my father was out doing what he calls 'tomcatting,' when he met a woman who sweet-talked him, or something more basic, to get him to go with her somewhere, and she drugged him, and then they put him someplace, and he probably woke up with casts on his legs and all fucked up—excuse me—from the dope, and they're keeping him that way while they steal his money, is that about it?"

"Yes," Arthit says.

"And then they're going to kill him."

Arthit hesitates and then nods. "So far that's how it seems to have gone."

Edward starts to say something, clears his throat, and says, "He must be frightened."

"Arthit," Poke says. "A while ago you said something about how long the men were held between the disappearance and the finding of a body? What's the longest period you know about?"

Arthit glances at Edward very quickly and turns to Poke. "Fourteen days."

Miaow says, "But Edward's father has been—" She breaks off and looks down at the table.

"Twelve days," Edward says. "Tomorrow it'll be thirteen."

"We'll do all we can," Arthit says. "All over the country." They're standing in the living room, on the way out. "And here in Bangkok I'll see that Poke gets everything Clemente and I can find, and I can lend him Anand and one or two other people, off the record, if it looks promising."

Edward nods. He seems remote, even stunned. There's a possible time limit now. He tries to say something and clears his throat instead. Says, "Thank you."

"And you need to call the American embassy tomorrow," Rafferty tells him. "They can put some pressure on the cops."

"Although the response," Arthit says, "will be mostly cosmetic."

They all hear the front door open, and Anna calls, "Hello? We're home."

"We have guests," Arthit says, a trace of warning in his tone. The door snicks closed, and Anna takes a few tentative steps into the room. She smiles a hello and raises her eyebrows at Arthit, a gesture that says, *Anyone else?*

"Just us," Arthit says.

"It's *Poke*," Anna announces to the air, stressing the name as though it's the information that will clinch a difficult deal. "And *Miaow*."

A moment passes, and then Treasure peers around the corner. She smiles at Miaow, nods to Rafferty, and then her eyes stop on Edward. She blinks so heavily that Rafferty can almost hear it.

"This is Edward," he says. "A friend of Miaow's."

"Hello," Treasure says. It's the only time in Rafferty's memory that she's been the first to speak to anyone.

"Hi," Edward says.

Treasure comes all the way into the room, and Rafferty's breath snags in his throat. When he initially saw her, in the house of her abusive, probably insane father, she'd been ghostly: tenuous, terrified, and almost emaciated. In the seven or eight weeks since he's been in the same room with her, she's gained weight. Her bone structure no longer pushes aggressively against her skin, and the mask of controlled muscle that defined her face for so long has relaxed, at least a little. She's straightened her spine. Her shoulders are no longer hunched protectively. She looks healthier and younger than she did that night in the home of her father. Whom Rafferty killed.

He says, "Seeing you here makes me very happy."

Arthit says, "She's making all of us happy."

Treasure's head is tilted down, eyes on the carpet, but she might be smiling, a little.

"Okay," Arthit says briskly, taking the spotlight off Treasure. "We've got a plan, of sorts, and we'll talk in the morning, yes, Poke? And Poke's right, Edward—call the embassy first thing tomorrow. It can't hurt, and you never know, it might even help."

"Treasure," Miaow says, "can I come over someday?"

Treasure nods. She glances up at Miaow quickly and says, "Yes." Her eyes skitter to Edward for a second and then away, toward an unoccupied spot in the room. "I'd like that."

"Done, then," Arthit says. He touches Edward on the arm. "We'll do what we can."

"Thank you," Edward says. "I'm sorry I was—"

"Forget it," Arthit says. "You had good reason." He's looking at Treasure, who has glanced back at Edward. Edward is studying the carpet, clearly somewhere else.

Miaow looks from Treasure to Edward. She says to Poke, "Let's go."

10

Chewing through a Wall

THIS IS WRONG. Every instinct she has is scrabbling for attention, like rats chewing through a wall.

Five thousand baht, she recites to herself. *Five thousand—*

He has his arm around her. He smells, a little, of meat.

She's told him her name three times now, in about twelve minutes.

Tonight is the night the bar was supposed to pay her. She has only 212 baht. Where can she sleep?

He's strong. When she tried to loosen his grasp on her shoulders, he didn't even use his arm strength to keep her in tow. He just tightened the fingers around her left shoulder and propelled her along.

"Pretty little thing," he says for the third time, and she remembers the slow, disconnected way his facial expressions had changed, and she thinks, *Get out of here.*

And then she remembers she's not that frightened little boy anymore. She hasn't run away from anyone in months and months. She *broke Ying's nose.* That cow. She tightens her grip on the backpack. He's tried to take it, to help her, he said. She doesn't need help.

No, she decides, her nervousness isn't hard to understand. What she's nervous about is the job she lost and the area they're in, a dim snarl of streets between Silom and Surawong, in which the only lit doors seem to open into bars featuring boy shows. It's not anywhere she's been before, not anywhere she'd have reason to go. And she's nervous about the identity card she'll have to leave with the security man who will be stationed in front of the elevators at the man's hotel. Since she's in Thailand illegally, she had to pay more than six thousand baht for it. It looked fine, it was a careful job that layered her face over a copy of another girl's card, and she hadn't noticed until the first time a guard pushed it back at her, shaking his head, that the other girl was twenty-nine years old. Lutanh is barely eighteen and doesn't look even that. After that she'd started wearing heavier makeup, and the card hasn't been refused since. So, she decides, that's all it is. The job. The neighborhood. The card.

At that moment the man, whose name is a syllable she's never heard before, maybe "Stan" if that's a name, takes a sudden left. He's pushing her up a couple of broad stairs and through a glass door and into a large, twilit room that seems to be the lobby of a small hotel, one she's never seen.

There's no one behind the desk. She's revising her guess—*might be an apartment house or a cheap condominium*—as he leads her across the room and toward a corridor, and she slows. He slows with her, looking down with his eyebrows raised.

"I think I change mind," Lutanh says.

"Just be nice," he says. "Half an hour, six thousand baht."

"Seven," Lutanh says. Maybe he'll say no. But with seven thousand she could pay all the rent she owes on her room and have enough left over to stay there for a week or two, maybe even negotiate a third while she figures out what to do next. Where to go.

"Seven," he says. "Because you're so pretty." He guides her into the even dimmer corridor, where she sees an elevator, its doors closed. In front of it is the security man's desk, and she's surprised at the disappointment she feels when she sees there's no one there. "Magic," the man says, making a show of pressing the button. The doors slide open. He puts his hand on the back of her neck to lead her in.

She simply stops moving, just puts her feet together in their rubber-soled running shoes and digs in. He tugs at her once, and when she resists, he drops his arm, steps back into the elevator, and runs the tip of his tongue over his upper lip. "Well, if you don't want to come . . ." he says. He lets his gaze fall to the elevator floor for a moment and takes his finger off the button. The door starts to slide closed, but he puts a foot out and stops it. "Wait a second." He rummages through his trouser pocket and brings out a wad of thousand-baht notes, maybe thirty of them, and he flips slowly through the bundle until he comes up with a five-hundred. He holds it out to her. "At least," he says, "get something to eat. And you need to clean up *here*." He touches her scratched cheek gently.

"I sorry," Lutanh says. She shrugs the pack over her free arm so it's no longer dangling from one shoulder, gently pushes the hand aside, and gets in. "I come with you."

"Good girl," he says. He steps back to give her more space and lets the doors close. "So," he says for the fourth time, "what's your name?"

Lutanh gives him her sweetest smile and says, "Sally."

He holds her eyes, and one muscle at a time as the elevator rises, he builds a smile. "Sally," he says. "Pretty Sally."

THE HALLWAY IS dim, and it smells like wet paper. The carpet squishes underfoot as they pass beneath the dripping overhead air conditioners. She can hear the plop of water farther down the corridor, and the odor makes her want to choke. The air is cold on her bare legs. Why does someone who carries around thirty thousand baht, who handles the bills like they were toilet tissue, stay in a place like this?

The fear peeks out at her again. He stops and inserts a card into a slot in the door—422, it reads, so she's on the fourth floor. He withdraws the card, puts the hand with the card in it on the horizontal door handle, and pushes down. At the same time, he slips his free arm around her neck, pulls her close, and half drags her into the room. He pivots to his right and kicks the door closed behind him, knocking her sideways with his hip as he snaps the lock into place and slaps a metal hasp over an exposed latch three-quarters of the way up the door.

I'll have to undo both those things, she thinks automatically as she backs away, *to open the door.*

The place stinks of meat.

The bed is a heap of blankets and discarded clothes, such suggestive piles that her imagination turns them for a moment into bodies. The pillows, their cases stained with what she tries to tell herself is coffee, are partly hanging off the couch. On the table in front of the couch is a low wooden table with serving trays on it, each containing a dinner plate bearing an uneaten mess of vegetables and rice, plus the bone from a steak, gnawed to where the red meat meets the bone. She thinks, with a jolt of terror, he hasn't let the maid into this place in—

She sees movement out of the corner of her eye and tries to jump, but he's on her.

He's got her backpack, but he's not snatching it away, he's squeezing the straps together, forcing her shoulders back until she cries aloud. Then one hand twists the left strap around her arm as she tries to shy to her right, and the other slips down the back of her shorts, his knuckles pressed into the base of her spine. He yanks her backward, the top half of her body folding forward from the momentum. At the moment her hands brush the carpet—trying senselessly to find something to hold on to, he hauls her, one-handed, straight up, as tightly angled as a jackknife, and lets her dangle. Things spill from the pack, and then it slips from her shoulders and hits the floor. She starts to scream, and he gives her a bone-rattling shake, as though she were a misbehaving puppy, and says, "You shut up, and I'll be nice, right? Say 'Right.'"

"Right," Lutanh says. "Right, right." Her head is filling with blood, and her heart is pounding so hard she thinks it will explode. The cosmetics and clothes from her bag are scattered across the carpet. "Right, right."

"That's better," he says. He lowers her, but her legs won't behave, and she crumples to her bare knees in the middle of her possessions, her weight snapping the wood in one of her wings with a sharp *crack*, a hot patch at her crotch telling her she's wet her shorts. She says to his legs, not daring to look up at him, "Please."

"This will only take a minute," he says. "Stand up."

"I can't."

He says, "You have no *idea* what you can do," and she gets her legs under her, leans on the edge of the wooden table, and manages to stand.

"Look at me," he says, and she does.

He shakes his head and smiles, almost affectionately, and then he says, "You little *faggot*," and his right arm comes up to his left shoulder, and he whips the back of his hand across her face.

Her head snaps around, bones at the back of her neck going off like popcorn, a lightning strike of pain announcing that the scratches Ying left on her cheek have opened more deeply. She topples to her right, but before she goes all the way down, he's knotted his hand in her hair and tugged her back up, and once she's upright, he sweeps her feet out from under her with his right leg and lets go of her hair.

And she's falling sideways, nothing to grab on to, toward the table and the fat, greasy red meat, but somehow she gets an elbow down and lands on it with most of her weight, the elbow dead center in one of the plates. The plate and its tray, with her elbow still on it, skid across the surface of the table—wet, she realizes, with her own blood—toward the couch, but somehow she manages to get her other hand down, trying to stop the slide, the fall, whatever it is, and something slices into her palm. Her fingers close around it spasmodically, and she recognizes it as a knife, one of the sharp ones for steak.

Her cry of pain is pitched so high it frightens her even more. She lets herself slide the rest of the way until she's splayed across the table, stomach down, her back unprotected and her nose bleeding into the nearest pillow, and he grabs the back of her shorts and lifts again, and when she folds forward this time, she doesn't resist it; instead she goes with it, and at the point where she's hanging, head down, closest to his legs, she sinks the knife into the big muscle at the front of his thigh, and then she jerks it free and aims it at his kneecap, feeling it hit something hard and complicated before it skitters aside, but then she's falling again, because he's dropped her and is stumbling back, bellowing, both hands finding the slice in his thigh and then, with another bellow, getting the telegram of pain from his knee.

On the carpet—in a defensive crouch that transports her instantly to her boyhood in the village—with the point of her knife aimed at him, Lutanh watches him back up, fast and off balance, until his hamstrings strike the edge of an armchair, and he goes down heavily into a precarious sitting position, the armchair tilting and almost going over backward, and then she's up, screaming again, except this time it's nothing but hatred, and she brings the edge of the knife down across his face on a diagonal, the blood coming instantly. She gets a foot under the edge of the chair and lifts, tipping him further back until it goes all the way over and slams into the floor, his howl of pain turning into a grunt, and she's running for the door, throwing the hasp aside, hearing the chair turn over sideways as, probably, he fights himself free of it, and then she's unsnapping the lock and yanking the door open. Then everything goes away for a moment or five or six, and she's in the middle of a kind of opaque, pearl-colored shining, and when she returns to herself, she's hurtling down the fire stairs: third floor, second floor, first floor, *the door* . . .

. . . and through it and past the elevators, past the man who's now sitting at the security desk, who's leaping to his feet and shouting after her, the blood from her nose pouring over her mouth and chin, and she slows just enough to take a giant slice out of the air in his direction, him putting his hands up and backing away from the knife, and then she's out through the hotel door and running, running, with no idea where.

Halfway to nowhere at all, she stops as though she's slammed into a wall and wipes blood from her face, thinking, My *wings. My bag. My wings.*

11

I Smell a Broken Heart

"S o y o u ' l l l o o k for his father," Rose says. She's lying beside him on the bed, wearing one of his ancient Sleater-Kinney T-shirts and a pair of loose cotton shorts, the glorious, heavy hair that falls to the middle of her back wrapped tightly in a damp towel, the second she's used since he got home. He's waiting for the air conditioner to make itself felt. Every now and then, without being obvious about it, he sneaks a sniff of her shampoo.

"He pretends not to be scared," he says, "but he is."

She says, "Mmmm," and touches the towel, checking to see whether it's time for the third one. She shifts a little against the ache in her back.

"It's going to keep me out of the house for a while." He's lying on his back, too, with one sock-clad foot up on the mattress and the other, the right, hanging off the edge with an untied shoe dangling from it. He straightens his knee quickly enough to flip the shoe end over end across the room, but it lands short of its mate.

"I understand that," Rose says, "and I appreciate it." They're speaking what Poke thinks of as their personal linguistic invention, a kind of Thaiglish that blends his barely passable Thai and her improving English. She says, "I'll miss you."

He turns his head to look at her. "Really?"

"Of course, I will. You know I will."

He goes up on one elbow and tries to kiss her on the forehead, but she lifts her chin and finds his mouth. Then she nods in satisfaction and lies back again. "I'm going out to lunch with Fon tomorrow."

"That's good," he says. "I worry about you being alone."

"I'm not—" she begins, but breaks off.

"I know, I know." He casts around for a new subject. "I think Miaow's getting serious about Edward."

"I see that," Rose says. "It worries me. He's too good-looking."

"He doesn't seem to realize it. The girls in Patpong were all yelling at him, and even Treasure—I mean, she said *hello* to him."

Rose turns to look at him. "First?"

"Hard to believe."

She raises both eyebrows. "Maybe she's getting better."

"She's put on weight. We need to have dinner with them, with Arthit and Anna. When you feel up to it, I mean."

"The girls at Miaow's school like him, too, or so she says. Maybe she's exaggerating it."

"I don't think so. When we were walking tonight, I was invisible as far as young women were concerned."

"You poor old thing," she says. "Get used to it."

The silence stretches out in a comfortable manner. When Rafferty shifts his weight, trying to roll his left sock down his calf with his right foot, she says, "What were you and Miaow talking about in the living room?"

"A play they're doing at school, about a street girl who becomes a lady. I downloaded it on her laptop, and my guess is that she's reading it in her room." He gets the sock over his heel, then presses his right foot over the sock's toe and pulls his left foot free.

Rose says, "Why don't you just sit up and take them off?"

"Anybody can do that," he says. "I'm different."

"I'll bet she's not reading the play," Rose says. "She's sitting there worrying about Edward."

He's begun work on the other sock. "He wants to be in it, too."

Rose says, "I smell a broken heart." She sits up, grunting a little at the pull in her back. "Last towel of the night."

"Then can I be the dryer guy?" Her routine involves a series of tightly rolled towels to get her hair to the point at which she can blow it dry it without turning on the heating element, and Rafferty loves to do that part for her, running the long, sleek, black hair over his forearm and watching it ripple and shine like liquid night as he directs the flow of air at it.

"Sure," she says. "You've been good." She listens to what she's just said. "I'm a very lucky woman," she says, "and I know it." She gets up, goes to the foot of the bed, and pulls his sock the rest of the way off, taking a swipe with her nails at the bottom of his very ticklish foot.

Rafferty says, "Yikes," and pulls his foot away. "Just throw them over near the shoes. They have things to discuss."

"You're joking. These need to be washed. Maybe twice."

"Takes time to break in a good sock," Rafferty says.

"The people upstairs can probably smell them." She picks up the other sock from the floor, letting them dangle from her fingertips, and drops both of them in the plastic hamper, which is full almost to overflowing. She squeezes the towel experimentally. "Got to do wash tomorrow."

"Well," he says, giving her an innocent expression she's certain he used often on his mother, "I'd be really happy to do it for you, but . . . you know, I've got to go out, to—" He stops because she's already left the room.

She has to go around snapping off the lights in the living room because Poke seems to believe either that electricity is free or that somewhere some luminous entity is tallying spiritual points, karmic gold stars, for those who use the most of it. The hallway light is off, but she can see the yellow strip beneath Miaow's door, so she knocks.

"*What?*" Miaow says, sounding like it's the fiftieth interruption in ten minutes.

"Just hello," Rose says, continuing down the hall.

"Oh," Miaow says. "Hi, Mom." The door remains closed.

Hi, Mom, Rose thinks as she pushes open the door to the bathroom at the end of the hall. *I have an American child.*

She flips on the bathroom light, unrolling the towel as she closes the door behind her. The face in the mirror is older than it used to be; in the six, almost seven years she's been living with Poke, she's lost what she had hoped would be an unusually prolonged youthfulness and she's become someone who finally looks her age. And, she thinks, leaning toward the mirror and studying the barely visible wrinkles at the corners of her eyes, maybe a little more.

It hardly seems fair. She'd had no idea she was beautiful until she was hauled down from a tiny, impoverished farming village in the northeast to work in Patpong, and now she's fading. Meanwhile Miaow is coming into her own kind of beauty as a teenager with a dangerously handsome boyfriend, and Poke looks exactly like he did when he met her. She's the only one who's getting old. And she can see the fear in her face.

Can he see it?

She has the dryer in her hand and is fanning her hair and letting it fall through the stream of air before she remembers that she's come in to towel-dry it and roll it up again, that she's told Poke he could handle the dryer. Well, she thinks, he'd hear it and come to the door if he wanted to take over. She likes the way he handles her hair, never snagging on it or pulling it.

But he doesn't. Maybe, she half hopes, he's fallen asleep. She sections her hair, damper than usual since she only toweled it twice, and lets the dryer range over it. The air is cool, almost cold on her shoulders, and there's something cold inside her, too.

And here she is. Where she chose to be all those years ago. With Poke and their adopted street child, hundreds of kilometers from home. And frightened.

Her parents' village was built beside a river. At some point, generations past, the people who first stopped there put up their huts and dug their rice paddies, thanking the spirits of the place for showing them a river that would provide nearly everything the village needed to remain alive. The river would water the rice and fill the wells. But in their first year, they learned that it flooded in the rainy season, washing away one of the year's three crops, and dried to a fine, red, waterless dust in the summer, endangering the second. The people adjusted, Rose thinks, to living on one, and sometimes two, harvests less. They adjusted their expectations, which were low enough to begin with. The poor have to learn to adjust. Only the rich can be rigid.

So there they were, in their village with their treacherous stream, and she grew up beside it, beside what they called Fools' River. People never knew until it was too late, she thinks, whether the place where they pitched their tent was on the banks of some Fools' River.

When she first realized she had Poke's child inside her, it announced itself in a dream: Fools' River, broader and deeper than usual, was flowing past her, coming around a bend, bringing something to her. She'd awakened in the middle of the night, certain that the dream had significance, and the next morning, on the phone, her mother had told her what it meant, had told her that she'd seen Rose pregnant in the street several times now only to find, when the woman turned, that it wasn't Rose at all. The river brought her the news of the baby.

That alone should have been enough to put Rose on her guard.

And now Poke is waiting for that baby. Sitting on the bank of Fools' River and peering around the bend, waiting for it to bring him the thing he wants most in life. Trusting it. *Depending* on it.

Her fingers snarl in her hair as the cramp returns. She yanks through the snarl and leans on the sink for a moment, looking at the knot of hair in her hand. Then she turns the dryer's fan to high to drown herself out and says aloud, to her reflection, "I'm terrified."

12

Ink

THIS TIME THE surface seems very far off.

He needs to breathe, he *needs to breathe*, but he knows he'll drown if he does. His lungs are screaming to be filled, but the water is dark and thick and swarming with unimaginable things.

He was a swimmer once. In high school, when his life was something to look forward to. He won races; he won medals. The butterfly, the breaststroke. He'd been slender; he'd been young, he'd had a different girlfriend every week and a shelf full of trophies because he could *control his breath*. Winning was about breathing; breathing was everything. In the last third of the last lap, when your lungs were fire, when you saw dark paramecia, amoebas, changing shape before your eyes, when the only thing your body wanted was a breath, you didn't break the rhythm to take one.

He strains against the weight of the water, pulling himself through it, asking himself, *Where is my fucking buoyancy?*

And then he breaks through, gasping in the dark, and opens his eyes.

What time is it?

Dark. The amber and yellow lights on the medical machines are blinking where they always blink. There are streetlights out there beyond the window, he knows; the upward tilt of the blinds turns their glare into pale horizontal stripes across the ceiling, straight as the lanes in a pool. He's gasping, stretching his mouth wide to admit more air, to pull his eyes even wider open, waiting for the veils to lift.

What the *hell* have they given him? This is the deepest it's ever been. Everything that happened before he went under seems to be on the other side of a thick pane of smoked glass.

His heart is slamming in his chest like a ball on a squash court. He slows his breathing. Pancake told him often, before she gave up on trying to help him, that slow, steady breathing would bring his heart under control and clear his head. He rubs his eyes. Pancake. He's been awful to her. Sweet, plain, dithery Pancake. He doesn't deserve—

He's rubbing his eyes.

His right hand is free. He reaches down, and sure enough, the back of his hand hits the cuff, still dangling from the bed rail. His left is still secured.

A thought approaches him on the other side of the smoked glass, and then it assumes a kind of shape. It's a familiar shape, and it's tinged with a familiar fragrance. *He's been here before.*

The sense of smell, he knows, drives nails through memories to hold them in place: Memories associated with scent last forever.

He smells his fingers.

Ink.

The last time he woke up like this, it was light. Either daytime or the lights were on, he's not sure. He had dark blue ballpoint ink all over his index finger. It had an odd kind of off-perfume, off-petroleum smell. He'd been holding a leaky pen. And now, if the smell is any guide, he's done it again.

And it's happened more than twice.

The thought jumps the arc, and he thinks, *Money. They're taking my money.* And there's not that much of it where they can get it.

When I run out, he thinks, *I'll be dead.*

He thinks, *How much is there? How much time do I have?*

He thinks, *Edward,* and the name strikes him like a blow. He yanks the cuffed hand hard enough to hurt, hard enough to make a sharp, metallic sound. *Edward,* he thinks again, and this time the name leads to another thought: *I've got to get out of here.*

He hears a sound in the corridor. Someone is coming. Frantically, he fumbles with the open cuff, trying to make it look like it's still locked. Another sound, just the give of an old floor under weight. As much as the giant doctor frightens him, he hopes that's who it is. He's absolutely terrified of the nurse.

The door to the room opens.

Part Two
THE BEND

13

Time's Wingèd Chariot

FRAN DEPENDAHL, THE wife of the man who had been found brain-dead in a *klong* with casts on his legs, lives in one of the new high-rise condominiums that have turned stretches of Sukhumvit into the most expensive areas of Bangkok and have sunk some long-familiar neighborhoods to the bottom of a canyon. Her place is on a floor high enough that Rafferty's ears pop in the elevator.

It's a little before ten in the morning, and after the gloom of the street, its early light blocked by the upper reaches of unfamiliar buildings, he's dazzled at the sudden sight of the sun peering through the big living-room windows behind her as the elevator doors open; she occupies, apparently, the entire floor. She sees his squint and laughs. It's a low, effortless laugh that sounds like it comes easily and often, and it's not what he'd expected from this woman whom he'd envisioned as a kind of widow-in-waiting.

"Go left, go left," she says, stepping back to let him pass. "Into the library, second door on the right. I keep the curtains drawn in there so the sun doesn't bleach the spines of the books. Be awful to go in for a book and find all the spines blank, wouldn't it?" She's following him. "Like a low-budget nightmare. Assuming, I mean, that you read. There you are, the door on your right, the closed one. It's going to seem dark in there."

"Dark would be nice," Rafferty says, still trying to blink away the black circle, the sun's negative, imprinted on his retina.

"Men are such sissies." She follows him into the room, both cool and dim, and snaps the light on. Floor-to-ceiling bookcases pop into existence left and right, taking up the room's longer walls. The far wall is swathed in thick, patterned drapes. She goes to a little huddle of comfortable-looking furniture and fiddles with an angular wrought-iron floor lamp, possibly from the 1930s. The parchment-colored shade goes a bright yellow. "Yours is in there somewhere."

"My—"

"Your book, silly. *Looking for Trouble in Thailand,* isn't that it? You haven't written a new one, have you?"

"Yes," he says. "But it's not available here yet."

"Right. Bangkok is the zone of late arrivals, isn't it? Coffee?"

"Coffee would be a miracle."

"Well, browse for a minute, and I'll be back."

She's gone, snapping off the overhead lights, before he realizes he hasn't actually gotten a good look at her. Slacks, something loose on top. He can hear her humming—he can't quite identify the tune—as she goes down the hall, making the *tock-tock* sound that suggests high heels—*right*, high heels. At this hour, in her own house. Not in his social zip code. The floors are some kind of polished stone, marble maybe, and he can't begin to imagine how much the place costs. He'd pictured some lonely, frail-but-valiant soul, both waiting for and dreading the funeral pyre, swathed in anticipatory black and stretching every twenty-baht note a yard long to remain here so she can keep her vigil until the shadow line between life and death has been crossed and she can burn the widow's weeds and go home again, tourist class all the way.

The light from the standing lamp shows him fiction shelves

that are heavy on biggies, including the writers he thinks of as the nineteenth-century marathon runners: Dickens, Trollope, Balzac, Stendhal, Tolstoy, Dostoyevsky, the Brontës (cumulatively), Austen, and, on the other side of the Atlantic, Twain, Henry James, and (a surprise) James Fenimore Cooper, all in volumes that look well read and well owned. Half a dozen of Dawn Powell's acerbic novels from the 1920s and '30s lead into a cluster of other women who wrote in the first half of the last century: Edith Wharton, Zora Neale Hurston, F. Tennyson Jesse, Virginia Woolf. Odds and ends of Fitzgerald and Hemingway, a weedy clump of heres-and-theres—novels that seem related only by their physical proximity on the shelves—then about two feet of shelf space given to a batch of contemporary thrillers, mostly in the British paperbacks that are easiest format to find in Bangkok.

It doesn't feel like the library of someone who's planning to move anytime soon.

He finds his own book in the company of a group of travel writers, both living and dead, whom he'd love to hang around with in person. He hears the heels again and is fighting to shove the book back in when she comes through the door behind him.

"Don't act so guilty," she says. "If I'd written one, I'd pull it out and look at it myself."

"It wasn't that, exactly." He wrestles the book onto the crowded shelf and turns to face her. She's almost as tall as he is, with the kind of posture that suggests a strict grandmother lingering indelibly in her past, eyes of a deep iceberg blue, and a head of short silver ringlets, chopped in a way that looks accidental and probably costs a fortune. Her clothes are mostly gray and, he thinks, very expensive, the scarf around her neck a deep purple silk, shading to black. She holds two china cups on saucers, and she extends one to him.

"Black," she says, "although I should have asked."

He accepts the nearer one. "I always think people who take stuff in it should stick to ice cream."

"Or tea," she says. "I'm sure there's much to be said for tea, but I won't be saying any of it. Then what *was* it? And please, sit down."

"What was what?"

"What you were doing with your book, if you weren't just looking at it for a little furtive satisfaction."

"Checking to see if it was a bootleg." He sits in one of two leather armchairs with a small round mahogany table between them, in the circle of light from the standing lamp. "Two out of every three sold here are. Bootlegs, I mean."

"I *was* following you," she says. "I suppose, on some obscure plane, being bootlegged is flattering." She sits opposite him and blows lightly on the surface of her coffee.

"I think of *royalties* as flattery," he says. "Nothing says sincerity like money."

Up close, she's younger than the silver hair suggests, perhaps in her middle fifties or a little more if her genes are good. Maybe she met and married the unfortunate Mr. Dependahl when she was much younger than he. She gives him a measured smile and sips her coffee, conveying politely that the banter portion of the conversation is over. She says, "And?"

"The people who gave me your phone number weren't sure whether your husband was still alive." The coffee is strong enough to make him sit up.

"If that's a question, yes, he is. In a manner of speaking. He's receiving hospice care, one of the few long-term patients to get hospice care, I suppose, but it was the least ruinous way to have him taken care of." She sips her coffee again. "Monitoring the vital signs, the drips, the antibiotics, turning him over from time to time, taking care of bedsores." She draws a deep breath and lets it go. "A doctor comes in every few days, mainly so he can testify that everything was on the up-and-up if, when, Stuart dies." She lifts her eyebrows in what feels like an apology. "Not something we can discuss lightly, so I thought I'd get the rough stuff over with."

"Must be hard on you."

"It's been a mixed curse, in a way. But you're not here to talk about me."

"I wouldn't mind."

"I'm fine, thanks," she says. She drains the coffee in three long swallows, then places the cup and saucer noiselessly on the mahogany table. Regarding him across the table, she purses her lips slightly, as though tasting something that she hasn't made up her mind about, and tilts her head a bit to the right. "*But,*" she says, "since you ask, and since you learned about him from that bunch of free-range gonads on Patpong, I'll tell you that Stuart pretty much lived for three things—me, money, and, oh, let's see, we'll just call it tail, since that's the way he thought about it: an isolated body part, although the path to it was more pleasant if it led through nice biological scenery. It had to belong to someone previously unknown to him, because, for Stuart, novelty was a powerful aphrodisiac. You would have thought that the female reproductive organs were much more different from each other, more *individual*, than they actually are. Like some of them can whistle Broadway show tunes and others discuss Goethe and Proust while others are . . . oh, who knows? Quick-draw artists. As for the person who possessed them, she had to be young and otherwise unknown, but beyond that it didn't matter whether she was an illiterate streetwalker or a Nobel laureate. No, that's not fair. I know he never had a Nobel laureate. He would have told me about it."

"Would he?"

"He told me about his poet, his ballet dancer, his corporate vice president, his stewardesses—he more or less minored in stewardesses—his charter-boat captain in the Gulf of Mexico, whom he apparently enjoyed miles from shore on the boat's deck, surrounded by large, flopping, freshly caught fish. Showed me a cut on his shoulder supposedly gouged out by the spear of a marlin, grabbing a moment during its death throes to get even." She smoothes the slacks over her thighs.

"But he managed," Rafferty says, "surrounded by dying fish and getting stabbed by a marlin."

"Managed?" she says. "Oh, yes, I see. Of *course* he managed. He could have managed on the floor of an elevator in free fall from the top of that building in Dubai, you know, the tall one. I can't actually dream up any circumstances under which Stuart couldn't have managed."

"Gee," Rafferty says, for lack of anything more insightful. "Says a lot for being single-minded."

"But with it—with his perpetual potency, I mean—came *his* end of our shared curse, which was that he couldn't stop testing it. Anyway, that's why I refer to the current situation as a *mixed* curse, because at least I don't have to nod approvingly anymore while he tells me about how he got it on during a parachute jump."

Rafferty says, "He didn't."

"No, silly, he didn't. But you wouldn't believe the circumstances under which he did. It was Peter Pan syndrome, of course, time's wingèd chariot and all that. He was fairly steady, almost monogamous, until he turned forty, if you don't count eight or ten dalliances—isn't that a pretty word? But from the moment he blew out the candles on that fateful cake, he was marching in terror to the ticking of a clock, like Captain Hook. Just feeling his potency draining away with each tick. Drip, drip, drip."

Rafferty sips his coffee, which has gone cold, and he barely avoids making a face. "I'd request permission to ask a personal question," he says, "except that I think we're probably past that point. I'm not getting much of a sense of how you felt about it."

"You know," she said, "one of the most common mistakes people make is thinking they can guess what goes on between the members of a couple, especially a married couple. In spite of its misleadingly simple name, 'monogamy' is the most complicated thing in the world." She sits forward, gives him a smile. "Want me to warm up that coffee?"

"I came to write a book," he says, aiming a thumb at the bookshelves. "That book."

"But you stayed." She blows on her coffee, although there's no reason to, since it's already cooled. It's a stall. "Why? You're a travel writer, and they travel, right? This was a just business, something to process and then move on. You didn't stay in the Philippines or Indonesia."

"Well, I got kicked out of Indonesia. Came up against an imam with a short fuse and a lot of friends."

"You're not answering my question," she said.

"You didn't actually—"

"Oh, don't be silly."

Rafferty says, "I stayed because I fell in love."

"Well, surely," she says, "that's not uncommon in Bangkok. People seem to be falling in love on every corner, if 'love' is the word. Makes Paris look like Akron, Ohio. Still, most people go home eventually."

"I've only been in love once. Well, twice."

"Both in Bangkok?"

"Yeah. I married one of them, and we adopted the other one."

Her eyebrows go up a barely measurable amount. "Adopted."

"She was a street kid. Nobody knows where her parents are.

Now we're—" He breaks off as it occurs to him how few people he's told about this. "We're expecting one of our own, I mean, *biologically* our own, my wife and I."

"Your first."

"Yes. It's pretty much all I can think about."

"But you're here. With me."

"As I said on the phone, it's for one of my daughter's friends. His father, who fits right in with the guys at the Expat Bar, is missing. He came here, the father, for the same reason Stuart did."

"And you think it might be the people who—" She stops. *"Who,"* she says.

"I think it probably is."

"Well," she says, "if you catch them, do something slow and horrible to them, just for me."

"If I get a chance. Why are you still here?"

"Let's see," she says, stirring the coffee again. "I like it here. The Thai people surprise me daily. And there's Stuart, obviously. It wasn't much of a marriage from some perspectives, but we were friends. Friendship usually lasts longer than love." She looks over at him. "In my case, at any rate."

"I don't know," he says. "You sitting here like this, waiting it out, it feels pretty permanent to me. What it feels like is love. How could friendship survive all that—what can you call it except betrayal?"

"You do keep coming back to that."

"I look at you, I see a woman who doesn't have to . . . to *settle* for things."

For a moment he thinks she'll change the subject. But instead she says, "Why do people love each other? There are a million songs about how *much* people love each other, but not so many about *why*. We *interested* each other. Stuart was a very interesting man, setting aside his compulsive behavior. He almost never bored me, and I bore easily. He could pick books for me, something no one else has ever been able to do. I could pick books for *him*, and you probably know how infrequently it goes both ways. He went clothes shopping with me and pretended to enjoy it. We sailed from San Diego to Honolulu, just the two of us under the sails, and when a storm almost sank us, he put his arms around me and told me he'd never been happier in his life. In the middle of the storm, with the hatches closed tight, he sang me to sleep." She looks at her coffee again, as if it might have turned into something else. "On my fortieth birthday, he gave me a check for seven million dollars because he comes from the kind of family whose members automatically contest one another's wills. I could go on like this for hours. He was my best friend. If it soothed some anxiety in his life to do the old in-and-out with strangers, what was I supposed to do? Deny myself his company? I might as well punch myself in the face."

"I guess."

She takes both cups off the table and starts to get up. "We've certainly pushed past small talk, haven't we?"

"Tell me," Rafferty says, "how you found out about Stuart. About . . . what happened to him."

For several seconds he doesn't think she'll answer, but then she says, "In stages. First, his bank here called me in the States to say that he was overdrawn and that he hadn't responded to their emails and phone calls. Thai banks very sensibly want several individuals they can contact for foreign accounts, and having met several of the foreign men who live here, I'd say that seems like a prudent policy."

She seems to realize that she's still holding the cups and saucers, and something that looks like rage stiffens her face for a moment before she stows it away. It's the first time he's seen a spontaneous emotion, and it confirms his suspicion that she's learned to keep what she cares most about locked in a small room somewhere, a skill she probably developed to survive the invisible battering she'd taken from Stuart, $7 million or no $7 million.

When she's satisfied with the saucers' placement on the table, she says, "It was a frightening call, since *I* couldn't reach Stuart either, so I called the embassy. Having a lot of money helps when you have to deal with the embassy. They talked to the police, who, as far as I can see, did fuck-all until Stuart was pulled from that canal. His photo, taken on some dreadful table, was sent to the logical embassies, and in the meantime someone here in Bangkok opened a newspaper and recognized the description of a tattoo Stuart had. One of those men at the bar, I think. He called the embassy, and the embassy called me. They emailed me that picture, to make sure."

"You must have been horrified."

"Yes," she says. "The picture was enough to frighten me half to death. But, to be totally honest with you, I'd been expecting *something* like this for years."

"Why?"

She clears her throat and then strokes it with her fingers, like someone trying to resist a cough. "Stuart didn't take sex seriously on an emotional level, but someone like him, sooner or later, is going to come up against someone who *does* take it seriously, A husband, a boyfriend, girlfriend, a father, the mailman. Who knows? I continually expected a call saying he'd been shot to death or run over by a tractor. He had a penchant for rural girls." She closes her eyes briefly, and when she opens them, she's looking at the bookshelf. "But I hadn't expected anything as . . . as *operatic* as this."

"So you came here and started to talk to people."

"With no real point. I knew I wouldn't learn anything valuable. I just wanted to get a sense of his world, by which I mean the last world he was aware of. So I talked to the fading sex addicts on Patpong because he'd mentioned 'the guys' at that bar, and they were surprisingly sympathetic. The one with the awful comb-over—"

"Bob Campeau."

"I suppose. He patted me on the shoulder. One of the most awkward gestures I've ever seen, but he meant well."

"Did he get up off his stool?"

"Yes. Is that unusual?"

"Close to unique."

"Well," she says, looking at nothing. "He did." Then she turns back to the table, picks up the china again, and says, "Maybe we should go see Stuart."

He knows traffic is terrible by now, and he doesn't want to look at his watch, but he says, "How far away is it?"

"Not far," she says. "Ninety, a hundred feet."

14

Cast Aside in the New Order of Things

HE FOLLOWS HER down a long hallway with a gleaming marble floor, past a kitchen half the size of his apartment, where two Thai women in blue jeans and T-shirts are loading an industrial-size dishwasher. "These are Ning and Som," Mrs. Dependahl says. The women turn at the sound of their names, and one of them smiles— the one on the left, Ning, Rafferty supposes, since we read left to right and Mrs. Dependahl named her first. Ning—if that's who she is—is in her mid-twenties and plump, with an intelligent, slightly apprehensive expression. The other, who has to be Som, is older and rail thin, graying hair pulled back mercilessly to make a no-nonsense bun with a pencil stuck through it, and bright, sharp-cornered eyes.

Rafferty says hello. Ning nods and extends the gesture into a very slight bow, as though she half expects a slap, rubbing her hands together a bit anxiously while Som gives him the measured nod and pursed lips of a teacher who's heard all about him and is just waiting for him to act up.

"They're angels, hospice people," Mrs. Dependahl says. "I don't know what I'd do without them."

"He's here?" Rafferty says. He'd figured the hospice was elsewhere in the city.

"Of course he's here. One thing I've got here is space." To Som she says, "I have a shopping list if you get time to go to Foodland."

"Villa better," Som says.

"I know you like Villa," Mrs. Dependahl says with a tiny measure of steel, "but I prefer the meat at Foodland, so let's go to Foodland today, okay?"

Som nods with the air of someone who's keeping score, then turns back to the dishwasher, and Fran leads him down the hall. "Som is the wife Stuart actually needed," she says. "He'd have been terrified of her." She opens another door, and the marble floor turns to unconvincing wood laminate, the bare walls painted a flat white. "Servants' quarters," she says unapologetically.

She goes to a varnished wooden door, but as she's about to turn the handle, Rafferty says, "Before we go in, does he . . . I mean, can he . . . ?"

"Is he aware? The doctors say no, but they would, wouldn't they? Otherwise they'd have to admit that they have no idea. That's what I'm most afraid of, actually, that he's *in there* somewhere, in a tiny little bright box, fully aware and screaming to be let out." She breaks off, chewing on her lower lip. "Som—who, as you might have noticed, is not the sunniest house on the block— Som thinks he hears everything, registers everything. She calls him 'Big Ears,' as though he eavesdrops on every word spoken within a mile, and she talks to him all the time, resuming one-sided conversations from the day before, telling him about the weather, the prime minister, the latest family ghost story, the price of a kilo of rice." She pauses for a moment, as though she's lost her place. "Telling him . . . ahh, what she and Ning are going to do for him moment by moment, like a play-by-play announcer, getting irritated with him when he's not being good."

"Being good?" Rafferty says.

"You know, when he's got drool on himself or—oh, I don't know, anything that she disapproves of, and she disapproves of everything. It upset me at first, but Ning, who's terrified of Som, says that it's what Stuart needs, he needs to be treated like everyone else. Ning, being Ning, plays good cop and tells him he's looking handsome each morning and, um . . ." She lowers her head, and he hears her draw a couple of deep breaths. "It's a blessing they're here," she says. "They give him, between them, a kind of community."

"And you," he says. "Don't forget about you."

"I try," she says. "I do what I can do. Let's go introduce you."

THE ROOM IS sparsely furnished, a long hospital bed, the back raised to an angle of about thirty degrees, a wheeled table, probably for food and palliative supplies, two barstools, high enough so that the people who sit on them are at eye level with the man in the bed. The walls are completely bare.

The man in the bed looks diminished in a way that suggests evaporation over a long period of time. He's on his side, facing away from them, so all Rafferty can see are the hunched shoulders and the slight frame beneath the white sheets and a close-cropped head of gray hair, just mowed back, it seems, with an electric razor.

Fran is talking before the door closes behind them. "Good morning, Stuart. It's hot as hell out, even for this time of year, and I've brought you a visitor, a man named Poke Rafferty—isn't *that* a silly name? Why are you called Poke?"

"When I was a kid," he says, "I poked my nose into things that didn't concern me. My father had an irritable side, and he called me Poke."

"Well, Stuart has spent his entire life, seventy-three years of it, without a single nickname, haven't you, Stuart? Not even *Stu.*" They've come around the bed now, and what Rafferty sees first are Stuart's arms on top of the sheets, the elbows bent and the wrists close together, like those of a man in prayer, except that one hand is a few inches higher than the other and both are crumpled into loose fists that look permanent. His nails need to be cut. There's something utterly defenseless about the position. The hands have a discarded, forgotten air, something cast aside in the new order of things.

Beneath the short, unevenly cropped hair, Stuart's face is still beautiful: an aquiline nose, fine cheekbones, a strong cleft chin, and an unexpectedly sensitive mouth. His eyes are closed most of the way, just the whites and the very bottoms of his irises visible beneath the long lids. He smells of sweat, staleness, and urine.

"Isn't he handsome?" She tugs the sheet, which looks like it's been ironed, out from under his elbows and arranges it up around his wrists. Half of his tattoo, the Tenniel illustration of Alice's caterpillar, protrudes above the sheet's edge. "The curled fingers?" she says. "That's a kind of atrophy of the muscles. You'd think they'd get looser, but instead they . . . umm, contract like that. There's something graceful about it, isn't there?"

"Very," he says, because it's the only word that presents itself.

"Stuart, I brought Mr. Rafferty in here to meet you because he's looking for the people who did this to you, and I thought you'd like to know that. Mr. Rafferty has written a whole book about Bangkok," she says, and then she uses the back of her hand to swipe at her cheeks, "and he knows it backward and forward. He can find *anybody*. He's helped lots of people, haven't you, Mr. Rafferty?" She sounds furious.

"I have."

She says, through teeth that might as well be glued together, "And you can find them, can't you?"

"I can."

"And you will?"

It feels like talking to a ghost, but the anger has risen to the back of his throat, and he says to Stuart, "I will."

"He's *exactly* who we need," she says to her husband, and now she's not bothering to wipe the tears away, although her voice is under control. "And when he's got them, Stuart, when he finds them . . . well, tell him, Mr. Rafferty, tell Stuart what you're going to do to them."

Rafferty comes to the side of the bed, heavy with fury, as he leans down to talk directly to Stuart. Speaking around what feels like a half-swallowed stone, he says, "I am going to *fuck them up.* I'm going to fuck them up so badly their shadows will try to run away."

Movement at the edge of Poke's vision draws his eye. The two Thai women from the kitchen are standing in the doorway. Ning's mouth is slightly open, and her eyes are wide. Som looks like she can't decide whether it would be impolite to look amused.

"And when he's done, Stuart," Fran Dependahl says, "he's going to come back here and tell you every single thing he did to them. *Twice,* if you want to hear it again." She looks at Rafferty expectantly.

"I will," he says again. And then, to the unmoving man on the bed, he says, "I promise."

15

Staring into the Glare

WHEN HE LEAVES, ten minutes later, Rafferty goes down the front steps of Fran Dependahl's sprauncy condo building carrying a cardboard box that once contained a dozen bottles of a red Bordeaux he's wanted to taste for most of his adult life. It's now filled haphazardly with a miscellany of documents, notebooks, paperback mysteries, folded newspapers, wallet contents, anything and everything with writing on it that had been in the apartment Stuart had been living in—not the present one—when Fran arrived in Bangkok. After Fran cleared it all out, she'd asked the police if they wanted it, but they had not expressed interest.

It's a hike to get to the Skytrain, and Fran had been telling Stuart the truth about the heat, so Rafferty flags a cab, shoves the box across the backseat, and slides in behind it. As the car pulls into traffic, his phone buzzes on his hip.

"Where are you?" It's Arthit.

"Sukhumvit, Soi . . . uhh, Twenty, give or take."

"Which direction?"

"South, essentially."

"Tell you what. Meet Clemente at Chu's in the Exchange Tower on Asoke. Second floor. Driver can drop you right there. She should be there about now."

"Okay, Chu's. Just talked with the woman whose husband is

brain-dead. Saw him, and I'll tell you, Arthit, it was rough." He leans forward to give the driver the new destination.

"Let Clemente go to Edward's later today," Arthit says. "It'll help get her feet wet, give her some experience with what we're looking for and a little emotional motivation at the same time."

"I'll work it out with her. I want to be there, too."

"Fine."

"Thanks for getting on this so quickly."

"Someone has to," Arthit says. "It's awful." He disconnects.

WHAT HE DOESN'T see through the restaurant's glass walls when he reaches the top of the escalator, lugging his Bordeaux box, is Clemente. But he immediately spots an unoccupied table for four with two storage boxes on it, both thoughtfully marked as police property in enormous Thai characters, just in case there's anyone in the restaurant who wouldn't already want to eavesdrop on the conversation between a *farang* and a brisk-looking, uniformed policewoman with enormous golden eyes.

Chu's is small, crowded, and deafening, but Clemente has obviously pulled rank. The boxes sit atop one of the few tables where people can hear one another, because it's up against the wall. When he goes in, a college-age waiter intercepts him and says, in English, "Five, ten minute, sir."

"I'm with the cop," Rafferty says, pointing his chin at the table with the boxes on it. He jiggles his own box as further credentials. "Where's my friend?"

The boy looks past him a bit anxiously, as though he fears the appearance of an entire uniformed division. "She . . . she in kitchen."

"In the kitchen," he says.

"She want to see how making food."

"Right, well, she's a member of the . . . umm, the food squad. Everything okay back there, all clean and everything?"

"Clean enough to whistle," the boy says.

Rafferty thinks about correcting him and then realizes he has no answer for the inevitable question, *What's so clean about a whistle?* So he says, "She shouldn't give you any trouble, then. I'll go wait for her. Coffee, black, please."

As he sits down behind the big boxes that say POLICE, putting his own carton on the chair beside him, he feels the curious eyes of the other customers. In a way, he thinks, this whole episode—since he spotted the boxes, minus Clemente, waiting for him on the table, the interaction with the waiter, all of it—is probably a good thing. It's allowed him to put a little space between him and the rage that rose up in him the moment he saw Stuart Dependahl in his perpetual, useless attitude of prayer.

The detachment lasts until he opens the first of Clemente's boxes and takes out a thin, battered wallet with the rigidity of leather that's spent some time in water. It's been relieved of any cash or credit cards it might have contained, but behind a piece of clear plastic—glued to it now by the coating on its surface—is a small color photo. A laughing woman in her early thirties, wearing a bathing suit, a big-brimmed sun hat, and dark glasses, sits on a dock that reaches out into what seems to be a lake. Gathered around her like baby chicks are two boys of four or five, twins from the look of them, and a little blonde girl, a toddler, probably two. The twins are laughing hilariously at something as their little sister watches them with her mouth open and their mother, despite her own laughter, squints a bit painfully at the camera. The photographer's shadow stretches toward them like a long, pointing finger; the sun was almost directly behind him, which explains his wife's expression: She's staring into the glare. On one level, Rafferty thinks, this is a family whose problem is that they'll get to their cabin or their hotel room and realize they had so much fun they forgot to slather the kids with sunscreen.

But their real problem, of course, is that Daddy is dead.

The picture could have been taken ten or twelve years ago, maybe even more; bathing suits and sun hats don't change all that rapidly. The little boys are towheads with mops of blond hair that wouldn't have looked out of place at any time, even during Rafferty's childhood. But the edges of the picture are still sharp and uncreased, and the colors are still crisp, and even in its present state the picture has a hard-edged digital quality. So let's say eleven, twelve years old. That would put the boys in their teens and in high school now and their little sister somewhere in the wind-tunnel drama of junior high.

Do they have any idea what actually happened to their father?

Do they believe he just paid a visit to Bangkok and mysteriously fell into a canal with casts on his unbroken legs? What story were they told? And why is all this stuff still in a box, in storage? This should obviously be an active investigation.

A slight drop in the conversation level makes him look up, and he sees Clemente threading her way toward him, people sliding their chairs aside in deference to her uniform and doing double takes at her face. In a country where most women have hair that shines and ripples like a conditioner commercial, Clemente's chopped thatch is thick, black, almost coarse, with no sense of direction: Despite high-energy brushing, it flies out toward all points of the compass. She has unusually broad shoulders for a woman so short, and a strong, pronounced jaw. In Bangkok this adds up to a highly distinctive appearance, but almost no one who meets her winds up remembering anything except the extraordinary eyes, the color of fine, pale amber, that seem to take up half her face. If she had barged into Chu's with a machine gun, blown out the windows, and killed half the customers, the only thing on all the identikit pictures would be a pair of eyes.

"What were you doing back there?" he says as she slides into the chair opposite him.

"I want the eggs Benedict," she says, in Thai, although her English is extremely good, "but with bacon, not ham, and I wanted to make sure I'd get lean bacon. I hate fatty bacon."

"I know *exactly* how important that is."

She gives him a level look that almost makes him push his chair back. "I put up with a lot from my fellow officers, the male ones anyway, to wear this uniform. The least it can do for me is get me some good bacon."

"Can you order me the same thing?"

In English she says, "I took all the lean stuff."

"Oh, well," Rafferty says. "I'm not really hungry anyway."

"Oh. *Right.*" She puts her elbow on the table and rests her chin on her hand. "*That's* right, you were visiting the guy who didn't die, weren't you?"

"And his wife. And 'die' is a relative term."

"Well, I didn't really take it all," she confesses, reaching up to flag a waiter and getting the attention of all of them. To the one who arrives first, she says, "Give my colleague some of my bacon, a reasonable amount, for his eggs Benedict. What kind of toast?" she asks Rafferty.

"Whatever they dare to serve you."

When the waiter is gone, he taps a finger on each of the police boxes. "Have you looked at these?"

"As much as I could, although I didn't have a lot of time."

"Did you see this?" He slides the wallet over to her.

"Yes." She closes the wallet to hide the family's smiles. "That was when I stopped looking."

"I'm amazed you've already scored two boxes."

"Well, the colonel," she says, promoting Arthit from his actual grade of lieutenant colonel, "called me after you left his house last night, so I started ringing up the stations right then and kept it up until about three. I found two more guys with casts, by the way, so the official number, although we're the only ones tracking it, is fourteen, and the colonel was saying there might be another."

"Might be, but he somehow lived through it. I'm going to try to track him down."

"So with fourteen or maybe fifteen cases—"

"So far."

"Right, well, I couldn't reach anyone that late at two stations that handled four of them, and for the other ten cases there are possessions from only two of them in various evidence rooms." She flicks a forefinger at the closer of the two boxes. "These two."

"Only *two?*"

"Some of the relatives came to Bangkok to take their . . . uh, loved one home for burial. Other people arranged for their embassy to handle it. The ones who came in person took the effects, meaning this kind of stuff, with them or left it in their hotel rooms or threw it out, no way for us to know what happened after it was given to them."

"They weren't held as evidence?"

She looks down at the table and doodles something invisible on it with her forefinger. "In those cases either it wasn't treated as a crime or it had been classified as unsolved and essentially closed, so the stuff would have been dumped. The people at the station who gave me these were a little sticky about it. They had to call supervisors for clearance, which, if I can judge from the end of the conversation I heard, was not easy to get. I could see that they were worried about being embarrassed."

"Because they were incompetent?" he asks. She looks at him as though slightly confused. "Or corrupt?"

Rafferty senses someone standing at the table and looks up to see the young waiter who had asked him to wait. He's got

Rafferty's coffee in his hand, but it's forgotten. He's staring at Clemente's eyes.

"You can put it down," she says briskly. "And I have an iced coffee coming. Are you all waiting for it to get cold enough?"

"Sorry." The waiter wheels around and almost bumps into another, who's holding a sweating glass of iced coffee.

"No, *here*," Clemente says, pointing at the spot where she'd like the coffee placed. To Rafferty she says, "I think corrupt is a better bet. These feel low-down, thugs operating on a small level, picking off everybody's least favorite tourists, shaking all the money out of their pockets and credit-card accounts, and then dumping them in a canal. My guess is that a couple of people at the stations in the districts where most of the bodies were found know who's behind it and are on the pad. They file the cause of death as 'heart stopped' and pocket part of the proceedings."

"My feelings exactly."

She gives him a quick smile, which he returns without knowing he's doing it. "The colonel's, too," she says. "So later today I'll contact the other stations and see what they've got, and I'll also go over to the kid's house, your daughter's friend's house. About his father."

"I'll go with you," Rafferty says. "Miaow usually gets home from school around three-thirty, and I've left her a message asking her to have Edward—that's the kid—call me to say what time he'll be at his house."

"I can do it alone," she says, and there's a bit of prickle in her tone.

"I'm sure you can," Rafferty says, "but I already know Edward. He's ashamed of his father. He doesn't like the way his dad is with women. It'll be awkward for him to explain it to you. If I'm there, it'll all be out on the table from the beginning. Save you a little emotional tiptoe."

She thinks about it for a second and gives him a small, unreadable smile that he doesn't mistake for agreement. "Okay."

He pushes the nearest box, the one with the wallet in it, a few inches down the table. "What are you going to do with all this stuff?"

"Try to make sense out of it." She reaches into a bag at her feet and comes up with a tablet, which she flicks into life. "I started looking through the first box while I was waiting for them to dig out the second one." She swipes the screen and tilts it toward him. "This was the first thing I thought of. It's simple, but it might show us something." What Rafferty sees are four vertical columns: one of numbers, one of people's names, both Thai and non-Thai, written in the Roman alphabet, a third that seems to contain places—addresses, street names, what might be business names— and a fourth, which is empty. "It's just a spreadsheet," she says, sounding apologetic. "I'm entering all the numbers, whatever they are, in the left-hand column and all the names and other stuff in columns two and three, and when I'm done, I can just tell it to arrange the numbers on the left lowest to highest, and all the repeated numbers, if there are any, will be stacked on top of each other."

"And you can also alphabetize the data," Rafferty says.

"Exactly. And the fourth column, the one that's blank right now, will have a number that will correspond to the one I write on the box that entry came from. That way if the same phone number, address, whatever, pops up two or more times, we can look at the box numbers and see which victim entered it and whether more than one did."

"My, my," Rafferty says.

Clemente passes a finger over the screen, making the figures scroll up. She's input several screens' worth already, so she's been hard at it. "I was in charge of most of the computer stuff at the first station I worked at, the one where the colonel met me before he rescued me and moved me downtown. I had pretty good database software there—by police standards anyway." She looks at the screen, her mouth pulled over to one side. "This is kind of primitive by contrast, but it should work, don't you think?"

"I'd be doing it on bits of paper," he says, "so I'm the wrong guy to ask."

She blinks at him once, apparently weighing her response, then says, "Do you even *have* a spreadsheet program?"

"I guess." He thinks for a moment. "Open Office?"

"That'll do it. Better than Microsoft because they'll never upgrade you without asking."

She looks up. "Ahh," she says, "food."

"HOW DOES HE seem to you?" Rafferty says. The place has emptied out some, and they can hear each other without shouting.

"Compared to what?" A few bits of substandard bacon have been shoved to one side of the plate, possibly for reevaluation.

Rafferty reaches over and takes one, and she points the tines of her fork at him in a businesslike threat. He says, "I don't know. Does he seem happy?"

"You've known him longer than I have," she says. "To me he's the colonel. I don't see him personally, the way you do."

"Not so often these days," Rafferty says.

"I'm not sure what you're asking," Clemente says, and then sits back so quickly a jack-in-the-box might have popped open in front of her, and she blushes. "Oh," she says. "You mean you've seen him less since he . . . he married . . ."

"It's complicated," he says. "He's still my closest friend, but . . . well, we've both got things, you know, pulling at us."

"He's a remarkable man," Clemente says. "If you let that

friendship wear out, or however you'd put it, I think that would be—excuse me—foolish."

"You're right," Rafferty says. "You're absolutely right."

"Is it . . ." She lowers her face to her plate as though she thinks she might have spotted something worth eating.

"Is it what?"

"Nothing."

"Boy," he says, "look at us tiptoe."

"Please excuse the question. Is it your partners? I know that sometimes when men stop being friends, it's because the partners don't like each other."

"No," Rafferty says. "It's my fault. It's entirely my fault. The only thing my wife has to do with it is that she's pregnant, and it's . . . I don't know, it's very emotional."

"Is she worried about the pregnancy?"

Rafferty sits back and looks at the emptying restaurant without seeing any of it. "You know," he says, "she is. I think she's worried sick."

16

Soi Nowhere

FON HAS CHOSEN to meet her at a little elbow-bend *soi*, full of food vendors and their carts, one of the few "food streets" the government hasn't bulldozed to make way for the ugly, upscale concrete of new money that's gradually making Bangkok look like every other town with big bucks and bad taste. The moment Rose gets out of the taxi—Rafferty made her promise not to take a moto—the smells from the *soi* take her back years, to her arrival in Bangkok, with the mud of Fools' River still between her toes. Her first friends in the bar had taken her to places like this, on little streets so indistinguishable from one another that she thought of them all as "Soi Nowhere." The women had sealed their friendship by lending or even giving her the small amounts of money it took to eat there. At the time she'd been terrified of the work she was being paid to do, but some of her happiest memories are of those meals, with girls who knew their way around this horrible, bewildering, wonderful city and had survived all the experiences she dreaded with their souls intact. More or less.

She'd scoffed at Rafferty's insistence that she take a cab, but now she feels like phoning him to say thanks. Even the taxi ride had been too bumpy for comfort. She feels as though there's something heavy and syrupy rolling around in her abdomen, something that wanted to keep moving when the cab slowed and that practically towed her into the front seat when the driver finally stopped at the curb. Once out of the car, she grabs a deep breath and crosses the width of the sidewalk. It seems to take a long time, during which tiny, bright fireworks go off in front of her, and once across she leans against a building for a slow, shaky moment, the fireworks yielding to gray flowers that bloom in her field of vision. The heat is so extreme it seems personal, a slap in the face, and the scent of the food almost mocks her with the contrast between who she is now and who she was when she first smelled it. It seems stronger now, less appetizing, almost . . . the smell of all that *meat* . . .

She forces herself to breathe through her mouth, slowly and evenly for a count of ten in and ten out, her gaze locked on the sidewalk because the motion of the cars going by pushes her to the edge of vertigo. When she chances breathing through her nose again, she finds that the odor of the food has gathered and concentrated itself until it's overpowering. Maybe this wasn't a good idea. Maybe she should have stayed home, in bed. Poke wasn't there, so he wouldn't have known how weak she'd been—

"Are you all right?" The words are in English.

She looks up to see a sunburned *farang* boy, a little younger than Edward, redheaded, beaky, skinny, and angular, in a T-shirt and a pair of jeans. Braces glint on his teeth. Behind him, looking at her uncertainly, is a neatly dressed woman, wearing too many layers for a day so hot, who has to be the boy's mother.

The mother leans forward and says, very slowly and a bit loudly, "He. Wants. To. Know—"

"I'm fine," Rose says. She blots sweat from her upper lip. "I mean, I *will* be fine, in . . . in just a minute."

The mother leans toward her, eyes narrowed assessingly. "I think you need to sit down," she says. It's the tone of someone who doesn't get a lot of argument.

"I . . . I don't think I can walk right now."

"There are lots of chairs just in this little street right here," the mother says, glancing into the *soi*. "There are even some in the shade. Willis and I can help you, one of us on each side. If we leave you here, I'm afraid you'll fall, and you're . . . well, you're so tall. It's a long way down."

"It's just a few steps," Willis says. "I'll be over here, and Mom will be over there, okay?"

"I'm very good at this," the mother says. "I was a nurse for centuries. Here. Put your arm around my shoulder and lean a little on Willis. He's stronger than he looks."

Willis says, "Jeez."

"I don't know," Rose says, and then the sidewalk dips a bit beneath her feet, and she says, "Thank you." She edges uncertainly away from the stability of the wall.

"I'm Joyce," the mother says, draping Rose's arm over her shoulders, "and you already know Willis's name."

"It's *Will*," Willis says, "not—"

"Yes, dear," Joyce says. "Here we are, up and moving; isn't this nice? Lean on me, lean on me. What's your name, dear?"

"Rose. That's—" She grabs a deep breath of air that's too hot. "That's my American name. My Thai name is Kwan."

"That's a pretty name," Joyce says, and Rose can hear, even through her unsteadiness, that it's the mechanical reply of someone who is focused on what she's doing. "What's it mean, dear?"

"Spirit," Rose says. The *soi* opens up in front of them, and to their right are the promised shaded chairs. They're all occupied.

"Isn't that beautiful, being called Spirit," Joyce says matter-of-factly. They're nearing the chairs around the closest table now, and the three young women sitting there look up and see them coming. One of them, a girl in her early twenties, leaps to her feet and pushes her chair toward Rose.

"Such nice people," Joyce says. "*Careful*, careful. The Thais are such—just a little to your *left*, dear—such nice people." The woman who surrendered her chair is moving at a near jog toward the closest cart. "Here we are . . . umm, Kwan," Joyce says. "Let's just turn you around with your back to the chair so you can sit, and we'll guide you down."

The other women have gotten up, too, looking at Rose with obvious concern.

"I'm fine," Rose says in Thai and then in English. "I was just dizzy."

"Thank you," Joyce says to the woman who had been sitting in the chair next to Rose and who has shouldered Willis aside to help Rose sit down. To Rose she says, "Do you want to bend forward, dear, put your head between your knees?"

Rose is sharply aware again of the fullness in her lower abdomen, and she says, "No, thank you. I'll be fine."

Joyce has knelt in front of her, peering into her face. "Have you eaten today? Do you think it's the heat? Oh, *look* at this sweet thing." Rose looks up and to her right to see the woman whose chair she's taken, whose short-chopped hair is streaked with blonde, approaching with a cup in her hand, full of something cold enough to make the cup sweat in the humidity.

Rose can smell her own perspiration. Her hair is hot on her back. The other two women, one with a tight ponytail and the other with the guileless face of a twelve-year-old, are creating a ring of chairs so Joyce and Willis can sit facing Rose. Then Blonde Streaks is there with the cup extended, and Rose reaches for it, but the American woman—Joyce, Rose thinks—intercepts it and says, "Just a few sips at first, dear," and then hands it to her.

The water is ice cold, and for a moment it creates a bright red spasm of pain in the center of Rose's chest. She must have reacted somehow, because Joyce says, "See? Slowly, slowly."

Willis says to his mother, "She's so pretty."

"She understands English, Willis," Joyce says, and Rose looks up to see Willis go sunset red. Ponytail and Twelve-Year-Old laugh. Blonde Streaks says, "She *is* pretty, isn't she?"

Joyce takes the seat opposite Rose, and Ponytail makes little sweeping motions with the backs of her hands, scooting Willis toward the remaining chair. Willis says, *"Kob kun krup."* One of the women, maybe Blonde Streaks, says, in English, "Oh, very good," and at that moment some of Rose's dizziness dissipates.

"The heat," Twelve-Year-Old suggests.

"Have you eaten anything?" Joyce asks again, and Ponytail says, "Some rice? Something light?" and Blonde Streaks says, "Just suck on the ice in the cup. That'll help."

For a dizzying few seconds, Rose is back in her village, in the middle of the ring of friends and neighbors who materialized to surround anyone who was hurt or ill, offering assistance and advice, often conflicting, and she finds herself blinking back tears. A familiar voice says, in Thai, "Always the center of attention." Rose lifts her head, feeling the chair spin beneath her, to see Fon pushing in between Ponytail and Twelve-Year-Old. Behind her is an older woman with deep-set eyes, a downturned mouth, and thinning gray hair. She looks familiar.

Fon was Rose's—Kwan's—first Bangkok friend. When Kwan appeared, wide-eyed and lost, in the bar—tricked into the journey down to Bangkok by a woman who befriended her and lied to her about *everything*—Fon was the one who opened her arms to the newcomer. She shared her room with the new girl, navigated her through the Borgia-like personal politics of the bar, and after Rose, who had no sexual experience, failed utterly to please her first customer, an influential cop, Fon was the one who taught her the "pet tricks," as Rose thought of them, that would satisfy even the high standards of the Bangkok Royal Police.

"You look terrible," Fon says in Thai. Then she says it in English for the benefit of Willis and Joyce.

"No, she—" Willis begins, but his mother silences him with a glance. To Fon, Joyce says, "I don't think she's eaten anything."

"Sure she has," Fon says in English. "She's had her awful yogurt, haven't you?" Fon was never a conventional beauty, but there's a kind of relaxed harmony in her face that makes her prettier than most of the baby dolls strenuously mimicking the Japanese and Korean starlets who have become the templates for female beauty in so much of Asia. Fon's face announces that she's someone who can be depended upon.

"I ate," Rose says. "Really, I'm feeling much better now."

Joyce is studying her. "Stay there for a minute more," she says.

Fon moves aside, and the woman behind her steps forward and, without a word, extends both hands. The gesture is a command of some kind, and Rose automatically reaches up. The woman grasps her wrists and turns her hands over to study the backs and then rotates them again as though she's about to read Rose's palms. She says, "Mmmm-hmmm."

"I told you," Fon says to the older woman.

"Told her what?" Joyce says.

"She's pregnant," Fon says, "and it's a problem." There's a spattering of syllables all at the same time and from all directions, and Rose can't tell from whom.

Joyce says, in a more businesslike tone of voice, "Do you hurt anywhere?"

Rose says, "No," and then, "Yes," and then she says again, "*Yes*," and begins to weep.

The group goes silent, and the three women who gave up their chairs take an instinctive step back to preserve Rose's privacy, but Joyce says, "Have you had problem pregnancies before?"

Rose nods, and Fon says, "Two."

Ponytail must have moved close again, because she puts a hand on Rose's shoulder, and Rose says, "I'm going to lose this baby, too," and then she's crying loudly, not caring who hears it, not caring about the people at the adjoining tables, feeling the cold truth of what she's just admitted open up beneath her, eager to drag her down. There are more hands on her, on her back, on her shoulders, and someone, maybe Twelve-Year-Old, rubs the center of her spine in light circles, but there's no controlling the sobs, not just for this child, not just for her and Poke and Miaow, but for the other two as well, the two children she left in the dark without ever bringing them into the light of day. The unborn ghosts of her failed womanhood.

There are arms around her from all directions, and Joyce says, "Go get . . . um, Kwan some water, Willis," and Willis says, "She's already got water. That lady just—" and Joyce says, "Water, Willis, *now*," and Willis says, "Sheesh," and gets up, and a couple of wadded-up napkins are forced into Rose's hand, and then it's just crying until, finally, it stops.

Rose focuses on breathing as the others wait to see whether they'll be needed to comfort her again, and the older woman— Rose recognizes her now, doesn't know her name, but she's a doula who assisted a number of bar workers through childbirth—says, in English, "She needs a doctor. Now."

"Are you . . . I'm sorry," Joyce says. "Are you a medical professional?"

"She's a doula," Fon says briskly. "Are *you* a doctor?"

"She's a nurse," Willis says from outside the circle.

"Get something to *eat*, Willis," Joyce says. "And don't tell me you're not hungry." When he's gone, she says, "How far into your term did you lose them?"

"About now."

"How far is that?"

"A little more than four—"

"A doctor," Joyce says in English and the doula says in Thai.

"You don't understand," Fon says. "She doesn't *want* anything to be wrong."

"It's not about you," Joyce says sternly to Rose as Twelve-Year-Old takes the soaked napkins and gives her two dry ones.

"Her husband doesn't know she's—having problems," Fon says.

"It's not about him either," Joyce says. "It's about your *baby*."

"You have to try to keep the baby," Ponytail says. And Twelve-Year-Old says, "Yes, you can't—"

"But I don't . . . I don't think there's any way—"

"Listen." It's Joyce, and there's no arguing with her tone. "There's a—"

"Can save, maybe," the doula says, glancing at Joyce, and Joyce opens her mouth and closes it again. "You talking stitches, yes?" the doula asks.

"Yes," Joyce says. "It's an outpatient—"

"New," the doula says.

Joyce closes her mouth and looks deferentially at the doula, and even in her emotional state, Rose can see that it's not an easy thing for the American woman to do. On the other hand, there's a brightness in her eyes that indicates a willingness to shove herself back into the discussion anytime it goes awry.

The doula says to Joyce, "Please. You tell."

"If you are going to lose the baby," Joyce says, "and there's no guarantee you will, it'll be because your cervix—do you know the word 'cervix'?"

"Yes," Rose says.

The doula nods briskly, and Joyce says, "It's usually because the cervix is dilating early, like it's made a mistake and it . . . it thinks the time has come for the baby to be delivered."

"Have good doctor here," the doula says, with the kind of certainty Rose has always envied and never possessed. "Not far."

Joyce gives the doula a doubtful glance and gets a stony gaze. "So," she says, "they can look, do a pelvic, maybe an ultrasound. Sometimes, depending on . . . on what they see, it's enough for you just to go to bed and stay there, and sometimes they do a procedure, they take a little stitch, just to narrow the opening, do you understand?"

Rose realizes how intense her own expression is and that Joyce has mistaken it for incomprehension. She breaks her gaze, looks around, and realizes that the women in the circle all seem like people she's known for years. "I understand. A . . . a stitch—"

"Or maybe two, *little* ones, just to make the opening narrower. Then you can take it easy, not too much walking or jumping around, stay in bed a lot, and when the baby is due—"

"Cut thread," the doula says, miming a pair of scissors.

"*Wow,*" someone says, and Rose looks up to see Willis over Ponytail's shoulder, staring wide-eyed at the doula. Rose can't help it; she starts to laugh, then stops as she cramps again, putting a hand where it hurts.

"Where is the doctor?" Joyce asks.

"Two, three kilometer," the doula says.

"You stay here," Willis says. "I'll get you a cab," and he wheels and takes off at a run, and in his voice, even through her cramping and her fear, Rose hears the satisfaction of a male who's been proved indispensable after all.

She says to Joyce, "You have a fine son."

"And so will you, dear," Joyce says, patting Rose's shoulder. "You'll have a strong, healthy child."

17

The Next-to-Last Cough of Someone with Tuberculosis

Everything HURTS.

Her nose is a numb spot, dead center in an island of ache, and she knows it's broken. *Again.* The skin in the hot, reddish-feeling circle that includes her nose and mouth and chin has dried blood on it. When she grimaces, it cracks as though her face is tearing. Her neck is stiff from the way the Meat Man's slap snapped her head around. The big scabs on her knee and elbow have hardened. Her back and hips ache from the hard, cold pavement she slept on.

And her eyes feel like there's a whole handful of sand in each of them. She starts to rub them with the heels of her hands and then thinks, in panic, *My new lenses.* She was told to take them out for the first few nights, until she was used to them. Has she rubbed one or both of them out of her eyes? From her shelter beneath the park bench, she focuses on the morning distance, and there it is again, the world in all its new and bewildering, hard-edged detail, maybe a bit foggy. The lenses are still in place, even if they're cloudy because the pretty little case and the liquid in which they should have been soaked overnight are in the back-pack in the . . . the Meat Man's room.

Once out of the hotel, she sprinted, in as straight a line as possible, the long kilometer and a quarter to Lumphini Park, looking behind her for him repeatedly even though she knew he couldn't possibly be chasing her. Craning back for the eighth or ninth time, she slammed into a light pole, took two staggering steps backward, and went down on her butt, and then, half a block later, tripped on an uneven sidewalk paver and pitched forward to take all the skin off her left elbow and her right knee, bare beneath her shorts. She didn't even glance down to check the damage before she was in flight again, zigzagging between the people strolling on the sidewalk and charging full out whenever she hit an empty stretch, dodging traffic across the streets, the pounding of her heart pushing her along like a marching drum. She'd been beaten up and humiliated before, when she was a boy, but this was something new: not stupidity, not insensitivity or the bullying malice of boredom, but *hate*, and all she knew was that she needed to be somewhere with hiding places, lots of hiding places, somewhere relatively dark where no one would see her bloodied face and remember it, where she could be an animal in a safe hole. Sooner or later that . . . that man would come after her. Or call the police. She knew that people would remember her, bloody, disheveled, and practically flying, but in her mind she erased the path behind her, speeding as she passed people to give them the shortest possible look at her, doubling back briefly two times so there would be confusion about her direction if—when—questions were asked.

She felt as though she were breathing fire by the time she reached the edge of the park and angled left to avoid the lights of the night market that would remain open until about 1 A.M. The sight of a darker entrance, wide and inviting, slowed her, and she plunged in. The paved, curving path took her toward the park's center, away from the headlights and the noise of the street. The relative darkness stilled some of the urgency in the middle of her chest. She slowed to a walk, knowing that her injuries were harder to see here, but it wasn't until she was absolutely certain she was unobserved that she peeled off the path, heading at a blind run again for the areas around the man-made lake where the trees were thickest.

The water's edge stopped her, pulled her up short. She stood there, slack and vacant as an empty bag, watching the city's lights gleam, sinuous and upside down, on the water's surface. She was still breathing heavily, and her pulse banged in her ears. She thought it might give her some relief to cry, but the remaining bits of Keo, the boy she had been, wouldn't permit it.

After a few numb moments, every bit of her attention focused on the lights reflected on the dark water, she sat slowly down at the lake's shoreline. Not until her muscles had relaxed, not until she was no longer on the verge of flight, did she give way and begin to sob.

She had no way of knowing how long she sat there crying, but by the time she carefully wiped away the tears, avoiding her nose, and pushed herself to her feet, her joints were stiffening, especially the knee she'd cracked on the sidewalk. Without making a conscious decision, she moved toward the darkest area in sight, a copse of trees on the lake's long curve, and then through that into another grove of bigger, older trees, so thick with foliage that it blocked completely the lacework of moonlight that had dappled the ground as she walked. At the edge of the little wood, she claimed an empty bench, far enough from the nearest source of light that neither she nor it threw a shadow, and she climbed onto it in a gingerly fashion, new centers of pain flaring into existence with every cautious move. She sniffled a couple of times, almost experimentally, the air feeling oddly icy in her damaged nose, and then decided she was cried out. So, for the first time, she began to think about her situation.

The nose could be fixed. The bruises and scrapes would heal, even Ying's claw marks. What wouldn't change was that the Meat

Man was a *farang* tourist, probably American, and as such a protected species, while she was a *katoey*, a prostitute, and an illegal immigrant with a forged identity card, about as low in the Thai pecking order as it was possible to go. Not much question about whose side the police would find more profitable.

She yielded to a small wave of self-pity, let it wash around inside her for a moment, and then banished it so she could keep her head clear as she considered her position. She didn't see anything that raised her hopes. He would call the police and say she attacked him and probably that she stole money from him. He would undoubtedly send the cops to This or That Bar, where several girls would gleefully tell them where she lived, and then the cops would go to her room, which she couldn't get into anyway without paying the landlady. One of her enemies in the bar, probably Ying, would give the cops the name of Lutanh's closest friend, Betty, who worked at another Patpong club, which meant that she couldn't, in good conscience, even ask Betty to take her in. She could see no clear path to refuge in any direction.

For a moment she thought what her life would be like in prison, winced at the images that came to mind, and decided she would kill herself before she'd let them send her there.

The only wisp of hope she could find was that he might be so embarrassed by the whole thing that he wouldn't want it on any official record. He might not want the attention. He might be one of those odd men for whom *katoey* were a dark secret. She pulled that hope over her like a thin blanket and drifted into sleep.

In what felt like just minutes, she snapped awake to the sense of something crawling on her. Bent over her, prodding the area where her breasts would be if the hormones had kicked in, was a filthy, vile-smelling man of indeterminate age with meth blossoms all over his face and wearing layers of old clothes despite the heat. His breath was feverish and foul, his nose only inches from hers.

She struck twice, without thinking: a knuckle-popping blow to his throat and then a full-out kick, all the strength she could put into straightening the leg with the bad knee, directly into his gut. He'd stumbled back with a shuddering grunt, looking startled and almost comically offended, clearly too drunk to remain upright. She'd leaped from the bench as his feet tangled beneath him, and then she'd taken off at top speed, heading even farther into the park, the man's aggrieved complaints following her until they faded into silence and she realized he wasn't going to come after her.

The night was still surprisingly hot, the air close and damp, almost as motionless as it was in her room. How she'd hated that room, and how badly she missed it now, how much she wanted to go back, to lock the door behind her and crawl onto the hard, narrow, lumpy bed and curl herself into a ball and cry until she used up all her sorrow. Only yesterday morning, she thought, as the dawn's first light began to sift like fog through the trees, she'd had money in her pocket, a place to stay, a job—even if she hated some things about it—and *more* money coming at the end of the day, and she'd been good as Peetapan, and, and there had been something else, something wonderful. What had it—

She'd met Edwudd. She'd looked her absolute best with her new violet dress—lost now, abandoned in her backpack—and her new violet eyes. She'd been the prettiest she'd ever been. He'd glanced at her twice when Miaow wasn't looking at him. He was so *beautiful.*

And look at me now, she thought, lightly passing her hands over her face, the losing fighter in a Muay Thai match, someone who had blocked her opponent's best kick with her nose. Hurting, frightened, soaked in sweat, she halfheartedly searched out another bench, started to lie down on it, and then decided instead to crawl beneath it. Just a few hours' sleep. Things, she told herself, would be different with a few hours' sleep.

* * *

WHEN SHE FINALLY opens her eyes, things *are* different. For
one thing, the sun is well above the horizon. For another, she can
hear music from the front of the park, where hundreds of people
gather for aerobics. Must be past nine, maybe even ten or ten-
thirty.

And one more thing that's different: She's being stung by ants.

She slaps at the side of her neck and brushes at her bare legs,
accidentally scalping the newly formed scab on her knee. As she
rolls out from under the bench, her right hip, which already hurts,
gives out an especially sharp pang, and she puts her hand there
and feels the outline of her phone through the pocket of her
shorts.

The morning seems to brighten in every direction. Her phone
wasn't in the backpack she'd left when she escaped from the Meat
Man after all. And then she has a sudden memory of reaching into
the pack to retrieve her forged identity card in anticipation of
showing it to the security guard, and she slaps at her right front
pocket and finds it there in its little plastic supposed-to-be-leather
folder. *He doesn't have my picture,* she thinks, and it seems as
though her heart expands a bit in the center of her chest, easing
a kind of cramp she hadn't even been aware she'd been feeling.
Drawing a deep breath, she pulls the phone out and powers it up,
and her spirits sink: 14% POWER, it says, and she knows from experience that fourteen percent is like the next-to-last cough of
someone with tuberculosis. She might manage two short calls, but
to whom? With only two calls left and nowhere to plug in, she
needs to think. She powers off again, slips the phone back into her
pocket, and thinks, *First, stop looking like a nightmare.*

Around the lake, to her left if she's in the right place, there are
some bathrooms. The question is how to get to them without

attracting attention. Moving in a way that she hopes looks idle and uninteresting, her bloody face downward, she chooses the largest tree near her, pauses as she picks out the next one, and walks on. Aside from the throng doing aerobics far behind her, the park is still mostly empty, and only once does she have to go slowly enough to keep one big tree between her and a woman who is walking in the opposite direction on the path that's thirty or forty meters away. Joggers work the perimeter, but they're not looking at anything except their next twenty meters.

One of the buildings housing the restrooms is in sight now, but she has to get across a wide, grassy, relatively open space to reach it. Just as she sets off onto the lawn, one hand to her brow to mask her face, one of the restroom doors begins to open, and Luntanh accelerates and veers to the right so she can stand beside the building, behind the opening door. When the door is fully open, she grabs its edge and darts through it, pulling it closed and locking it.

She's alone behind a locked door, surrounded by concrete walls. There's a toilet to sit on. She collapses onto it, noting the dried blood that's stiffened the front of her shorts, and the sight triggers an overwhelming reaction, as though everything she's been keeping down, everything she's been pushing aside so she can see her way to the next moment, has been compressed into a single gigantic ball that's rolled down a steep slope just to knock her flat. All her plans, all the momentum that has brought her this far, is knocked out of her, as her breath was when one of the village boys sucker-punched her. The whole world is reduced to the ugly, dim little bathroom and the echoes of the sobs she didn't know she was making. And at this moment, something in her recognizes, she's safe enough to give herself entirely to crying, so she does. And when she feels as though she might be dramatizing it just a little, she stops.

* * *

A SMALL MIRROR, but it's big enough to give her the bad news. She looks as if someone hit her in the face several times with a brick. It's not going to be just a matter of getting the blood off. Her nose is so swollen that its narrow, expensively constructed bridge is thicker than her thumb, and the skin around one of her eyes—the left, the side where he hit her—is turning an ugly purplish brown. There's even bright red blood in the eyewhite. Her lower lip, which she doesn't even remember him hitting, is twice as fat as usual, and Ying's claw marks make it look like someone attacked her with a rake.

So she does what she can. She pulls off her T-shirt and gently bathes her face with cold water, then takes a paper towel, wets it to make it softer, and begins very lightly to move it in small circles across her cheeks and down to her mouth and chin. It takes several passes, and it hurts whenever she gets close to her nose, but eventually most of the blood is gone, or so she thinks until she lifts her chin and sees the blood-tinged water making rusty trails down her throat. When *that's* clean, she cups water in her hands and dips her nose into it, breathing out through her nostrils until all the water has leaked between her palms. Then she does it again and again, until she can use a sopping towel to scour the blood, very, *very* gently, from the bridge of her nose and from her nostrils.

By the time she's using hand soap to scrub the front of her T-shirt, several people have knocked on the door, so the park is filling up as the morning wears on. She gives herself one last unhappy look, wets her fingers, and uses them to pull her hair lower on her forehead and forward on the left and right, closer to her nose and mouth. Then she studies the effect, wishes for the big movie-star dark glasses that had been in her backpack, and pulls the T-shirt back on. The area that begins beneath her chin and stretches down to the center of her chest is wet and still slightly brick-colored with dried blood, so she turns it around and wears it backward.

Nothing she can do about the angry-looking skinned areas of her knee and elbow, but in a town where people regularly go down on motorbikes, they won't attract attention.

Someone knocks again, impatiently this time.

"One minute!" she calls out. She grabs the wet paper towels that she's dropped everywhere, wads them up, throws them into the basket, and pushes them down so they're not too conspicuous. Then she debates for a moment whom to call: Betty and her friends from the bar will be asleep until noon, and Miaow is in school. *And so what?* she thinks. *I'll leave a message.* As she steps out through the door, her head down over the phone and her hair hanging forward to conceal her face, she sidesteps the waiting woman and powers up the phone. Her eyebrows rise; it's later than she'd thought, almost noon, which means the school lunch break is coming up soon. She dials Miaow's number.

Once she's left a message, she pauses and looks at the bright, hot day and tries to think of a single place she'd be welcome. For the first time since she set out on her journey, she misses her village.

18

Behind Every Drop of Sour Lemon Juice

HE'S LEFT CLEMENTE in Chu's, where she was waiting for the waiters to clear everything off the table so she could start digging through the boxes, logging numbers and looking for photos of the victims, which Rafferty thinks someone might recognize in the bars they frequented. It seems to him that overlapping patterns are the only likely pointers they're going to find, given how far apart in time some of the murders are.

"We definitely need more pictures," she'd said, flipping through the nearest box as he got up to go. "Too bad we can't get the stuff the relatives trashed or took home."

"I don't suppose the morgue photographs—"

"No. They were floating facedown, in some cases for more than forty-eight hours." She fans a hand in front of her upper lip, as though clearing fumes. "The ones I saw were barely recognizable as faces, much less individuals."

"I'll see what else I can do."

He walks a few distracted blocks, thinking about Rose. It's just late enough that the shadow of the Skytrain, rising above the center of Sukhumvit, shades the curb edge of the sidewalk, and he aims for that to get out of the sun. People walking in the opposite direction have had the same idea, so there's some broken-field weaving, and in the end he just gives them the shade and settles for a clear, if hot, path.

He gets Rose's voice mail, which reminds him that she's out with Fon and who knows who else. He hopes she's having a good time. Her spirits have been so heavy lately that there've been times he barely recognized the woman he married. Clemente's question echoes in his head, and suddenly he knows with certainty that Rose's moods haven't just been hormonal, despite the male consensus that pregnant women are sometimes impossible. He's done a little reading of his own, reading she doesn't know about, and in an instant it's clear to him: She's worried.

He calls her again, if only to be doing something, and listens a second time to her message as though it might be coded, as though it might conceal something that would either confirm or soothe his anxiety. But all it sounds like is Rose, the *old* Rose, before her voice tightened and irritation seemed always to be just over the horizon.

He's an idiot.

But, he thinks, *not much I can do from here if she's not answering, and even if she were, nothing I try seems to work.* Someone bumps into him from behind, apologizes, and hurries past him, but Rafferty doesn't even look up.

He angles to his left, avoiding more collisions, until he's in front of a tailor shop. Shaking his head in the negative when the Indian man who patrols the sidewalk to buttonhole customers says, "Shirt, sir? Slacks?" he pushes speed dial for Arthit.

Arthit says, "Did you see Clemente?"

"Just left her. She's laid claim to the restaurant, and she's sitting there, working away." He explains about the spreadsheet.

"I have an eye for talent."

"Is there some way to get pictures of all these guys? I mean, weren't they photographed when they went through immigration?"

The Indian man says, "Nice suit, fits good," and Rafferty puts a finger in his free ear.

"The later ones were," Arthit says. "Some of them probably

entered the country before the government finally decided which cameras to buy, which is to say the ones with the highest graft markup."

"Can you get the ones who were photographed?"

"Not very quickly. I haven't got much weight behind me these days."

"Well, hell."

The Indian man is tapping his ring on his plate-glass window and gesturing at the somewhat dusty suit jackets hanging there. Rafferty moves three or four feet down the sidewalk but stops again, struck by a thought. "Most of these guys probably stayed here long enough to make visa runs, right? And probably most of them went to Phnom Penh. You're supposed to put a picture on your Cambodian entry form."

"Good thinking," Arthit says. "And those cops don't earn *anything*. Tell you what, I'll find out who to call and—can your client go five hundred US?"

"Sure. I mean, I haven't asked, but I can't see why not. Edward's father has money, and Fran certainly does."

"Fran?"

"The wife of the one who lived."

"Sir," the Indian man says.

"Fran? You've been busy."

"I have an active metabolism." There's a tug on his shirtsleeve. "What about the Americans? They should have pictures—"

"Forget it. Nobody gets anything out of the Americans. You need a security clearance to learn what the date is."

"Excuse me," Rafferty says. To the Indian man, he says, "I don't want a fucking suit. Leave me alone." The man backs up but then holds his ground, obviously evaluating the threat.

"Aaahhhh," Arthit says, "you're on *those* blocks. You really could use a suit. Maybe you could get one with little feet in it."

"Can you do it?"

"You mean get the pictures from the Cambodians? Sure, probably. Give me a couple of hours to work it out. Five hundred US is more than those guys make in a month."

HE'S GOT ABOUT two hours before he's supposed to meet Clemente at Edward's place, so he goes back home to change his shirt. He's saturated the one he's wearing with so much sweat that it smells like something that might be used to lure large carnivores into camera range.

When he pushes open the door to the apartment, he pauses for a moment, half in, half out—a habit he's developed, in part because there've been times when he wasn't sure who might be inside and also because it drives Miaow crazy. The place seems almost supernaturally silent, as it always does when he's the only one in it. The three of them, he thinks, make a lot of noise, and then he amends "noise" to "music." He belongs to an intergenerational, intercultural trio, and they've been improvising their music, sometimes a bit stormy, sometimes romantic beyond the point of good taste, for . . . good Lord, *how* long now? He's been in this apartment nine years, Rose, the cello, a little more than eight, and the first violin, Miaow, about seven. He thinks of himself as the banjo.

Not since he left his parents' home in Lancaster, California, some twenty years ago has he lived anywhere this long; not staying in one place had been the most fundamental building block in what he then thought of as his life plan. And now, after nine years here, immobile as a tree, he can't imagine going anywhere.

He pulls off the offending shirt, tosses it onto the bed, and goes into the bathroom to grab a washcloth and do the minimum Bangkok hygiene routine, face, neck, chest, underarms. He turns to take the wet cloth out of the bathroom and through the kitchen to the hamper containing the things Rose said she was going to wash today, but he gets sidetracked by the lingering fragrance, maybe tea tree oil, of her shampoo. It's coming from one of the heavy bath towels she used last night, now abandoned forlornly on the edge of the tub, and he remembers suddenly that he promised to help her dry her hair but had fallen asleep with his jeans and shirt still on. Even so, when he woke in the middle of the night, the air conditioner—which Rose used to hate—had been making its low, metallic burr, the room was cold, and he had been covered with a spare blanket.

Small kindnesses, he thinks. There's nothing much more important than small kindnesses.

Washcloth and damp towel in hand, he goes back into the bedroom to retrieve the sweaty shirt. On his way to the little storage area in the kitchen where Rose keeps the laundry hampers, he makes a detour into Miaow's room, following one of the ley lines the three of them have put down, the straight paths they've taken thousands of times from room to room, from family member to family member. On her bed he sees a shuffle of loose pages, one of them half crumpled, undoubtedly the product of the little inkjet on his desk. Figuring, *If she didn't want us to see it, she'd have put it away*, he goes over to take a look. The type is very heavily marked up, mostly with multiple question marks, exclamation points, and what look like angry scribbles, and he uses the washcloth to smooth the crumpled page—at least he can say he never touched it—until he can read what's written there. He sees:

THE MOTHER: How do you know that my son's name is Freddy, pray?

THE FLOWER GIRL: Ow, eez ye-ooa san, is e? Wal, fewd dan y' de-ooty bawmz a mather should, eed now bettern to spawl a pore gel's flahrzn than ran awy athaht pyin. Will ye-oo py me f'them?

He can't help it, he begins to laugh. He should have warned her. It's the first scene of *Pygmalion*, and Shaw, who was nothing if not meticulous, begins the text with an attempt to present phonetically the cockney accent his flower girl, whose name is Eliza Doolittle, will gradually lose over the course of the play. Even as he's laughing, he feels a sympathetic pang for his daughter. She's a sponge for language; with a few notable exceptions she has hacked her way through the thorniest thickets of pronunciation and the contradictory rules of grammar and spelling that mark English as a hybrid, assembled from a dozen other languages, ancient and modern. He's heard her at night reading out loud in her room, and he's sat with her the following morning as she repeated the passages to him so he could offer corrections. He worked with her endlessly on Shakespeare when she played Ariel in *The Tempest*. And then, with some well-hidden trepidation, she opens *Pymalion* and first thing out of the box she gets this . . . this *cipher*. It must have looked hopeless, and Miaow—who has tried desperately to leave behind the dirty street child she once was—has never wanted a role as much as she wants this one. It's *her* story.

It's going to be a bear for her, he thinks, and the phrase "life lesson" pops into his head.

A favorite topic of conversation for his father, whom Rafferty does not think of with much affection, could be indexed as *Life lessons, comma, benefits of.* Frank Rafferty was fond of using his son's (and his wife's) occasional failures as an opportunity to urge them to learn from reversals, although he wasn't quite so benign when it was his own problem. *Behind every drop of lemon juice*, he once said to Poke, whose girlfriend had just dumped him, *is a lemon blossom.* Poke had replied, *And a whole fucking lemon, too*, but Rafferty's mother, who was fast on her feet, had gotten between them in time to prevent an escalation that could have made the little house seem very much smaller for weeks to come.

Life lessons. Who's had more life lessons, and handled them with more grace, than Miaow? He immediately adds, *And Rose.* Not many lemon blossoms back there either. His own life, by comparison, feels like he was sentenced at birth to Beverly Hills. And now here he is, in love with two people who have become themselves in the hardest possible ways.

He makes himself two silent promises. First, he'll find a way to be helpful to Rose without getting underfoot all the time, and second, he'll help Miaow with this accent, no matter how many thrown objects, how much Sturm und Drang it takes. The accent is the only stumbling block. Other than the accent, she was almost literally born to play Eliza.

He tosses the dirty stuff into the hamper, briefly thinks about putting it all into the washing machine, and then abandons that plan because it could be construed as passive-aggressive criticism. Instead he goes into the living room and powers up his printer.

HIS NICE CLEAN T-shirt is soaked by the time he's walked the six blocks to Leon and Toot's. He's perspiring so heavily, and the air is so humid, that he feels the way he felt when he'd just arrived in Thailand, when he was always the wettest guy on the block. Thais seem somehow to perspire in secret, and he grew used to slogging along slowly to conserve his strength, spritzing like a fountain, with water dripping from the tip of his nose, as the Thais glided by looking as cool as ice-skaters.

"Hot, yes?" is the first thing Toots says as he's wilting his way toward a barstool.

"You noticed," he says. The newly printed pages of Shaw's play rolled up in his right hand are limp and damp. "Can I get a soda water, heavy on the ice?"

"You look hot," Campeau says, unashamed, as always, to state, or even restate, the obvious. He sits on his stool as though he made it himself. He seems to have been there ever since Rafferty's first day in Bangkok.

"Just out of curiosity, Bob," Rafferty says, looking at his watch, "what time do you usually get here?"

"Right after opening," Campeau says. "Miss the heat that way."

"Nobody else is here?"

"What's-his-name is in the john," Campeau says, miming wavy hair just above his head.

"Glad it's not—sorry—glad it *wasn't* just Leon and me."

Campeau sights him suspiciously over the top of his glass. "Leon and you what?"

"Who couldn't remember the name of—*Hey*, there," Rafferty says as the guy with the hair comes into the room, wiping his hands on his pants.

"Poke," the guy with the hair says, investing it, as always, with a kind of radio-announcer solemnity that makes the name sound ridiculous in Rafferty's ears, but this is the way he says everything: like an actor who has entered, a bit late, a mystifying scene to which he and only he can reveal the key, except that he might have forgotten his lines. He sounds exactly the same when he asks for a refill.

"Hold on," Rafferty says. "Me first." He downs the icy club soda and extends his glass for another. When Toots has taken charge of it, he says, "The guy who got beaten up so bad and went to Phnom Penh. You remember, some bird name."

"Finch," Campeau says, "Larry Finch."

"Right. Do you know how to get hold of him?"

"Louis does, I think." Louis is the Growing Younger Man.

"Where *is* he?"

"Sheesh," Campeau says. "Guy's got a life. What do you think, we all just sit around here waiting for you all the time?"

"Of course not."

"We got lives," Campeau says reproachfully.

"Is your adorable daughter," the guy with the hair declaims, "still thinking about trying out for that play?"

"Yes, I mean, yeah. Yeah, she is."

"The accent," the guy with the hair says, putting quite a lot of himself into the word "accent," "will be an obstacle."

"Yes, it will," Rafferty says. "A life lesson, as it were. But, you know, behind every drop of—"

"Hold on," Campeau says. He's fiddling with a phone the size of a man's shoe. "Can't hear myself think."

"Think louder," the guy with the hair says, apparently making a serious suggestion. Rafferty has never heard him talk so much, so he takes a closer look and sees that the man is squinting at his hands, folded in front of him on the bar, as though guessing how far away they are. He's absolutely poached, a conviction that's reinforced when Toots plunks down in front of him a glass of something amber and served straight, shaking her head in disapproval. To Rafferty he says, "Do you believe we think in words?"

"I have no—"

"Or, perhaps, pictures." After a moment he nods, as though he's been waiting for a simultaneous translation of what he said, and it just arrived via his earphones. "Or," he says, leaning in to emphasize the word in a way that suggests it's the most interesting thing anyone will say all day, "something *between* words and pictures, something, something . . ."

"Wictures," Rafferty suggests, not very kindly. "Or maybe purds."

"Poke," Toots says reproachfully.

"Or maybe they *are* images, like the ones in dreams," Rafferty says, "but tied up in little bitty hyperspace knots so they take up less space and arrive faster. Dreams are supposed to be really short, you know. A dream that seems to take hours happens in a couple of seconds. Maybe *that's* what we think in. Loops."

Toots blows air between her lips to make a rude sound.

The guy with the hair thinks for a moment and then says, "Huh." He blinks slowly, his eyelids coming down at different speeds.

Campeau says into his phone, a bit sharply, "*Yeah*, now. You telling me you got something more important to do? 'Cause if you do, I'd like to know what the hell it—"

Raising his voice to be heard over Campeau, the guy with the hair says, "What's all that wet paper?"

"It's . . . um, it's the play, Miaow's play. I'm going to try to help her with the accent."

"You're a good father," the man with the hair says.

There's a moment of silence that Rafferty devotes to a silent expression of contrition.

"Okay," Campeau says, putting his antique phone down with a clunk. "Louis gave me the number for Larry Finch. A little later I'll call Larry and ask him to call you."

"Why don't you call him now?"

"Because I don't feel like it." He taps the side of his glass. "Busy, you know?"

"Great," Rafferty says. "Great." He puts some money on the bar and gets up, saying to Toots, "Let me buy this round. One, make it two, all around."

"The accent," the man with the hair says as Rafferty opens the door. "It's going to be an obstacle."

19

Lala

THE HOUSE, LIKE a lot of newer, upscale Bangkok homes, seems to have been assembled from chunks of several other aspirational houses, a kind of structural *Reader's Digest*: classical columns, arched windows, and roofs on several levels, the slanting edges of which, in a nod to the traditional Thai house, bend inward a little toward the middle to create a curving, inverted V at each apex. The whole thing, phantasmagorical enough to serve as the setting for an urban production of *A Midsummer Night's Dream*, is, up close, made from stucco and has been further anchored in the real world by being painted a color that falls in some industrial workaday spectrum between gray and taupe. From where he's standing, outside the gate, it seems to Rafferty that in addition to their many other plagiarisms the builders have borrowed one brilliant idea—from, of all places, the Parthenon—creating a false perspective that makes the structure look taller by narrowing the whole building slightly as it rises.

He has purposely arrived fifteen minutes before the time Clemente is scheduled to meet him and about twenty before he figures Edward will get home from school. He wants to take a look at the house's security, searching for the way Edward said the housebreakers got in. It's not that he doubts the boy, but he's not in a frame of mind to trust assumptions.

So there's a forbidding wall, about seven feet high, broken by a double-wide gate at the street end of the driveway. The gate is made of wavy diagonal lengths of black metal, about four inches apart, that create a watery impression. Easy to see through but difficult to get through or over. He tugs it toward him and then pushes it away. Locked. There's a buzzer with a microphone beside it. Thinking there's a chance Auntie Pancake might have come back, he presses the button, but there's no responding voice or buzz.

To his left the wall makes a ninety-degree turn to follow the property line between Edward's house and the place next door, a sort of Rubik's Cube variation on this one but with even more glass, much of it mullioned. That house has no wall, so it's open lawn the entire way, and Rafferty can't imagine that the thieves just strolled over the grass, in front of all those fancy windows, so he heads right.

Since the house stands on a corner, the wall that surrounds it hangs ninety degrees left to parallel the junction of the streets. About fifteen yards after he turns the corner, he sees, like a transplant from Tuscany—almost the only place on earth the builders hadn't already borrowed from—a gate made of rough-hewn natural wood held together by bands of black wrought iron, dimpled irregularly with little ornamental dings from a ball-peen hammer. It obviously swings inward, because it's standing about four inches ajar.

He pushes it the rest of the way open, surveys the backyard for a count of ten or so, and goes in. No lock, not even a catch, on the inside of the gate. It's consistent with the lax approach to life he's come to associate with Edward's father. He cuts across the yard toward the big mango tree where, according to Edward, a nail has been driven into the trunk above eye level with a key hanging from it. The nail is there, devoid of the key. Ahead of him are the driveway and the corner of the house, so he follows the paved surface, hot even through the soles of his shoes, to the rear door and sees unpainted putty, obviously fresh, surrounding a new and heavily fingerprinted window that's probably never been washed.

Everything just the way Edward described it. Poke relaxes a little, and he's surprised to realize he'd felt any doubt.

Compared with the apartment he's just been thinking about, this is a mansion. He and Rose and Miaow are crowded together, living happily—most of the time—in one another's pockets, while here, in this space of perhaps four thousand square feet, are three people who, according to Edward, don't even like one another very much, each with volumes of empty space separating him or her from the others, each revolving in his or her own solitary orbit: the unwanted kid, the auntie who's anxious about being exiled from the palace, and the father who doesn't seem to have deep feelings for anyone. Poke wonders for a moment how his own family would do in a place like this and decides they'd probably all wind up in the kitchen.

He's ambling along the driveway, trying to picture Miaow here, when the gate grinds into motion. It swings toward him, and there's Edward eyeing him, wearing the white shirt and dark pants his school favors. Behind him, looking slightly disconcerted, is Clemente.

"Your friend said you might have gone in," Edward said. Over his shoulder Clemente gives Rafferty the small, private shrug of a conspirator.

"No lock on the wooden gate. Not exactly a challenge."

"Did everything check out?" He seems a little irritated at being doubted.

"Just wanted to look around it. Hot, isn't it?"

"When isn't it hot? I guess we might as well go in. I think I forgot to ask why you were coming."

"We wanted, Officer Clemente and I—sorry, this is Officer

Clemente—to let you know where we were on the investigation and what we were doing."

"And to go through your father's things, if we could," Clemente says in her best English, which, while accented, is as functional as Rafferty's. "Ask you a few questions."

"Well, thanks for trying." Edward steps aside to let Clemente precede him. "Let's get inside. I think the only reason it's not raining is because the water evaporates on the way down."

"NOTHING JUMPS OUT at me," Edward says. "At least not yet."

They're in the room Edward's father uses as an office, a medium-size space with a big picture window and a highly polished wooden desk that has a laptop sitting on it. In the corner beside the desk, bolted to the floor right through the beige wall-to-wall carpeting, stands a safe the size of a big microwave oven. Its door hangs open. There's also a leather couch, and Rafferty, who's gradually getting stuck to it as he pages through Edward's dad's bank statements and, noting contact numbers and balances on the backs of the damp pages of *Pygmalion*, is wondering why anyone buys a leather couch in this hot, humid climate. Every time he sits forward, pulling his wet back from the cushions, he makes a dull smooching noise that draws Clemente's eyes. Edward is occupying his father's swivel chair, tilted back against the desk's edge with Clemente's tablet on his knees, skimming the columns of the spreadsheet. Clemente sprawls on the floor with her notebook on her knee and the pulled-out desk drawers surrounding her, happily rooting through them. Rafferty is working on a beer, since it's a little after four, and the others are drinking some kind of iced tea that's scented vaguely with cinnamon.

"You've got a lot of stuff here," Edward says, scrolling down on the tablet.

"It's the kind of work I like," Clemente says, peering inside an envelope and putting it aside. "Repetitive, meaningless, and boring, until suddenly it's not. If you're lucky."

"Doesn't seem boring to me," Edward says. "Sort of like hunting for game."

Clemente gives him a quick glance, looks back down, and says, "How do you mean?"

"Everybody leaves tracks," Edward says as though it were the most obvious thing in the world. "You're looking for the places where they overlap, right?"

"That's very good," Clemente says. "You're not—What's that thing," she asks Rafferty, "about pretty faces?"

"Not just a pretty face," Rafferty volunteers, and is somewhat relieved to see Edward hunch down a little bit. He's never sure about handsome boys, about how aware they are of their impact. The teenage dreamboat who stole his girlfriend dropped her a week or two later, and Rafferty eventually came to believe that the boy had broken two hearts simply to stay in practice. That memory is the main reason Rafferty has been uneasy about Miaow's infatuation with Edward.

To Clemente, Edward says, "Give me a break."

Clemente comes up with a piece of paper that's been folded diagonally, like a napkin, and opens it. To Edward she says, "Put the entries in the number column into numerical order and then look for a phone number that begins with 318."

The boy expertly slaps the screen around for a moment and says, "What's the next number?"

"Seven."

"Nope. Two that start with 318, but no 7."

"Oh, well. Take this number down in the second column, and over in the right-hand column put the number four."

"Why?" But he's keying in the number.

"I've partially searched three boxes, which are sources one through three. This house is source four."

Edward hits the keys and says, "Three boxes of what?"

Clemente looks over at Poke, her eyes wide.

"Effects," Rafferty says, choosing the most remote word he can find.

"You mean . . . from, umm . . . ?"

"Yes."

Edward looks up from the tablet's screen at Clemente and then back at Poke. He says, "People who . . ." And then he says, "Oh." He drops his eyes to the screen again, clearly not seeing it, and then picks up his glass of tea and drinks it with his eyes closed.

"THE THING IS, they *have* to go on honoring his checks," Rafferty says into the phone. He's just finished reading the names and phone numbers of Edward's father's banks, plus his account numbers, while Arthit wrote them down. "None of your guys in the field has come up with anything, so we have to take this possibility, the canal possibility, seriously. Sooner or later the people who have Buddy Dell will walk in with a check that would overdraw the account. If whoever it is gets a bounce . . . well, that's not going to be good news."

"But what can I do about an overdraft?" Arthit says. "If I tell the bankers they have to honor it, they're going to ask me who's going to cover the money. I can't run down and make a deposit."

"I actually think the first time they *get* a bounce—" Rafferty says, and he breaks off as he feels Edward's eyes swivel to him. "I think . . . I mean, I think—"

"They'll kill him," Edward says. "Maybe they'll try another bank first, but if that bounces, too . . ."

"It won't end well," Rafferty says. To Arthit he says, "Isn't there some way the police can guarantee that the overdraft—"

"Not at my level," Arthit says, "and I'm not eager to make the case to Thanom."

"No," Rafferty says, "not Thanom." Thanom, Arthit's superior, has never forgiven Arthit for saving his ass four or five months earlier.

"Mr. Rafferty," Edward says.

"Hang on, Arthit."

"I can write checks on two of my father's accounts. My signature is on them. As long as there's money in those two, I can get to the other banks and make a deposit to cover whatever the overdraft is."

"Did you hear that, Arthit?"

"What if those accounts are the ones that—"

"Jesus," Rafferty says, "one thing at a time."

Edward is waving his hand in the air.

"I've got a credit card, too," he says. "It's got a high limit, six or seven thousand US. It's an emergency card—Dad calls it my 'get out of jail card'—but I guess this qualifies as an emergency."

Arthit is silent for a moment, and then he says, "I wouldn't mind having a kid as quick as that."

"I'll tell him you said so. Do you think you can do it?"

"I can try. I'll call the banks, give them an alert. They're to call me if someone cashes a check and see if they can get whoever it is on video without being obvious about it. If it's an overdraft, I'll tell them it'll be covered within . . . within how long?"

"Edward," Rafferty says, "how fast do you think you can make a deposit if you have to?"

"An hour or two? The problem is school. By the time I'm out of school, if traffic is bad—I guess I could stay home for a few days."

Arthit says, "I never heard a better excuse."

"Edward," Clemente says. She's got a piece of pink paper in her hand. "*Edward.*"

Rafferty says to Edward, "Do you think it would help if Arthit called the school?"

"I don't know. It would cause kind of a ripple, and people would worry about me. *Notice* me. Maybe Miaow could get my assignments, just tell my teachers I'm sick or something."

Arthit says, "Ask him if he wants a job on the police force."

Clemente says *"Edward"* a third time. She's waving the piece of paper at him. "Look at the column with the names in the second—"

"I'll start making calls," Arthit says.

"—and see if you find 'Lala,'" Clemente says.

"Okay," Rafferty says. "I'll give you a ring if we—"

"L-a-l-a?" Edward says. "I don't even have to look. That's not a name I'd—"

"Hang on a minute," Rafferty says to Arthit.

"It's here somewhere. Right . . . here." Edward holds up the tablet.

"I think we've found something," Rafferty says.

"Then try this phone number," Clemente says. The enormous eyes are on fire. She reads the number and waits, one foot bouncing rapidly.

"Oh, boy," Edward says. "Twice. But one of them is in a row that doesn't have 'Lala' in it."

Clemente says, "Jackpot." To Rafferty she says, "Give the colonel this number and tell him—I mean, *ask* him—to check the reverse directories."

"Four sources, three hits," Clemente is saying, loudly enough for Arthit to hear. "Two victims, one of them Edward's father, wrote down 'Lala,' probably close to the time they disappeared, since one of them had only been here for a month. Edward's dad and one other wrote also down the number."

Rafferty says, "How far apart in time are they, the ones who wrote either the name or the number?"

"Because—oh, right," Clemente says, "Lala's age. If it's even the same Lala, that sounds like a name that could get passed around. Hold on a minute, all I have to do is get the dates off the death certificates."

"I'll make a new column," Edward suggests. "It'll let you look at the . . . the murders in sequence."

"Great idea," Clemente said. "Hang on, I'm looking. First put the date your father disappeared. He's row four."

"Got it." He looks down at the tablet, probably, Rafferty thinks, at the date he's just written, and swallows.

"*What* are they entering?" Arthit says.

"The dates the victims were found. We've got three so far, plus Edward's father. Can you get the dates for all of them? Clemente could only get two boxes of effects today, and I brought Dependahl's with me."

"Sure."

"And we need more effects. Clemente got some pushback."

"Nothing I can't handle," Clemente says. "I should be able to get two or three more."

Arthit says, "You heard her."

"And finally, can you talk a hotel into letting me in under an assumed name? I mean, *they'll* know my name and they'll get my credit cards, but they need to route calls to me under a different name."

"You think the phone numbers are alive?"

"Hang on." To Edward he says, "Have you guys got those dates in?"

"Yes."

"What was the date when the one who wrote down Lala's name turned up in a canal?"

"Ummmm . . . 2014, May 2014."

"And the one who had the number but not the name?"

"That was 2011."

"Six years ago and three years ago. Yeah, the number might still be working. And the name, Lala, that's in Edward's father's things. So *she*—"

"Or maybe *they*," Clemente says.

"Right, she or they are still active even if the number has changed. If you can get me a business name or something to match the number and give me a running start at a conversation, I can call them."

"And?"

"And see what I can find out, what kind of business they say they're running, whatever. Unless you want the cops to do it, which would make me very happy."

Arthit is silent for a long moment, and Clemente is looking at Rafferty and shaking her head decisively, the corners of her mouth pulled down, the "no" unmistakable from twenty meters away. "There have been . . . a lot of these," Arthit finally says. "No solutions, not even a suspect. We're not *that* hapless. I think it's very probable that money changed hands, possibly several times. The cops who got it and the cops they shared it with are going to pay close attention to anyone who stirs this up." He says, "What?" and it's evident he's talking to someone who's come into the room. "Hold on a minute, Poke."

Rafferty waits, trying to pull himself slowly enough off the back of the couch that he won't make that rude noise. He's just succeeded when Arthit says, "Phone number's no good. It's a mobile, and it's a burner. They're being careful."

"And they have good reason. So I'll place a call," Rafferty says. "Put me in a good hotel, one that says I have enough money to get their attention."

20

Hates Hates Hates

L ALA HATES THIS heat.

She's believed for years that she was reincarnated from a cold country, where there's lots of clean white snow covering up all that irritating color and taking the edges off the landscape, where the stars gleam in the winter skies as though they were frozen in place, where everyone wears lovely layers of soft clothes. Where people never sweat and they have pale skin and red, red cheeks.

She hates how dark she is, dark as a sunburned rice farmer.

She hates the town she fled from, and she hates Bangkok. She hates that you can only see vistas in the city by going to the top of a high building. Some of the tall new ones have bars and restaurants on their roofs so you can get a cold drink in this awful heat, maybe even feel the breeze, and see for miles. She's felt hemmed in ever since she got here, always afraid she wouldn't see the enemy coming until it was on top of her, and there's always an enemy *somewhere*, so she likes vistas, but . . .

She hates heights.

And she hates the Thai Ploughman's Bank. The line in front of her is so slow it's as though the bank won't wait on you until it's your birthday. This is the part of the game she hates most because it's the most dangerous. But she has to do it. Kang certainly can't. And it's not only that he refuses to talk unless it's absolutely necessary; the voice is the lesser problem. Nobody who *sees* Kang ever forgets him. Someone who's lost an eye and won't put a patch over the socket, who outweighs three average people combined, and looks like he can bench-press two hundred kilos with his ears, someone like that stands out in people's memories. Lala may be dark and short, but that can be taken care of temporarily with creams and powders and high heels, and she has the ability to look like half a dozen other women, depending on what she's wearing. When she puts on certain kinds of clothes, when she lightens her skin and darkens her lips, when she slides her feet into heels and chooses a wig that goes with the clothes, she feels herself turn into that other woman. Her voice changes, her intonations change. Now that she's in her mid-thirties—well, mid-*late* thirties—she feels like a whole gallery of other women, women she can slip into and out of like slipping into and out of a bathrobe.

It's a skill she learned as a cherry girl. No two men want exactly the same girl. And even the steady customers usually want something new; they want the same girl to be a *different* girl. So she learned how to do that. She learned how to be the gentle sweetheart, the shy schoolgirl, the confidante, the comforter, even the confessor. She learned what to do for the ones who wanted to hurt her and what to do for the ones who wanted her to hurt them. After letting an especially persuasive customer get her hopes up ten or twelve times, she learned to distrust and dislike them all equally, a democracy of loathing.

She'd learned a great *many* things at Cherry Girls.

The customer at the head of the line is finally waved forward by one of the somnolent tellers, and Lala's heart accelerates. She feels the prickling of sweat in her underarms. She hates hates *hates* this part of the game.

When she first fled the northeast for Bangkok, with the police after her for almost killing her father, and owning nothing but the scraps on her back, she let a man take her in and give her a place to sleep in one corner of a filthy, leaking, plastic-sheeted plywood shack in the poorest part of Klong Toey, where any food left unattended for more than two minutes simply disappeared beneath a squabble of rats. After he forced himself on her three times (he was her first, if you didn't count her father's fumblings) and her novelty wore off, the man told her she'd have to pay her way by working the sidewalks of Sukhumvit, but she stood out because of her age. Worse, because she hadn't gotten herself an in with the cops, she was run off repeatedly and was taken twice to a station where policemen put her in a cell and took turns with her for several bruising days. Finally she let the only cop who'd ever seemed friendly buy her coffee, and he told her about a place she could work where they *wanted* young girls and the police wouldn't bother her.

So she went with him to a building with a neon sign that said CHERRY GIRLS MASSAGE. Watching him pocket the fee the mama-san gave him without offering a baht of it to her, she felt a dull ache in her heart, its edges ringed by a fine, bright flicker of fury. He was the only person in Bangkok who had been polite to her. He left without looking back.

It had been almost six in the evening when he took her there. By the time they closed the doors at 3 A.M., she felt as scooped out as a melon. She'd had seven customers. She was seventeen years old.

Once again the line is at a dead stop. The bank is so silent it could be underwater. For the past year, she's been telling herself it's time to quit. Their luck can't last forever. It's time to tell Kang that she's close to quitting. It would be a good idea, she thinks, to be well armed for the conversation. To take her mind off the bank, she begins to organize her approach.

Even before Cherry Girls, her first few months in Bangkok had taught her quite a bit. When she arrived, like many young people, she had assumed that the sexes were much more similar than they actually are. But the men she met in the city taught her otherwise. The city was rich in lesson opportunities. She learned one lesson from the slum dweller who welcomed her to the city by raping her and turning her out as a street whore. She learned others from the few she snagged on the sidewalk before the cops got her; some of them hated her the moment they were finished with her, and others found it amusing to throw her out without paying.

She learned an enormous amount in the police station, from the cops who lined up to take her in the cells. They competed to mount her differently, in front of one another and the prisoners in the other cells. They called out encouragement to one another, entering her through all the available orifices, applauding or laughing when one of them did something novel. When they thought she was too dirty even to rape, they hosed her off right there in the cell. It had been an intense learning experience.

An icy stab of panic snaps her into the present. *Where's the check?* She finds it folded neatly in the Vuitton purse and glances reflexively at her Rolex, a real one. Bank tellers can spot fakes more quickly than customs agents. A quick glimpse of the real thing works wonders on a teller's attitude.

She realizes she's shifting from foot to foot and doesn't want it to be seen as anxiety, so she checks the watch again, and this time she actually reads the time. Getting late. This is the main thing she was worried about, the reason she has risked changing her routine. She always makes the two stops in the same order: ATM and then bank. The ATM is a low-risk warm-up, getting her ready for the bank. But it had been late by the time she got away from the current patient, and her bus couldn't move in the traffic, so she'd broken the rule, gone to the bank first and let the ATM wait. Standing here in this eternal line, she regrets it.

She hasn't *done it in this order* before. Doing things in order is the safest way to stay alive.

As she came to realize—even before she wound up at Cherry Girls—how little of her life she could control, she developed a secret magic to avert disaster. Its fundamental tactic was to remember a situation in which things had worked out well and then duplicate her conduct as closely as possible, every time the situation arose. By now she does it without thinking about it, unless, as now, she's forced to deviate. She sits in the same chair for dinner every night, goes around the block in the same direction, has one sip of liquid before she eats. In a thousand little ways, she follows scripts only she knows, follows them *every time*, and they work. Look at her: All these years and she's still playing the game.

But. She should have gone to the ATM first. The perspiration beneath her arms runs down her sides. Sweat has popped into being at her hairline, hidden for the moment beneath the wig. She'd mop it, but she might knock the wig crooked, and then she'd be remembered.

In one way Cherry Girls was a survival course. As much as she'd disliked her customers there, she was forced to compete with the girls who in other circumstances she would have tried to befriend. The massage parlor felt like a dinner for twenty where there was only enough food for ten. She had to keep her own customers and, beyond that, steal some away from the other women. This meant that for the first time she had to focus on the customers as *individuals*, even when she was accommodating eight or nine a night. If she wanted them to come back to her, she couldn't just see them as dicks with legs. They sensed it when a girl did that, and they wanted to feel *special*, even the ones with the most repulsive demands. She saw how many men lit up when their girl of choice greeted them by name, but most of her customers were *farang*, and all foreign names sounded the same to her, so she assigned each of them the name of an animal he somehow resembled. She had a whole menagerie: a water buffalo, several breeds of dog, a sheep, a couple of fish, a snake, many kinds of birds, even some insects. She ran through most of the animals that a farm girl is familiar with, plus a few exotics, such as a unicorn—a guy who always entered the room visibly ready to go—and one of those dinosaurs with the huge body and the tiny head. (Years later, seeing a Disney cartoon in which a platoon of little animals pitched in to help the heroine do her chores, she had laughed out loud.)

So she didn't have names, but she had a way to tell them apart, and she had *dates*. On a calendar over the bed, she wrote the Thai word for each animal who showed up on that day, and when he came back, she could smile and say, "I get *lonely*. I don't see you for *eight day*." Those customers tipped more, but that didn't make them smell any better, weigh any less, or want to do less humiliating things.

The big room flickers and brightens, and Lala realizes that the bank has turned on its fluorescents because the day outside is beginning to dim. So she was right about one thing: If she'd gone to the ATM first and then walked here, the bank might have been closed when she arrived. The realization doesn't relax her.

Cherry Girls was run like a factory: men in, men out, no drama, no shouting, no unsatisfied customers. Eat when it was possible, go hungry when it wasn't. To keep the girls acting cheerful and innocent, the mama-san had hired three muscles. As Lala would later learn, all houses had muscles, who were generally kept out of sight until needed. The girls talked about the muscles. Two of the muscles could be won over, for a time anyway, with a quick one on a slow afternoon, but the third, a silent, one-eyed giant who was the biggest man Lala had ever seen, demonstrated no interest in the girls. He looked at them, if at all, as though they were furniture that might eventually need moving.

The giant gave her one of the worst frights of her life late one night when a regular customer, the stork, was leaving. She'd followed him into the hallway, telling him to come back soon because she'd miss him, and as soon as he'd disappeared around the corner, she spit on the carpet. Then she did it three more times. When she turned to go back to her room, the giant was standing there, his right eye gleaming in the fluorescents, the socket of the left pink and dusty-looking. For a moment she thought her heart would stop, but he just shook his head slowly and passed her by, pausing to grind her spit into the rug with the sole of his shoe. Just before he followed the customer around the corner, he turned back to look at her again, for a long, breath-holding moment.

After three years of working seven days and nights each week at Cherry Girls, she'd been told she was through, she was too old. So she'd asked the mama-san for the portion of her earnings they'd told her they were banking for her and was told that her room and board had eaten most of that up and there wasn't cash on hand to pay her the remainder. When she said she'd wait until they had the cash, the mama-san called the big one, and the giant had picked her up, thrown her over his shoulder like a sack of rice, and carried her to the tiny room she worked and slept in. He'd tapped his watch and held up five fingers to tell her how many minutes she had to get everything she owned, and then he went away. She sat on the bed, feeling like someone who had opened her front door only to discover that the world had disappeared. She'd hated Cherry Girls, but at least in there she knew what to expect. She'd barely been outside since the cop sold her to the mama-san. She didn't even know where in Bangkok she *was*. When the giant came back in, carrying an empty brown supermarket bag, he found her exactly where he'd left her. He opened the bag on the bed, right beside her, and started picking things up.

He'd hold something up and point at her, meaning, *Yours?* If she said yes, he'd drop it in. When the room was empty, he sat beside her, so close she thought he was going to take her by force since she no longer officially worked there. Instead he put his mouth to her ear and said, in a whisper so ragged it might have been dragged over a sidewalk for miles, "You sure all this is yours? Mama's going to check." She'd closed her eyes for a moment to dispel the mixture of anger and panic that owned her from head to foot. When she opened them again, she took out two blouses she'd borrowed from another girl and put them on the bed. Only then did she begin to cry.

The tears were mostly fear and frustration, but the giant misunderstood. "Won't do you any good," he whispered. The voice was *awful*. "Got any money?"

"No." She could barely look at him. The sight of the empty eye socket made the room spin.

"Too bad," he said. He rifled through the bag, taking things out one by one and holding them up again, waiting for her to nod or shake her head. When he was through, he handed her the bag, leaned so close that his lips brushed her ear, and said, in that gargling whisper, "I'll tell Mama I double-checked. Go out and turn left. Walk to Soi Seven and turn there. Go to the Heart Clinic. Tell them Kang sent you."

It was the longest speech she'd ever heard him make. Since she had no alternative plan, she did as he suggested, and when she unpacked her things in the Heart Clinic, where all the girls were dressed as nurses, she found a five-hundred-baht bill folded into a tight, tiny square at the bottom of the bag.

Eight months later *everything* had changed.

She's been in the bank more than twenty minutes, but she's finally getting a hello from a teller. It's the same one who waited on her the last time she was in this bank, a sallow young woman who looks infinitely pregnant, with circles beneath her eyes that are so dark they could have been photocopies. Lala hoped for any other teller in the bank, but so far there's no flicker of recognition. Lala looks nothing like the woman the teller waited on nine or ten days ago.

"Hot out," Lala says, putting the Vuitton bag up on the counter in plain sight and rummaging needlessly through it. She wants to display both the bag and the Rolex, show the teller a wealthy woman who's disorganized, unprepared, who might need a little help. After they'd been together a few months, Kang had told her she "radiated distance" and that she needed to learn to make people feel closer, make them feel, at the very least, that she knew they were there.

"Unusual for this time of year," the teller says politely.

"Don't know why I carry all this stuff," Lala says, with just a touch of cherry girl: wide-eyed and unequal to the challenge of the moment.

"It's a beautiful purse," the teller says. She places her left hand on her stomach as though the child has just kicked. "It wouldn't look so nice if it were empty."

"*That's* what I'll tell my husband," Lala says. "He's at me all the time, as though I'm packed for a week's vacation, but he bought me the bag. I'll say, 'It needs to be full to look its best.'" She pulls out the check. "Finally."

"Straight deposit?" The teller glances at the check as Lala slips it beneath the glass.

"No, I'm cashing it. Let me get my ID."

"Take your time," the teller says, studying the check. "I need a moment." She turns away.

Lala doesn't lift her face, which is tilted downward so she can continue to rummage through the bag, but her eyes follow the teller, who angles across the space behind the customer stations and stops in front of a desk. Behind the desk sits a heavy man with three chins, fat lips, and hair combed forward like a Roman emperor's, a pathetic attempt to mask a receding hairline. He's on the phone. As Lala's heart plays a tiny timpani in her ears, he holds up a finger—*wait*—without glancing at the teller. Even through her fear, Lala feels a flare of loathing erupt in her heart. Officious prick. She reduces her fear by envisioning him strapped naked to the bed as she makes him up to look like a female pig, attaching little pink suction cups on his chest like nipples, using a whole tube of lipstick on those fat, wet, pendulous lips. With a tape of squealing pigs on the sound system and more serious indignities to come. Keeping her face empty, she brings out the Coach wallet with the excellent driver's license, the name and the number valid but not hers, and waits for the pig to give the teller a moment of his precious fucking time.

She *hates* men like this one. This is the kind of man, self-important and probably self-loathing, who drips sweat like a faucet when he fucks, who likes to slap cherry girls around, either because they're "starfish" who, under the pretense of being innocently unfamiliar with the act of love, just lie there or because they simulate passion badly, with the empty overreaching of bad acting. This is the kind of man she had the hardest time handling until the day she finally came up with a little two-person play in which a powerful and irresistible man gradually and unexpectedly awakens passion in a frightened girl, a girl who has no idea what is happening to her and who in the end weeps with gratitude. And if this man were the customer, the first thing he'd do after he had his pitiful little spasm would be to go to the small mirror on the wall, congratulate his reflection, and comb his hair forward with his fingers.

He'd probably stiff her on the tip.

He hangs up the phone and takes the check from the teller's

outstretched hand without meeting her eyes. He looks at it and turns it over. Lala's heart rate doubles.

The fat-lipped man snaps a question. The teller shakes her head, saying something, but he cuts her off with an upraised hand and thrusts the check at her. The teller wheels away, back toward Lala, and the fat-lipped man gets up grudgingly and follows, but not closely. When the teller is back at the window, he stops about two meters away.

"Is there a problem?" Lala can't believe how steady her voice is. What's waiting on the other side of this moment, if it goes wrong, is the death penalty.

"No, no, it's just over my limit, that's all. That's your identification?"

"It is." Trying to look amused at the situation, she holds the driver's license up to her face to demonstrate that it's her photo in the corner. Her knees are shaking but her hand is motionless. She slides the license under the pane of glass. The teller looks down at it and up at her, then picks it up and turns toward the fat-lipped man as though inviting him to look at it, but he shakes his head, dismisses her with the back of his hand, and waddles toward his desk, his pants caught in the crack of his ass, as Lala thinks how much better he'd look with a cast on his leg.

BEING A NURSE was *much* better than being a cherry girl.

Where cherry girls were damp and submissive, nurses were dry, brisk, and *in charge*. The Heart Clinic looked inoffensive enough from the outside—the sign was a giant pink neon heart with a tidy little Band-Aid on it—but inside, it pandered to a spectrum of specialties sorted by room, with the less exotic practices—ranging from relatively innocent variations on playing doctor to ultrahygienic hand jobs—in the front rooms. The rooms farther from the entrance hosted more complicated costume play with clearly defined roles and high-priced pain. In the smaller, darker, and *much* more expensive rooms at the back, behind two concealed doors, were immobilization and long-term stays for the wealthy and the warped. Here Lala learned to administer medications via IV bags, how much fentanyl was usually safe for someone who'd built up a tolerance, how to create an expert bandage on an unharmed arm, how to counterweight a traction device, how to put a functional cast on a leg.

She enjoyed the work. It suited her. She was inherently tidy and strong-willed, and her stay in Bangkok had done nothing but intensify the loathing for men that was her father's only lasting gift. She *liked* having them immobile and dependent on her, liked the apprehensive expressions they wore when she came into the room with her mask on, especially after she started putting her lipstick on the outside of the mask rather than on her lips. She liked the fact that they had to call her "Nurse," liked it as they tried to see how big a dose she was injecting into the IV bag, and most of all they liked the fact that it was agreed in advance that she, and not they, decided when the game ended. Sure, they had a "safe word," but the ones who used it too soon were, generally speaking, not encouraged to return unless they tipped *very* well, so over time a kind of evolutionary mechanism weeded out the weak and moved the general customer population toward the deadly serious end of the long, ever-darkening line that connects love and pain.

Then Kang had shown up and seized control of the business in a short and remarkably bloody coup that included negotiating a sign-off from the cops. A few months later, he'd taken her to the small apartment building he'd purchased beside the *klong*—in which he occupied the only unit in use—and, in careful stages, told her the idea that had made them both rich.

With the bank's money stowed safely in her purse, she steps out onto the hot, stinking sidewalk again, wondering whether she's imagining the fat-lipped man's eyes on her back. She literally has to shrug off the impulse to turn and look. She modifies the aborted movement into a fluff of her wig where it falls onto her back, a piece of mime that's expressive of the heat. Then she looks at her watch again, just to be doing something, and turns right.

It's nearly six. The day is dimming, and the sidewalk is jammed. Lala can smell the people, their dirty hair and underarms. Three hairy-legged foreign men in shorts jostle past her, a German, maybe, and two Arabs, towing behind them a triangular wake of body odor.

He might have been on the phone, the fat-lipped man, by the time she stepped outside. Not going to the ATM first is feeling more and more like a serious mistake; the bank was mostly empty by the time she left, and if she'd gone to the ATM first, she wouldn't have had to wait in line for a teller, might have gotten a different teller with a higher limit, might not have had to . . .

Stop it, she tells herself. *It's over. There's just the ATM to go, and that's easy.* Then she can go home, get this stuff off, and take a long shower.

Why did the teller need approval? The last check was for a little more, and there hadn't been a problem.

She passes two big banks with a scattering of ATMs in front, gleaming like big, bright, hard candies in the spotlights that have just snapped on to illuminate the area. The ATMs she uses in this part of Bangkok are five long blocks farther off. It will be dark when she gets there. Any of these machines would probably do, but there will be *no more changes* to the routine.

So she's relieved when she sees the ATMs, sees that no one is standing at the one she needs. She walks past it, her head still but her eyes everywhere, and then pauses in midstep, clearly someone who's just remembered something, and turns and goes back to the

ATM, shaking her head at her own forgetfulness. She unzips the purse with her right hand, always her right hand, and takes out the orange plastic card that says HERBERT DELL on it. She looks right and then left—she always does it, even though she knows it's a signal that she's about to make a withdrawal and is checking her surroundings. She did it without thinking the first few times, and now it's an inescapable part of the script, and anyway, she pities the street thief who would try to take her purse. The card, now in her left hand, slips into the slot easily, as though it's been allowed to go home at last, and Lala hits WITHDRAWAL, keys in 60,000 BAHT, and enters Dell's security code. The machine whirs a moment and then makes a noise she hasn't heard before, and the card slides partway out, as though the machine is sticking its tongue out at her.

The screen says DECLINED.

There's a roar in her ears, her stomach is suddenly in knots, and she feels sweat on her forehead. She pushes it all aside and repeats the entire sequence. Maybe she got the code wrong, maybe she inverted—

DECLINED.

She doesn't look around to see whether anyone is watching. She stands there for a slow count of four, breathing evenly to dissipate the cold ball of panic in her gut, and then reaches down and mimes taking cash out of the slot and retrieving the card. Bending to put the card and the imaginary banknotes into her purse, she catches a whiff of her own breath, and it's sour with fear.

When she's all the way around the corner and sure no one is watching her, she pulls her phone out of her purse and holds down one key. When Kang picks up—without a spoken greeting, as usual—she says, "We have to get rid of him. Tonight." She doesn't expect an answer, whether he agrees or not, but she waits anyway. After a few seconds, he disconnects.

Part Three
THE RAPIDS

21

Yes, I Not Know

ARTHIT HAS BOOKED Rafferty, under the not-very-likely name Richard Milton, into a fancy room at the Landmark on Sukhumvit, up one long block—although not quite long enough for Rafferty—from the three-story stack of skin emporiums on Soi Nana. He's heading down the hallway toward the front door of Edward's house, dialing Rose for the fourth or fifth time, when an electronic cricket chirps somewhere in front of him. He stops abruptly at the sound, and Rose's voice mail picks up his call as Clemente, toting the box of Edward's father's things she'd declined to let either him or Edward carry, bumps into his back and says, "Excuse me."

Edward, who is ushering them out, steps around him and pushes a button beside the door. Above the button a small and very bright screen pops to life, and Rafferty sees Miaow, looking even shorter when seen from above. Behind her is a slight girl wearing a big floppy hat, a loose, familiar-looking denim dress, and a huge, movie-star-size pair of sunglasses.

"Hey there," Edward says, apparently into a microphone. He pushes the release button, and there's a buzz. Rafferty watches Miaow and her shrouded companion come through it as he disconnects from Rose's voice mail without leaving another message. He feels a little squiggle of unease chase itself in figure eights in his gut—this is an awfully long lunch; what if something went wrong?—but he pushes it away and steps aside as Edward pulls the front door open for Miaow and her friend. Miaow's mouth narrows, not in a smile, as she sees him.

"What are you—" she says, as he says, "Have you heard from your—" but then he recognizes her companion and says, "What in the *world* happened to you?"

"Man," Lutanh says, miming hitting herself. "Him . . . he . . . *he* . . . boxing me."

"A *man* did this?" Clemente says. She drops the box where she's standing, and Lutanh jumps straight up at the sound. "Take off the glasses."

Lutanh shakes her head. "Ugly too much."

"Take them off." Clemente's tone does not invite argument, and Lutanh very carefully eases the glasses from her face. Edward draws a quick breath, and her eyes dart to him and then away. Her eyelids are a mottled purple and pink, swollen almost shut, and her nose is thickened and lopsided, knocked about fifteen percent off vertical so it now drifts to the left as it approaches her split upper lip.

Clemente steps around the box to get a closer look "Where did this happen?" She's biting the words off. The golden eyes glow like roadside reflectors. "Do you know who—"

"Happen in ho—"

"On the street," Miaow says over her. "Near Silom. Big guy. *Farang.*"

"When?"

"This *morning*," Miaow says, all but shoving Lutanh to shut her up.

Clemente gives Miaow a long glance and leans toward Lutanh. "*Do* you know who—"

Lutanh says, "Yes," and over her Miaow says, "No," and Lutanh says, "Yes, I not know who he is."

"Why would he hit you?" Clemente says.

"Him want . . ." She falters, grabs a deep breath, and ventures, "My money?"

Clemente turns to Rafferty and shrugs a sort of irritated hopelessness.

"We can talk about all this later," he says. "Lutanh, have you used any ice? Do you have any open cuts?"

"No," Lutanh says, looking at Miaow. When no prompt is forthcoming, she says, "Yes. Have." She points to her lips. "Here." Then she indicates her right elbow and her left knee, both of which are covered, and says, "Have here, too."

Clemente says to Lutanh, "If you know who he is—"

"Not know," Lutanh says, and she sounds like she's on the verge of tears.

"I'll get some ice," Edward says.

Miaow says, "Good idea. Lutanh, *go with him*. Maybe he can . . . you know, do something about the swelling. Maybe some antiseptic for the scrapes."

"Okeydoke," Lutanh says. "Where going, Edwudd?"

"Kitchen," Edward says, turning to lead her. "We have a refrigerator that makes ice twenty-four hours a day. It's absolutely impossible to run out of ice." Lutanh says something in reply, but they're out of earshot.

Rafferty says, "Your dress looks good on her. So does Rose's hat."

"I thought they were cute," Miaow says. "And, look, she's almost the same *size*—"

"So you took her home before you came here."

"Well, her . . . um, her clothes were all bloody, and she—"

"Was your mother there?"

"Mom?" Miaow looks surprised. "No. She went out to lunch."

"Have you heard from her?"

"I haven't checked my phone, but—"

"Check it."

"Yes, *sir*. Hang on."

Clemente says, "Those injuries did *not* happen this morning."

"No," Miaow says, lowering her voice, her fingers a blur on the phone. "Last night, but don't tell Edward." She looks at the screen. "No calls."

"It's been too long," Rafferty says, glancing at his watch.

"She's with her friends," Miaow says, "and she *never* gets out of the apartment."

"If it happened *last night*—" Clemente says, but Miaow is shushing her, so she lowers her voice. "If it happened last night, what *else* is she, or the two of you, lying about?"

"I don't think we actually told you any—"

"You *didn't* tell us anything." Clemente leans forward, a movement that manages to be simultaneously intimate and aggressive. "What's the big secret?"

Miaow says, in a half whisper, "He doesn't know she works in a bar."

"He?"

She lifts her chin in the direction that Edward took.

Clemente says, "This is about *teenage love?*"

Rafferty says, "Why did you bring her here?"

Miaow gives him the wide eyes that mean, *Dumb question.* "She can't stay with *us*. You know . . . Mom. And she can't go home."

"Why not?"

"The cops—" She looks at Clemente and puts her fingertips over her mouth.

"Did she steal something?" Clemente demands. She slides the box up against the wall with her foot. "Did she injure him?"

"Oh, *no*," Miaow says, "she just sat there and let this big bag of shit beat her up. What do you *think* she did? But she's a bar worker and he's a *farang*, and guess who'll go to jail?"

Clemente says, "How badly did she hurt him?"

"Stabbed him in the knee."

"The *knee?*"

"She was dangling *upside down*, okay? He'd punched her in the face and knocked her down, and then he picked her up by her belt and she grabbed a steak knife—"

"Lower your voice," Rafferty says.

"Do you really think," Miaow says to Clemente in a fierce whisper, "that she assaulted a guy who weighs like a hundred kilos? Look at her, she's a blade of grass."

"So what you're saying, or at least what you *would* be saying if you could calm down," Clemente says, "is that a customer took her to his hotel to beat her up."

Miaow eyes her for a moment. "That's what I'm saying."

"Does she remember what hotel? His room number?"

"Of *course* she does."

"Well, then," Clemente says, and her throat sounds tight. "Maybe a personal call is in order."

"He's got her wings," Miaow says to Rafferty.

"Her wings?"

Miaow looks at the carpet. "Never mind," she says. "It's not important."

Edward comes bustling out of the kitchen and makes a sharp right to go upstairs. "Her contacts, the blue ones—"

"Violet," Miaow says automatically.

"Fine, violet. Well, they're still in, and her eyelids are so swollen I'm afraid they'll scratch the surface of her eyes. My dad wears contacts, so he's got all that stuff. We need to get her lenses out."

"Edward," Clemente says.

He's halfway up the stairs, but he stops and turns, gazing down at her, and Rafferty is struck again by the boy's good looks.

"You did well today. You helped us quite a lot."

Edward blinks a couple of times and then ducks his head in acknowledgment. "Thanks," he says. "Just find him, okay?"

CLEMENTE HAS TRUDGED off to her car, toting the box, and Miaow and Rafferty are on the front porch, watching her go. The door behind them is ajar. Miaow sighs.

"Are you sure about this?" Rafferty says.

"Look at her," Miaow says. "She slept under a bench in Lumphini last night. Some meth mutt tried to paw her while she was asleep. She can't go home, because the guy who beat her up is probably going to complain to the cops, and the people in her bar will tell them where she lives and who her friends are and where *they* live. She can't come to our—"

"No," Rafferty says, "she can't."

"And here's Edward," she says, "all alone in this big house, with food and water and bedrooms that no one has ever slept in." She opens her mouth to say something else but falls silent.

When the silence is getting awkward, Rafferty says, "You *are* aware that she likes him."

"*Everybody* likes him," she says, sounding slightly bitter. She shoves her mouth to the right and chews on her lower lip. "But you know," she says, "they're my friends. Both of them."

Rafferty wants to hug her, but he's learned not to, not unless she invites it. So instead he makes a high musical humming sound with his lips tightly closed, moves his head right and left as she watches him uncertainly, and then he darts in and kisses her, very quickly, on top of her head.

She scratches her head. "What was *that?*"

"That?" he says. "Oh, *that.* You've just been bitten by a kiss-quito. They're rare, but once one bites you, you stay bitten."

"Yeah? If they're so rare, how come one just bit me?"

"They follow me around," he says. "I have no idea why."

She glances at the front door. "So what happens if one bites you?"

"First you smile, and then you give yourself the pleasure of admitting what a terrific person you are when you've done something selfless."

"That's silly," she says, but she's grinning at him. "*Kissquito.*"

"I know. I stopped trying to be cool around you when you were eight."

"Seven," she says. "Should I go inside?"

"Do you think you can help? Can you make her more comfortable?"

A shrug. "I don't know."

"Would it be rude to leave without saying goodbye?"

She nods. "It would, wouldn't it?"

"Should I go in with you?"

She says, "Call the kissquito again."

"They don't just come when you call."

"No," she says, "but if *you* do . . ."

He makes the humming noise as she watches, and then he darts in and kisses her in the same spot. "Salty hair," he says.

"That's what I've always wanted to hear," she says. She pulls the door open and leans on its edge, scuffing the sole of her shoe on the porch and making a gritty noise. "But thanks. Okay, then, bye."

"I've got some ideas about *Pygmalion*," he says. "We'll talk about it tonight."

Going inside, she says, without turning back, "Promise?"

"What time will you be home?"

"Early," she says. She glances at a bright yellow watch he realizes he's never seen before. "Before dinner probably." She grabs an audible breath and closes the door behind her.

22

Adjusting the Balance

ROSE'S PHONE RINGS again.

Fon doesn't even take it out of her purse. It'll be Poke again, or maybe Miaow. They're both probably getting worried. But then Fon's a little worried, too. Across the room the foreign woman—Joyce, she thinks—glances over at her. "You're not going to look?"

"It's her husband again."

Willis takes his eyes from the screen of his phone long enough to say, "Poor guy."

"She has reasons for not telling," Fon says. "Or thinks she does."

They've been in the hospital for almost an hour. The doctor to whose office the doula took them had done a brief examination and then come out, saying he believed it was best that she have a procedure immediately and he couldn't do it there. Should he call an ambulance, and could she pay for it if he did? Joyce had looked worried, as though she were debating whether to volunteer the money, and Fon had said, "I have it. I have money, credit card, everything."

So Fon and Joyce and Willis had ridden to the hospital in a cab and Rose had gone in the ambulance, the doula riding with her. They'd found their way through the white corridors to the correct waiting area and then settled in for what proved to be a very, very long hour, broken only by occasional beeps and cackles from Willis's phone games until his mother had snapped at him to kill the noise.

After a while the doula had come out and shrugged at them; she'd been barred from the room.

And now it was *more* than an hour; it was almost an hour and a half, and then it was two hours, and the chairs got harder, and there were no windows so they had no sense of the day, and the doula excused herself to go see another patient somewhere else in the city, and Willis said he was hungry, and Joyce said he was always hungry, and Willis went back to his game, his stomach growling at them reproachfully, and Fon said to Joyce, "You don't have to wait. I can take care of her," and Joyce said everything would be fine if they could just *feed the beast*, and Willis had said, "Jeez," and Fon smiled sympathetically at Joyce and got a surprisingly warm smile in return, considering how bony her face was. All female *farang* except the very young seemed to Fon to have bony faces, but Joyce's seemed to be *all* bone, except for the part that was nose. Still, when she smiled, she was very pretty.

Fon said to her, "You very pretty," and Willis looked up, startled, as Joyce shook her head and said, "Old lady," but she was still smiling.

Willis said again, "I'm hungry," and then he said, "Do you think it should take *this* long?"

In the silence that followed, a nurse opened the door and looked in, saw no one she was searching for, and started to back out, but Fon stopped her and asked where the boy could get something to eat.

"You like Thai food?" the nurse asked dubiously.

"I love it," Willis said.

"You come with me," the nurse said. "First I looking for some-body. I find, I take you to cafeteria. Have hamburger, too," she added. "Thai food hot."

"Thai is fine," Willis said, and the two of them went out. The door closed, leaving just the two women and the silence in the room.

After a minute or two had passed—time seemed to Fon to be

lurching by in fits and starts, and she couldn't really gauge it until she checked her phone—she said to Joyce, "You know about this. Is taking too long?"

Joyce had opened her mouth, closed it again, and looked away. Then she said, "It might be."

AFTER A LONG, hot slog looking for a cab and wishing he'd hitched a ride with Clemente, Rafferty settles himself in the backseat, sniffs at his shirt, and gives the driver the address of the Landmark. He needs to check in, talk to the desk and the people on the switchboard, make sure everyone understands about the name, Mr. Whatever It Had Been. Mr. *Milton*, Mr. Somebody Milton.

Richard. Richard—

He waves both the name and the errand aside and leans forward to give the driver a new address, the one for Aspirin, the auntie nobody likes. She sounds suitably difficult to handle, and that's what he wants now, something difficult, something that will involve him completely. He can handle the hotel on the phone, give them a credit card, do everything except show them his passport, which he probably doesn't have to do anyway, because Arthit was the one who made the reservation. What he has to do at the Landmark isn't urgent enough, compelling enough. *Distracting* enough.

Auntie Aspirin might be.

He has to face it. He's not just worried. He's frightened.

It's not only that no one has heard from Rose today, although that's what's brought it to a boil. His reply to Clemente, when she asked about the pregnancy, had been completely disingenuous. She'd invited him to talk about it before he was prepared to. Saying something *out loud*, he feels instinctively, magically makes it real. So he hasn't discussed it with anyone, not even Arthit, but that doesn't mean he's not worrying about Rose all the time; he knows she's having a difficult pregnancy, and he knows she's afraid she'll lose the child. At night, when she's asleep, he's gotten out of bed to open the books he bought, to search out her symptoms online, and he knows that what they're most likely to indicate is a miscarriage. And he knows that her fear of that is the reason she's locked him out of what she's going through—why she's seemed, for the past month or so, to be in a different room, behind a closed door, even when she's sitting beside him. He supposes it's because she's afraid he'll hold the baby's loss against her, although he can't think what he's done or said that would make her believe that.

Because losing the baby, much as he dreads the possibility, *isn't* what he's most afraid of. He's most afraid that something will go wildly wrong and he'll lose *her*. He knows that it can happen, and it's no comfort that the odds against it are high.

Why hadn't he *dried her hair*? What kind of an asshole *is* he anyway? You can't just roll over and fall asleep when there's an . . . an *opportunity* like that. There's no way to know, he thinks, because life isn't kind enough, or cruel enough, to tell you when it's the last time you'll dry your wife's hair, when it's the last time you'll say good morning to her, argue mildly about her refusal to give up Nescafé in favor of the beans he buys and grinds daily, talk about Miaow with her. When it's the last time you'll look at her across a room when she's not aware of your gaze, hear her laugh when she's on the phone with a friend. Listen to her breathe when she's asleep.

The apartment that feels so small for the three of them would be immense without her in it. He and Miaow would rattle around in it like Edward, all alone in that big empty dump his father bought. His life is unimaginable without her. She's as fundamental to him as gravity.

There's a blur at the side of his field of vision. A moto taxi zips by, going too fast, and so close that the driver's shoulder bumps the rearview mirror on the driver's side of Poke's cab. The young woman passenger laughs, although it might be the surprised laughter of someone who is momentarily amazed at being alive. He watches them zip off, weaving through traffic. The driver was young, the woman, in the glimpse he got of her, was pretty, so the driver was showing off. He supposes people risk their lives for less every day.

Rose is not—*is not*—risking her life to have this child. This isn't the nineteenth century.

And yet it happens. All his reading has made him an expert on the ways pregnancy can go awry. There can be infection, then sepsis, the infection finding its way into the bloodstream, invading other organs and systems of organs . . .

"How much farther?" he asks the driver. He has to say something, do something.

"Not much," the driver says. Bangkok is as flat as the floodplain on which it was built, but it slopes very gently downhill when you're approaching the river, and Rafferty can feel that now.

"Do you have children?"

The driver catches his eyes in the mirror. "Five."

"Wow." He realizes he's leaning forward so far he probably looks like he's about to climb into the front seat, and he forces himself to sit back. "They're all healthy, your kids?"

"Sure," the driver says. "And they eat *all the time*."

"And your wife, did she . . . I mean, were the pregnancies easy for her?" He realizes what an odd question it is and says. "My wife is pregnant. First time."

The driver smiles in a way that looks more like sympathy than celebration. "Not easy," he says, "Second time, third time, easy. Fourth time, fifth time, nothing. First time, the world stops."

"Yeah," Rafferty says. "It does."

"You worried?"

"Am I *worried*?" Rafferty is stunned to feel tears come to his eyes. "I'm terrified."

"Your mama alive?" the driver says.

"Yes." He blots his eyes with his shirt.

"Your wife mama alive?"

"Yes."

"*You* alive?"

"Of course."

He shrugs. "Well, then."

"It's not going right," Rafferty says aloud for the first time.

"What can I say?" the driver says. "It's between her and the baby. Tell her you love her. It won't help, but it can't hurt."

THE VOICE ON the other side of the door is unexpectedly sweet. He was expecting something like a nail on slate. "Who is it?"

He says, in Thai, "I'm here to talk to you about Herbert Dell." The corridor is lit by about half the number of fluorescents it requires, and an actual path has been created in the center of the dirt-brown linoleum, wearing away the surface to reveal the paler material beneath. It looks like a ghosts' highway.

The closed door says, in English, "Who?"

"Umm. Buddy. Buddy Dell."

"Oh, *Buddy*." There's a silence. "Has he come back?"

"No. We're looking for him."

"Well," she says, an undercurrent of stubbornness coming into her lower tones, "*I* don't know where he is. Who are you?" Her English is almost unaccented.

"Just a friend. I . . . um, I'm good at finding people. Listen, can you please open the door? Just give me five, ten minutes."

"Stand in front of the door. In front of the *middle* of the door."

He does as she says, and he hears something heavy sliding over the floor inside the apartment. A second later a little bright hole about the size of an American quarter appears in the center of the door. The place is nowhere near fancy enough for a peephole with a lens. An eye is put to the hole. It looks him up and down.

"Name."

"Philip Rafferty. Look, you can call Edward at Buddy's place and ask him about me. He'll tell you I'm okay."

"Edward," she says, the way she might say "mildew." The little hole in the door goes dark again, and whatever it was slides back over the floor. A moment later the door opens.

Auntie Aspirin is a plump little doll of a woman of the general type often seen in advertising wearing an apron and baking some homey sweet. He was expecting something out of *The Addams Family*, an angular vamp with, perhaps, black fingernails, so he mentally kicks himself for stereotyping and says, "Thanks for talking to me."

"No problem." She steps aside to let him in, kicking a small step unit a foot or so farther from the door. She's barely five feet tall, and her face is pleasant enough except for her eyes. Rafferty thinks, *If I tossed a handful of coins into the air, she'd have them counted before the money hit the floor.*

"This way." She turns and leads him into the living room, which is small, crowded with furniture that's covered in densely patterned prints, and almost as dim as the corridor. The builders saved a fortune on window glass; the day's last light leaks into the room only through two panes about a meter high and as narrow as medieval arrow slits. On the outside the glass is the kind of dirty that sometimes inspired Rafferty when he was a kid to write WASH ME on someone's car.

"Cozy," he says. It's the word Miaow used, sarcastically, to describe Edward's father's place.

"Good enough for me." She stands in front of the overstuffed couch, neither sitting nor inviting him to sit, and gives him a long, assessing look. He feels like he did in church back in Lancaster, the day his Catholic mother introduced him to the priest—that everything he'd ever done wrong in his life had been waiting patiently for that moment and had manifested as facial acne. "You're married," she says.

"I am. I'm the most married man I know."

"Don't you find marriage complicated?" She sits and waves him toward an uncomfortable-looking chair.

"Oh, I don't know," he says. "Not compared to, say, metaphysics." The chair is *much* more uncomfortable than it looks.

"I don't know what that is," she says. "I don't think I need to know. So . . . no sign of Buddy?"

"None, but we think he's been taken, and we think we know by whom, and we don't believe he'll be alive much longer if we don't find him."

"Who's 'we'?"

"Me and some other people."

The eyes flicker, and he realizes that his evasiveness has angered her. She says, "*How* much longer?"

"At the outside twenty-four hours."

She nods. "You're right," she says complacently. "That's not much longer." She's wearing a blouse with outsize buttons, surprisingly cartoonish for what seems to be her deeply unwhimsical personality, and she's toying with one of them. "But if you say you know who has him—"

"In general terms. We're about ninety percent sure they've taken other men in the past, and all those men but one or two are dead. That's why I want to talk to you."

"Why would I know anything about it?"

"How long have you been with . . . um, Buddy?"

She sits back, increasing the distance between them. "*With* him? I'm not with him. I make myself available to him from time to time, but I'm not *with* him. I don't share *anything* with him except my time, when he needs it."

"Which is on a regular basis, according to—"

"He's a creature of habit."

"Does he talk to you?"

She gives him a slow, patient look that probably doesn't last as long as it feels like it does. "That's all he does, talk."

"Really. Probably because your English is so—"

"No," she says. "Time is wasting. Ask me questions."

"So your relationship is different from the other—"

"From anyone, but especially that bunch of old slags, the aunties. My appeal is on a different plane." She uses her index finger to rub very lightly at the tip of her nose, as though to defeat a slight itch. "Buddy is a bad boy," she says, with no change of tone. "He's always been a bad boy. He's selfish and cheap and small-hearted, and he's uncontrollable where women are concerned. Look, he's abandoned a wife, a daughter, and a son, even if Mama eventually sent the son back by return mail."

"So you're what? A confessor?"

"No, not in the sense you probably mean. Why do you think I can help?"

"There aren't that many people who know him. 'Small-hearted' is exactly the way I'd describe him. The night my wife met him, he more or less abused the woman he was with—"

"That would be Pancake. She's the one he takes out in public. She's so homely that people see him with her and think, 'Well, at least he's not looking for beauty. He must be deep.' Your wife is Thai?"

Rafferty suddenly finds himself very unwilling to talk about Rose with this woman, but there's no way to avoid answering the question. "She is."

"Beautiful?"

"I think so."

She gives him a lopsided smile. "Pretty little doll?"

"Not even close."

Aspirin waggles her head side to side, the equivalent of a shrug. "And you're satisfied with only one?"

"I am," he says, his face feeling both stiff and hot. "Completely satisfied."

"Well, Buddy isn't. Buddy's a man who's dying of thirst in a . . . in a water-bottling plant and who is *completely* convinced that the water tastes different in every single bottle that rolls off the line. So he's constantly discarding bottles, and like most men who have a lot of women, he finds that his tastes have grown more . . . well, specialized. Harder to satisfy. So he discards even more bottles. And because he also thinks he's more interesting than he is, he believes that he's somehow *hurt* all those tossed bottles."

"Bangkok has a lot of guys like that."

"But Buddy's different from most of them, because somewhere in him his inflated sense of how interesting he is is rubbing up against his conscience. Like a short circuit. He feels *guilty*, cheating all those women of the splendor that is Buddy. And the world doesn't punish him. That's where I come in."

"How?"

"Well, on the one hand, you have someone who feels guilty and undeserving, and on the other hand, you have the world that keeps *giving* him things. I adjust the balance." She crosses her legs and glances down at the big buttons.

"What does that mean?"

"I give him the comfort of retribution."

Rafferty says, "Aaaahhhh."

"So it might have been a good idea to have someone come to see me a *week* ago. A session with Buddy begins with me taking his wallet and everything in his pockets, including all his money. His wallet is one of the ones with a little notepad in it. He knows I'll read it. That's where my questions come from. In other words, I know things about him that nobody knows."

"Has he said anything about—"

She holds up a hand. "How much?"

It's Rafferty's turn to give *her* a long look. She doesn't faint or clutch at her heart. She doesn't even blink. He says, "How much do you want?"

"A thousand US."

He gets up. "Bye, then."

"I thought you wanted to—"

"He's not exactly a friend, and it's not like I have an expense account."

"Seven-fifty."

"Haven't got that much with me."

She smiles up at him. "But you're good for it. If you tell me you'll pay me, you'll pay me. I can spot honesty a mile away."

"I'll pay you if it's worth it."

"Sit."

"Not on that thing," Rafferty says, with a thumb toward the chair.

"Buddy likes it," she says.

"That's Buddy's problem," he says, thinking, *Poor Edward.*

"How much do you have on you?"

"Seven, eight thousand baht."

"Let's start with five thousand. That's about a hundred fifty US. You'll owe the rest."

"Fine." He pulls the money from his pocket and counts out five thousand. Then he folds it once, slips it into the pocket of his T-shirt, and says, "I'm listening."

She moves down to the far end of the couch and pats the cushion she's vacated. "Please," she says, and he sits.

For the next twenty minutes, clearly enjoying herself, she tells him things he wishes he weren't hearing.

23

A Real Girl

LUTANH HATES SCRAMBLED eggs, but she's eating them for two reasons. First, Edwudd made them for her, and second, he said it was what his mother always made him when he didn't feel good. She'd been thinking, *That's so sweet,* when he said, "*She* couldn't cook either."

"Taste good," Lutanh says, even though it doesn't; the only thing she likes about scrambled eggs is salt, and he forgot it. She doesn't want to insult him by pouring some on, and anyway, it hurts to chew. Something's not quite right with her jaw, and her throat feels too narrow—bruised inside, as though the Meat Man had squeezed it smaller. She doesn't remember him doing it, but he must have, because there's a little flare of pain, like a striking match, quickly blown out, every time she swallows. On the table in front of her, embarrassingly ugly, is the wet, bloodstained ice pack she's been holding to her nose. Edwudd has seen her nose— he even looked *up* it at one point to see what was blocking her left nostril, which turned out to be dried blood. So there's not much about her nose he doesn't know, but the ice pack, with its pink, diluted patterns of blood, still makes her feel ashamed. She'd throw it away, but the wastebasket in this enormous kitchen seems to be hidden. Edwudd sits opposite her, not even pretending he's not looking at her. They're at the table in the middle of the kitchen, the table he called "the island." She'd never known kitchens had islands, but if he says this kitchen has an island . . . well, this kitchen has an island. She'd betrayed her surprise involuntarily by saying, "Island?" but rescued the situation by pretending she didn't know the word in English. So at least he doesn't think she's too poor and too ignorant to know that kitchens have islands.

He's left the cooking mess on the stove, piled on top of other dirty pots and pans, like someone who's never had to clean up after himself, and now he's resting his chin on his hand, watching her eat. This means that she has to disguise the two moments of pain, the chew and the swallow, that punctuate every mouthful. There's been a silence for a minute or two that has only served to emphasize to Lutanh how noisily she swallows, and she's experimenting with tiny, less painful chews with the objective of turning the food into a paste when he says, "How long have you known Miaow?"

Miaow had left about forty minutes earlier, after trying once again to phone her mother. She'd seemed upset that the call hadn't gone through. It's dark now on the other side of the kitchen windows, but even with the evening rush, Lutanh thinks, Miaow is probably home. Lutanh had recognized that something changed in the room when Miaow left, and instead of what she might have expected—the room feeling larger with one fewer person in it—it feels smaller; and although she and Edwudd are no closer to each other now than they'd been before, he *seems* closer. She thinks she can almost feel his body heat, thinks she could close her eyes and know where in the room he is. Even with her lids shut tight, he'd be a warm orange glow.

For a moment she's afraid the feeling shows in her face, so she makes a grab at his question, whatever it was—and there it is, patiently waiting for her, complete with answer: "I meet her same day I meet you, when you do first play. But I meet you at night, she come daytime." She parks the scrambled egg in her cheek to clear her speech and delay the pain of the swallow and says, "She come my house. Show me how to *act*. How to be other girl."

"Act?" he says. "Oh, *right*, you go to Miaow's acting class. You were going to do something yesterday, right? You had wings, I think."

"Peetapan," she says, feeling a twinge for her lost, broken wings. She waves it away. "My teacher famous too much."

"How was it? *Peter Pan*, I mean. Did it—" He scratches his head, obviously figuring out how to formulate the question. "Did it go well?"

"Go okay," she says. "Two girl wery cry." She waits, but all he does is duck his head in acknowledgment. "*I* cry when Miaow dead."

He says, "Excuse me?"

"That night I meet you," she says. "In play. In your school. You *boy* in play, yes? And Miaow is girl, and she die, she come back, she look around. Say goodbye, goodbye everything. I cry. Have—" She brushes her cheeks, very lightly, with her fingertips. "Makeup. For look white." She tracks tears down her cheeks. "Make all foofoo, have to do again."

"I remember when I met you."

"You *do*?" She can feel her eyes widen. "Yesterday you say—"

"I didn't recognize you yesterday," he says. "And all I was thinking about was my . . ."

"No problem. You thinking your papa." She swallows the mouthful and sticks her fork back into the eggs because he's watching. "So you now, you acting more?"

"Maybe," he says. "I don't know."

She touches the bridge of her nose to see whether the swelling has gone down after the ice, but it feels as wide as a highway. "For you, acting good. You look same-same movie star," she says, running it into a single word, "moviestah."

"Me?"

"When I look you, I think moviestah." She fusses with the eggs, her head down because she's afraid to see his expression. "You . . . you first person I see."

"First person you—what do you mean?"

She taps the plastic case with her contact lenses in it. "After I buy eye," she says. "I look around, you first person I see."

He says, "Oh."

"I think you wery pretty. Good luck for me. Happy I not see ugly person first, have bad luck." She's just rattling, so she breaks off and lets silence claim the room.

He's looking at her eggs, too. After a moment he says, "Want another aspirin?"

"No. Have enough. Make me . . ." She rubs her belly.

"Yeah, makes mine hurt, too, but it helps with the swelling."

She says, "You have beer?"

"HE WASN'T — I mean, he *isn't*—much of a father," Edwudd says. "But he's the only one I've got. And I don't want to go home."

"Home."

They're in the long, dim living room, lit only by the big-screen television, on which the female villain of a Thai soap opera is plotting, probably for the fiftieth time, a bad end for the heroine. The sound is off, and neither Edwudd nor Lutanh is watching it. Lutanh is on her back on the thickly carpeted floor with her legs up and her calves resting on a big, soft footstool, with Miaow's denim skirt tucked demurely between her knees. She's feeling the pain fade, courtesy of the aspirin. Two-thirds of a bottle of beer has eased even *more* pain, and she'd like another. Edwudd is halfway across the room, also lying on his back, on one of the two couches. They're talking in a desultory fashion, but what they're looking at is the ceiling.

"America," he says. "Where my mother is."

"Oh." She digests this for a few seconds. America is just a movie to her, a movie where people shoot each other a lot. "You like Thailand?"

"I didn't think I would," he says, "but I love it."

"Me, too," she says. She lifts her head enough to bring the bottle to her lips without spilling on herself. The bottle feels light. She swallows and says, "Love too much."

He shifts his back on the couch, as though scratching it on the upholstery. "Well, sure, you're Thai."

"No Thai," she says, "me Lao."

He rolls onto his right side to look at her, and she fights the impulse to use her free hand to hide her swollen face. While they've been staring at the ceiling, with the television to distract them once in a while, she's forgotten what she looks like. "Really?" he says. "Where in Laos?"

She wants to yank her hair out. If it weren't for the beer, she'd never have told him. "Small, little, small."

"How small?"

"Not have name." She laughs. "Have pig and people. And dog."

"But your family—"

"Not have movie, not have big store, not have—" She almost says, *Bar*, but deflects it and says, "Movie."

"You already said movie."

"Not have two movie," she says. "Not have many, many movie."

"When did you come to Bangkok?"

"Oh," she says. She should have seen this coming the moment she said she was Lao, but it's too late now. "Three, four year," she improvises. "When I fourteen."

"So now you're—"

"I nineteen," she lies, adding a year. "Lao age. America age eighteen."

"I'm almost the same age."

She lets that pass and then says, "We get more beer?"

"No, I've still got some." He holds up the bottle and sights through it at her as though to check the level but doesn't drink. "Why did you come?"

"School better here," she says promptly. It's what she tells the customers. They like to think of her as being in school.

"Wasn't it hard, getting used to a new system?"

"No problem," she says. "I smart."

"What grade?"

No one has ever asked her this before; the image of her in a school uniform has always been potent enough to reduce her customers to silence. "Eight?" she says. She hears the question mark and overwrites it with a confident, "Eight." She hoists her bottle and sends him a mental message to drink, but it doesn't seem to get through. "Why you not like Papa?"

"All he wants is women."

"Many man same-same."

"Yeah, but he doesn't even *like* women. All he wants is . . . you know."

"Him old man," she says, making it up as she goes. "Some old lady, they want baby, baby, baby. Sometime have many man, look for baby. So some man—"

"It doesn't have anything to do with babies," Edwudd says. At last he takes a swallow of his beer, and she follows suit, emptying hers. "He hates babies."

"Cannot hate *baby*," she says. "Everybody like—"

"He says the best way to become invisible, if you're a man, is to be carrying a baby. Women don't even see you. Carry a baby, push a baby carriage, he says they look through you like you're a window." He drinks again and then sticks his index finger into the neck of the bottle and dangles it over the edge of the couch. "But maybe he's wrong. He was never as handsome as he hoped he'd be, and I think he hates women because all they ever wanted was his money."

She doesn't want to get into men paying for companionship, so she blows into the mouth of her bottle, making a low, hollow flute sound. He glances over at her and blows into his, which produces a sound high enough, she estimates, to make it one-quarter full. She blows into hers again, and the two of them hold a kind of beery harmony until he runs out of breath.

"You're easy to be with," he says.

"I," she says, and has nothing to add; the comment has taken her off balance. So she gestures with her beer bottle at the big-screen. "You look Thai teewee?"

A glance at the screen and a shrug. "Not much."

"Why? Girl wery pretty, some man wery handsome. Have nice cloe."

He looks over at her, "Cloe?"

"Shirt," she says, sitting up a little and tugging at Miaow's dress. "Pant. *Cloe*, okay?" She settles back in. "If *I* have teewee this big, I look-look-look."

"I watch DVDs sometimes."

Her eyebrows go up. "*Deeweedee?* Have *Iron Man?* Have *Mulan?* Someday I want act Mulan. Have *Chucky?*"

He says, "*Chucky?*"

"*You* know," she says, holding her hand, palm down, a couple of feet above the carpet to indicate Chucky's height. "Him—him little, same-same doll. But have big knife, make *foom-foom-foom*," she says, miming stabbing herself in the stomach. "I wery like *Chucky*. Make me *brrrrrrr*." She illustrates the word by rubbing goosebumps on her arms.

"You like being *scared?*" Edward says. "Why?"

"Because," she says, "when movie finish, everything okay. Not same, ummm . . ." She makes a big circle with her hand, indi-cating the real world. "You know?" He doesn't reply, and suddenly her stomach is in knots. "I not talking about you papa," she says. "Him . . . him okay. I know, him okay. So you—" She ransacks her mind for a new subject."You not like teewee, look deeweedee."

"Sometimes," he says. "Mostly I read."

She says, "Oh." She presses her thumb against the bottle top, shakes the bottle, and puts it to her ear, hoping there's enough left to fizz but not hearing anything. Then she does it again and licks the beer taste off her thumb. "You smart."

"Yeah," he says. "Smart."

"You read comic book?"

There's a pause, and she can feel him looking at her. Then he says, "Sure. I love comic books."

"Same me," she says happily. "When I small? My papa, always he angry me. I read comic book, comic book."

"Why would that make him angry? Didn't he want you to read?"

"No, him want me read bang-bang book, like boy. But not like. I like comic book with love, comic book with princess."

"And that made him *angry*?"

"Yes. Him want me be *boy*. Him not want—" She breaks off, feeling a sudden wave of certainty make the floor move beneath her. *He doesn't know?*

"He wanted a boy?" Edwudd asks, but she barely hears him.

It's never occurred to her that he doesn't know. She looks like a girl, sure, she *is* a girl, but not quite yet. Not all girl, not yet. And he hadn't . . . She has a swift, dizzying, shrinking feeling, as though she's growing very small, very fast, and she realizes exactly what she and Edwudd have been doing, where they've been going, where she's been half-intentionally *leading* him. But he doesn't know she's a *katoey*, he thinks she's a *born* girl, he'll probably be *angry* when he finds out, he might be disgusted. He might hate her. And she's so ugly now—what has she been thinking? And then another thought steamrolls itself at her, from a completely different direction, and with a sensation like a spike driven through her heart she thinks, *Miaow.*

If she were a girl, she thinks, with a wave of self-loathing. Or if he'd *known* she wasn't, and if he, if he *liked* that . . . she would have, would have betrayed . . .

. . . but what would it have been like to be with someone she *wants* to be with, someone who's good, someone who's beautiful, who's not old and drunk? What it would have been like to hold—

What, she thinks, *would it have done to Miaow?* Everything on her body that hurts attacks her at the same time, and she accepts it. She welcomes it. She *deserves* it. She puts the bottle down and rolls over and, a little stiffly, gets to her feet. "I need go to bed now," she says. "Can you show me room?"

24

An Honest-to-Jesus Bobby Pin

KANG HATES TO talk.

It's not because he's not articulate. He isn't—or at least not very—but he doesn't care about that. What he *cares* about, and keenly, is his flutish little cartoon-mouse voice, so at odds with his height and bulk. Until the sudden spurt of growth that kicked in when he was fifteen, he was comedy material for his peers, good for a cheap laugh whenever they tricked him into speaking. All a kid had to do to get a hand was to mimic him in a tremulous falsetto.

Later, when it was clear to him that the growth spurt wasn't one of nature's little jokes and that he was destined to *remain* bigger and stronger than almost anyone, he took his time about settling scores: breaking the comedians' noses, splitting their lips, aiming a bare-knuckle punch at the precise spot where the skin on the face is thinnest to explode a single eyebrow into a furry little archipelago of eight or ten pieces that some surgeon either would or wouldn't be able to sew back together. In several cases he waited so long that his victim had no memory at all of the laughter he'd caused. But *Kang* remembered, and that was enough.

Still, the voice remained a problem. He hoped, during the time it seemed to his apprehensive classmates that he was doubling in size each year, that he'd tow his voice along with him, but ultimately he accepted that his voice had changed as much as it ever would, and even if he looked like a gunboat, he was doomed to sing soprano. The saving grace was that, big as he was, he looked even *bigger* close up, and he discovered at the age of seventeen that his preferred conversational gambit was to get more or less on top of people and force his voice into a kind of choked gargle, big on the back-of-the-throat rasp that makes some Middle Eastern languages such effective vehicles for swearing. And it worked.

And after the loss of his eye, a lucky thumb plant by someone who was seconds away from a broken spine, his physical impact was intensified, especially since he declined to wear a patch. When he dealt with people face-to-face, he found, he had a marked advantage; the simple proximity of someone who looked like a mountain and sounded like a strangling parakeet persuaded most people to end the discussion or negotiation quickly and, for him, satisfactorily. If necessary he'd give them the side of his face with the bad eye and bring it very, very close. A real deal sealer.

The telephone, however, presented problems.

So: big, frightening, ugly, and uneducated, but nowhere near as dumb as he looked. Add to that combination a surprising indifference to pain—rare among bullies—and a flair with knives that was almost musical in its delicacy and virtuosity, and by the time Kang was eighteen, he was highly employable in the darker sectors of the Thai economy.

Muscle is a necessity for businesses that trade in women. Any good pimp knows that the two most important aspects of managing a string of pros, some of whom are not volunteers, are protecting them and threatening them. Kang excelled at both. The sheer menace projected by the enormous body, the tiny voice, and the empty eye socket was usually enough to get pissed-off johns to appreciate management's point of view while simultaneously keeping even the angriest, craziest, most drugged-out working girl in line without marking her, thereby necessitating unprofitable recovery time.

With these assets Kang had effortlessly scaled the ladder of the red-light world until, at the immensely profitable Cherry Girls, he'd met the business partner he needed, a harmless-looking little scoop of ice cream who was even colder than he was. He'd watched all the new girls as they came into the stops on his climb, rarely speaking to them, just letting his bulk make the necessary impression until the girl did, or tried to do, something that required a more complex interaction. They rarely required it twice. As the places changed—from run-of-the-mill whorehouses to tag-team joints, to "gentleman's clubs," to relatively mild fetish bars, to whipping shops, to Cherry Girls Massage, and then to the moral black zone of the Heart Clinic, so did the fees the men paid and the unpredictability of both girls and customers. By the time he was running the Heart Clinic, Kang began to regard the back rooms—where people paid large money to be immobilized, filled with dope, and mothered, nursed, titillated, or tormented—as the potential first step to a much more profitable conversation. Why not go private, cut loose all the girls but one, and take literally everything the customer has, one punter at a time?

He's still a bit pissed that Lala got so rattled at so little this afternoon. Disaster wasn't the *only* explanation. Maybe the check took the account close to overdraft and the teller had to get approval for it. Maybe the credit line on the card had been maxed. Maybe the patient had missed a payment. In spite of Kang's best efforts, the patient hadn't been very precise about his finances. He had the careless attitude toward money that comes with never having needed any.

But Lala wants the man upstairs finished, and she's the one who has to go into the banks, so if Kang isn't in the market for a fight, it's his responsibility to do the finishing. But he'll insist Lala

run each of the other credit cards first, all the way to the *real*
limits.

So he goes into the triple-locked drug room he's created from
the kitchen in one of the vacant apartments and mixes the bye-
bye cocktail for the man upstairs, which has to be strong enough
to let them manhandle him and then throw him into the water
without a bunch of time-consuming resistance. He uses fospropofol with a little of the opioid compound called fentanyl, being
as precise as always about quantities and proportions. Such a
useful drug, fospropofol. A water-soluble version of the drug that
carried off Michael Jackson, it was developed because propofol
sometimes causes significant pain when it's injected, and pain is a
memory marker. Propofol had seemed perfect for Kang's purposes,
because people who were given it rarely remembered what they
did when they were high, but the injection pain, to an extent,
counteracted that. As he'd been told by a mistress in a whipping
shop, pain produces something called *adrenaline* that hangs a
bright yellow tag on the memory of what happened to cause it.
According to the whipper, a tiny little thing who called herself
Eiko although she was no more Japanese than larb kai, adrenaline
makes sure we remember the things that hurt or frighten us.
Without it, she'd said, most of us wouldn't survive childhood.
Kang, who rarely laughs out loud but whose childhood had been
one mercilessly prolonged nightmare, had been caught by surprise
and released a girlish tee-hee.

So people who are given fospropofol remember very little,
which means they're far enough under that they don't know
what's happening when they sign the checks, and the same is true
when they're being towed out at the end of their stay, until they
hit the water, by which time it's too late for them to do anything
about it. The patients' first reaction when they land in the relatively cold canal is invariably a reflexive inhale, but they're

facedown with the cast's weight pulling them deeper, and what they get is a lungful of water that speeds things along. The addition of the opioid to the mix knocks them out so deeply that he can tote them downstairs, but—if Kang doesn't overdo the fentanyl—the patient will also be able to bear some of his own weight when it's time to walk. As much as he hates to admit it, Kang's deteriorating spinal disks are a constant reminder that he's not getting any younger.

Once he's got the precise mix he wants, he opens a new package of fixed-needle syringes. There are ten of them in five bright, playful colors, two in each hue to reduce the likelihood of accidental sharing among groups of self-injectors, not that most of them, Kang thinks, register anything as subtle as color. If more than five are shooting up, tough luck. These are low-dead-space syringes designed to fill completely and deliver precise and unvarying doses, and Kang was delighted when they hit the market.

He draws the fospropofol mixture into three of the syringes, caps the tips, and cleans up after himself, washing the small graduated beaker in which he mixed the doses and putting everything back into the safe that looks like a garbage-disposal unit beneath the sink. Then he puts the three full syringes into his shirt pocket, the tipped caps protruding, locks the room behind him, and goes out through the empty, unfurnished apartment and into the dim hallway, which is sharp with the smell of dust. He figures he's earned a beer.

There are six apartments, each with one bedroom, on the ground floor, and four, identical to the ones on the ground floor except that each has an additional, smaller, bedroom, on the second. He and Lala occupy adjoining ground-floor apartments at the end of the building that angles closest to the *klong*, an arrangement that was originally for convenience—they were in and out of each other's rooms frequently in the beginning—but which over time has evolved into a way he can keep track of her. All the other apartments on that floor are dark and empty behind windows blocked with tinfoil. Same with the ones upstairs, except for the patient's room.

When they started the business, they kept the disposal simple. He just waited until three or four in the morning, sent her out to make sure no one was around, and carried the uncomprehending patient to the edge of the *klong*, tossed him in, and let the weights planted in the foot of the cast do their work. But as his back got worse, with increasingly sharp pains that were diagnosed as a degenerating disk or three, he bit the bullet and spent a month of miserable nights digging a tunnel that leads from the space beneath his kitchen sink to a spot a little more than halfway to the edge of the canal, running dead straight for about six meters and ending in a clump of very well-fertilized, well-fenced bushes. Dead center in the garden, surrounded by other bushes, is a flat trapdoor, actually a shallow box, set into the opening so that when the box is full of earth, it's the same level as the ground. A couple of stunted plants are fixed to it. He sprayed them green, and from a few feet away they look alive.

People might miss the tunnel's opening, behind the cabinet doors and a sliding wall panel, in a hurried search, but anyone with time will find it. Kang figures, though, it will give him and Lala time to get out before anyone goes through the place carefully. The passageway is just big enough around for him to crawl through it on hands and knees, pulling the patient behind him on the lightweight plastic creeper, originally designed to allow auto mechanics to slide beneath a car. Now it's the patient's last ride. Even with Kang's bad back, the tunnel gets him part of the way to the *klong*, the creeper carries the patient through it, and the dope mixture gives the patient just enough control of his legs so that after a couple of focusing slaps he can bear part of his own weight.

Lend a guy a hand.

Getting old is no fun, Kang thinks.

At the end of the hall, he opens the last door on the right, into his own space. The refrigerator hums away, singing its one-note song about beer. He pauses for a moment to listen past it. The patient's room is directly above him, but, of course, he, Kang, can't hear anything. Problem is, when they put the place together, they wanted the patient to believe he was in a hospital—at least at first—so they bought the machines and put them in the patient's room and got the uniforms and made a recording, to be played in the hall, of doctors being summoned to far-off emergencies.

So the illusion wouldn't be ruined by the noises Kang and Lala made downstairs, Kang pulled out the ceilings in his apartment and put in three layers of one-inch lightweight foam, followed by an inch of SonoLite, which is used to absorb sound in recording studios. So now, after all that work, they've abandoned the hospital pretense, and the only lasting result is that he can't hear anything above him. It irritates him almost daily, even though, with the patient handcuffed to the bed, the best he could possibly do is knock something off the table with his elbow.

The "hospital," as it turned out, was a waste of time and money, an unnecessary holdover from the Heart Clinic. The idea had been to keep the patient from panicking or getting violent, loading him up with dope to harvest signatures, leaving only muddled memories in the victim until it no longer mattered what he remembered. But it became obvious reasonably quickly that the sooner the patient realized it really wasn't a medical facility, the sooner he cooperated, the sooner he started trying to buy his way past Khun Death, grinning at him from the other end of the room, through the lipstick on Lala's mask.

Lala. She's stored up a lot of venom over the years. If this is the last patient, as it well might be, he'll have to be careful of Lala. She's been taking some of her cash after every bank and ATM run, but the rest of it has gone into a joint account to cover expenses. He's never talked to her about how much money the account holds, but knowing her, she's kept a running total of everything they've brought in on some calculator somewhere, with multiple backups, and he's going to need all his tact when he explains to her that her half of it is actually about thirty-two percent.

Or maybe he'll just kill her.

He removes the three hypos of the fospropofol mixture from his pocket and lays them side by side on a careful bed of paper towels, smooth enough to have been ironed, and then he opens the refrigerator. Lala will be back soon, and she's going to want to know that the patient has had his first two shots and is on the way to dreamland. The third can wait until fifteen or twenty minutes before the heavy lifting. Kang takes a long pull on the beer, puts it down, and picks up the first hypodermic. Then he figures the hell with it, life is short, and he settles in to enjoy the beer. It's exactly the right temperature. He'll give himself a few minutes before Lala gets back.

HE CAN'T DO it. It isn't possible. His fingers are cramping into permanent claws. And he's barely made it through five inches of the cast.

The open handcuffs dangle from the bed frame behind him. Beside the machines on the bedside service table is the bobby pin that must have been one of those that secured Lala's nurse's cap, the bobby pin he found today on his sheet, maybe six hours ago, although it's hard to tell when you're loaded and there's no good view of the sun. But there it was, an honest-to-Jesus bobby pin.

Paper clips are a little stiffer and might have been better, but so would a key, and the bobby pin is a gift from God. A long time ago, a swimming teammate of his, the only guy in the league who could get anywhere near him in butterfly, had taught him a party trick, guaranteed to impress any girl with a few drinks in her. Have her put a cheap set of cuffs on you, good and tight; it actually helps if the cuffs don't wobble too much. Take a paper clip or a bobby pin and straighten it out, then make a tiny oblique angle, say sixty degrees, at one end—he'd done this with his teeth—then make another one just above it in the opposite direction to create a sharp little zigzag, left and then right, that looks like a tiny step. Slip the angled tip into the keyhole, find the point of resistance, and move it. Then get the girl to let you put the cuffs on her so you can teach her the trick. After a while.

But it's been *years* since he did it, and he wasted most of a precious hour trying to figure out whether the movement should be clockwise or counterclockwise, trying and failing until he was brimming over with panic. Finally he'd done the deep breaths he'd always taken before a race, filling his lungs, holding it, and then blowing out, forcing oxygen into his bloodstream, and after eight or ten fumbling tries and much cramping of the fingers in his free hand, the one he'd been shoving back up under the cuffs at the head of the bed, whenever he heard them coming, muscle memory finally took over, and the lock popped.

Enos was the guy's name, the guy who had taught him, if you can imagine any parent naming his kid Enos, with the inevitable rhymes, but Enos was big enough and fast enough in the water that he was spared most of the nicknames and the limericks that occurred to absolutely everyone else Buddy met. Buddy had done the trick the first time he tried it, at a no-parents party, and it had given him the little push he needed to get past small talk and down to business with what-was-her-name, the bleached-blonde cheerleader with the big chin and the bigger chi-chis. What the hell had her name been? Why could he remember all the Enoses and Daves and Jasons and Justins and Joshuas and Jakes—the whole fucking J-crowd—and none of the girls' names?

So say it had been been noon today when he found the bobby pin in his bed, and he'd wasted an hour waiting, thinking they might bring him something to eat, but they hadn't bothered, and then it had taken him another hour to get the fucking bend right, and *then* he'd screwed it up so badly, trying to slide it in the wrong direction that he'd had to bend the other end of the hairpin, start all over again, sweat dripping off the tip of his nose as he tried to cajole the lock, convince the lock, *finesse* the lock, because if he breaks the pin off inside, he's dead.

Dead. He knows he will leave this place dead unless he somehow leaves it on his own. How he can do that, he has no idea in the world, except that whatever the steps will prove to be, they'll have to begin with these goddamn handcuffs. Thank God he was relatively clear when he found the bobby pin, that his metabolism had processed most of whatever they'd given him the previous evening, and at least he could focus. But the focus didn't last long—in fact, he was drifting a little as he worked, and he had to pull himself up sharp a couple of times and remember to *listen*. Listen for the click of the lock on the cuffs, listen for someone coming outside.

And then the lock popped open. He had both hands free. He'd pushed the cuffs side by side on the bed frame so he could get back into them quickly if need be, and then he'd sat up, feeling the muscles in his back, lazy after so long, pull as though they might seize up, so he put both feet on the floor and slowly bent forward, stretching those muscles before they could tighten into a spasm. Then, carefully as an old man, he stood up, wrapped his hand around the wheeled stand from which his IV hung, and slowly, *slowly*, dragging the heavy cast so it wouldn't make a noise when he put down the foot it covered, tugged the stand across the floor to the chair that his jeans and shirt had been on for however long he's been here. He picked up his jeans and walked, still sliding his feet on the floor so he wouldn't be heard downstairs, back to the bed. He got in, put the IV stand precisely where it had been before he moved it, folded his blankets over his knees so he could snatch them up quickly if he heard someone coming, and tested his theory. The theory that he'd been turning over for days, the theory he was sure would work if he could just get to his jeans, except that they'd been eight feet away and for all the good it did him, it might as well have been eight miles.

Carole, her name had been Carole; the cheerleader's name had been Carole. With an *e*. "Carole with an *e*," that was how she'd introduced herself to him, as though remembering that silent letter were important for some reason. Imagine thinking that anything that didn't threaten your life was important.

He'd been holding his breath without knowing it when he stretched one side of the zipper as tightly as he could, a good steel zipper in a prime pair of Levi's. So he exhaled slowly, put the zipper's serrated edge against the top of the cast, over the center of his left quadriceps muscle, and began to saw it up and down.

And was instantly rewarded by a fine sifting of white powder on his thigh.

His breath exploded out of him with a rush, as though he'd just done an entire length underwater, and he sat there, breathing deeply, until the spots before his eyes were gone, and then he went back to work. And here he is, God only knows how long afterward, with all of five inches cut into the plaster.

The plaster's not the problem—well, that's stupid, of *course* the plaster is a problem—but the real issue is the goddamn linen gauze beneath the plaster. The fibers snarl in the spaces between the zipper's teeth and have to be pulled out. And even five inches down, he's having trouble getting his bottom hand far enough under the cast to give his saw a little travel space. So he's going to have to do step two considerably earlier than he wanted to. He'd hoped to have sawed down another couple of inches; the deeper he's cut, the easier it will be for him to snap the plaster.

He has four fingers, palm up, wedged between the the cast and his thigh, six to eight inches from the place where he's cut it. Four deep breaths, close eyes, and *pull straight up.*

Oh, my God. He's holding a triangular piece of the cast in his hand. The skin on his thigh, newly bared, feels cold.

Now he has a second starting point, and for the first time he thinks it might work. He puts the zipper's edge to work again, instantly snarls it in linen, clears it while doing a lot of inventive silent cursing, and starts back to work. His left calf, the one in the cast, chooses that moment to cramp again, and he has to choke off a groan. He can't possibly lengthen the muscle to fight the cramp; he just has to let it have its way with him.

At that moment he hears heavy footsteps coming up the stairs at the end of the hall. It's the Other One.

Jeans under the covers, laid flat. The knee without a cast raised up to cover the bulge. Pull the bobby pin from the cuffs, put it in his mouth. Wrists in cuffs, cuffs closed. Shut both eyes.

Is the IV stand in the right place?

The door opens, and the giant comes in. He hits the overhead light, lets the door swing closed, and kicks the bed to rouse the patient.

Buddy opens his eyes, blinking against the light. The chair to his left, the one his jeans were on, suddenly looks enormous, conspicuous, and as empty as outer space.

The big man doesn't even glance at it. He extracts an orange syringe from his breast pocket, pulls off the little cap at its tip, and slips it into the intake for the IV bag. He follows it with a yellow one. Then he gives Buddy a long, pensive look, shakes his head once, as though in regret, and leaves the room.

Buddy waits to make sure the footsteps go all the way down the stairs, and then he fishes the bobby pin out of his mouth again. As soon as he has both cuffs off, he turns to yank the IV needle from his wrist, and he's already closed his fingers around it before he remembers that pulling it out sets off an alarm. He thinks for a moment about trying to crimp the line, but that requires one of his hands when he needs both, and he's not sure that wouldn't set off the alarm, too. In the end he decides the only thing he can do is to work as fast as he can. He clenches his teeth and begins to saw at the plaster, but six or eight minutes in he stops sawing and sits slumped over, feeling it coming, feeling it round a bend and come straight at him. The hand holding the jeans seems to dance away in front of him. Whatever he's been given, it's arrived. And it's a fucking *train*.

TEERAPAT, THE SCREEN on his phone says. Kang puts down the new beer, rejects the call, and sends Teerapat a text that says, WHAT?

He waits, tension twisting at his gut. Teerapat is a well-fed police lieutenant with fat, short fingers that are too thick for texting but slip easily into other people's pockets. After a moment Kang reads, NO POSTCARDS LATELY.

Greedy son of a bitch. STILL WORKING THE PATIENT, Kang writes.

GET SOMETHING NOW, Teerapat writes. THEN RID OF HIM. NOT A GOOD TIME.

Suddenly Kang is sitting bolt upright. He puts the beer down and reads the message again. He keys in, CALL ME, and waits. In a minute the phone rings.

"Why?" he demands before Teerapat can say hello.

"An inquiry. From Phaya Thai station. Hand-carried by a police-woman."

"What does she want?"

"Well, at first I thought maybe you'd cured the current patient and he'd been fished out. Got my blood pressure right up there, since you hadn't sent me any—"

"What does she *want?*"

A pause to let Kang know that Teerapat has registered his tone and dislikes it. "Personal effects. Everything they had."

"On how many—"

"As many as she could get. We gave her two."

Kang sits back, thinking, and then he registers what Teerapat has said. "*What?* Why did you—"

"I wasn't here when she came," Teerapat says. He sounds testy, although he always does. "But she had enough rank, she had ID, she had an official request for the material."

Kang rubs the skin on his forearm, which suddenly feels cold enough to be wet. "Interesting."

"It gets worse. She asked what we knew about the bodies from other stations' jurisdictions. A bunch of ones I knew about." He pauses. "And a couple I didn't."

"It's a mistake," Kang says. "There aren't any you don't know—"

"Because, you know," Teerapat says over him, "I'd hate that."

Kang gets up and takes slow and deliberate paces into the living room. "There haven't been."

"Wonder what she meant, then."

Kang says, "I have no idea."

"What about the one you've got now?"

"We've only taken a little so far. He's not as rich as some of them." Kang clears his throat. He doesn't usually talk this much.

"I believe you, of course," Teerapat says. "But if you're wrong about how wealthy he is, or if you've miscounted the take, let me know and send something along. And in the meantime you might want to empty that room and keep it empty until we learn who's so interested."

"How are you going to learn that?" He's looking around at his wretched little apartment. He's always disliked it, but it's offered him a kind of life: stability, money, a woman, no one staring at him all the time.

"I've got someone on the woman cop," Teerapat says. "She met a *farang* in the Exchange Tower around noon, and a few hours later she went to a big house, a new one, in Thonglor. She spent a couple of hours there." He pauses.

Kang says, "Yes?"

"Your guy with the small bank balance wouldn't be from there, would he? Some nice new houses there. Lots of money."

Kang says, "Goodbye."

"House she went to is owned by a guy named Dell. Sound familiar?"

"Like I said, good—"

"Just trying to help. If the current guy, the one I saw when I dropped in about eight days ago, is named Dell, two things: First, take whatever else you can get, right now, and get the hell out of there, and second, send me my share. I'd hate to have to get involved in the investigation."

"Like I said," Kang says, and disconnects.

A little rill of rage, like a fast-moving ripple on a lake, runs through him. Fucking fat-ass cops, thick, greasy thumbs in everything, collecting money they do nothing for, ready to bust you and then help you commit suicide in the cell if you've got any evidence that might give them an uncomfortable moment or two. *Dropped in,* the son of a bitch, always checking to make sure he's not getting cut out, nothing is being sneaked past him. Then Kang stops in the middle of the room, thinking, *I should give the guy upstairs the last shot of fospropofol.* He stands, irresolute. As angry as he is, a quarter of one will help him relax, think more clearly. He hardly ever uses it himself, no more than once a week, but this is an unusual occasion. He takes the remaining syringe out of his pocket.

25

No Accounting for Taste

AFTER ALL THIS time in Bangkok, Rafferty was certain that
he was past being deeply shocked, but some of the things Auntie
Aspirin said to him made it literally impossible for him to maintain eye contact with her. And yet, as awful as much of it was, he
finds himself experiencing a small—a *very* small—pang of pity for
Buddy Dell. No one, he thinks, could actually want to live that
way. And he realizes that some of the concern he feels is for
Edward.

He settles back in the—what? fourth? fifth?—cab of the day.
His head aches, and he suddenly realizes he's hungry. Except for
whatever he nibbled at Edward's house, he hasn't eaten since he
was at Chu's with Clemente. Well, he's on his way to the Landmark at last, to take care of things there. He can grab something
to go in the ground-floor restaurant before . . .

Before what? He's had no response from Rose, and his reaction
to the silence has slowly begun to eclipse everything else he's said
he'll do. He dials Miaow, and the moment she picks up, he says,
"Everything okay?"

"You mean since we saw each other, has there been a tragedy
that I haven't called to tell you about? No."

"You got home all right?"

There's no response, but it's the kind of no response that *is* a
response, and he has to remind himself that she survived alone on

the streets of this city for years, beginning when she was probably three. She'd gotten home all right even when there wasn't a home to get to, and she's being *patient* with him. "Are you sure," he says, "that you don't have a phone number for Fon?"

For a moment he thinks she's going to let him go unanswered again, and he feels a little blink of irritation, but then she says, "Can I go through Mom's drawers?"

"You can pull them out and turn them upside down as far as I'm concerned."

"That's not good enough," she says. "I need you to give me permission and promise to take the blame if she gets pissed off."

"I do and I will." Her apprehension about Rose's being angry reassures him. She's not as worried as he is.

"I'll call you back."

He forces himself to sit back yet again, thinking, *How do I keep getting into this position without even being aware of it, as though I'm about to climb into the front seat and grab the wheel?* Out loud he says, "Yikes." The driver, probably not knowing the word, looks at him in the mirror, eyebrows raised in inquiry. "Sorry," Rafferty says. "Nothing."

At a loss for something to do, he flips through the printout of *Pygmalion's* first act, now dry again but rippled from exposure to the day's humidity. The backs of several of the pages are scrawled with his notes. He finds what he's looking for, a phone number copied from a business card in an eye-splitting pink that Auntie Aspirin had appropriated from Buddy Dell's wallet. It features a bright pink clock face with something like twenty hands, pointing everywhere. Beneath that, in a fancy, flowing script, are the English words *"Good Times,"* and below that, *"Any time is a good time to call!"* He dials the number.

And gets a truncated electronic burr representing a ring and then a burst of the kind of bright, tinny music he associates with cheap Japanese anime, yielding to a woman's voice—almost as bright as the music—telling him that she's away from the phone at the moment, but if he'll leave a message, she'll get right back to him, and she *knows* he'll be happy he called. She's speaking American English, pretty well, so either she had a script and a good ear or she's spent a lot of time with Americans. He doesn't want them to hear a hang-up, get curious about it, and possibly call him back, so he says, "Hi, my name is Richard Milton, and I'm at the Landmark. I didn't memorize the room number, but they'll ring you through. Just call when you get a chance." He hangs up.

And once again finds himself sitting forward, one hand on top of the driver's seat.

He slides back across the upholstery and imagines Velcro on his shirt, keeping him in place where he belongs, thinking that he might have just heard Lala's voice. What would she look like? Tall, short, in between, glamorous, cute, nymphetlike, ripe, motherly, young, old, slight, willowy, voluptuous, built like a linebacker? Would the stuff of Buddy Dell's fantasy world be memorable, or would she be someone he, Poke, wouldn't notice if he passed her on the street?

She could, of course, be any of those things, plus dozens of others he hasn't thought of; he's learned that the spectrum of what men want in a temporary companion, paid or not, is much, *much* broader than he'd once assumed, in terms of both the kinds of experience the customer wants and the ideal appearance of the person who, in his fantasy, will provide that experience. Decades ago, when Poke was in his early teens, his normally volatile half-Filipina mother, Angela, had suspected her husband of cheating on her (again) and had limited her protest, at least while Poke was in earshot, to the expression, repeated quite often and about a vast array of things, *There's no accounting for taste.* It was, in its way, more intimidating than a screaming match and infinitely more flexible. She used it to describe everything: choosing a car, picking a TV show, changing a hairdo, wearing a certain shirt, selecting from a restaurant menu. Inoffensive topics, all of them. But Poke, sitting in the backseat, saw his father's ears go red; saw, in the living room, the muscles bunch in his father's jaw; and finally, one night in bed, heard all hell break loose. Years later, after his father had deserted them, he learned who had been the object of his mother's suspicion, and he'd been flabbergasted: She was, to his eyes, so ordinary as to be invisible. His mother was once a great beauty.

Rose had once said to him, "There's *nothing* that some man, somewhere, won't pay for."

Where the hell is Rose?

He's seen dozens of variations on this theme of unexpected preferences among his acquaintances in Bangkok. Few things, he's come to realize, are less predictable and more inexplicable than someone's sexual tastes, especially when that someone has had the time, the license, and the means to indulge them for a while. Rafferty had thought there wasn't much he hadn't heard about, but Auntie Aspirin, in her soft, cotton-candy voice, had shone a light on new and deeply unappealing continents of bad conduct.

He texts the Good Times phone number to Arthit with a few words to explain its provenance and to request an address, if one exists in this age of mobile communication. He's just pressed SEND when the phone rings: Miaow.

"Found it," she says. "At least I think I did. It says 'Fon' anyway."

"In what?"

"Her phone book, where did you think?"

"I didn't even know she had one."

"It's really a calendar book. She puts phone numbers in the back."

"Right. I think I remember—" He finds he's once again surged up against the back of the front seat, so he slides to the rear, thinking, *It's not productive to be this keyed up.*

"You might not have paid attention to this," Miaow says, as though he weren't talking, "but she doesn't have a lot of friends these days."

It hits him like a splash of cold water. "She doesn't?"

"As I was looking through the book? I saw all these names, people she never mentions anymore. It surprised me. It made me kind of sad. So I guess *I* wasn't paying attention either. And, you know, she went to *meet* Fon and maybe one or two other girls from the bar days, and it seems like that's all she's got left."

"Got it," he says. "Oh, *boy*."

"I felt the same way," Miaow says, "but then I thought about it, and you know? If it's true, she chose it—I mean, she chose *us*—it's not like you built a wall around her or kept her on a leash or anything."

"Still makes me sad."

His daughter says nothing. The silence stretches just a little too long.

"She'll be okay," he says, pumping it full of assurance.

"I know. She's strong."

"She is." This time he can't think of anything reassuring, so he says, "Well, thanks. Talk to you later," and rings off. The moment he does it, he thinks, *I didn't get the*—and the phone rings.

"You didn't get the number," Miaow says. She starts to laugh but then doesn't. "Are you ready?"

"I was just testing you," he says, fumbling with his pen. A moment later he says, "Go," and she reads the number.

Then he and Miaow share another discouraging moment of silence until she says, "Bye."

Fon's phone just rings. No pickup, no voice mail. He dials it again and gets the same nothing, so he calls Rose, for perhaps the twentieth time since he left the apartment that morning. When her voice mail kicks in, he just says, "Me. Getting worried," and hangs up.

He's practically in the front seat again.

Suddenly he can't stand the idea of going to the Landmark, dealing with minutiae. Eating something when he's actually not all that hungry; he's got a little layer of fat around his middle, he can live on that. He calls Miaow again.

"What?" she says. "Did you hear anything?"

"No. No answer. Listen, go get your mom's calendar book." The cab eases to a stop, and Rafferty looks up to see they've pulled up to the Landmark, so he says to the driver, "Keep going."

The driver says, "Where?"

"I don't care. Around the block, just go." The driver pulls away from the curb, and Miaow says, "Got it."

"Okay. Read it. The names, I mean."

"Out loud?"

"If I wanted you to read it silently, I wouldn't be tying up my phone."

"Okay, *okay*," she says, and she begins to read, flatly, just getting through them. Rose has apparently written many of the names at full length, including some interminable last names, and to Rafferty's ears it's a speeding freight train of virtually meaningless syllables.

"It's just a *list*," he says. "You could be reciting the alphabet. Even a name I know might slide past me." It gives him an idea. "Make it *interesting*, give me some variety."

"Like how?"

"Like . . ." He thinks about it for a moment. "Okay, you read those lines in *Pygmalion* last night, right?"

"Yeah." She sounds cautious, like he might be setting a trap.

"Well, when you do the accent in the play, because you're going to get the part, what you're probably going to do is make the accent thick at the beginning to startle the audience and to demonstrate how wide the gulf is between the way Eliza talks and the way Henry Higgins does, and then you're going to thin it out some so the audience doesn't have to work so hard. Following me?"

"Don't ask me if I'm following you when you haven't said anything hard to understand. But yeah, that's what I'd do."

"When it's thick, the accent, I mean, you're going to have to visualize what you're saying. Have you got the script there?"

"Sure. That's what I'm *doing*, looking at—"

"Read it."

"It doesn't *mean* anything."

"It does. Read it. Start with her third line."

"Sure, he says *read* it. Hold on a second. Okay, here goes: 'Ow, eez ye-ooa san, is e? Wal, fewd dan y' de-ooty bawmz a mather should, eed now bettern to spawl a pore gel's flahrzn than ran awy athaht pyin.'" She's sounded out every syllable with exactly the same emphasis as the ones that preceded and followed it.

"That's what your mom's phone book sounded like to me when you read it. Now, look, here's what's happened. Eliza, she's selling flowers on the street because she's so poor, but they're *rich* and they speak with . . . umm, rich accents, and the son, Freddy—"

"That's the part Edward wants."

"Freddy has just stepped all over her flowers—sorry, *your* flowers, without saying he's sorry, without even looking down at you, and he's run off to get a cab. How do you think Eliza feels?"

"I know *exactly* how she feels," Miaow says. "I had rich people practically poop on me all the time."

"Well, what Eliza is *saying* is, 'Oh, he's your *son*, is he? Well, if you'd done your duty by him as a mother should, he'd know better than to spoil a poor girl's flowers, then run away without paying."

He listens to nothing for a long moment, and then Miaow says, "*Oh.*"

"So when you've got the accent and you're doing it, you'll see all of that in your mind as you say it, and it'll be twice as clear to the audience what you mean."

She reads the lines again. It's not cockney, but it's more intelligible.

"We'll work on the accent later. For now read me the names in your mother's address book, more slowly, and try to visualize the ones you know, or make up a picture for the ones you don't. Think of it as an exercise."

"Okay, here goes." She sounds a little stilted at first, but then she puts it together, and he can hear the names begin to represent individuals, and he knows some of them. He writes one down and tells her to stop and give him the number.

"That's Peachy," Miaow says. "They haven't seen each other in months. Not since she told Peachy she was pregnant."

"They were close, they were business partners, maybe they've talked. What's the number?"

As she reads on, he can see some of the people who go with the names; he's known some of them almost as long as he's known Rose, although he's seen them infrequently: Lek, Ning, Noi, Coke, Jah, Kai, Champagne, Marilyn, Nit, and half a dozen others, the friends she made dancing in the bars. Mrs. Pongsiri, the older woman who lives down the hall. Anna, Arthit's current companion, plus eight or ten more.

"That's it?" he says.

"And she doesn't even talk about these lately," Miaow says.

"Okay," he says. "I'll call around."

"She's with *Fon*," Miaow says, as though it ends the discussion.

"Can you think of anything *else* I can do?" He looks up to find that they're stopped in traffic and that half a block or so in front of them, on their left, are the neon-lit hordes of Nana Plaza, so either traffic has been terrible and they've barely moved at all or they've already gone around the block once and are into their second circuit. "But Fon's not the only one," he says. "Maybe there was a group of them, maybe they're still together and one of them—Lek or Noi or someone—has her phone with her, who the hell knows? What time is it?"

"Look at your watch."

"I'm in the back of a cab, and it's dark, and don't tell me to look at my phone because I'm talking to you on it."

"Wow," she says. "Nine-forty *already*."

He gets a beep on his phone and looks at the screen. It says BLOCKED.

"I gotta go," he says, punching the buttons.

A man's voice, a tight, nervous voice that snips off the syllables as though he's saving part of them for future use, says, "Mr. Rafferty?"

"Yes. Who's this?"

"You asked someone to have me call you," the man says. "My name is Larry Finch."

26

Stooo-art

L A R R Y F I N C H I S still talking, but a horn is blaring behind Rafferty's cab, probably someone too eager to get into a Nana bar to wait and too lazy to walk. Rafferty says, "Hang on a second, Mr. Finch. Don't go away." To the driver he says, "Please turn into the Nana parking lot."

"You want go Nana Hotel?"

"Not really," Rafferty says, "but what the hell." He pulls out a hundred-baht note; the meter says sixty-three, so he hands it over the back of the seat and says, "Thanks," and gets out of the car. Into the phone he says, "You still there, Mr. Finch?"

"I am."

"Can I have your number, in case I lose you?"

"No."

"But if we get cut off—"

"If we get cut off, it'll be because I hang up. I don't know much about cell phones, sonny, but I know some people can figure out where you are when you're on one."

"That's fine," Rafferty say. "Just give me a minute, because I need to get someplace where I can hear you."

As Rafferty goes into the lobby, one of the Nana's ancient bellmen snaps awake long enough to stand up, looking around for Rafferty's luggage. Rafferty waves him off and hoists a thumb to the left, the direction of the coffee shop, and the bellman sighs and sits down again. It's a big, cavernous, run-down lobby, just shading into dinginess. In a cluster of armchairs at the far end sit a bunch of men, possibly the same gaggle of old guys who were there last time Poke was in the hotel, maybe two years ago. He knows that some of these men have arranged to live here until they die.

In the empty coffee shop, he heads for a seat at the window that serves as a wall, unnoticed by the waitresses, who are lolling around the cash register and telling jokes. On the other side of the plate glass, the parking-lot girls are already out in force, flagging down the lonely, the miserly, and the impossible to satisfy as they head back, solo, from the bars to their rooms. Three more of the hotel old-timers cluster at their usual outdoor table, their backs to the automatic sliding door so they can watch the unchanging show. As Rafferty sits down, the man nearest the door, who is in a wheelchair, backs it up a few inches and activates the door, which obediently slides open for no one, admitting an unwelcome puff of hot air.

"Okay, this is better," Rafferty says. "And you're right, I don't need to know where you are."

There's a pause on the other end of the line. "What *do* you need?"

"Well, Campeau said—"

"You mean Bob?"

"*Yes*, Bob. He said you'd had some trouble here and then disappeared."

"And I'm going to stay disappeared," Finch says. "Why does this matter to you?"

"Didn't Bob—"

"I'm asking you."

"A man has been missing for nearly two weeks now. He's got a lot in common with a bunch of other men who also disappeared and then turned up dead."

"He's a punter," Finch says bluntly. He doesn't make it sound like a compliment.

"And he's got a teenage son who's a friend of my daughter's, and—"

"Part-Thai daughter? Got a Thai mother?"

The automatic door slides closed again. Instantly, on the other side of the window, the man in the wheelchair rolls back, just enough to reopen the door. Rafferty can't see any reason to begin a conversation about Miaow's being adopted, so he says, "Yes."

"You've got what I wanted, you son of a bitch," Larry Finch says. "When I first got there, I wanted to get married and have kids, fifty-fifty kids. They're so beautiful. How old is your daughter?"

"Fourteen," Rafferty says, although no one knows for sure.

"Smart?"

"Smarter than I am."

"And the boy? The son of the guy who's disappeared? Is he a half-and-half?"

"No, he's American. His father came here to live, and his American wife sort of sent the kid to him by express mail. So if his father doesn't come back—"

"He won't," Finch says. "Not unless he was born with a four-leaf clover up his butt."

"Well, that's why I'm bothering you. We're going to try to lend him a hand. I'm hoping you can give us something that'll help us find him."

"Who's 'us'?"

"I'm working with a couple of cops."

"Uh-uh," Finch says. "Goodbye." He disconnects.

Rafferty sits there, staring at his phone. Automatically tries to return the call but gets BLOCKED again. He shakes the phone, as if that'll do any good, and then drops it onto the table as a wave of weariness sweeps over him, a tangled knot of exhaustion: worry about Rose, worry about what will happen to Edward, frustration at the idiocy of his raising Edward's hopes by thinking he could help when time is so clearly running out. He closes his eyes and rests his face in his hands, and after a long moment of something close to despair, intense enough to feel as though it might be permanent, a jolt of anger snaps him upright and he grabs the phone.

When Toots says, "Leon and Toot's Bar," he says, "It's Poke. I need to talk to Campeau."

"In toilet."

"When he comes out, give him the phone."

As he waits, the sliding door opens again. The fidgety guy in the wheelchair has been joined by a couple more male friends wearing the many-pocketed photographer's vests, mail-order linen shirts, and cargo shorts that make up the informal uniform of longtime expats, an outfit that always suggests to him that they're anticipating the return of the tropical swamp that's pressed beneath the weight of Bangkok. Standing in front of the table, facing in through the glass and obviously just killing time, are two of the more mature parking-lot "girls," women carrying too many pounds and too many years for the clothes they're wearing but whose faces are lively and kind and even sympathetic. *How can they look like that*, he thinks, *after all they've been through?*

Campeau says, "So?"

"So your friend Larry Finch just hung up on me."

"Yeah, well, he wasn't sure he wanted to talk to you anyway. How'd you piss him off?"

"Where is he?"

"Nope," Campeau says. "And I'm not nuts about your tone."

"You met Edward. Did he seem like a nice kid to you?"

"As kids go."

"Well, if his father lives through tonight, *Bob*, he'll have outlasted everyone else these people abducted. He's going to die very soon, if he hasn't already."

"He shouldn'ta wore white shoes. So how'd you piss Larry off?"

"I mentioned that I was working with some cops."

"That'd do it," Campeau says. "He said cops were in and out while those assholes were holding him."

It feels to Rafferty like his heart has stopped. He sees Clemente, out there on her own, after going to three police stations solely to shove sticks into the beehive.

"Nice of you to tell me."

"We haven't had much time to chat," Campeau says. "You don't come around so much these days."

"Give me Larry Finch's phone number."

"No can do." Rafferty can hear the satisfaction in Campeau's tone. He's never really forgiven Poke for marrying Rose, "taking her off the market," as he once put it. Rafferty has always attributed the man's anger to his obvious unhappiness—he's someone whom life has let down so hard he got dented—but Rafferty is too pissed off to think about that.

"Listen to me. You can either give me the number or you can tell Finch that the cops I'm working with are on the right side, but they've got the same skills as the other ones, and for not too much money under the table they'll locate him, and when they do, I'll turn his address over to Lala. Make sure you mention Lala. And I'll *do* that if he doesn't call me back."

"Third option," Campeau says. "I tell you to go fuck yourself and then I have another drink."

"If you like Larry Finch *at all*, you'll do what I just said. How long—cops in Southeast Asian countries being as infinitely corruptible as they are—how long do you think it would take them to locate him in, what? Phnom Penh? Siem Reap? Maybe a couple of hours and a few hundred bucks? Just tell him. Help him out. Be a pal, for once in your goddamn miserable life. If he doesn't want to help me, he can hang up again."

He disconnects, thinking, *That might not have been the right tone,* but he's so furious his throat feels like it's closing up, and he knows he can't control what he says when he's that angry. Either Campeau will call Finch or he won't. There's nothing more he, Rafferty, can do about it now.

He watches the group on the other side of the window for a moment. The two older parking-lot women have been joined by a third, somewhat younger, with a long, clearly defined pirate's scar down her right cheek. She's wearing a thick mask of foundation makeup to conceal the scar, a sharp, embossed slash from cheekbone to jawline, as though someone had tried to cut her head in half. It's a dull red, and despite the makeup just enough of the color has leaked through to go a slightly livid purple in the yellowish light of the parking lot. Did some customer give her that?

The thought of a knife reminds him of Lutanh, and that in turn reminds him of Clemente, and as much as he doesn't want to tie up his phone, he calls her.

"Just thinking about you," she says.

"It was mutual. I just learned that Larry Finch, the guy who got away, said that there were cops in and out of the place where he was held."

"Not an enormous surprise. In fact—"

"So I was thinking about you, showing up at all those stations and—"

"In *fact,*" Clemente says over him, "I think I might have someone behind me."

"Well, shit."

"I've called Anand. I'm doing a kind of loop now, and there might or might not be a car with tinted windows back there. I'm going to keep looping until Anand calls to say he's in the neighborhood and heavily armed, and I can pick him up."

"Anand is a good guy." Anand is the cop Clemente was dating last time Rafferty saw him, but this isn't the time to ask whether they're still valentines. "So why were you thinking of me?"

"Your little *katoey*. The guy who hurt her needs to be talked to. Kind of forcefully. And unofficially."

"I can't argue with that."

"She gave me the name of the hotel and his room number. Since there's nothing I can do right now except try to dodge whoever's behind me, I called a couple of times, but he's not in."

"And this concerns me because . . . ?"

"Because your daughter, who's obviously nicer than you are even if she bends the truth once in a while—"

"She's had a mixed history with cops."

"Everyone has. But the point is, she helped the *katoey*, and she's your daughter, and if I talk to the jerk, I thought maybe you'd like to be part of the conversation."

"Sure, if there's nothing I can accomplish about Edward's father."

"I think the *katoey* should be there, too."

"Lutanh, her name is Lutanh. Let's see what happens in the next hour or two." He finds himself thinking it might actually be a good idea to get Lutanh out of Edward's house. They're both young, they're both beautiful, Lutanh has an obvious case on Edward, and as Poke was just reminding himself—in another context—there's no telling what people will do. He'd been unenthusiastic when Miaow announced the plan; now he thinks it's a potentially terrible idea.

"Okay." Clemente pauses. "There's definitely someone back there." She sounds pretty calm about it. "What it looks like is a police SUV."

"Do you want me to call Anand? Or Arthit?"

"No, Anand's on his way, and don't bother the colonel. Well, I'd better pay attention to this." She hangs up.

Rafferty says, "Be careful," into a dead phone.

The woman with the scarred face has just poached a cigarette from the guy in the wheelchair, who lights it for her and then celebrates his generosity by wheeling back far enough to open the door again. A waitress, who's apparently had more than enough of the sliding door, trots past Rafferty's table, saying, "Moment," as she passes. Within ten seconds she's reseated the table so the guy in the wheelchair is on the left and the one nearest the door is on a stationary stool. She takes a step back, inadvertently opening the door again, and stands there, arms crossed in a no-nonsense elementary-school-teacher pose, making sure they're not going to play musical chairs the moment her back is turned. Then she comes in again and smiles at Poke, who orders a pot of coffee, a Diet Coke, and a dish of crisp basil, pork, and chili—*phet maak maak*—very hot. He looks accusingly at his phone, willing it to ring, and then gets up, doing a little *I go out, I come back* pantomime to the cashier, who had looked over when she heard his chair legs squeak on the floor.

He'd almost forgotten how sweltering the evening is until the atmosphere in the parking lot, an oven-force mix of gasoline fumes, body odor, and makeup, punches him in the face. The guy in the wheelchair glares up at him, but he glares at everybody.

"Buy you all a drink?" Rafferty says.

"Let's see," one of the other guys says. He takes a little notebook out of one of the pockets in his photographer's vest, opens it to a blank page, and says, "Whaddaya know? Today is open. *Bier Sing.*"

"Hold on," Rafferty says, gesturing for the waitress. "This is important. You don't want to trust my memory."

"You buying for the ladies, too?" asks the man in the wheelchair. It's a challenge. He sounds like he hopes he's picking a fight.

"Sure," Rafferty says, and the woman with the scar says, "I have friend."

"She have many many friend," one of the other women says. "They all thirsty."

"Just you three," he says. "When there are too many beautiful women around, I get dizzy."

"Sweet mouth," says the one with the scar.

"Have a seat," says Mr. Notebook.

"That's okay, I'll stand," Rafferty says. "I'm just bribing you. I'm looking for a few friends."

"Who isn't?" says the man in the wheelchair.

"These are specific guys. Any of you know Buddy Dell?

There's a pause, and then Mr. Notebook says, "White shoes?"

"Exactly."

"Sure, I know him. To say hello to anyway. He's a friend of yours, you said?"

"Not a close friend."

"Good, because he's kind of a dickhead. Sorry, ladies."

The woman with the scar makes big eyes and clamps her hands over her ears, and one of the other women laughs politely.

"So why you looking for him?" It's the guy in the wheelchair.

"He's missing," Rafferty says. "His son is a friend of my daughter's, and the kid is worried."

"Good Samaritan," says the guy in the wheelchair, not making it sound like praise.

"What about a guy named Stuart Dependahl?"

There's a brief silence, and then the announcer in the open-air Hooters that stands between the Nana Hotel and Soi 4 shouts into a microphone, "Say *'yee-haaaa!'*" No one says *"yee-haaaa!"*

"Fucking asshole," says the man in the wheelchair. "Not your friend, that clown in there. People get up on that windup bull, he tells everyone to say 'yee-haaaa,' and no one ever does."

"I knew Stuart," says one of the men in a vest. "Sad thing."

"Yeah," Rafferty says.

One of the women, the oldest of the three, says, "You say Stooo-art?"

"Yes."

"Take many, many lady," the woman says.

"I wouldn't be surprised," Rafferty says.

"Same time," the woman says. "Many lady same time. Bed too small, him sleep on floor."

The other unscarred woman is nodding. "Big bed," she says. She laughs. "Room cold, air-con too much. Five lady warm in bed, him cold on floor."

"Stooo-art," the one who first mentioned him says fondly. "Good heart."

"They ever catch the guys who . . ." asks the guy with the notebook, letting the question peter out.

"No, they didn't. What about—" Poke has to close his eyes to concentrate, and there it is: the name of the man whose family had squinted into the sun in that snapshot taken on the dock. "Hayden Williams."

General headshaking, although the woman with the scar shoots him a brief, troubled look.

"Okay," he says, giving up for the moment. "Thanks."

"Thanks for the drink," Mr. Notebook says.

"Let me ask one more," Rafferty says, turning back. "A woman this time. Name is Lala."

The response is total silence, but the scarred woman is looking at her feet. He says to her, "Do you—" but his phone rings, and once again it says BLOCKED.

"Lala," he says to all of them. "Hold that thought."

To Larry Finch he says, as he goes back inside, "Let me tell you why you don't have to worry about me."

27

The Tug That Tells Her You're Stuck

"SON OF A bitch was bigger than Idaho," Larry Finch is saying. The phone is on speaker, and Rafferty has the wrinkled copy of *Pygmalion* blank side up on the table, a pen in his right hand and a spoon in his left. In front of him, a glass of Diet Coke gets warm as the ice melts and a cup of coffee gets cold.

"What was his name?"

"No idea. I just thought of him as the monster. Biggest Thai I ever saw. There weren't any introductions. Mostly it was me alone in that bed while they played the same fucking tape over and over again in the hall."

"Tape of what?"

"Hospital shit. 'Dr. Jones to surgery,' that kind of shit. 'Calling Dr. Kildare.' And every now and then, they'd inject some kind of whoopee juice into my IV and I'd go somewhere in my head. Later, after I got away, I learned how many checks I'd written on my accounts here—I mean *there*, in Bangkok—and they'd maxed my cards."

"How much did they get?"

"Forty-five, fifty thousand US."

"How long did they have you?"

"Near as I can figure, six days. Might have been seven. It was hard to keep track."

Rafferty stirs the cooling food around, trying to crowd a bunch of the little red chilies onto his spoon. "So to back up for a minute, you phoned Good Times. Why?"

"Whaddaya think? You been through it, too, probably. You been here awhile, you've done everything you can think of and a bunch of shit that never even occurred to you before you got here, and one night you remember this website, and it's right there on the fucking front page, with the biggest link leading to the Bangkok area of the site. 'Good Times,' all in pink, and it's got like five hundred customer reviews, and they're almost all five stars. And they say things like, 'Think you've done everything? Think again,' shit like that."

"Lot of reviews," Rafferty says, just to keep him talking.

"They gamed it, I figure. Don't know how I could have been such a sucker, but that's what happens when you think with ol' Johnnie instead of your head. They just jammed these fake reviews into the Bangkok part of the site, supposed to be like Amazon for sex. So you call, and it's Lala, and you meet her, and . . . and it's not like she's the most beautiful girl in the world, right? But she knows how to use the old can opener, and while you're still working on your first drink, you're telling her things you've never told anyone, talking about things you want to do, and she's looking at you like you're wonderful, like all this pathetic crap you're talking makes you a man of imagination and daring. And all the while, of course, she's sitting dead center in her web waiting for the tug that tells her you're stuck."

"Did she ever send you a picture?"

"Sure, first time I called her, but don't get all Sherlock about it, because they took my phone."

Rafferty is thinking, *Take another look at those laptops*, but what he says is, "How did it work?" He signals a waitress, points at his Diet Coke glass, which is mostly ice water. The chilies are hotter than usual. Like a complete neophyte, he'd asked for *hot*, and he's willing to bet there are people laughing in the kitchen right now.

"Basic honey trap," Finch says. "We met in a bar at Nana, and she made me feel like George Clooney. She was good at it, listened so close it was almost awkward, but she remembered everything. Second time I saw her, she was asking me questions about things I said the first time. Remembered where I grew up, my kid sister's name. Kind of flattering to a guy nobody's ever listened to. So I took her out a couple times, and she made me feel interesting, and she banged me brainless, but she did it really nice, like what they used to call a 'girlfriend experience,' remember those? Jeeeezus, how pathetic is that? You, too, can come to Asia and pay for a girlfriend experience. Not that they were usually free in the West, were they? Free sex is always the most expensive, right?"

"So I've heard," Rafferty says. "A couple hundred times." A whoop of laughter goes up from the waitresses dawdling around the cash register.

"Somebody there?" Finch says.

"I'm in the Nana—"

"Lucky you."

"And the cashier is apparently hilarious."

"Anything except wait on people. So . . . Lala. She did me right, got past all the defenses and the 'She's a pro' fence we always put up, and then, when I felt like we . . . you know, *knew* each other, she said she could take me someplace special, someplace where there were beautiful girls who would do *anything*. She said it in English, and she made the word last like fifteen minutes, the same way my older brother, who has what you might call *food issues*, says 'fried chicken.'"

"How old is she?"

"Who can tell with Asians? She only *looked* twenty-two,

twenty-three, far as I was concerned, didn't look like she'd been ridden around the block a few hundred times the way some of them do—even some of the young ones, know what I mean?"

Rafferty is liking Larry Finch less with each passing moment, but he parks his judgment, stores his incredibly spicy food in his cheek, and says, "Sure."

"I put up a little resistance, told her she was enough for me, I didn't need anybody else, all that shit. Gave her some money, like a present. Fact was, I was kind of frightened. About what would be offered."

Rafferty says, "About whether you'd do it."

"What's that supposed to be? *Insight?*"

"Sorry. Just trying to put things together." He looks around for the waitress, for *any* waitress, to refill his glass. "So you go with her to this . . . this building, and when you get there, somebody—"

"Had to be the monster. Minute we go through the door. *Bam.* Like the ceiling fell on me."

"And then you come to in the hospital bed, they've put the cast on you—"

"Part of it," Finch says. "They started with one leg, built it about as high as a gym sock, know what I mean? Couldn't move my ankle. They did that, the first part, after I was conscious again, so I'd know what they had in mind for me. Getting my attention, right? I'm flat on my back in the bed with the monster sitting on my knee, practically broke the fucking thing, while she did the work. Then she told me if I was good, they'd take it off, and if I was bad, they'd build it all the way up and do the other leg, too."

"What does 'be good' mean?" His empty glass disappears and is replaced by a new one, but he's too engaged making notes even to look up.

A pause. "Sign the checks, I suppose."

He stops writing, takes a gulp of cold Diet Coke, follows it with some tepid coffee, and thinks for a second. "But you were loaded when you signed—"

"Yeah, yeah, yeah. All I can figure is that someone, someone before me, fought the dope. Or maybe . . . who knows? Maybe I was the first one they used the dope on. What do I know? And the dope, I can't be sure about this, but I don't think the dope was like the hypnosis in some bullshit 1950s movie, you know, took away your will, made you a slave. *'You vill do vot I vant.'* Not like that. It sure as shit fucked with your memory, though."

"Then how do you know—"

"Can I get a minute to breathe once in a while? About a month after I got out, I started having dreams about it. Nightmares. I'm in the bed, it's dark in the room except for a little circle of light, and *he's* standing behind me. I can hear him breathing—asshole breathed like a swimming-pool vacuum—and I don't want to sign the check, and she says—Lala does—she says, 'Hit him,' and the monster hits me."

"The pain," Rafferty said. "Pain is a memory marker."

"I heard something like that." There's a pause, and then Finch says, "Once, after they put the stuff in my IV but before I went all the way under, I heard the door to the room open, and when I looked over, I saw a couple of cops, those fucking brown uniforms. The monster brought them in to *look* at me, like I was a snake in a cage or something. They might have been there more than once. I'm a little foggy about it."

"Would you recognize them?"

"No. What I saw was uniforms. Just cops."

Rafferty takes a moment to catch up on his notes and come up with the next question. Outside, the old expats are still at the table, but the cast of women has changed. There are five of them working the guys now, younger and putting a little more back into it as the evening wears on, while behind them the hotel's other guests stream in from the bars, each with the honey or honeys of the evening in tow. There's been an explosion of ladyboy bars at Nana in the last few years, and some of the men have made their choices from those establishments. These girls, older and more obviously trans than Lutanh, are often more stylishly dressed than the biological women in their jeans and T-shirts. As a tall, willowy ladyboy ambles past Rafferty's window with her john, she makes a remark to one of the women working on the men at the table, and the girl whirls and her hands come up, teeth bared, fingers curled into claws. The ladyboy laughs lazily and accompanies her customer into the hotel, tilting her head cozily onto his shoulder. Rafferty sees hatred in the rigidity of the other woman's back. There's a lot of anger, a lot of repressed violence, in the sex trade. Not always repressed either.

"What was the room like?" he says. "What kind of building? Anything more you can remember?"

"It was like . . . like a million other places. Just an old apartment house, small, crummy, a couple stories. Maybe wood on the outside, maybe cement. No color I could see. I mean, you know, it was dark. In a nothing neighborhood with a canal going through it. One of those parts of Bangkok that don't feel like a big city yet, no skyscraper in the front yard. My . . . um, my feeling about the building is that it was empty except for me and them. Door to my room opened into the hallway; there was a kitchen setup against one wall, a little bathroom, a bedroom no one ever went in; that was it. You know, a small, crappy apartment. There's a trillion of—"

"Windows?"

"Yeah, one, to the left of the bed and about ten feet away."

"What could you see?"

"Not much, because I was cuffed to the bed. But there were some treetops and some buildings behind them, tall ones, farther away—and . . . uhhhh, one of them was that whopper, the really high one with the kind of needle on top."

Rafferty sits up straight. "The Baiyoke Tower, the Sky, whatever it's called? The hotel?"

"Maybe."

He closes his eyes and tries to visualize it. "Very high rectangular building, but then it goes round under the spire for a couple of stories, like a hypodermic? And the round part beneath the spire lights up?"

"That's it."

"How much of it could you see?"

"Don't know. There were other tall buildings between me and it, but it was taller than all of them. Maybe eight, ten stories at the top, the layer cake, and the spire."

"In what direction?"

"Well, the sun set behind it."

"So west of you. How far away?"

"Who can tell? Far enough so I could see the top of it."

"Could be miles. I mean, it would have to be, for you to see the top through a small window, right? I think it's the second-tallest building in the city. Do you have any idea where you were, what roads you took to get there?"

"No. I was kind of occupied. She was keeping me busy."

The point of Rafferty's pen tears the paper, and he forces himself to sit back. "*Think.*"

"I *am* thinking. Third or fourth day I was there, she saw me looking out the window. That night they doped me. Next morning there were blinds. Closed."

Rafferty exhales so loudly that Finch can hear him.

"I'm trying, I'm trying," he says. "If it helps any, the spire on that hotel, if that's what it is, pretty much cut the sun in half."

"Canal, in a nothing area, due east of Baiyoke. Maybe within two or three miles." His knee is bouncing up and down as though of its own will.

"The canal," Finch says.

"I just *said* the canal—"

"Wait, wait, hold it, I . . . I know you said the canal, but I remembered something while you were talking, and my wires got crossed. One thing, when we were driving in. The block where we were ended in the back of a sort of medium-size building. And when we drove in, I saw a word, part of a word, in the headlights on the front of the building, or a sign in front of the building, and it caught my eye because you know how you can hear your name in a roomful of—"

"Yeah, yeah, got it."

"So yeah, there was this *sign* in front of the building, and when the headlights hit it on a bounce, I saw the end of a word, *i-t-y*, and then blank space, which is how I knew it was the end of the word. Anyway, when I was a kid, I had a T-shirt with that sideways eight on it, because I'd watched *Cosmos* and I thought it was cool, and I spent half my time for about six months explaining it meant infinity and then trying to explain infinity, which I wasn't very good at. So those letters, they sort of jumped—"

"Right. Anything special about the building with the sign? High, narrow, octagonal, tapering, tons of glass, a bell tower, *anything?*"

"No. Just a building. Wide, but only two, three stories high. No lights on. Just a big dark box."

"Which direction from where you were? If Baiyoke was to the west—"

"Gotcha. Woulda been to the . . . to my left. What's that if you're facing west, south? Mostly south, anyway."

"Well, well." Rafferty is drawing it all on the back of the *Pygmalion* script: the canal, the small apartment house, the building with "ity" on it, the setting sun, the high Baiyoke tower. A compass in one corner. He says, "My, my, my."

Larry Finch says, "Yeah?"

"Maybe, maybe not. I don't know. So tell me how you got away."

"First thing was—did I tell you about the mask?"

"No."

"When I was there, in the hospital bed, she was wearing a nurse's uniform and she had a surgical mask on. Always had it on. At first I figured, okay, she's dumb enough to think I won't recognize her, and she almost never talked, so I wouldn't hear her voice, and I thought it meant they might eventually let me go."

"Even though she'd taken you to the—"

"You grab at straws," Finch says. "When all you've got is straws, you grab at them. But then it just stopped making sense, no matter how desperate I was, and I realized I was *supposed* to think that, that it meant they weren't going to kill me. So all I could think *then* about was how to escape, but by then the cast was halfway up my thigh. A couple nights later, the last night, they doped me extra good. I mean, usually it felt like sinking into a soft bed, but this was like getting tossed off a roof. I actually thought for a second I was going to die right then. I went *under.* I think you could have pulled teeth, you could have circumcised me with a pair of pliers, I wouldn't have noticed. But then the monster dropped me."

"Dropped you."

"He tripped, I guess. One minute I was out cold, dead to the world, and the next I was tumbling ass over elbow down the stairs with the monster falling on top of me. For once in my life, I had the brains to do the right thing, I just lay there facedown at the bottom of the stairs with my eyes closed. He kicked me once, for the inconvenience, I guess, and picked me up and took me out and tossed me into the canal."

"How far to the canal?"

"Thirty, forty steps. Really *big* steps. But see, what he didn't know was that my cast had cracked open above the ankle, maybe on the edge of a stair, and when it started to pull me down in the water, I was able to hit it against the cement on the side of the canal, and that was hard enough to break it the rest of the way open so the bottom part of it slipped off, like a shoe, and then I rose to the surface. I grabbed one gigantic breath the minute I could, then rolled facedown and let the current take me until I had to breathe again. By then I was out of sight. It took me forever, maybe an hour—but who the hell can tell in a situation like that?—before I could grab hold of something and get out of that sewer."

Rafferty had drawn a thick box around his map as Finch told the story. "So," he says, "the casts are weighted." Arthit had mentioned that, he thinks.

"Yeah, I figure there's weights in the foot. They're to keep you from trying to get away and then to make you sink."

"And your reaction to all this, once it was all over and you were safe and sound, was to run away."

Finch's voice rises. "The fuck would you have done? Go to the cops? The cops fucking *visited* me. And Lala and the monster, they knew I hadn't been found, so I obviously wasn't dead. Bet your ass I ran away. I called a friend, stayed at his place while the embassy got me some new papers and I figured out where I still had some money, and then I came here. *Here*, meaning where I am now, and that's all you need to know about it, it's where I am now."

"Okay," Rafferty says. "Can you think of anything else? When you took Lala out, did you choose the places you went or did she?"

"I did, maybe she did once."

"Where? Did they seem to know her there?"

"No, just a . . . uhhh, a Brazilian steak house, you know, a meat palace, 'cause I said I wanted meat, over near Sukhumvit. Around Asoke. There were a million people, but no one seemed to recognize her or anything. Just, you know, eat and go."

"I know the place." He finished writing and looked at the three scribbled pages. "If you think of anything else, anything that might help, let me know."

"Okay, and to square things up, you do something for me."

"Sure."

"If they get her, if they get both of them, tell Bob. Tell Campeau. Ask him to call me. I'd like to go back there, maybe stay with him while I find a place. I'm lonely here."

"Will do, I promise. Thanks."

He waits until Finch has disconnected, then makes a quick outline of what matters most. He takes a photograph of the map he's drawn and emails it to Arthit. As he starts to dial Arthit's number to discuss it, the phone rings.

28

As Temporary as a Rash

THE ROOM KEEPS *tilting.*

He feels like he's in a boat, adrift on an unending series of high, long swells that come from all directions. Just as he learns to anticipate that the next one will roll in from the left, they shift and begin to come from behind him or in front of him. Dealing with the rise and fall of the room distracts him from his work, it slows him down, it makes him sick to his stomach. And when the movement comes from in front of him, it terrifies him.

Back when he was in high school and winning all those swimming medals, he took a brief stab at diving. The really good divers got all the prime fluff. Being a swimmer, where your body is invisible in the water most of the time, was like being the bassist in a rock band; being a diver, rotating slowly, gracefully through the air as the girls gasped at your abs, was like playing lead guitar. Divers didn't need handcuffs.

But the dives where he had to go off the board backward, straight up into the air *facing* the board and then flip forward and down toward the water—those dives scared him senseless. He could visualize the moment of impact as his forehead struck the board, and in his vision the board simply scalped him, baring the white bone of his skull as he dropped through the air, leaving his skin and his hair dangling from the tip of the diving board like a victory flag, like a trophy: Board 1–Buddy 0. Once he imagined that, his diving career was over.

And that's *almost* what this feels like at the times when the swells approach from in front of him. Like he's about to pitch forward, helpless against the tilt of the room.

Whatever they gave him . . .

Here it is again, coming from in front of him, and he has to lean into it, and his hand, a cramping, knotted claw now, loses the zipper yet again. *I'm not making enough progress.*

Whatever they gave him this time, it was different. In the seconds after the stuff hit his veins, he felt like he was dissolving down a drain, a sensation of disintegration and swirling and free fall with the room above him getting smaller and smaller. A kind of awful *warmth*, as though he'd somehow pissed himself all over, bloomed from the top of his head to the end of the foot in the cast. And then he was just *gone*, off to the place where they keep the dark and the silence, not a glimmer, not a shadow, not a paling, not an edge. Darkness with a *texture*, like a warm, soft blanket, and him drifting through it weightless, the softness opening in front of him and closing behind him, maybe like the dream of a baby that's still inside its mother.

And now the rocking intensifies, and with a jolt he comes to himself again, fast and hard, because he's *going to hit his head on the end of*—Snaps his eyes open once more for, what? The thirtieth time? The room so out of focus it could have been a picture by that guy who painted all those fat naked women with the sunlit haze around them. *Renoir.* If Renoir had painted a dark room. With a terrified guy in it.

There. Renoir. Who *said* he was stupid?

A *baby*, he thinks, and for a moment he's back in the time, pretty hazy itself and always seeming sunlit, when Edward was a baby, and then, later, when Bessie—oh, pardon me, *Elizabeth*—was a baby, when they were more important than anything else, when he could be *good*, as he thought of it, because what could make a man happier than a family with a baby in it? What more did a man need than a beautiful—if occasionally difficult—wife and two little kids who adored him? What kind of fool would endanger that kind of happiness? Well . . .

And of course, as his own father said, nothing lasts forever. *Happiness*, his father had said, was a practical joke played on people with arrested development who continue to believe in fairies and Santa Claus and miracle cures; for the rest of us, happiness was just something we use later to measure our unhappiness against. Happiness was as temporary as a rash, and it ended worse.

Good old Dad.

So, naturally, the Bessie/Elizabeth thing became an issue. Both children had royal names, although he'd barely recognized the fact when Sophie insisted on them. He'd responded to the revelation—after the fact—by saying, *Sure, no problem*, which was the best tactic when arguing with Sophie. He thought of it as his "yield immediately" strategy. It didn't win him any arguments, but when Sophie was on the other side, it felt like a victory just to have the issue, whatever it was, behind him. So Edward and Elizabeth it had been.

Except that Elizabeth was *such* a Bessie. When he dreamed of her, her name was Bessie. Edward, on the other hand, was definitely Edward. Not remotely an Ed or an Eddie. Even as a small child, he'd had a distance to him. Where Bessie reached up to everyone in a room, Edward didn't invite hugs. He responded to his mother's baby talk with raised eyebrows. He was the cleanest child in history; when he was five or six, he began to criticize the way the laundry ironed his shirts. In the meantime Bessie was a human puppy; she wanted love from everyone. Naturally, she became Sophie's favorite. Sophie identified Edward's distance with Buddy's own, and after a while she referred to her two children as "Bessie" and "the boy."

And then Edward had shown no interest in the sports his father had imagined him playing. His father is thinking about winning medals, and the kid announces one day when he's twelve that he might like to be an actor. So there he is, with a mother who refers to him as "the boy" and a father who's worried that he might be a fairy. Jesus, poor kid.

A swell comes from the right. He closes his eyes, but he can manage them when they're from the right. He waits until it stops, draws a few deep breaths.

But the babies. The way they'd smelled. How small their hands were. The way they'd looked at him when he came into the room. He *had* loved the babies.

He is certain he had loved the babies. He's positive he had.

He looks around at the dark room in which he figures he'll probably die. All this, just because he wanted someone to smile at him again, the way women used to, to *want* him again, as though he were still beautiful, as beautiful as he'd once been. As beautiful as Edward.

And yet again, with a pinching around his heart, he thinks, *Edward*, and then the swells begin to come from the front, and he chokes down some air and lets the movement take him. His consciousness thickens, and once more he's afloat on a sluggish ocean of pitch. At some time (maybe twice), he turns his head to vomit.

When he comes back to himself in the puke-stinking room, he makes a fist with his right hand, squeezing so hard it drives his nails into his palm, stretches his fingers out, makes a fist again, willing the hand to do what he needs it to do. Then, for what feels like the millionth time, he takes the top end of the zipper between thumb and forefinger and slips it *just* into the cast, at the end of the short new cut he's made, grabs the other end in his left, and begins to saw back and forth, the movements tiny, hampered by his inability to move the hand he's jammed inside the cast more than half an inch at a time. But he's broken off two new pieces of plaster since the first time he came out of the dope, so he's making progress. He's sawing, with agonizing slowness, to a spot a few inches below his knee—he's close to breaking off more, to the point where he'll be able to flex his knee, he'll be *able to flex his knee*—when, downstairs, a door slams.

It takes him a second or two to process it, and then he has to pull himself together; he has to *be completely here* to hide everything, get the jeans flat beneath the blanket, and lie on top of them so they won't be visible if she peels the blankets down, *more* time to rearrange the blankets, fumble with the handcuffs—and it feels like it takes a full minute for his hands to *begin* to do every single thing he wills them to do, however simple it is. He *knows* that he won't be ready when they come up; he knows he's about to be—

But they're both still down there. Yelling at each other. He remembers to put the bobby pin back in his mouth *footsteps on the stairs* fastens the first cuff *coming down the hall, heavy, so it's* fastens the second cuff *it's the big guy* and closes his eyes just as the door opens.

Lala looses a tangle of angry syllables at the big guy, and the big guy startles him by hitting something, the door or the wall, hard, and so loud that Buddy flinches and thinks, *I'm dead*, so he plays it a little, groans, turns his head on the pillow.

Keeps his eyes closed.

They're definitely arguing, volleying sharp-edged snatches of the Thai he's never bothered to learn, and the big guy seems to be getting the worst of it. She makes a sound of disgust, a sharp *pfffff*, probably in disapproval of the way the room smells, and she says something that seems to be a joke, because the big guy makes a kind of snort that might be a laugh. After an absolutely immeasurable amount of time—could be a minute, could be ten—the door closes. He counts to fifty, even though he hears them going away down the hall and then on the stairs. He needs to be completely sure that one of them isn't standing right there looking at him.

And then he counts to fifty *again*, getting lost once and starting over, and when he's done, he opens his eyes just the tiniest amount. Through the thicket of his lashes, he sees that the room is empty.

This is all *different*. The drugs are different, the argument was different, her coming home and going out again, which he's pretty sure she did, *that's* different. Before, when she came back here, she stayed here, so that's another change in the routine. Changes are not good news.

He's certain that this is as far as he goes. This is the night they'll kill him.

If he can just maintain focus. He was always focused, it was one of his strong points—one, he supposes, of the few: He kept his eye on the ball. He kept the end in sight. He can *do* this now, he knows it. He *will* live through this. With the only surge of optimism he's felt since he first woke up in this bed, he uses his tongue to work the bobby pin out of his mouth, spits it into his cuffed right hand, and watches it slide out of his palm, bounce soooo *slowly* off the edge of the bed as he scrapes his wrist raw against the inside edge of the cuff trying to catch it, and then it obeys the law of gravity, all the way to the floor. A million miles down.

Part Four
THE FALLS

29

Define "Idiotic"

THE PHONE DISPLAYS a picture of Miaow he took when she was rehearsing for *Small Town*, the play in which she and Edward played kids falling in love. She hates the picture, but as he told her, it's his phone. Rafferty sweeps aside the hand-drawn map he was going to discuss with Arthit, parks in his head the things he wants to share about his conversation with Larry Finch, takes a deep breath to clear his head, and answers.

"Fon called me," Miaow says, without a greeting. There's an edge to her voice he can't recall having heard before.

"Why not me?"

"How would *I* know? But she says that Mom wasn't—isn't—feeling well, so they went back to Fon's—"

"Not feeling well? What does that mean?"

"I'm telling you what she said. She wouldn't stay on the phone."

"Do you know where Fon lives?"

"No."

"Well, did you ask about the baby, whether anything happened—"

"What do you *think* I asked about? She said I shouldn't worry, they'd be home later."

He's up and signaling for the waitress to bring him a check. Outside, the party of old-timers is down to two. The man in the wheelchair is asleep, slumped back in the chair with his chin on his chest, a spill of beer in front of him, dripping off the edge of the table onto the knee of his pants. "Then what? She hung up?"

"*Yes,* she hung up. What do *you* do when you don't want to stay on—"

"Okay, okay. Did you call her back?"

"Poke," Miaow says. She rarely addresses him by name. "If I'd called her back and she answered and if I'd learned anything more important than what I just said, don't you think I'd have *told* you about it?"

"So she *didn't* answer. When you called her back."

"That's right." There's a pause, and he can see her, alone in the apartment, probably dead center on the couch. She always claims the whole thing when she can. After those years on the street, space and silence are still luxuries. "She said I shouldn't be worried, but I am," she says. "Fon sounded . . . she sounded *scared.*"

"Well," he says, swallowing, "there's no point in you and me being—"

"Don't *father* me. I know how worried you are."

"Okay," he says. "We'll be worried together."

She says, "I'm *frightened.*"

After a moment of arguing with himself about being the reassuring adult, he gives up and says, "So am I."

"Can you . . ." she says.

"Can I what?"

"Can you come home?"

"Not right now," he says. "I have to meet somebody, I really do. But as soon as it's over, I'll be there. And anytime you need to talk, call me."

"Okay," she says. "I guess."

"Tell you what. I'll be there in an hour. Is that okay?"

"What do you have to do?"

He doesn't want to talk about separating Lutanh and Edward. "Something you'd approve of. I'll tell you about it later."

When she's no longer on the line, he stands at the table hearing her voice in his ear. It has sounded higher, younger, more vulnerable than usual in the past year or so, since she began to act. He makes a rough estimate of the amount of money he owes for the food, adds some to it, and waves the money in the air at the cashier before running out through the sliding glass doors and down to Sukhumvit to find another in an unending line of taxis.

"IT'S ME," HE says, "Poke." He puts the phone on speaker and goes back to studying the Google map of Bangkok he's brought up on the screen. Whoever occupied the cab before him had broken the rules and smoked, and it stinks.

"Hi," Edward says. "What's happening? Is something wrong?"

"I need to talk to Lutanh." The cab makes the zigzag across Sukhumvit that gets his attention every time, into lanes that run the opposite way during rush hour. Once he knows he's going to live, he opens the window to thin the stench of the smoke and looks down again at the map. It's *tiny*. "Is she . . . I mean, can I talk to her?"

"She went to bed," Edward says. "I gave her something to eat, and . . . and she was tired, you know, she got beat up pretty bad." He hesitates, and then he says, "Do you *really* need to wake her up?"

Catching himself leaning forward again in the cab, Rafferty sits back. He says, "I do," and lets out an enormous breath that surprises him. It tells him how much tension he's been tucking away for the past few hours. There is, he thinks, *a closed door* between Edward and Lutanh. If Miaow's heart is going to be broken, at least it won't be tonight or tomorrow. His spirits rise a little, and he uses the energy to wonder where in the house she is. He'd gone upstairs only as far as Buddy Dell's office, which was the first door in the hallway, a long hallway. The place had seemed, from the street, to have a lot of upstairs rooms.

After thirty seconds or so, long enough to climb a flight of stairs, he hears Edward knocking and then knocking again. "I'm pretty sure she's asleep," the boy says, and then knocks a third time and says, more loudly, "It's Miaow's dad."

I've become Miaow's dad, Rafferty thinks, enlarging the map as much as he can. He's just beginning to locate things when Lutanh says, in a voice like a truckload of gravel, "Hello?"

"I need you to get up and get dressed," he says. He considers for a moment whether to tell her where they're going and decides she might refuse to go anywhere near the man. "We have an errand to run. It's important."

"THEY'RE BEHIND US right now," Clemente says. "Where are you?"

"Half a mile away from Silom, heading toward the guy's hotel. Traffic's the shits. Have they made any attempt to get closer or pull you over, anything aggressive?"

"No. They're being careful. They're usually five, six cars back, but they get close enough from time to time that we can't miss them. I think it's mostly a power show: *We know what you've been doing.* We've been zigzagging, stopping every now and then to pretend to run an errand. When we take a *soi,* they wait until we've gone a little way before they turn behind us."

"Are you sure there's only one car?" Lutanh is staring at him out of her blackened and swollen eyes, openmouthed—perhaps because she can't breathe through her nose—looking like she's debating whether to jump out of the cab. She'd started getting nervous when he told the cabbie he wanted to go to Silom. When he'd explained the purpose of the visit, she'd argued with him, her voice as high as a biologically female soprano's. The cops were no good, she'd said, not even that lady cop. They'd just demand money from the *farang* and then let him do what he wanted with her. The cops didn't care about people like her. A Thai commits murder, they arrest a Lao or a Burmese every time. She wanted to go back to Edward's.

He reaches over to put a reassuring hand on her wrist, and she snatches her own hand away as though he's on fire. She's sitting right up against the door. If it popped open, she'd pitch sideways into the street. Looking at her face brings back to the surface the rage he felt when he first saw her, but he smiles and says, "Seat belt."

Lutanh ignores him and for the ninth or tenth time passes her fingertips down the bridge of her nose as though assessing the damage. On the phone Clemente says, "I always wear one, but thanks for the thought." Anand says something Rafferty can't quite hear, and Clemente laughs. "Yeah," she says, "there's only one car, as far as we can tell."

"When you stop to do your errands, what happens?"

"First and second time, they pulled over, too. Third time, which was the last so far, they went past us as though we weren't there, but a minute or two later we drove past *them* and they pulled out behind us again."

"How many people inside?"

"Minimum two, in front. Could be another two in back. Windows are tinted, we didn't get much of a look."

"What I'd like to—" His phone buzzes to signal an email. "Let me put you on hold." He presses to accept the incoming message, which is from Arthit, clicks on the email link that's the only thing it contains, and finds himself looking at an image. No text, just a detailed, magnified map of a section of Bangkok, upon which has been imposed a long, narrow, very acute isosceles triangle in bright orange with the base—the narrowest of the three sides—ending at the right side of the screen: due east. He enlarges it and sees that the apex, the point, is at the Baiyoke Tower. The phone buzzes again to signal a call, but Rafferty is already at the edge of his technological expertise, so he blinks a couple of times and says to Lutanh, "I've got three calls at the same time."

She says, "And?"

"And I don't know what to do."

"You give me," she says, extending her hand. She takes the phone and glances at the screen, squints at him dubiously, and says, "This . . . email?" She makes it sound like something he should have wiped off his shoe.

"Yes."

"You think email get angry, you say bye-bye?"

"Um," he says, and she closes the email and looks down at the display. "You want Arthit?" she says.

"Yes, but try not to lose—"

"Here." She hands it to him.

"Where are you?" Arthit asks. Lutanh has put the phone on speaker.

"On the way to Silom."

"Did you see the map?"

"Looking at it as we speak," Poke says, wondering how to get back to it.

"Well, keep yourself available," Arthit says. "I've got three people working on that triangle right now."

"Shouldn't be too hard to find him," Rafferty says, "with a word fragment like 'ity' in the equation."

"I'm sure that will reassure them. Think how nice it would be if it were the *beginning* of the word."

"There are only so many words—"

"One of them, unfortunately, is 'city.' Why are you going to Silom?"

"I live there," Rafferty says, feeling truthful and evasive at the same time.

"Do you want to be around when this thing goes down?"

Lutanh pinches his arm, and he glances over at her impatient face and raises a hand that means, *Wait a minute.* "It's *Edward's father*, remember?" he says to Arthit, seeing Lutanh's eyes sharpen when he says the boy's name. "The kid came to me. Plus, I'm the one who has to answer to Miaow."

"I'll be back to you." Arthit hangs up.

"You maybe find Edwudd papa?" Lutanh says to Rafferty.

"Well, we've got a triangle. Hold on a minute."

He's found his way back to Arthit's map, and Lutanh is looking at it with him, squeaking a little each time she tries to inhale through her nose, when the phone vibrates again and Lutanh says, "You want talk other friend?"

The display says CLEMENTE. "Yes," he says. She does something to the screen, barely glancing at it, and he says, "I'm back. That was Arthit."

Clemente says, "He doesn't know what we're—"

"No. Of course not. But I gave him some information a little earlier that might help him figure where the murdered men were held."

"You think he might locate the place tonight?"

"Possibly. I mean, I hope so."

"Could be a full evening," Clemente says. "What do you want to do about our little parade?"

"I thought it might be fun to get behind *them* while they're behind *you*. Tail them kind of closely."

A man—has to be Anand—says, "Fun? Are you crazy?"

"Well, if you don't want me to . . ."

"For what possible reason?" That's Clemente.

"I don't know. I'm just pissed off. I want to fuck with somebody."

Lutanh says, "Talk bad."

"Mr. Rafferty," Clemente says, "fucking with somebody is the whole point of this errand."

"I don't feel like waiting."

"Are you in a cab?" In the front seat, the driver sits up.

"Yes."

"Well, forget it. No cabdriver is going to—"

"Ahhh," Rafferty says, letting it go. "I know that. But look, you don't want these guys to be at the hotel while we're upstairs. They could screw everything—"

"I've been thinking about that."

"See? I'm not useless."

"But what can you—Wait, tell me you're not going to do anything idiotic."

Rafferty says, "Define 'idiotic.'"

"Getting these guys angry. Getting yourself killed. Getting *me* killed."

"Angry or killed. Okay, I promise. Are they staying right with you or is it sort of elastic?"

"Elastic."

"Good. Where are you?"

"On Surawong."

He thinks for a second. "Okay. Give me about five minutes, get an extra few car lengths ahead and dick around with them to kill a little time, and then do a few loops to wind up heading east on Silom. Get to Patpong and take it through the snarl at the end of Patpong, to where the traffic begins to move again, and then keep an eye on the rearview mirror. Are they in one of those silvery cars, a white one, or a black-and-white SUV?"

"I told you already. The SUV."

"And you?"

"The little white one with no acceleration."

"Okay. Across Patpong keep your eyes on the mirror, and when they stop, you get lost. And I mean *lost*."

Anand says, loudly, "Nothing stupid."

"Me?" Rafferty says. After hours of nervous frustration, he feels like a battering ram. "Stupid?"

IT'S JUST AS much of a knot at Patpong at eleven-thirty as he hoped it would be: lines of avaricious taxi drivers quoting ridiculous fares to guys who are half frantic to get back to their rooms with their new conquests, people with suspect blood-alcohol levels wobbling in the street, the occasional brave and/or foolish soul fording the traffic in an attempt to cross but getting stuck at the center divider, looking for a hidden opening like the one Rafferty and Miaow use. "This is fine," he says to the driver when they're at the center of the clot, where there's barely room to move. "This is perfect." He leans forward and hands him a couple of bills, tells him to keep the change, and says to Lutanh, "Open the door."

She gives him a long look and then turns and scans the crowd pouring out of Patpong, clearly looking for someone who might be a threat. He says, "Out, out. Don't worry, I'm with you." She regards him without conspicuous confidence, but a moment later they're on the sidewalk.

"Ice cream," he says. He's checking the crowd, too. She's drawing glances, but he's pretty sure it's only because she's been so badly beaten up. "Right there, Häagen-Dazs. Get yourself a big cup and sit in the back, facing away from the window. Give me ten minutes."

She takes the five-hundred-baht bill he's holding out. "Maybe I run away," she says.

"You can't. We need you with us. Without you we won't know we've got the right guy."

She shakes her head. "Cop no good."

"Really. I suppose they're better in Laos."

"Lao cop no good," she says, her eyes on the crowd. "Thai cop no good, too."

"These cops are fine," he says. "Listen, we *need* you if we're going to fuck this guy up."

"Bad talk," she says again. Then she blinks. "Fuck up?"

"You bet."

Whatever she's looking for in his face, it would seem that she sees it, because she nods. She says, "I get ice cream."

HE'S FIVE OR six layers of people back in the crowd, behind a posse of tall and very drunk Aussies who are singing three different songs at the same time, when the little white police car goes by, Clemente at the wheel and Anand with the window down, looking for him. He pushes the button to dial them as they pass by, says, "I see you, keep moving," and elbows his way into the people gathered at the end of the night market that straddles the center of Patpong 1, trying to position himself to face the traffic. Before he can weave his way through the last bit of the crowd, someone bumps him from behind; it's one of the Aussies, miffed that Rafferty pushed between them.

"In a hurry, mate?" says the Aussie who bumped him. Rafferty ignores him and looks back at the traffic.

It's already been twenty seconds, thirty seconds, the cars are *crawling* past, and he's beginning to think the cops trailing Clemente gave it up when, five or six cars down and inching through the crowd, he sees the tall black-and-white SUV inching toward him.

The Aussie taps his shoulder, hard. "I asked you a question, Jack."

Rafferty thinks, *Why not? This is better.* Giving the SUV a little more time to get nearer, he turns to the Aussie and says something almost under his breath. The Aussie's friends both say, "What?" and Rafferty clears his throat, then waves the tallest one down, and when the man bends toward him, Rafferty plants an open hand on his face and shoves hard. The tall Aussie staggers back and goes down, but his friends leap forward, and with them at his heels Rafferty takes off at a diagonal run, weaving between people with the shouting Aussies grabbing at his shirt until he spots the SUV, and then, shrugging off a restraining hand, he charges directly at the front fender of the SUV, which is traveling at about three miles an hour, slaps the the panel as hard as he can with his hand to simulate impact, and leaps up onto the hood, landing on his side and rolling back until he's lying flat across the windshield. He hears the Aussies shouting at each other to get the hell out of there, a woman obligingly begins to scream, and the SUV jolts to a halt.

He's just slowly beginning to move when the driver's door opens. A second later, a pair of hands grasps his ankle and yanks him across the hood to the accompaniment of a grunt from the cop who's pulling him. He doesn't resist, just lets himself slide and then crumples to the street on his back, an out-thrown arm beneath the SUV.

He looks up, past a round, brown-clad belly, at a tight mouth, a pair of wide nostrils, and two furious, deep-set eyes. "You hurt my car," the cop says, bending down. The cop grabs his shirt, drags him out from under the SUV, and then, with a low, beer-scented grunt, pulls him to his feet and shoves him against the front fender. "You crazy!" he shouts in English. "You drunk?"

"Men were chasing him," someone says in accented Thai, and over the cop's shoulder Rafferty sees Lutanh. She has her hands knotted anxiously in front of her heart, but she takes a step forward. "Three men."

A woman, a bar girl on her way out, pulls her arm free of her customer's to say, "I saw it, too. Big men."

"There," Lutanh says, pointing at the three Australians, who are frantically trying to shove their way back into the anonymity of the crowd. "Those men."

Rafferty can almost see the cop think, *One versus three*, and decide to pick on the solo. "Why they chase you?" the cop demands.

"They pushed me down," Lutanh says from a couple of yards away, still in Thai. "They laughed at me and pushed me down. He pulled them off me, and they start to chase him. They wanted to—"

"Okay, okay." The cop's focus moves from Rafferty, and he looks after the three Aussies. He would have to run through the crowd to get them, and he'd be outnumbered, and it's the last thing in the world he wants to do. He's searching for some way to save face by being right. Rafferty decides to make it easier.

"It was my fault, not your driver's," he says, sticking to English. "I was running away from them and not looking. If there's any damage to your car, I'll be happy to take care of it."

"Mmmm," the cop says. He's a captain, Rafferty registers, not a rank likely to be out cruising the tourist areas. He thinks, *Someone is worried about Clemente.*

"Here," the cop says, pointing at a scratch on the fender that's at least three feet from where Rafferty hit it. The cop tilts his head, assessing the damage. "Four thousand baht," he says.

The bar girl who'd backed Lutanh up makes a fart sound with her mouth and links her arm again through her date's to lead him away. The show is over.

"Fine," Rafferty says, reaching into his pocket and wishing he'd given less to Aspirin. "Thank you, Colonel."

The cop doesn't correct him on the rank, just stands there, hands on his hips, looking at Rafferty. For a moment the mean little eyes narrow, and Rafferty guesses he's replaying the incident, looking for a little more money, regretting not having asked for more, and also weighing whether the whole thing might for some reason have been intentional. His eyes flick to Lutanh, and Rafferty can almost see the train of thought: a *farang*, three drunk men, witnesses, Patpong— what could it have to do with the cops he'd been following? Rafferty takes out his wallet, where he keeps a wad of emergency money, counts out five thousand-baht bills and says, in Thai, "A little extra for your inconvenience."

The cop nods, grunts, palms the money, slips it into his pocket. Rafferty has been trying to sound out the characters in the name on the tag pinned over the pocket and comes up with "Teerapat." To Lutanh, Teerapat says, "What happened to you?"

"Boxing," Lutanh says. "Boyfriend."

"You fight too much." He extends a hand. "ID card."

Lutanh hesitates and then reaches into the pocket of Miaow's denim dress. Rafferty watches her take out a laminated card and look at it unhappily as she reaches into the pocket again. When her hand comes out this time, there's something tightly folded in it, and Lutanh slides it beneath the card and hands it to Teerapat.

Teerapat glances at the card, lowers his head to look at it a little more closely, and his eyes come up to Lutanh's. He pushes his lips out, clearly thinking, and he uses his thumb to slide the card aside. When he looks back down, Rafferty's five-hundred-baht note is visible there. He says, "Don't get in fights," and extends the hand with the card protruding between thumb and forefinger. She slips the card out, leaving the bill in his palm, and he closes his fist on it and then lifts his hand and turns it palm down to check his watch. "Look at the time," he says. He takes a last, unhopeful glance in the direction Clemente was going, nods at Rafferty, scans the crowd once—it looks reflexive, automatic, to Rafferty—and turns back toward the SUV. Rafferty stays where he is until the vehicle is halfway down the block and then heads to his left, as though to follow it on foot. Passing Lutanh, he says, without looking at her, "Ice cream."

I've Always Been Partial to "Putting Things on a Firmer Footing"

RAFFERTY'S WATCH READS a few minutes after 12:40 A.M. when the little white police car makes the turn into the dim, narrow street where the hotel is. Anand and Poke are shoehorned in the backseat, their knees high against the back of the front seat. Clemente is driving, and Lutanh is riding shotgun and calling out directions, in response to Clemente's inspired suggestion that she should be their guide, even though they all know where it is.

"Uhhh," she says, shifting in her seat. "That's it. There." The bottom has dropped out of her voice; it sounds like it's coming from inside an empty bottle.

"Where should I park?" Clemente asks, trying to put her back in charge.

"I . . . we, before, with man, I walk."

"Well," she says, "why don't you and Poke and Anand get out here and wait for me, and I'll be back in a minute."

Lutanh says, "I stay in car. When you go, I want stay in the car."

"But we need you to—"

"And Poke stay with me. I want." She reaches over and puts both hands on the handle of the door beside her, as though to hold it closed against anyone who might try to open it.

"You have to come," Clemente says. She leans over and

brushes a wisp of hair from Lutanh's forehead. "You're the only one who can tell us we've got the right man."

"I have a gun," Anand says, taking the male approach. "Clemente has a gun."

"Here's what's going to happen, sweetie," Clemente says. "We're going to go in and talk to the person behind the desk—"

"Nobody there before," Lutanh says, her voice as tight as a wire.

"We'll *get* him there. I'll talk to him, and you can stand a little away, between Anand and Mr. Rafferty. And then we'll talk to the security man at the elevator—"

"Him not there, too. But then, *after*, I come out, him there. He *see* me."

Rafferty says, "Lutanh, he'll be too busy pissing his pants to think about you."

She cranes around to look at him. She says, "I don't *know*. He . . . he . . . nobody *ever* hurt—"

"We do know that," Rafferty says. "That's why we're here. Look at us: you, two people with guns, and me." She breaks eye contact, and his heart sinks. He hasn't thought this through at *all*. "I know, I know. The last time you helped me, you got hurt."

"You were a hero," Anand says to her. He'd been there, although too far away to help.

"But this time—" Rafferty breaks off beneath the sheer weight of it. He says, "Maybe you're right. Tell you what. Anand and I will go in, and you and Clemente—"

"Hold it," Clemente says. "This is personal for me. Anand can stay with you. I want you with us, but Anand—"

"Why is it personal?" Lutanh says.

"*Nobody* beats up women when I'm around," Clemente says between her teeth.

"I'm *girl*, not woman," Lutanh says. "Why not?"

"I won't talk about that," Clemente says. "Because I'll cry, and then you *really* won't have any confidence in me. But I'll tell you one thing: It's why I'm a cop."

Lutanh says, "I have con-confence in you."

"Me, too," Anand says. "Of course, I've seen her in action and you haven't."

The car is silent for a moment as Rafferty holds his breath, and then, Lutanh says in Thai, "Who *cares* where we park? You're a cop. Let's just go."

ALTHOUGH RAFFERTY'S NEVER been here before, he knows everything he needs to know about the place within five seconds of following Clemente and Anand through the door. They're moving in a tight cluster because it seems to calm Lutanh, who's beside him. The scene of the crime is an old, cheap apartment house, given a surface-deep renovation decades ago and reincarnated as a hotel to take advantage of the tourist bonanza of Patpong. The lobby floor is gritty and needs sweeping, a couple of the overhead fluorescents need replacing, the artificial flowers need dusting, and the man behind the counter needs more sleep than he seems to get, because he's yawning when he comes out of the back room at Clemente's insistent pounding on the bell.

He stops yawning when he registers the uniforms. His eyes do a quick tour of the four of them, slowing when they come to the wreckage of Lutanh's face, and he sighs. He's small, slope-shouldered, and prematurely balding. On his chin a big black mole sprouts black hairs, like a spider on its back. He chooses Anand as the person in charge and says, "How can I help you?"

"How's your license?" Clemente says, stepping in front of Anand.

The counterman blinks. "You'd have to ask the owner."

"And the papers for the conversion into a hotel? And the back taxes? I suppose they're all in order?"

She gets a head shake and a shrug. "It's been a hotel as long as I've been here."

"Get a lot of minors?"

The man spreads his hands. "Not while I'm here."

Clemente says, "I can arrange some."

"I'm sure you could. But why bother? There's nothing you could ask me to do that I won't, if it's within my power."

"The man in 422," Clemente says. "Four things. First, I need the key. Second, I need your photocopy of his passport. Third, he is never to be allowed back into this place, not by you, not by anyone. Fourth, we're going up to see him, and he is *not* going to know we're coming. Am I making myself understood?"

"Yes." He tries on a smile, but it doesn't fit and he drops it. "Which do you want first, the key or the photocopy?"

"The key. If you contact him in any way, when I'm going up there—if I even *suspect* he knew we were coming, I will put you in jail and lose you there. You'll stay lost until—Do you have children?"

The man swallows loudly, and his eyes go to Lutanh again. "Yes. Two."

"How old?"

"Nine and eleven." Out of the corner of his eye, Rafferty sees Anand moving quickly toward the corner where the elevator and the security guard, probably, are.

"Well," Clemente says, "by the time we find you again, they'll both be married."

"He won't know," the counterman says. "Not from me."

"Fine. Give me my stuff. Go back to sleep."

When she has the key and the photocopy, she turns to go, slowing when she sees that Anand isn't in sight. She takes a few steps in the direction of the elevator anyway and waits for them. Rafferty starts to follow, but he feels a tug on his sleeve. When he looks down at Lutanh, she takes his hand.

He squeezes it and says, "Do you know the English expression 'piece of cake'?"

"I like that one," Clemente says. She's moved around to Lutanh's other side.

Lutanh says, "No. I know what is cake, but—"

"It means 'This will be easy,'" Clemente says.

From the direction of the elevator, they hear a grunt and a bang like a chair going over. Clemente takes Lutanh's free hand, and the three of them head toward the noise.

The bang wasn't a chair, it was a whole desk. Standing behind it, his eyes wild and the neck of his shirt knotted in Anand's hand, is the guard who's tasked with recording the ID numbers for the broad variety of hookers whom the hotel guests take up to their rooms. He looks at Lutanh, who has slowed at the sight of him, and he shakes his head in what looks like resignation.

"Four-two-two," he says without being asked.

"We already know that," Clemente says. She puts her arm around Lutanh's shoulders and eases her forward. "Is this the man who was on duty?"

Lutanh says, "Is," but it's barely a whisper.

"Let me see your book," Clemente says. "Our young friend here went up to the fourth floor last night, so naturally you checked her card, signed her in, made a note of the room."

"I . . . you see, I . . . I couldn't—"

"Then how did you know she was old enough? Look at her. Are you telling me you didn't even *ask* to see her card?"

"I was in the bathroom."

"So," Anand says, "you're saying there's nothing in that book."

"No. No, there—"

"Well, this is your lucky day," Clemente says. "Anand, help the man with his desk."

Anand steps back and studies it for a moment. "Looks easiest from this side," he says, making a *Pick it up* gesture with both hands.

Clemente says, "Here's the catch. You do *not* call up to 422. Got it?"

"I hope you throw him out the window," the guard says, hoisting his desk. "He's terrible."

THE WET-PAPER SMELL, the dripping air conditioner, the squish of the carpet underfoot—everything is just as it was. When she was still a boy, Lutanh had a nightmare that came back over and over, her mother turning to her and smiling to bare a mouthful of long, pointy teeth. After a certain number of times, she learned to wake herself up before her mother pulled back her lips to reveal her tiger's mouth. But that won't work here, so she squeezes Rafferty's hand hard enough to make him inhale sharply, and he slows down, saying, "It's all right, I promise, it's all right."

"This is the plan," Clemente whispers as they approach the door. "You two stay out here until we call you." She says to Lutanh, "When we call you, it *will* be safe."

Lutanh nods, standing very close to Poke. She's studying the carpet.

"Here we go," Clemente says. Unexpectedly, she reaches down and puts a finger beneath Lutanh's chin to tilt her head up, then leans down and whispers, "Not many people have a chance to get even. *I* never did." Then she puts both hands up, just a moment's silent pause to give everyone a chance to center and prepare for what's to come. She nods at them all, turns to the door, and puts her hand on the handle. Anand unholsters his gun.

Lutanh says, in a shaky whisper, "Two lock. One inside."

Clemente says, "Anand?" and Anand comes up beside her. She whispers, "And one, and two, and *three*," and on *"three"* she inserts the card in the slot and jams the handle down, and Anand raises a leg and kicks the door open so it slams against the wall behind it. Clemente and Anand shove their way through the door, guns in hand, saying, "Don't move, don't move, don't *move!*"

The door starts to sigh closed behind them, and Rafferty steps forward and stops it with his foot. Lutanh stays where she is.

Inside, Clemente says, *"You.* Into the bathroom and close the door and stay there." A terrified-looking someone in under-clothes—boy, girl, Rafferty can't tell which—bolts toward them, throwing a surprised glance at Rafferty and Lutanh, standing in the open door, and disappears to their right. A second later the bathroom door slams.

"In the center of the room," Clemente says.

A man's voice begins to bluster, but before he can get more than a couple of words out, Clemente says, "I'm going to *show* you why." More loudly, she says, "Mr. Rafferty?"

Rafferty says, "Ready?"

"Okay," Lutanh says. She reaches out, squeezes his hand again, and lets it drop. "You first."

He hesitates for just a second, thinking she still might run, but she's looking up at him, the swollen eyes and split lip shocking him yet again, and she shakes her head. "Me okay."

"No wonder Miaow admires you," he says, and goes in.

The heat slows him—the man doesn't have the air-con on— and then Rafferty smells the meat, not rotten, not really spoiled, but heavy, oily, oppressive. What he thinks of is a fine spray of blood in the air, but then he's all the way in and he tunes it out in self-defense.

The man wears white underpants. He's big and soft, with a butterfat body concealing a muscled frame. The plumpness clashes with the military shortness of his hair. Heavy bandages, already soiled, are wrapped around his tattooed knee, and there's a large butterfly dressing, greasy with food, on one cheek. He gives Rafferty a puzzled look, and then Rafferty steps aside.

The man says, "Oh." He looks everywhere but at Lutanh.

Lutanh says, a bit shakily, "Hello."

"She . . . she stabbed me," he says to Anand. "She stole from me."

"After you beat her half to death," Clemente says in English.

In a corner at one end of the couch, Rafferty sees a backpack. Protruding from it are some broken bits of wood with something filmy and reflective—plastic food wrap—clinging to them. He nudges Lutanh.

"Those were my wings," Lutanh says in Thai. "They were already broken when I got here, but he made them worse." She looks at Clemente. "Make him *move*. I want my wings."

Clemente lifts her chin and scoots the man farther away with both hands, and the man steps back. There's a kind of sullen satisfaction in his face, the expression of someone who has always expected the worst and has finally been proved right.

"More," Clemente says. "Back to the wall."

He backs up, sliding his bare feet on the carpet. As Lutanh crosses in front of him, his eyes follow her with no interest at all.

She picks up the backpack and stands there, looking down at it. Tugging at the end of a piece of wood, she pulls out a wreckage of wood and plastic and regards it. Her chin suddenly wrinkles, and Rafferty holds out his arms, and she comes to him, and he holds her.

She's shivering. He says, "You can still fly, Lutanh."

"Okay, she's got it," the man says. "Now what? Two cops and whoever *you* are," he says, nodding at Rafferty, "that's overkill, don't you think? For a fucking ladyboy. She robbed me and stabbed me and cut my face, and now you've helped her get her shit back, so what now? Capital punishment?"

"Where's your wallet?" Clemente says.

"Of course," the man says. "All Thai cops, all the same. In my pants. Over there." He indicates the couch behind the coffee table with the line of partially eaten meals on it.

Anand goes over and gets it. He opens it and flips through the currency. "About fifteen thousand baht."

"Take twelve. Give it to Lutanh."

When Anand has handed the bills to Lutanh, Clemente holds up the photocopy of the man's passport. "You asked what now. This is what now. You have until six this morning to be on a plane out of Suvarnabhumi to somewhere, I don't care where. The money you have left will cover your cab fare and give you a little extra."

"Small change. Fucking crooks." He squints at the paper in Clemente's hand. "What *is* that?"

"Come take a look. A plane leaves Thailand about every twenty minutes. Be on one of them. This is going to Thai immigration. You're never coming back."

The man stops about three feet away. "That's my passport. You can't do that."

Clemente says, "You're not taking me seriously. Poke, is there an English expression people would use to announce that a threat is serious? That it has something behind it?"

Rafferty says, "I've always been partial to 'putting things on a firmer footing.'"

"'Footing'? Is that a word?"

"It is."

"Fine," she says. She takes two steps toward the man and says, "Putting things on a firmer footy—"

Rafferty says, "Footing."

"Sorry, *footing*. Putting things on a firmer footing." She transfers the copy of the passport from her right hand to her left, shifts her weight slightly, brings up the right, fist tightly clenched, and delivers a very short, very fast punch, dead center on the man's nose.

The man stumbles back, blood pouring down over his chin, and falls into the chair he hit after Lutanh stabbed him. In a voice so strained that it sounds like she's being choked, Lutanh says in Thai, "He likes it when you push the chair over." Anand takes a couple of steps, raises a foot, and shoves the chair over backward. Then he leaves the room, and they hear him knocking at the bathroom door. "You can come out now."

A reedy voice says, "I want my clothes," and Anand comes back in and goes to the bed, where he gathers up a pair of jeans and a T-shirt, then bends to retrieve a pair of shoes and a small purse.

As he heads back to the bathroom, Clemente bends over the man. "Do you know how old Lutanh is?"

Still on his back in the armchair, he wipes the blood from his face and looks at it. In a shaky voice, he says, "Nineteen, twenty."

"Not nineteen, eighteen. Well, eighteen *Thai* age, because Thais—and Chinese, too—say you're one the day you're born. In your country she's seventeen. And, of course, she's a boy."

Lutanh had opened her mouth as though to argue about her age, from which Clemente has shaved a year, but resisted the impulse. Now, though, she says, "Not boy."

"By the standards of *his* country, you are." To the man in the chair, Clemente says, "So you've raped a minor, and guess what?

You're gay, which apparently doesn't sit well with you. You should see a therapist. By this time tomorrow, Thai immigration will have a police form identifying you as a pedophile, which your country takes seriously, so you want to be out of here before they get it. You won't come back, and if you ever do, you'll be stopped at the airport and a call will be made to the American embassy: 'Come and get your child molester.'"

"A world of trouble," Rafferty says.

Clemente says, "Sorry?"

"English expression. Problems without end."

"A world of trouble," Clemente says to the man. "Be on one of those planes. Immigration will notify me one way or the other. Lutanh?"

"What?"

"Do you want to kick him a couple of times?"

"No," Lutanh says. "I finish with him." The bathroom door opens, and a slight, small-framed person who appears to be a girl runs to the room door and out into the corridor.

"They're expecting you to check out soon downstairs," Clemente says. "Don't disappoint them."

Rafferty says to Lutanh, "Do you want me to carry your wings?"

To RAFFERTY'S SURPRISE, when they go back into the street, the asphalt is shining with rain, an increase in the humidity that makes the heat more personal, turns it into a heavy, muggy shroud. The rain must have been coming down harder a few minutes earlier, but now it's a fine, bath-temperature drizzle that needles the darkness and hangs halos on the streetlights.

Clemente steps back under the sagging awning at the top of the four steps to the street, puts her hands over her head like a little hood, and says, in English, "Great. As though my hair isn't curly enough already."

"Give me the keys," Anand says. "I'll get the car."

"Fine." She flips them to him. "But I'm driving." With obvious affection she watches him jog to the car.

"You guys getting along?" Rafferty asks.

"Oh, yes," Clemente says. "Just among the three of us"—she nods at Lutanh—"we're getting along just fine. But don't tell *him*."

"It's our secret." Rafferty takes Lutanh's arm and says to Clemente, "I'm going to walk home, so say goodbye to him for me, okay? And excuse us a minute."

He and Lutanh go down the steps into the drizzle. In Thai, Rafferty says, "Was that enough money to get back into your room?"

Her eyebrows go up. "My *room*?"

"Sure. You hadn't paid the rent, and—"

"I don't need *that* much." Lutanh's eyes shift past him and then come back. "But . . . but the . . . um, the police—"

"You're *with* the police. They'll take you home and go in with you. It there's any problem, they'll take care of it." She's looking up at him as though she's trying to translate what he's said, and he feels a twinge of uncertainty about what he's doing—surely he should allow the two of them, Lutanh and Edward, to work it out for themselves. And he will, he thinks, tomorrow. Just not tonight. Tonight seems too saturated in possibility for him to be comfortable with it. He takes out his last couple of bills and gives them to her. "Use the asshole's money for the doctors, and if you need more, come talk to me. Clemente will take you home."

"Home," she says. She nods as though something has been confirmed and looks down at the wet pavement. Up the street, they hear Anand start the car. She says, "I see."

"I'll call Edward and tell him you're okay. And tomorrow I'll have Miaow give you a call."

It takes a few seconds, but she says, without looking up, "Okay. Say hi for Miaow."

He hands her the backpack. "I think it's a good idea," he says. "You and Miaow, you're older than Edward, not in years but you've had . . . you've had bigger lives. He's still a kid in some ways, and I think it's a good idea to give him a little time, at least until this thing with his father is over. Don't you?"

She nods and then puts her arms through the straps of the backpack. When she's done and the broken bits and pieces of cane bristle up behind her shoulders, she says, "Yes."

In Thai, Rafferty says, "You're a good girl."

In English, Lutanh says, "I know."

31

You Don't Have to Be Just a Piece of Candy

THE SUDDEN SPATTER of rain on the balcony startles her, pulls her out of a world of alien vowels used by people speaking rather odd English, impossibly fast. She has the sliding glass door wide open. Both she and Rose are more comfortable with the heat than Rafferty is, although lately Rose has seemed almost American, her energy fading visibly when the temperature scales too high. These days the air-con in the bedroom, which Rose has always tolerated for Poke's sake, has often been on even in the daytime, with the door to the living room standing wide open, just to blunt the heat's edge.

Without getting up she slides down to one end of the couch so she can see past the flat-screen TV to the balcony. The ironwork is slick and shining. She loves the way Bangkok looks when it's wet and at a distance—it almost seems clean. After taking it in for a moment, she grabs a long breath of freshly washed air and slides back to the middle of the couch. She backs up the movie on her laptop, plays a few seconds' worth, hits PAUSE, and says aloud, "'Ooo's troying t'deceive you?" Again she says "'Ooo's" and nods, satisfied, and then says "troyin'." This time she shakes her head. "Not *trying*, not really *troyin'* either." She brings her hands to her cheeks and opens her mouth wide, the pose from one of Rafferty's favorite paintings, *The Scream*. When she's got it out of her system, she says,

"Why am I *doing* this?" and then she sighs, backs the film up, and listens again.

Where in this big, wet city is Rose?

For at least the twentieth time since she got home, she checks her phone. *Yes*, the ringer is on. *No*, it's not in airplane mode. *Yes*, it's still charged. *No*, no missed calls, no voice mail. She wants to call Poke, but that's stupid. He's more worried than she is, he'd call her if he knew anything, and if she calls *him*, he'll go into heart spasms the moment his phone rings, thinking either that everything is all right at last or that the worst has happened: *baby and mother, both gone*. Either way she'll be an anticlimax.

Most of the movies she's seen and the books she's read present women as being more emotional than men, but Poke's emotions are so close to the surface she can almost see them moving around under his skin at times. Rose, on the other hand, can be as practical as a pair of pliers.

She's all right, Rose is. Miaow is certain she'd know *instantly* if something bad happened to Rose. But the baby . . . she doesn't know about the baby. Until recently she's had mixed feelings about the baby.

Like Miaow before Poke and Rose took her in, Eliza in the play doesn't seem to have a mother. She has a father who drinks a lot and who, Miaow supposes, is intended to be funny. A *lot* of it seems to be intended to be funny, but she can already feel some long stretches where the audience will cough and fidget and the smaller kids will probably talk out loud.

Once the real story starts, though, once the frog begins to turn into a princess, the place will quiet down. She'll *make* it quiet down.

She sprawls out, precisely dead center on the sofa with her bare feet on the glass table, the loose pages of the script— reprinted to replace the ones Poke took—scattered around her, and her MacBook Pro on her knees, open and on. She's thinking about vowels and half listening to the drips of water from the balcony above pinging on the steel handrail of their own balcony.

About an hour ago, long before the rain started, she'd despaired of ever being able to figure out what Eliza is supposed to sound like. Out of sheer desperation, she'd sought help on YouTube. There she discovered an ancient movie version of the play that stuck pretty close to the script and was so old it wasn't even in color. Most of the actors have a kind of look-at-me phoniness that makes her think they wish they had a cape they could swirl around themselves or a mustache to twirl; they seem to be saying their lines to someone a hundred yards away, and they don't listen to each other. But the girl who's playing Eliza is *amazing*. Two minutes into the first scene, Miaow became aware that her mouth was hanging open, and she's been consciously closing it ever since.

The name of the girl playing Eliza is Wendy Hiller, and Miaow has already found out that Wendy Hiller is dead. She died when Miaow was one or two, which Miaow thinks is kind of sad. On the other hand, Wendy Hiller kept acting until she was tremendously old and not so pretty, so what Lutanh always says—if you're a girl and you want to be a movie star, start early, because no one will want you later—isn't necessarily true. Wendy Hiller won an Oscar when she was practically a hundred. Well, fifty, but then she kept working forever, and that means *this can be a long-term job*. You don't have to be just a piece of candy for ten years and then disappear.

Not that Miaow thinks she's pretty enough to be a piece of candy.

She pushes the PLAY icon and listens to the line again. It's a *nothing* line. It's the third or fourth time Eliza has tried to make the very same point, to people who are socially far, far above her: that they're treating her badly and that she's a person, too. It's repetition, almost filler, but it tells the audience that Eliza is stubborn and that she'll stand up for herself, two qualities that will be very important later in the play. After being in two plays and watching a million hours of television, Miaow knows that some lines—lines such as these, that aren't big surprises, that don't lead to action, that just say something about a character—are like bookmarks: They tell the audience where they are, but they're not very interesting. She also knows that moments like this one are harder to play well than the big emotional scenes where you get to scream and throw yourself around. In fact, she's come to think that an actor who's interesting when he or she is doing *these* lines is an actor worth watching, and Wendy Hiller makes every one of these nothing sentences feel different from the one that went before and the one that follows.

"'Ooo's," she says, giving it a more defiant emphasis. "'Ooo's troyin' t'deceive you?"

Picture something, Poke had said. Wendy Hiller, Miaow thinks, is picturing something different on every one of these lines, boring on the page but not when Wendy Hiller says them. Maybe the thing to do is to forget about the accent for now and think about what's behind the words Eliza speaks.

Resentment, sure; Eliza practically lives in the gutter, compared to Freddy and his mother. And she's probably more than a little humiliated to be so lowly and dirty in front of young, handsome, clueless, *clean* old Freddy. Freddy is a sap, but, Miaow thinks, Edward is pretty enough to make him interesting on the stage, at least to the girls in the audience.

Edward and Lutanh. What's happening over there?

She pushes aside the thought, and the little knot in her stomach it engenders, and pops into her mouth the last in Rose's only remaining jar of maraschino cherries, something Miaow is sure her mother will hate in a week. It's sweet enough to make her tongue shrivel in self-defense, but the sugar is keeping her awake. She'll have to sneak out and buy a new jar tomorrow; this one was unopened when she took it out of the refrigerator.

Lutanh and Edward. Don't think about it.

Edward is a good choice for Freddy because he's handsome and he's smart and he always seems so *clean*. Even his shoes don't get dirty, and his hair always smells like some kind of flowery shampoo. When she asked about it, he stammered as though he'd been caught in something and said it belonged to Auntie Pancake.

How is Poke doing with finding Edward's father? He's been gone all evening. *Something* must be happening.

She knows what it is to be dirty in front of people you envy. She experienced that for years, beginning when she was two or three and her parents used a piece of twine to tie her wrist to a bus bench and went away forever. After a few hours, a dirty, wildhaired boy came by, cut the twine, and took her with him. With half a dozen other homeless kids, she lived on the streets for years, so filthy she smelled and scratched all the time. Scratching was worse than stinking; they all had fleas, they all had lice, they all had snot on their upper lip, they all wore clothes that looked like they'd been washed in coffee grounds. The *clean* people, the rich and well-to-do of Bangkok, gracefully stepped aside to avoid getting near them, averted their eyes from the unsettling experience of looking at them, or, with wrinkled noses, tossed a few coins into a paper cup, or—even more insulting—onto the sidewalk, the same way they might toss food to a dog they're not sure about. Don't *touch* it; it's dirty. It might bite.

When the person refusing to look at her was a kid her own age, or even a little younger, a kid who'd never been filthy in his or her life, it was *unbearable*.

So *yes*, Miaow knows how Eliza feels when Freddy steps on her flowers without apologizing, how she feels when she has to grovel to sell them a blossom or two, only to be told they haven't got change that's *small enough* for the value she puts on her flowers.

Every cell in her body knows what it feels like.

She reads the lines of dialogue again, her mouth moving silently. Before, they'd looked like cards in a deck, one following the other almost at random—you could shuffle them without changing anything—but now she begins to see a pattern, to understand why Eliza chooses these words and in this order, how much it costs her to keep begging from these thoughtless twits who didn't do anything but be *born* in order to have pockets full of money, nice clothes, perfumed skin.

Free of bugs.

She realizes she's scratching her head and stops.

It's *important* that Eliza is stubborn. Through the whole play, no one except Freddy will ever be kind to her, but she stays there in Higgins's house and takes the nastiness, soaks it up and uses it for energy, because Higgins can teach her to talk. He can teach her to sound like a *lady*.

She closes her eyes and says a little prayer of thanks for Poke and Rose. They snatched her off the street, allowed her to shower to her heart's content—sometimes four or five times a day, using all the hot water—allowed her to have clean clothes, with their own tiny room to hang in, to have more than one pair of shoes, and *real* pairs of shoes at that, pairs where the left and right look alike. She suddenly remembers sitting on the floor in her new bedroom (*her bedroom!*), not long after she moved in, with the door shut—she'd never had a door to shut before—just lining up her three pairs of shoes, straight as soldiers. She'd done it over and over again.

And now she's in school. Now she speaks good English and

she's been in a play by Shakespeare and another one by an American, and she is—she *is*—going to play Eliza in *Pygmalion*.

Last night she hadn't even known what the play was about.

It's a different world. And without Poke and Rose, she'd be cutting purses on the sidewalk. Or dead from an overdose. Or a cherry girl in some massage parlor. She knows girls who did that. Her own *mother*, her adoptive mother, Rose, did, although she worked in bars, which was the next rung up, because the girls could say no to the customers they *really* didn't want.

The rain strums more loudly against the balcony. The pages of the play are everywhere. She's gotten pink dye from the maraschino cherries on the pages she's been studying. Pages from the play she'll star in. She has a future. She's in a room she loves.

For a terrifying moment, she's pierced by a thought: *I've lost my second mother. I've lost Rose.*

She's sitting bolt upright, her hand over her pounding heart, when she hears a key in the lock.

32

It's Worldwide Don't Answer Your Fucking Phone Night

IT'S RAINING HARDER, naturally. He shouldn't have said he'd walk, but he couldn't be stuck in the car with them anymore, couldn't keep hiding his anxiety under a blanket so he could pretend to carry on a conversation. He'd come out of the fog of worry briefly, while Mr. Awful was getting what he'd earned, but now the situation hits him twice as hard, a punch in the gut.

He's always believed that there are things that can be *done* in difficult situations. He thinks that fretting is a waste of energy that could be better used elsewhere and that there's always a way out of a box, no matter how tightly sealed it may seem. He's never been an advocate of *waiting*. It's passive, it's ineffectual, it accomplishes nothing other than fertilizing your anxiety. He lacks—he decides, as he does absolutely nothing but get wetter and wetter—*waiting skills*.

He's splitting his skin with anxiety, and there's fuck-all he can do about it.

A dripping ATM comes up on his left. He stops, fishes for his wallet, and slips in a card. He makes a mental note, for the fourth or fifth time this week, to transfer some money from his American bank accounts; he's getting too low here in Thailand. The Thais may top the list of the world's most charming people, but they're not noted for their eagerness to offer large amounts of credit to foreigners. This might have something to do, he thinks, with some of the foreigners their country attracts.

He withdraws ten thousand baht. Tomorrow is Friday, so he can take care of the transfer from the States. And by tomorrow they'll all be back together. Everything will be fine. All this will be behind them. They'll be *together*.

Reclaiming the card from the machine makes him think about Buddy Dell. Has Arthit gotten new information from the banks that issued the missing man's bank cards? Has he made any progress with the location—

His phone rings.

He slaps at the pocket where his phone is, so eagerly that he drops his wallet onto the wet pavement. Without even looking at the display, he punches the button, covers the wallet with his foot and says, *"Hello?"*

"We're moving on a couple of fronts," Arthit says, and Poke's heart plummets at the sound of his friend's voice. He'd *known* the call would be about Rose, maybe even *from* Rose. "A woman cashed a check on Dell's account at Thai Ploughman's Bank just before closing time, although it's hard to tell what she actually looks like. But that's not as important as it sounds, because I think we know where they're keeping him."

"Well," Rafferty says, squeezing his eyes closed in an attempt to focus, "that's good, right?"

"I'm pretty sure it's solid. I'm rounding up a small group I can trust to go in and get him. Do you have any idea where Clemente is?"

"Yes, they're—*she's*—over here, near Patpong. I was just with her. And Anand, too. They're taking Lutanh home."

"Two police officers," Arthit says neutrally, "taking a bar girl home."

"They're off duty."

"And, apparently, enjoying an evening out with you. No one invites *me* anywhere."

"It's a long story." He bends down and picks up his sopping wallet.

"Spare me. The word your witness saw part of is 'Trinity,' and the sign is outside a building that houses the Bangkok office of a Christian adoption organization that offers godly homes to heathen children. Trinity House. It's on a little dead-end stub of a *soi* bordering a canal, a few miles east of Baiyoke Tower."

"Matches like a fingerprint." Rafferty is fishing wet pieces of paper out of his wallet, many of them receipts that are printed on the thin, infuriating thermal paper that glues itself to everything in sight when it gets damp. He'll never be able to separate them.

"You don't sound very excited."

"I am, I am. I'm just worried about Rose."

"She's not back *yet?*"

"No, and no one can reach her. Listen, what time is it?"

"One twenty or so."

"Jesus." Rafferty blows out a couple liters of air.

"Do you want to hang up? Is there something you can do about locating her?"

"If there were, I'd be doing it."

"Of course you would. Out of curiosity, why were you with Anand and Clemente?"

"We were being frighteners."

"And the frightening. Was it legal?"

"Not even remotely." He's patting the receipts a little drier on the underside of his shirt. It won't help him pry them apart, but he knows from long experience that pointless activity, while it never accomplishes anything, can temporarily minimize anxiety.

"Well, then," Arthit says, "was it *justified?*"

"Totally."

"Good. Be awful to know that my cops are committing illegal

acts that aren't justified even by the standards of a moral code as flexible as yours. Maybe you should go home."

"And do what?" He hears movement behind him and turns to see a *farang* who is considerably wetter than he is waiting for a crack at the ATM. He steps aside and keeps going until he figures he's out of earshot. "Miaow is there. She'll call me if anything happens. Hell, for that matter, Rose and *Fon* could call me if there were anything to say."

"Do you want me to have someone check the hospitals?"

"*Would* you?" He wants to slap his forehead. Why hadn't he thought to *ask*?

"I've got Rose's full name. Do you know Fon's?"

"No. But Rose is the one who's having a medical problem."

"Fine. I'll get it started right now, and then I'm going to line up a couple more people—more than Anand and Clemente, I mean— and head out there. Do you know why they're not answering their phones?"

"Because it's Worldwide Don't Answer Your Fucking Phone Night, that's why. Why should they be any different?" He stops walking and tosses away the wad of receipts. "Wait, wait, wait. We all turned our phones off before we did the frightening so they wouldn't ring and tip the frightenee. They might have forgotten to turn theirs back on."

"You didn't."

"My whole *world* is on the other end of this phone, Arthit. I didn't even turn it off when I was told to."

"So if I can reach them, do you want me to have them come by and pick you up?"

"Sure. I'll go down to the entrance of the hospital on Silom. Tell them I'll be at the far end of the driveway."

"I'll call you after I talk to them, assuming their phones are on, and I'll get someone on the hospitals right now. You're not armed, right?"

"No, Arthit, I'm not armed. I'm almost *never*—"

"Good," he says. "When a foreigner shoots a Thai, even a rotten Thai, it's always a mess."

THE SHOCK, WHEN it happens at last, is so head-spinning that he almost passes out. He can *feel* it. It's *right there*.

It's taken him God only knows how long to get both legs dangling over the side of the bed, and he's had to cross the cuffs, on their too-short chains, one over the other, to allow him to roll over. Stomach side down, with his waist bent, he can move his feet much more easily. The one with the cast on it is obviously useless, except for accidentally booting the bobby pin to hell and gone, so he's keeping it motionless. The position he's in is one he won't be able to get out of in the amount of time it takes them to climb the stairs. If they come up, he's dead.

But he's dead *anyway*, he thought, and he forced himself to stop listening for them and direct all his attention to using the bare toes on his unencumbered right foot to search the dirty floor. At first he swept his foot slowly from side to side, but when he realized how much crap was down there, he lost confidence in his ability to distinguish the bobby pin from the dust rats and pieces of paper and bits of old dried food and whatever else the litter is made of, so he'd wedged the cast in place against the table leg, put his weight on the elbows sunk into the mattress, and very carefully raised his right foot and put the toes down again, raised it, put it down an inch or two to the side, then raised it . . .

If he kicks it under the bed, it's hopeless. He has no way to angle his leg so he could reach under . . .

There it is. Beneath his foot. Colder than the floor. Hard-edged. Now what?

He knows he needs to think the whole sequence through before he begins it. One slip, one mistake, will cost him the only chance he has. He relaxes his neck, lets his head droop for a moment, and it's a huge mistake. The room lurches and rocks, launching the swell, a big one, at him from the front and slightly below, and it takes him away. When he's back, trying not to vomit whatever is left in his stomach, the bobby pin isn't there anymore. He has to fight not to scream his rage.

Learn. Don't look down. Get calm. No matter how heavy your head gets, *don't let it fall forward.* The fluids in the inner ear, they feel the change in position as a wave, and for some reason that *brings* a wave, a druggy, internal, terrifying imitation of the real thing. Got to keep that fluid still, don't let it slosh. Picture it as the bubble in a carpenter's level and keep it *dead center.*

When he graduated from high school and faced the plans the old man had made for him, every year accounted for, his college major chosen for him, his grade-point average mandated at no lower than 3.5 if he wanted to keep his allowance coming, he rebelled. Told the old man he'd decided to work with his hands, to make something *real*, not jerk around with pieces of paper all his life, dictating memos that affect no one, compounding intangibles. To his surprise, the old man had gotten him a job with his friend Milt Eichenwald, a builder who ran a sweet scam, making rock-bottom bids for state and federal grants to put up low-income housing and then skimping at every turn: materials, foundation, insulation, wiring and plumbing, structural safeguards—slipping a little something every few weeks to the inspectors to keep them happy. For four months Buddy had worked on the site as an apprentice carpenter, and that damn little bubble became the symbol of his self-esteem. When they were done, what they'd built, beneath the cheerful coats of paint, was a straggling row of tacked-up, soda-cracker shacks that could have been blown to bits by a Big Bad Wolf who smoked six packs a day, but they were all fucking *level.*

Keep that little bit of fluid level.

He's on his third or fourth pre-race breath—in slowly, hold a few seconds, out slowly, concentrating on keeping his head still—when he hears the first ticktock of rain on the roof.

What does it mean? Will it complicate their plan to get rid of him or make it easier? Fewer people out in the rain to see anything, visibility is worse, but it has to get heavy, he thinks, to give them any real advantage.

So it gets heavy.

It doesn't *matter* whether it's raining. It doesn't matter whether it's a local sprinkle or the epicenter of a nationwide, a *continent-wide* storm. It doesn't matter if the whole city is swept away into the gulf, skyscrapers tumbling end over end in front of two-hundred-foot waves. What matters is one bobby pin.

Holding his head up, he lifts his bare foot, moves it a few inches to the right, and slowly puts it down. Paper. He sighs without even hearing it, focuses his eyes on the dark window to keep his head still, to prevent the room from spinning, and then raises the foot and lowers it again, an inch or two farther to the right. Nothing. Does it again and again.

And again.

The rain hammers down. Over the noise he thinks he hears an argument downstairs. Sometimes when they fight, they come up to take it out on him. If they do, he's dead. If he can't find the bobby pin, he's dead. Dead to the left, dead to the right, stand up, sit down, fight, fight, fight. He sends a promise in the general direction of God, or maybe just the rain: If he gets out of here, he'll be a better man. Inside, someone—one of the Buddys who caused all the trouble in the first place—says, *Sure you will,* and he remakes the promise, right on top of the sneering inner voice, and raises his foot again.

Holds it in the air, thinking. He can't go much farther to the right without moving the foot that has the cast on it, and he doesn't want to touch the floor with *anything* that can't send him the tactile information he needs to recognize the bobby pin. So instead he moves the upraised foot as far to the *left* as he can and gently lowers it just beside the cast on his left foot, feeling the roughness of the plaster on the ball of his ankle and the side of his foot, and then— touching his toes to the floor—he feels the edge of the pin.

To make sure it's the bobby pin, he points his foot straight down, the way he learned to do for a racing dive, and brings it down *very slowly* onto the pin. Then he slides it an inch to the right. It *moves*; it's not some obscure part of the hospital setup, a construction staple to hold cords in place, something like that. It slides. He can almost feel its shape, the little U at the bent end.

He starts to lower his head to relax a little but stops in a flash of panic, remembering the bubble in the carpenter's level. There's a small swell, a ripple, but it's nothing he can't handle, and he rides it out, holding himself as immobile as possible. In order to do the next step, the *big* one, he has to get up on the mattress again and roll over, untwisting the short chains on the cuffs, so his back will be on the bed when he puts his foot down to try to retrieve the bobby pin. He needs to be facing *away* from the bed to pick the thing up and flex his knee to lift it. He works up some saliva, not easy with all the dope drying him out, and spits it down onto the sheet as a marker. His head spins as he leans down, but he tries to position the spit exactly beneath his left shoulder joint. Near as he can figure, that's directly over the bobby pin.

Now comes the part of the task he *hadn't* envisioned: getting onto the bed and turning himself on his back again without shifting the position of the sheet.

And he looks at the sheet, which is loose and bunched and twisted, and realizes he won't be able to.

33

Easy Peasy

"I DON'T SEE you," Clemente says on the phone.

"I'm not there yet." Rafferty looks up at the rain and gets a faceful of water. "You're not as far away as I'd figured."

"Kid lives pretty close."

"Is she all right?"

"All tucked in with her big stuffed panda bear."

"Good. Thanks for taking charge of her."

"No," Anand says into Clemente's phone, "thank *you* for telling the colonel about it. He had the radio operators tell us to turn on our phones."

"Oh, well," Rafferty says. "What's he going to do, fire you? Listen, the driveway is a long, shallow U. Go on in and pull over in front of the building, near the front doors. I should be there in a minute, minute and a half."

"In this rain? Why don't I come to you?"

"I'm a minute away. Just hang on." He breaks into a trot, running past street vendors huddled beneath their plastic sheeting to pack up the unsold stuff. They barely glance at him; it's late, they're getting wet, and a running *farang* is nothing they haven't seen a thousand times. One or two of them look back to see whether anyone is chasing him and then, disappointed, go back to their work.

The rain hasn't cooled the air much, so Rafferty is both soaked and sweating when he climbs into the back of the car. The air-con is on full, and the chill is enough to make him sneeze. He says, "Excuse me," having learned not to wait for any Thai person to bless him. When he'd asked Rose about it, long ago, she'd said, "Would you expect someone to bless you if you farted?"

Rose.

"You getting sick?" Clemente says, pulling the car into traffic.

"No, but I appreciate the concern."

"No problem. If you were, I was going to suggest you take a cab."

Anand says, approvingly, "Such a sweet mouth."

"It's a small car," Clemente says. She makes an expert swerve. "Good. Traffic has thinned out."

"How long will it take?"

"Barring any of the Bangkok usuals—traffic jams, police activity, some rich kid flipping his Maserati and waiting in the middle of the road for his daddy's lawyers—maybe twelve to fifteen minutes."

"What's the drill?"

Anand says, "Are you armed?"

"Why does everyone keep asking me that?"

"Then stay behind us," Anand says. "If one of us shot you, Arthit would be furious."

"Well, I'd certainly hate to be the cause of something like that. So what are we doing? Driving in and knocking on the door?"

"We're *walking* in," Anand says. "The building is on a dead end with no through traffic, and we don't want to announce ourselves. The map people found another little street on the other side of the canal, and we can walk from there to a bridge that's close to the adoption center at the mouth of the *soi*, and we can go over it on foot and walk right in."

"Are there kids at the center?"

"We don't know. It's closed at this hour. The colonel has someone trying to track down a supervisor, and we'll be knocking on the door when we get there. In the meantime we'll behave as though there are. As much as possible, no fire in the building's direction."

"And Arthit? Where will he—"

"At the bridge. He's got a couple of street cops with him, real tough guys, apparently."

Clemente says, "Be still my beating heart."

"Wow," Rafferty says. "Where'd you learn that one?"

She catches his eyes in the mirror and says loftily, "First used in 1705 by William Mountfort in his five-act tragedy *Zelmane: or, the Corinthian Queen*."

"*Very* impressive."

"Awww. A girlfriend of mine said it once when a really edible guy walked into the restaurant we were in. I thought it was funny, so I looked it up."

Anand says, "And waited fifteen years for someone to ask you about it."

"Six," Clemente says. "But it was worth it."

"Play sounds like a corker," Rafferty says.

"Five acts," Anand says. "Didn't those people have anything to *do*?"

"I bet it was in verse, too," Rafferty says. "An opportunity to experience eternity without having to die first." His nervousness often expresses itself in mindless chatter.

Clemente says, "The whole line is actually 'Ha! *Hold* my brain; be still my beating heart.'"

"Was someone standing there to hold his brain?" Anand asks. "You'd really have to trust whoever it is if you're going to hand him your brain."

"There are brains and brains," Clemente says.

Rafferty leans forward, putting his head over the back of the seat. "*Is* there a plan? Or is it more productive for us to discuss eighteenth-century—"

Anand says, "Soon as we meet up, Arthit's two guys will head toward the entry to the street and wait there, in case someone tries to get out that way. If they hear gunfire from our end, one of them will run in to help and the other will stay where he is. We're going to do some creepy-crawling before we start shooting people because they've probably got the guy, your daughter's friend's father. We don't know where he'll be, so we have to be care—"

"Actually, we do know where he'll be," Rafferty says. "I found someone who got away. The room is upstairs, and the window faces west. Across the canal."

Anand turns to look at him and says, "Nice of you to share this with us."

"It's been kind of a fast-moving evening. Maybe you should tell Arthit."

"*What* a good idea," Clemente says. "But *you're* the one who knows about it, so why don't *you* call him?"

"Two-story building, second story, facing west. There are two people holding him, a woman and a giant. They live downstairs. There. That's what I know. Give him a ring."

While Anand is dialing, saying, "A *giant?*" Clemente turns on the cherry lights and takes a slow, drifting left against all the stoplights through an eight-lane intersection, as though she does it every day. Several cars heroically manage to miss them. "If you've got someone who was there," she says, "maybe we should get him to come with us, sort of a guide. Might save a life or two."

"I don't know where he is. I talked to him on the phone."

"Phooey," Clemente says. "But wait. Can you phone him?"

"I can try."

"FaceTime," she says. "That thing you're holding *is* an iPhone, right?"

"Right. Don't know if his is, but we'll see." He hits an instant-redial key.

"Leon and Toot," Toots says. She yawns. "We close now."

"It's Poke. Is Bob still there?" In the front seat, Anand has obviously hit a rocky patch in his conversation with Arthit. He's using hand gestures to get his point across.

"Him have one more wit' the road," Toots says.

"*For* the road. Can I talk to him?"

"If okay wit' him. You please wait."

"Jesus," Campeau says. "There's no getting away from you."

"Call your friend Larry Finch and tell him we've almost got them and I need him to call me."

"Really? I'm proud of you, but don't let it go to your head. Stay off the phone." He hangs up.

"Here," Anand says, holding out Clemente's phone. "He wants to talk to you."

Rafferty says, "Be still my beating heart," and takes the phone. To Clemente he says, "How much longer?"

"Six, seven minutes." She makes another turn through a red light.

Into the phone, Rafferty says, "We'll be there in—"

"I heard her," Arthit says. "Is there anything else you'd like to share about where we're going? You know, something that might keep us all from getting killed?"

"Hang on, I'm thinking. Apartment house, away from the . . . whatever it is, the adoption agency, two stories, he was on the upper floor, his window looked west, toward—"

"If it's the same room."

"He said he had a strong sense that the place was empty except for him and the two of them. Said he never heard their footsteps on the stairs and in the hallway unless they were coming to him, never heard anyone walk past his room, never heard any doors on his floor open or close."

"So they live downstairs."

"Well, he usually heard them on the stairs before they came into his room, so they *started* downstairs. Once in a while, they'd argue, and it would get pretty loud, and that was always downstairs. What else, what else? Yeah, he was hooked up to an IV on a hospital bed. Handcuffed to the bed frame. He . . . uhhh, he said the other one, the man, was a giant."

"Giant or not, only the two of them?"

"Except once, when he woke up, there were a few cops in the room, just looking at him."

"Not entirely unexpected," Arthit said. "Even the *Bangkok* cops would have caught them by now if someone weren't on the pad."

"'On the pad'?" Rafferty says. "'Be still my beating heart'? I worry for the future of Thai culture. Did I mention, in the email where I sent you the map, that he knew her as Lala?"

"You did."

"That's the name Edward's father wrote down," Clemente says, finally sounding excited. "This is beginning to smell really good."

"You're going to stay back, right?" Arthit says. "I don't want you getting shot by one of my cops."

"I always stay back."

"Yeah, and the dish ran away with—"

Rafferty's phone vibrates. It says UNKNOWN.

"Hold on," he says. "Call you back."

Larry Finch sounds like he doesn't know whether to laugh or scream. "You got 'em? You really—"

"We're on the way. I want you to help us."

"How?"

"Just to take one last look at the place, see whether there's anything you forgot to tell me."

"How am I supposed—"

"Is that an iPhone? Do you have FaceTime?"

"Yeah." It's a cautious "Yeah," the "Yeah" of a man who's not going to commit to anything.

"Hang on." To Clemente he says, "How long now?"

"Three minutes maybe. No stoplights."

"I noticed." He says into the phone, "Can you call me back in FaceTime, since you don't want me to call you?"

There's a silence, and then Finch says, "When?"

"Two minutes."

"That fast, huh? Well, do me a favor, wouldja? Shoot them a bunch of times for me."

HE SITS ON the edge of the bed, pulled awkwardly to his right by the short chains on the handcuffs. The cuffs were less limiting when he was lying down; he'd had a foot, a foot and a half, of movement. Now that he's sitting, he has to twist his torso sharply toward the head of the bed, to his right, because his left arm is pulled across his chest by the cuff, while his right hangs almost comfortably from its own chain. The disparity in the apparent length of his arms, the left feeling so much shorter, bothers him, interferes with his actions. It throws him off and brings the dizziness back. He finally decides to hamper both hands equally and knots his fingers together like someone pleading for something, perhaps his life. The notion almost amuses him.

They've been moving around down there. Making noise.

He arches his back and slides his hips over the edge of the bed until the cast touches the floor. Since the bedsheet moved all over the place, he's reverted to guessing where the bobby pin is. He thinks the cast will be within a few inches of it, but when he puts his bare foot down, it's not there.

It's all right, he tells himself. *It's all right. It's here somewhere.*

A door slams downstairs, loudly enough to echo up the stairway. He tells himself to forget it, lifts the foot and puts it down, lifts the foot and . . .

. . . finds it.

He has an irrational impulse to laugh.

When he was a kid, he was very, very good at picking things up with his toes. He's about four decades out of practice, but it's got to be like riding a bike, doesn't it? Once you've done it, you can do it again, right?

Right?

Well, *no*. The pin is lying flat. For it to be vertical enough for him to pinch it between his toes, it has to be on its side. Which is impossible. He needs something to push it against so it can't move, and then he has to find a way to slip something else *under* it and flip it up onto its side, and then he needs to find a way to keep it there until he can get it between his big toe and his second toe, and it's fucking impossible.

He's dead.

For only the second time in his adult life, he begins to weep. He sits there, twisted to his right with his legs hanging over the edge of this hellish bed, one foot on a bobby pin that's only *four feet* from where he needs it to be, and it might as well be on the surface of Venus, and he's crying, not well-bred little sniffles but full-out gulping, tear-shedding, snot-snuffling weeping. He's dead.

And what will happen to Edward?

The last fucked-up act of a fucked-up life. Stranding his only son here with no one to care for him but the aunties, all of whom will grab what they can and run for the hills, and the kid's mother, who practically kicked him through the front door she was so eager to get rid of him. And once his son got here, once they were together, what was important? Lala.

Lala.

He groans, loudly enough to be heard by someone just outside the door, but he doesn't care. He's dead. And Edward . . . well, Edward seems to have a strength of character, obviously inherited from his mother; whatever else you might say, you can't says she's weak. Maybe Edward will be better off without him.

But the memory of him as a baby . . . of him and Bessie . . .

His foot has drifted off the pin, and he has the sensation that the foot is slipping across the floor too easily, as though it's riding on something smooth, even slick. He remains absolutely motionless, up on his right elbow, his torso still twisted to the right, evaluating what he's just experienced, and then he experimentally pushes his toe down and slides it to the right. It *glides*.

Paper. His toe is on a piece of paper. Instantly he can see the progression: With his bare foot, push the bobby pin up against the hard surface of the cast so it can't move; use the bare foot again to slip the edge of the paper beneath the pin; push the paper *up* to put the bobby pin on edge; then let the paper fall back to the floor, leaving—*maybe* leaving—the bobby pin standing on its edge; slide the cast aside, praying that the bobby pin doesn't fall over. Pick it up in his toes and cross his legs to bring the pin up to the edge of the bed. Then one final, agonizing torque with his torso to force the foot holding the bobby pin over the mattress, and drop the pin there. Get his full body back on the bed, without knocking the bobby pin off again, and then *bring the pin to him* by tugging on the top sheet with his teeth. Pick it up in his mouth and spit it, *much* more carefully this time, into his right palm so he can go to work on the cuffs.

Simple, he thinks, and then he actually does laugh. He's made plans more complicated in his life, with even more steps to them, some of them arching across years of enterprise. He abandoned them all, of course, diverted by something that was briefly more appealing and easier to get, but he *is* good at breaking a complex task into simple steps, to be taken one at a time. And there's not going to be much to divert him this time.

Unless he's interrupted.

Fear isn't going to help. The only way to allay the fear is to focus on what he'll do once the cuffs are off. Break the cast at the lowest point of the line he's sawed into it and see whether it will let him bend his knee. If it doesn't, saw like hell and break *more* plaster until the knee is clear, get out of bed, not letting the cast thump on the floor, and figure out how to get out of the building.

Maybe they won't have killed him by then. Maybe the dope will have faded.

What floor is he on anyway? Seems to him the building was only two stories high. Must be the second.

Easy peasy.

He uses his big toe to slide the bobby pin up against the cast. He closes his eyes and puts his toes on the piece of paper. A muscle in his left side, stretched out for too long, cramps, and he inadvertently turns his head in its direction, and the fluid shifts. Closes his eyes in despair.

This is a *really* big wave.

34

The Enemies Are Gravity, Movement, and Emotional Upset

"I LIKE YOUR apartment," the beaky, orange-haired American boy says, and then he rolls his eyes in embarrassment at how he's opened the conversation. He's perched on the hassock, so tentatively he might be waiting for it to explode. That sentence was obviously the only thing in the world he could think of to say.

Miaow is trying with all her being to hear what's happening on the other side of the closed door to Rose and Poke's bedroom, so she says, "*What?*"

"The, uhhh . . ." His voice fades away, and he goes a deep, deep scarlet. Now he either has to repeat himself or think of something else, and from the look on his face there *isn't* anything else. Miaow knows that *she* blushes, too, on occasion, but not like the warning light in a cockpit; the darker hue of her skin mutes the red. "The apartment?" the boy says, making it into a question. His knee is bouncing up and down, almost too fast to see.

"Yes," she says. "The apartment. What *about* the—Who *are* you? Where have you been? What's wrong with my—"

He gives her a rapid-fire sequence of defensive blinks. "I think . . . I think *they* should tell you. They kicked me out a lot. Like now, when they left me out here. With you. Not that . . . uhhh—I'm pretty sure she's all right."

In fact, Rose hadn't *looked* all right when she was towed in, supported by Fon on the left and, on the right, a *farang* woman whose nose announced her as the boy's mother. Rose had a paper-white pallor that made her look like someone who has given far too much blood.

Miaow makes a conscious effort to relax her voice. "But I've been waiting all night. Going crazy. At least tell me where you—"

"Where? Well, we went from someplace with a lot of food stands, which was where your mother was when she almost fainted—"

"She *fainted?*"

"No, no, she didn't. We . . . um, kept her up, and then we got a chair, and a bunch of women, they . . . So anyway, we went to a doctor's office, because the other Thai lady, your mom's friend, said your mom was pregnant and there had been a problem before, and the *other* other Thai lady, who came with your mom's friend, she said she was maybe going to lose the baby—your mom, I mean. She was—the other lady—was, like, somebody who helps people have babies? A doo-wop, something like that?"

"Lose the *baby?*" She sits forward, and several pink-stained pages of *Pygmalion* fall to the floor.

He nods, registers what he's doing, and shakes his head instead. "But that was *before*. I think she's okay now. We went to a doctor and then the hospital—"

Miaow says, "I'm going in there."

"You can't. I mean, my mother says you can't, and the . . . the doctor said, after the procedure—"

"What do you mean, a *procedure?*"

"It was in the other room, where the doctor was, and my mom and your mom's friend—"

"Fon, her name is Fon." She raises her voice. "What *kind* of pro—"

The boy holds a vertical finger to his lips and says, in a

semi-whisper, "They want us to be quiet. Your mom needs to rest. The doctor said so, after we went back to him."

"All right," she says, but what she wants to do is to barge through the closed door and demand to know what's going on. Still, Fon *had* told her to wait, and so had the boy's mother, who has an air of command Miaow hasn't seen since her fifth-grade teacher, who could quell a buzzing roomful of hyperstimulated kids with a single raised eyebrow. And she figures they wouldn't order her around that way, right in front of Rose, unless there was a reason. And even if Rose *did* look kind of half there, they wouldn't dare to keep Miaow on the wrong side of the door unless that was what *Rose* wanted, too. "Just tell me," she says, and she's whispering, "why did you have to go back to the doctor?"

"I shouldn't. They want to be the ones who—" He breaks off. "I'll get it wrong. Like I said, they kept kicking me out."

"Just the most obvious thing that happened. You don't have to *diagnose* it or anything."

"My name is Willis," he says, and it sounds like a desperate dodge. "I mean, Will. What's yours?"

"I'm Miaow, I mean, Mia—no, forget it, I'm Miaow." She has failed to get the kids at school to go with her new name, so she's abandoning it. "Just the most *basic* thing."

Willis turns back to look at the balcony. He says, so softly she can barely hear it, "Bleeding."

"*Bleeding?* You mean, from . . . from . . ."

"Her . . . her lady parts," Willis says, and now he's red enough to stop traffic.

We're probably the same age, Miaow thinks, *but I'm a thousand years older than he is,* and she finds herself on her feet, dumping the rest of *Pygmalion* on the floor. "I'm going in."

"You . . . you shouldn't. My mom, she—"

"Be *quiet,*" Fon says, coming through the door. "If there's one thing in the world your mother needs right now, it's sleep. She's been poked and stitched, and she's had some anesthetic—"

"And she's been terrified for weeks," Willis's mother whispers, closing the door behind her. "It's a miracle she hasn't had a nervous breakdown."

"What about . . ." Miaow says, sitting again. She swallows. "The baby?"

"Oh, honey," Fon says. She rubs her eyes and sighs. "Move over. Joyce and I are tired, too."

"Sorry, sorry." Miaow grabs the pages from the floor, lines them up and sharply taps the bottom edge of the stack on the table to straighten them, apologizes for the noise, then scoots to the end of the couch. With another sigh Fon settles beside her, and Joyce, if that's the name Miaow heard, sits at the end.

Passing the buck, Fon says, "Joyce?"

"It was pretty close," Joyce says, leaning forward so she can make eye contact with Miaow. "She might have been on the verge of losing it. A friend of Fon's is a doula. Do you know what a doula—"

"Yes."

"She took us to a gynecologist, who did an exam and a procedure. I can explain it to you if you want, but the idea is just some stitches to tighten the . . . the passage the baby will come through, give it time to develop in the womb until it's viable. Do you know what 'viable' means?"

Willis says, "It means—"

"I know what it means," Miaow says. To Willis she says, "Sorry. I didn't mean to sound like that."

"So we had the procedure, and your mother, who was already in shaky shape, was exhausted. We thought we'd bring her back here. But then she began to cramp again. She said she was bleeding. We called the doctor and got his service, but he called us back and we met at his office. He took her into the examination room, and we waited for about an hour, and when he came out, he said he'd looked at her again and given her a mild sedative—"

"*Mild,*" Fon interjects. "She was in outer space."

"—and he said she needed to go to bed and stay there. So we got into another cab, but she got carsick—"

"In about half a mile," Fon says.

"And Fon's . . . um, apartment was much closer, so we took her there, and she slept there for a few hours."

Miaow says, "Why didn't anyone call me?"

"Well, first," Joyce says, in the exact tone of voice Miaow remembers from fifth grade, "it wasn't *about* you. It was—it's *still*—about your mother and the baby. And Fon knew you'd call your father, and then we'd have him to deal with, too. Fon says he's . . . excitable."

"Where Rose is concerned, yeah," Miaow says. "*Shouldn't* he—"

"Of course he should. But we can't have that. *She* can't have that. For the next eight or ten hours, she needs to sleep and she needs to be in bed. Right now the enemies are gravity, movement, and emotional upset."

"But my father—"

"Don't call him. When he comes home, explain what's happened and ask him to leave her alone until she wakes up on her own. He should sleep out here—this is a perfectly nice couch. Maybe you could put some—"

"Yeah, right," Miaow says. "But you don't know what he's been going through."

Fon leans forward and, in her sweetest and most cheerful tone, says in Thai, "You're being unforgivably rude. These wonderful *farang*, who don't even know your mother, have given up their afternoon and their evening to help her. They've been with her for almost fifteen hours, and Joyce hasn't even eaten. They may have prevented something terrible."

Miaow closes her eyes for a moment. When she opens them, she lowers her head and makes a *wai*, her fingertips almost touching her forehead, and says to Joyce, and then to Willis, "Forgive me. My Auntie Fon has just reminded me that you were my mother's angels today. I was rude and . . . and—"

"And frightened," Joyce says. "We would have been frightened, too. We *have* been frightened. But please, listen to us and don't call your father. There's no reason to upset him now. He can't *change* anything, whether he's here or not, and the best thing you can both do for your mother is to leave her alone until she's awake again. Let *her* decide how and when to talk to him. If she were in here with us, she'd ask the same thing. Will you promise me not to call him?"

"Wait," Fon says. "Miaow. Your mother told you about this, didn't she? About the first pregnancies—"

"She said one," Miaow says.

"Well, there were two. But she told you she'd miscarried before, didn't she?"

Miaow is studying her the way she might look at a chess opponent. "Yes."

"Have you told your father?"

Miaow looks from her to Joyce, then to Willis. "No."

"Why not?"

"Because she made me promise not to."

"Because," Joyce says, "she's the one who has to tell him. And you know what? He'll be home soon, anyway. It's probably just a matter of an hour or two. Isn't that right?"

"I suppose," Miaow says.

"Oh, and when she *is* awake," Joyce says, "take her whatever she wants. What's she eating a lot of lately?"

"Tangerine slices and yogurt." Willis makes a face. "And . . . ummmm, maraschino cherries?" The empty jar is right in front of her on the table, silently reproaching her. What kind of daughter *is* she anyway?

"That's ghastly," Joyce says. "But if that's what . . . Do you have those things here?"

"The tangerines and the yogurt." At least she, Poke, and Edward had gotten *those*.

"Two out of three," Joyce says. "But I'll tell you, that's no diet for a healthy pregnancy. Are your English reading skills at the same level as your conversation?"

"I read better than I talk," she says.

Joyce, glancing down at the pages on the table, says, "George Bernard *Shaw*? My, my. I'll send over some pamphlets tomorrow, dietary stuff and—"

"I'll bring them," Willis says.

"Yes, Willis, of *course* you'll bring them." Joyce is clearly amused, and Willis sees it and stares a hole in the floor.

"Thank you, Willis—*Will*," Miaow says. "I'd like that." Willis glances at her and then turns again to the balcony, which he seems to find fascinating. "So," Miaow says. "Just so I'm sure I understand, Rose is okay? The baby is okay? For now, I mean?"

"Absolutely," Joyce says in English as Fon says approximately the same thing in Thai, and Willis says "Yes" to the balcony. Joyce adds, "But it's a fragile situation, especially emotionally. You don't want to do anything to upset the applecart."

"The apple—"

"It's a saying. Just, you know, don't disrupt the order of things. If you keep reading Shaw, you'll find he wrote a play with that title."

Miaow says, "Oh."

Joyce looks at her watch, and a vertical line appears between her eyebrows. "Where *is* your father anyway? Look at the time."

"Where he is . . . it's hard to explain. But he's not doing any-thing . . . *you* know."

"I should hope not," Joyce says. "That young woman in there doesn't need drama. She needs love, she needs quiet, she needs to be waited on, and she's going to have to spend a *lot* of time in bed for the next six or eight weeks, at the very least. Is your father up for that?"

"He's up for anything," Miaow says. She taps the phone in her pocket without even knowing she's doing it. "It's my *mother* who's going to be the problem."

FIFTY MINUTES AFTER they've left, she overrules all of them and pulls out her phone. She dials Rafferty's number and listens to it ring. When it kicks over to voice mail, she hangs up, feeling a little ripple of uneasiness radiate out from the center of her chest.

35

You Could Fold Him Up and Mail Him

"GOT EVERYTHING?" KANG asks.

"Of course I do. It's in the Jeep, most of it." She's jumpy. He's never seen her jumpy before. "What about you? Did you get the machines?"

"I'll do that last. That'll tip him off. A change like that—"

"If you dosed him, he's out cold," she says. "You could fold him up and mail him, and he wouldn't know."

"Right," he says, feeling the quarter dose of dope flowing smoothly through his own system. It would have put a smaller man under, but at his weight it just softens the edges. Maybe he should go up and give the guy the last three-quarters of the syringe. Make him easier to handle. "I'll . . . uhh, I'll go up and check on him."

"Just get the fucking machines. They'll slow us down."

"Okay," he says, but he stays where he is. He wants either to give the shot to the patient or use it on himself. At this point he's pissed off and apprehensive enough that it sounds like a good idea to take a little more edge off.

She shifts from foot to foot. In anyone else it would look uneasy, but she doesn't *get* uneasy. "If the cops are really getting involved—"

"You think I'd make that up?"

"—and we're not coming back here," she says, "I want my money."

Here it comes. "I've only got part of it."

She goes as still as a photograph, her eyes fixed on his, and he remembers with some force just how dangerous she is. "Why do you only have part of it? How much of it *do* you have? Where's the rest?"

"Someplace safe."

"You asshole," she says in English. "You've spent some."

"No, no, I—"

"Or you're going to cheat me. Is that it, you big freak? After what I went through to get the money, to be with those men, to go to the banks? Are you *seriously* thinking about cheating me?" And she reaches down to the table beside her and grabs the handle of a teapot and swings it upward, inscribing a fan of pale brown liquid that seems to hang glittering in the air as she brings her arm back and heaves the pot at his head. Cold tea slaps his left cheek and gets into the empty eye socket, and the pot hits the wall beside him in an explosion of pottery shards and tea. "I'll kill you," she says, leaning toward him, her hands rigid at her sides and her fists clenched. "Do you think I won't?" She picks up the Louis Vuitton purse, and her hand comes back up with a little black automatic in it.

"Right," he says. "Good idea. Shoot me. Then *you* get rid of him, *you* carry out the machines and the other stuff, *you* finish wiping the place down. Oh, yeah, and *you* figure out where the rest of the money is."

"Why isn't it here?"

"Because," he says, his voice grating even more than usual, "you never, *ever* put all the money in any single place. Suppose we couldn't come back here? Suppose somebody found it? Suppose the building burned down? Suppose, suppose."

"How much is here?"

"About a hundred fifty thousand US."

"That's *nothing*," she says. The gun is pointed at his very con-siderable center mass. "We've taken almost nine hundred—"

"You take it all," he says. "There have been some ex—"

"Of course I'll take it all, and then another . . ." She closes her eyes for a moment, and he tenses for a jump, but they open again. "Another four hundred. That'll leave you three-fifty."

This is not the time to raise the issue of sharing expenses. "You'll get it."

"You bet your life I'll get it. Now, bring the heavy stuff down to the front hall so we can drag it out."

I T M I G H T H A V E been an hour since the sound of the Jeep had cut through the fog of the drugs and grabbed Buddy's attention; the engine was loud and the valves tapped, and he'd heard it before, but only once or twice. He thinks the two of them keep it garaged somewhere and come and go mainly in taxis. Even then, they get out of the cab at the building at the intersection and then walk the rest of the way in. He never hears an engine, never knows one of them has arrived until he hears the front door close. So the Jeep: it's *another* change, and certainly another piece of bad news.

The way he figured it when he heard those valves clacking away, he had two choices: He could let it discourage him or he could let it terrify him. He chose terror—not that it was entirely in his power to do otherwise—because he thought the fear might spur him into an even tighter focus, even more productive activity. And it has; he's been furiously busy since then, with a couple of drifty, nauseating intermissions for the dope to have its way with him, but when he's back, he works feverishly. Stretched thin by his new level of urgency, he jumps halfway out of his skin when he hears something bang into a wall downstairs. There have been arguments before, shouting at times, but he's rarely heard anything that suggests personal violence. Maybe, he hopes, one of them has killed the other.

As frightened as he is of the monster, he hopes *she's* not the one who's still alive.

The bobby pin is in his mouth, the cast is sawed down to a few inches below his knee, probably enough, probably time to quit, after he breaks off this last piece. The bed is full of plaster dust and linen threads, and he's taken all the skin off the bleeding knuckle of his right index finger, scraping it over and over again across the broken edge of the cast to get the longest possible draw on the saw. In between the interludes of focus, he's still occasionally caught off guard by an opioid wave or two, but they don't disorient him as much as they used to. Plus, he's heaved out everything that was in his system, so vomiting is no longer a problem.

But the bang on the wall demands attention. One or both of them might . . .

He snaps the potentially final piece from the cast, but there's a lot of linen beneath it, and it won't come free in his hands. He's twisting it back and forth, trying to break the threads, when he hears the heavy steps on the stairs.

There isn't time to do everything, so he chooses the big ones: lay the Levi's flat beside him, pull up the blankets. No time for the cuffs. They're gaping open and empty, so he slides his hands back beneath them, scraping the index finger yet again, slipping a finger into the curve of each cuff to tug it, he hopes, out of sight, with the backs of his hands resting on the rail four inches below the one from which the cuffs hang. If the big man doesn't turn on the light, if this is just a quick bed check from the door, he might get away with it. Otherwise it's over. Assuming it's not over already and that's why the big man is coming. He closes his eyes, wills his body to stop shaking, and waits.

The creak of a hinge announces the door's opening, but then there's nothing. Maybe he's in luck and it's just a final look in preparation for . . . well, for whatever they plan to do.

But then the giant begins to walk toward him, his weight prompting complaints from the cheap floorboards. Normally he goes to Buddy's right, where the IV setup is, but this time he goes to the left, the side where the chair that once held Buddy's Levi's is—now, in Buddy's imagination, the size of an aircraft carrier and empty, empty, empty. Surely *this* time the man will notice.

He keeps coming, though, until Buddy can feel the sheer bulk, the *gravity* of the man standing beside him, only a couple of feet from the head of the bed, not moving. Then there's the almost inaudible susurrus of skin moving over cloth, and the man grunts slightly. Buddy knows the giant is bending down, because he can smell the beer on the man's breath. Something touches the outside of his arm, just an inch or two up from the lower end of his biceps, *pressing*, feeling for, for . . . what? The *whatever* it is apparently isn't there, because the fingertip—and that's what it is, a fingertip—is lifted, and then it touches him again, an inch or so farther up the muscle, and he hears a satisfied grunt and then feels a prick and a burning sensation. Inadvertently, he moans.

In English the big man says, "Shut up," and wobbles the needle back and forth a few times out of sheer spite, yanks it, and turns away. Buddy hears him return to the door. "Sleep tight," the man says, and the door closes.

He didn't use the IV. Why wouldn't he . . .

Because, Buddy realizes with a jolt that seems to send ice water coursing through his veins, the IV is *slow*. It's a drip, and the anesthetic is diluted by the saline solution that carries it.

They're in a hurry.

Injected directly into a vein, he remembers from the bad old days, a drug reaches the brain in less than a minute.

He forces himself to remain still, almost hearing the clock of his consciousness tick, until the heavy footsteps make the turn on the stairs and continue descending, and then he sits up, flips the blanket down so he can rip off that final piece of plaster, the one that will let him bend his knee, that will . . . that will . . . let him . . . So, not

not

diluted, but *straight*. Not

(*a wave*)

dripped but

all at once.

How fast will it

will he have enough time to

The thoughts are gone as though they've popped like soap bubbles, as though they've slipped down a mental mail chute, and all he's left with is the pressure of his fingers on the plaster cast, the resistance as he tries to tear the linen holding that one last piece, and then the dope picks him up sideways, twirls him in the air like a lariat, and slams him into a solid wall of hard gleaming black shine.

36

The Perfect Dive

THE CANAL IS wider than Rafferty imagined it would be, five or six meters across with a two-foot wall on either side, and it's black and sluggish, and it *stinks*.

"A breath of old Bangkok," Arthit says. "Miles of sewage." He's standing at the foot of the three steps leading up to the bridge, his iPhone in his hand. He's had it to his ear, obviously waiting for something, and he lowers it as they approach.

Standing behind Arthit and peering at the latecomers are two cops Rafferty doesn't know, two battered long-haulers rather than—judging from the disappointed twist of her mouth—the broad-shouldered, flat-bellied warriors of Clemente's mental stereotype. They both have the dragged-behind-a-car look of lifers who've lost a few rounds. Softly, Rafferty says, "Be still my beating heart," and is rewarded by a snicker from Anand, who is behind Clemente.

Looking at Rafferty, Arthit says, "What's the phone for?"

"Right, well, this is someone whose name I can't tell you and who would prefer it if you don't see his face."

From the phone's speaker come the words, "I'd disguise my fucking voice if I could."

"This is the cop in charge," Rafferty says to the phone. "He's a friend of mine." He holds up the phone to show Arthit a man with a brown paper shopping bag over his head. The bag has eyeholes cut into it, and a pair of glasses rest on a papery nose bump, the glasses' wings pressing the bag against the sides of the man's head. "Meet the one who got away," Rafferty says. "He's going to tell us whether we're in the right spot and give us the benefit of whatever else comes to mind if we are."

"Have you got earbuds?" Arthit says. "The phone is too loud. And can you turn down your screen brightness? No point in actually illuminating a target for them."

"I knew you'd be pleased," Rafferty says. "No, I don't have any goddamn earbuds."

"I do." Anand thumbs back over his shoulder in the direction from which they've come. "In the car."

"Hurry," Arthit says. To Rafferty he says, "Hold on." He puts his own phone to his ear and says, "You there?"

Rafferty's phone says, "She brought me in via the road. From what I can see, I got no idea where you are now."

Clemente says, "Tell your friend he doesn't have to look so silly. He can just put something over the camera on his phone."

"I'm okay the way I am," Larry Finch says.

Obviously getting no response on his own phone, Arthit takes Rafferty's, puts it to his free ear, and says, in a low voice, "Thanks for your help. We're going in on a bridge over the canal from the far side because we think they'll hear us if we come up the road. Hang on a minute, and I'm going to turn the camera toward the building that's the first thing on the road. We're in back of it, and it's pretty dark, but—"

"What's it called?

"Trinity House."

A pause as Arthit pans the phone over the dark building on the other side of the bridge. Then the man with the bag over his head says, "That's *it*. I'm ninety percent sure. *Trinity*. Unbelievable. A Thai cop who can do the job."

"It arranges adoptions," Arthit says. "Did you ever hear children?"

"Oh, Jesus," Larry Finch says. "Is that what it was? I thought it was probably a school."

Clemente says, "So there could be kids."

"I haven't been able to rule it out," Arthit says. He holds up his own phone. "Waiting right now to find out for certain."

Clemente says, "Great."

Arthit says into Rafferty's phone, "The entrance you went through when Lala took you inside. Which end of the building was it? The one facing the adoption agency or the one on the other side?"

"Other side, the far side."

"So if we have guns pointed at that door, we'd be shooting in the direction of the adoption agency."

"Yeah," Larry Finch says. "But there could be a door on the other side, too. They took me in where they took me in, and next thing I knew, I was upstairs, and after that I was chained to the bed, but there could be—"

"We'll certainly take a look," Arthit says. Anand is suddenly back with them, handing a pair of earbuds to Rafferty. Rafferty puts one earpiece in, leaving the other one dangling.

"This okay?" he says to Arthit. "I'll jack it into the phone when you're finished and relay what he says."

Arthit nods approval and hands him the phone. "Stay back, Poke. Don't get between us and the buildings. I'll stick near you now, just in case your source there sees anything that might be helpful as we move into position, but after that you'll be on your own. You two," he says with a nod at the other cops, "get going." To the one on his left, he says, "You knock on Trinity's door and see whether any staff or kids are inside. If they are, you know the drill—get them to the building's far side, away from windows." To the other one, he says, "You take the middle of the road and hold it until you can't anymore." He says into his phone again, "Got anything?" and shakes his head and disconnects. He takes a slow look at everyone in the circle. "Is your guy certain, Poke?"

"Like I said, ninety percent," Larry Finch says. "And tell him to kill them both."

As HE CLIMBS the stairs to the bridge, Rafferty has to hold his nose against the smell, but he can sense it even when he breathes through his mouth. The rain has turned to a fine drizzle, and although the clouds are starting to break up and drift apart, they're still masking the moon. It's dark enough so that the two older cops disappear into the gloom as soon as they go down the steps and head for the building that's occupied by Trinity House.

"Stay close together until we're there," Arthit whispers. "Then at least a couple or three arms' lengths apart. No point in making it any easier for them than it has to be." He has taken the lead, and Anand, Rafferty, and Clemente follow him across the canal. When they're on solid ground, Rafferty inhales again, and even over the stench of the canal, he gets the sharp edge of Anand's perspiration. He wonders briefly whether Clemente, just behind him, can smell his.

"Where are you?" Larry Finch says in his ear. "Can't see nothing."

"It's cloudy, and we're under some trees," Rafferty whispers. "You'll see better when we get a little moonlight."

"Good. Only four of you?"

"Six, counting the two at Trinity House."

"Not very many."

"I really can't chat now, Larry. I'm going to hold the phone in front of me so you can see where we're going. Call out when you recognize something."

"To the left," Arthit whispers. "Follow the canal." He's coming back from a short look ahead. "No talking." He has an automatic in his hand, and Anand unholsters at the sight of it. Behind him Rafferty hears the snap on Clemente's holster, too.

"Wait for me, Poke," she whispers. "We'll walk together until we get closer. You shouldn't be in front of anyone with a gun."

He steps aside until she's beside him, and at that moment the moonlight shoulders its way through a small opening in the clouds and Rafferty sees a curl of heavier drizzle, like the ripple of a shower curtain, angle toward them, and then it cools his face. With the moon's help, he can see the other building about thirty yards away, just an unadorned shoe box of indeterminate color. There are lights on, in one or two ground-floor rooms at the end nearer to Trinity House, a pair of pale rectangles about ten feet apart, maybe in different rooms, maybe not. Everything else is dark.

"Can you see this, Larry?" Rafferty whispers into the phone, and he holds it up, the camera pointed at the building.

"Looks right to me," Finch says. "What I saw best was the door, so let's get around to the far side."

Arthit has heard the whispering and drops back. Rafferty says in his ear, "He says it looks good so far. Wants to see the entrance."

"Does he?" Arthit says, clearly thinking about something else. He snaps his fingers, and Clemente and Anand both turn. "Anand," Arthit whispers, "get up there and check the road. Make sure Kunchai is there." Anand takes off at a run.

Rafferty touches Arthit on the shoulder, points to the phone and then to the far side of the apartment building. "He wants to see the *door*," he whispers.

"Surely we know we're right by now," Arthit says.

Clemente says, "I'll go with him."

"Do what she says," Arthit says to Poke. He turns away, moving in the direction Anand has taken.

"I'm in the lead," Clemente says brusquely. "Keep it like that."

Rafferty says, "Yes, ma'am." Into the phone he whispers, "Here we go."

"If they've got somebody in there," Finch says, "hurry."

Gun in hand, Clemente precedes him. In his head Rafferty instinctively maps the area from above: to his left the straight black stretch of the canal; to his right the short street with the big building at the intersection and the small one at the dead end; the cop ringing the doorbell at Trinity House; the other one in the street, cutting it off as a means of escape. He envisions Anand going to make sure the cop named Kunchai is in position, Arthit between the buildings, waiting for Anand's return, and the two of them—he and Clemente—hurrying toward the smaller building, bearing left into the darkness and bending low as they pass the two lit windows. He says to Clemente, "Seems to me we're kind of spread out."

"Me, too," Clemente says, "but it's not my job to say so." The moon disappears again, and the night darkens considerably. Into her microphone Clemente says, "We're almost to the front of the building." Whatever Arthit says, it's audible only through the earpiece she's wearing.

And then they're there, and Rafferty says into the phone, "What do you think?" and Larry Finch says, "Absolutely. They're at the far right corner on the ground floor, and the hospital room is right above them, facing the canal. Get in there and *blow them to pieces*," and then there are shouts from the area of Trinity House, more shouts closer at hand, and over the confusion of voices, Rafferty hears a shot.

HE'S IN AND out, like the sand on a beach in between waves. There's a disorienting rush as the drug recedes, in some kind of rhythm that might be tied to the rate of his heartbeat, and there he is, out from under its weight again for a moment or two, alone in the room and *focused*, sitting up in the bed, tearing frantically at the linen, and then the drug comes on again, rushing over him, holding him under, and it's all he can do to remain sitting upright as the world whirls and disintegrates, leaving him with nothing except fear and, between his fingers, the texture of linen.

Learn to use the rhythm.

He's back, feeling the sweat slide down his body, using the cool spots where it evaporates as pushpins in his consciousness, points of location to give him a center in his own wet, slick skin, and the linen is frayed and thin now. If he had any strength at all, he could *rend* it like the garments people were always rending in the Old Testament, Abraham and Isaac, how could *any* father . . . and he's fading again, so he rubs the scalped knuckle over the broken edge of the cast *hard* and follows the flare of pain back to his task, and *there*, it's done. The piece has come free. His knee is bare. He sits there, rocking back and forth and weeping, flexing the knee, until he hears the footsteps on the stairs.

And he knows that this is the final visit.

So he's up, fighting for balance, grabbing his pants, not so much from modesty as a kind of confused gratitude because they've delivered him from the rigidity of the cast. The ankle and foot are still heavy and immobile in their plaster boot, but he can stump along on it, weighty as it is, and as he does, heading for the window and looking frantically for something he can pick up and use to defend himself, the footsteps get louder and closer, and then, like something bursting through a paper wall, there's *shouting* from somewhere down the street, men yelling at each other, and from downstairs Lala is yelling, "Kang! *Kang!*"

And then he hears a shot.

He pulls the blinds aside to see a world that, like him, is sliding in and out of light as ragged clouds admit and block the moon.

Below, between him and the canal, men are running, men in police uniforms, and he has a sudden vision of opening his eyes once to see two policemen peering down at him, and one of them was a fat-faced piggish man with wide nostrils, and as the moon gleams down again, pouring cold silver on the scene below, the cop in the lead looks straight up at the window—he knows *which* window—directly at Buddy; and that's who it is, the pig-nosed man. Their eyes meet, and then the cop is literally baring his teeth, glaring up, his teeth white in his dark face. Two other cops rush toward the pig-nosed man's group as though to join or, possibly, intercept it, and Buddy knows that he can't use *that* window—even if he doesn't break his neck, he'll drop into the arms of the cops. He turns and lurches toward the door of his room.

THE SHOT COMES from somewhere between the two buildings. It baffles and disorients Rafferty; he wastes a useless moment trying to convince himself it came from *inside* the house, but then there's another shot, also from between the buildings. More shouting, from the same direction.

One at a time, the lit windows in the house go dark.

Clemente says, "They're *in* there. But who the hell—"

Then there's a confusion of running men coming out of the darkness ten or fifteen yards away. One of them is Arthit, shouting orders that no one seems to be heeding, and then there's another shot, from the general direction of Trinity House, and Clemente grabs Rafferty and yanks him around the corner of the building to put its walls between him and the shooter.

"I'm okay," he says, but Clemente stiff-arms him, holding him in place against the wall until they both hear screaming from inside, and Clemente says, "A woman."

"Gotta be Lala," Rafferty says, taking advantage of her lapse in attention to sidestep her grip. But he doesn't go anywhere, just listens to Larry Finch shrieking in his earpiece, "That's *her*, the bitch! Get her, get her *get*—" Poke pulls the earplug out.

Another shot is fired, closer than the earlier ones, and then three policemen, their faces unfamiliar, round the corner, guns in hand, coming from the direction of the road, and head for the front door, which is unexpectedly yanked open from inside by one of the biggest men Rafferty has ever seen. The giant's single eye widens at the sight of the cops, and then the door bangs closed and there's the grating sound of some kind of bar being thrown across it, followed by the metallic snap of a latch.

The next shot nearly punctures Rafferty's left eardrum; it comes from a gun fired only three or four feet behind him, held by the cop he recognizes, with a shock, as the one at the end of Patpong— Teera-something, *Teerapat*, that was it—and he fires four times at the closed door, but the only results are little flares of wooden splinters exploding into the air. The cop furrows his brow as he glances at Rafferty and Clemente, but then his eyes widen and he brings the gun around to point it, two-handed, directly at them, but here comes Anand, at a sprint, and Teerapat backs away and literally screams in frustration, firing a couple of times into the air, perhaps a signal, then pops his clip and rams in another. The other three cops stare at him, confused and openmouthed, and Teerapat shouts at them to split up: two through this door and the other to go around and meet the men at the door on the other side, to take out the doors and go in, shoot anyone who resists, then meet in the middle and radio him when the building is clear. He whirls, gives Rafferty and Clemente one more furious glare, and runs in the general direction of the canal. Two of the cops charge the door with their shoulders, bounce off, and begin trying to kick it in.

Two more cops come into view. This time it's Arthit, with one of the veterans, Kunchai, in pursuit. He stops at the sight of them and says, "You all all right?"

"Sure," Clemente says. "The lead cop here followed me all over Bangkok tonight, but I thought we'd lost him."

"You probably did," Arthit says to her, "but your visits to get the boxes this morning tipped him off. He's probably here to erase the evidence." There's a shrill metallic protest from the bar the giant threw inside the door, and the two cops raise their legs and kick it once more, together, and it flies open and one of them screams, a mixture of surprise and terror, and they both fire indiscriminately into the corridor.

While they're still shooting, Arthit spreads his arms wide, leans forward, and rushes Clemente, Rafferty, and Anand, bulldozing them away from the open door, toward the street side of the building. When they're out of the line of fire, he says to Anand and Clemente, "Both of you, come with me. Poke, the action, if there *is* any outside the building, is going to be on that side, between here and the canal. I want you *right here*, on the street side of this building, hugging a wall and away from the windows, away from all of it, and I want you to stay there until you hear me call you."

A little cluster of shots comes from inside the building, followed by some confused-sounding shouting.

"*Now,*" Arthit says, grabbing Rafferty's shoulder and pushing. "Get around that corner and stay there, do you hear me?"

"Sure, but—"

"Go," Arthit says, giving him another shove, one that almost knocks him off his feet. He has to take a few steps to remain upright, and then he lets that turn into a run that carries him around the corner at the end of the building. He stops there a moment between the building and the little road, breathing heavily and seeing lights going on in windows that must belong to Trinity House. He hopes that's all about getting kids out of the line of fire. And then, as he shakes his head and steadies his breathing and works his shoulders to loosen them up, he hears glass breaking somewhere above him.

BUDDY IS ON his knees in the middle of the hallway, clutching his jeans to his chest, having been caught unaware by an enormous wave, a tsunami, that took him off his feet and down onto the point of one elbow, the pain bringing him back but also telling him *broken*. And as badly as it hurts, he knows that the drugs, which must be opioids, are shielding him from the worst of it.

Below him Lala is shouting at Kang, and Kang makes some strangled reply, and then Buddy hears pounding on the downstairs door—no, on *both* doors—and a head-to-toe pulse of terror brings him to his feet, the elbow forgotten, and he opens the door and barges through, dragging the heavy, weighted cast, to find himself, bewilderingly, *back in his room*—the bed, the machines—and he knows he's been turned around, that he must have lost it again when he fell, and as another wave of bone-shredding weariness picks him up and rocks him, he bites down on his tongue, *hard*, and he finds his way back into that hallway. The door he wants is opposite this one, on the other side of the hallway.

What sound like a million shots are fired below.

He pulls himself into focus and wobbles across the hall, dragging the jeans behind him without even being aware of it, hurrying for the first time without worrying about the thump of the cast. At the door he tries the knob. And—there *is* a God—it's unlocked.

Below him people pound up and down the hall, shouting at one another, kicking in what must be doors, and then there's a volley of gunfire, like amplified popcorn, followed by a command that sounds both furious and terrified, and he hears heavy feet, *booted* feet, at least two people, hammering their way up the stairs.

He steps into the new room and locks the door behind him as they make the turn on the stairs, and then time goes away again, and the next thing he knows, he's standing in front of the closed, dusty window, which (God is still here) isn't locked; the latch is harmlessly unengaged. But the window won't *move*, it won't budge. It's been painted closed.

The men who were coming up the stairs are on the second floor now. He hears the door of the room he was in bang against the wall, hears men speculating about the hospital bed and opening the closet, and then someone tries the knob of the door he's just come through, the door that's keeping them from him. There's an enraged burst of Thai and a heavy kick and then another kick, and someone hurls himself against the door, and Buddy has *no way to open the window.*

He wraps his hand in the jeans and swings at the glass with all his strength, but it's not enough, and the glass holds and the jeans slide over the window's smooth surface and he lurches forward, off balance, and his broken elbow hits the wall. Once again the pain sharpens him, but for what? The door behind him shivers in its frame again as he comes face-to-face with the end of everything: one thin, transparent pane of glass between him and the entire world, and he has nothing he can use to break it.

But he *does*, of course, he does. He puts a shoulder against the wall to steady himself, raises the foot with the extremely heavy cast on it, and puts it through the windowpane.

A HAND LANDS heavily on Rafferty's shoulder as the glass rains down, and he turns to see a cop he doesn't know. The cop's gun is unholstered, not pointing directly at Rafferty but close enough to cause discomfort. The cop, looking quickly back over his shoulder for reinforcements, nervously demands, in barely passable English, to know who Rafferty is and what he's doing there. It's obvious that the last thing he was expecting was a *farang*, and he's uncertain about the protocol.

The only thing that comes into Rafferty's mind is a game he used to play with Miaow when she was learning English and he was learning Thai, a quick-spoken mix-up of the two languages, nonsense but with enough badly pronounced Thai words laced into the English to keep her listening until she realized it was meaningless and started to laugh. All Rafferty wants to do is confuse the man further, keep the gun pointing away from him, but instead the man seems to be *listening*, leaning closer to Rafferty, his face screwed up with the strain of comprehending a stream of gibberish with just enough mangled Thai to make him think the failure to understand might be his, and as Rafferty is running out of inspiration, a shout goes up from the other side of the house, the side with the canal on it. More shouting, three or four voices now, and the cop shifts his weight from foot to foot and then makes a grab at Rafferty's arm, gets his sleeve but nothing more, and turns and runs to see what he's missing.

The sound of the glass forgotten in the aftermath of the encounter, Rafferty moves to follow, thinking Arthit or the others might need help. As he reaches the corner of the house, he hears an impact behind him, the kind of sound a fifty-kilo bag of rice might make when it falls from a truck, accompanied by the percussive *whuff* of someone having the breath knocked clean out of him, and he turns to see a man wearing a T-shirt, no trousers, and what seems to be a white boot pull himself up and take off at a limping, unsteady run around the far corner of the house, leaving a pair of jeans on the grass.

Startled and distracted by a concentrated burst of gunfire from the other side of the house and his concern about Arthit and the others, it takes Rafferty just a moment too long to put it together, to recognize what he's looking at.

* * *

YES, IT'S A canal. He was right all along, fuck her and her
blinds, it *was* reflected water, and there's a knot of policemen off
to his right, most of the way toward the door to the apartment
house he just jumped out of, but they're all focused on something
a little more than halfway between the house and the canal, a
little garden or something with a wire fence around it. He knows,
if they should see him, that he can't *outrun* them, but there's no
one who can keep up with him in the water, so he accelerates
toward it. His adrenaline and a now-unfamiliar surge of hope are
fighting the drugs, allowing him to keep his goal in sight, letting
him coordinate his legs so that even with the cast he's doing a
pretty good imitation of a run. He lopes to his left to get a little
farther from the cluster of cops surrounding the garden, recog-
nizing the pig-faced man, seeing him bend down and pull up a big
plant or something, like a box of dirt, and then he steps aside and
there's an outburst of gunfire and a long, wavering female scream.
But now Buddy is scrambling to the top of the low wall beside the
canal and feeling the muscles of his body, his young, undamaged,
unmarked body, stretch themselves into the ideal racing dive,
muscles lengthening, his entire frame elongating into *the perfect
dive*, an arrow that will pierce the surface of the water without a
splash, with virtually no loss of momentum, but he can't straighten
one arm, there's a whole fireworks show of pain from the elbow, and
he staggers, and his foot slips, and his momentum pulls him in sideways, and there's *something wrong with the water*, it's black and thick
and foul, and he's not swimming, he's being pulled down, and something heavy heavy heavy on his right foot is pulling . . .

IT'S A TUNNEL. They're shooting into a tunnel. Four of them,
just emptying their guns like hunters spotting their first prey very

late in the season. They're so intent on blowing to smithereens whoever's in there—and it can only be Kang or Lala or both— that they don't even glance at Rafferty as he hurtles past, wanting to call out to the man in the cast—Buddy, it has to be Buddy—but afraid of attracting their attention. He sees Buddy pull himself up onto the low wall and then totter and flail and go over, and his heart sinks at the thought of the water, but then he's on top of the barrier and over it and into the air, but he's already lost sight of Buddy. Buddy is down there in the dark, in the opaque muck of that awful water, and then, just as he feels a vibration in his pocket, Rafferty hits it, and it's colder than he expected, and he just has time to gasp before he goes under.

Paralyzingly dark, viscous, even *lumpy* in ways he absolutely refuses to think about, and he makes a few flailing, circling sweeps with his hands, hoping to touch Buddy, but then he needs to breathe; he had shut off the gasp because he was afraid of inhaling this water, and his lungs hadn't filled, so he pushes to the surface and scans frantically for a landmark of some kind, but the wall looks the same from yard to yard, and he doesn't even know which direction he's facing. There was a tree, he remembers, where they crossed on the bridge, but it's still quite a ways off even though he's moving slowly toward it, so there's one question answered: the path of the current. It's flowing toward the tree. Whatever that's worth. The moon reappears, right on cue, to show him that the tree is to his right now; it was to his left when he jumped in, but now it's to his right, so he must have turned around while he was under. It looked to him like Buddy hit the water only a foot or two away from the wall, but he could have drifted anywhere by now—across the canal, farther down toward the tree, he could be anywhere.

No.

The *boot*. The boot is weighted. It will drag him down.

The current has taken Rafferty six to eight feet from where he jumped in, and now that there's moonlight, he can see that the wall is darker and wetter where he and Buddy went in, and he strokes toward the splash marks, grabs a huge breath, and forces himself down into the dark, eyes tightly closed, waving his arms like a conductor, trying to explore the largest possible area, and just as he begins to surface again, his forearm hits something hard. With his lungs bursting, he brings the other arm around and finds cold skin—a shoulder maybe, and yes, above it a neck and a head—and fingers find his arm as he gets the man's neck into the crook of his arm and pushes for the surface.

But Dell is clawing at him, ripping at his skin with his nails, and when their heads break water, he screams and fights blindly, his eyes squeezed closed, and Rafferty tightens the arm around the man's neck and says, "*Edward*. Edward sent me, *Edward*."

The man goes absolutely inert. With his arm still around Buddy Dell's neck, Rafferty sidestrokes—dragging Dell behind him, just deadweight—toward the wall, where he sees Anand bending down toward them, his eyes enormous, and ten or fifteen meters behind him, in a circle of flashlights, Arthit in a heated discussion with Teerapat. In the scrubby little garden, a cop kneels to drag someone, a woman, from a cave of some kind. Anand reaches down, and Rafferty gives him Buddy Dell's arm, and Anand pulls him out.

Once he's on top of the wall, Rafferty watches the cop pick up the woman, who has the floppy jointlessness that comes only with death, by the ankles. He carries her, upside down, to the edge of the garden and drops her headfirst. She lands in a heap. It has to be Lala, but she's so much *smaller* than she'd been in his imagination. From here she looks like a child.

There's a choke and a cough from behind him, and Buddy Dell says, "*Edward*."

37

From Here

THE KNOB TWISTS beneath his hand while he's still trying to unlock it, and Miaow is standing there, index finger raised to her lips, but her eyes double as they appraise him—his filthy, dripping clothes, the pool of water at his feet, and then she takes a huge step back, raising a hand to cover her nose and mouth and using the other to fan the air away from her and toward him again.

He says, "Has she come—" but Miaow is already nodding, moving even farther from him and hissing, "But *shhhhhhhhh*."

"She's *okay?*"

"*Yes*, she's—" Miaow is halfway into the living room by now, with one hand still over her nose, and she's using a fierce whisper. "She's . . . Everything is okay, but she needs to sleep. I even called you, but—"

Rafferty holds up his right hand and uses his left to pull his phone, dark, dead, and dripping, from his pocket. He shows it to her and shrugs.

She takes another step back at the sight of the phone. "Where *were* you, in a pile of poop?"

"Yes," Rafferty says. "Just hold your goddamn nose and—"

She's waving her free hand, palm down, meaning *too loud*. "You have to let her sleep. She's . . . um, she's had a hard day."

"And . . . and . . . and she's okay, I mean . . ." He runs out of words. "She's—"

"Yes and yes. How can you *possibly* smell like—"

"It was Edward's father. But what about—"

"You *found* him?" Instinctively, she takes a step toward him but then backs away again. "Is he alive? I mean . . . does he smell as bad as you do?"

"Exactly the same." Without even being aware of if, he takes a step toward her. "Miaow, the *baby?*"

"Oh," she says, stepping backward and bumping into the edge of the flat-screen. "I would have told you if anything—"

He sloshes his way toward the couch, dropping the phone on the coffee table. "Thank God."

"You're not going to *sit* there, are you?"

"I'd thought about it."

"Don't. We'll have to throw it away."

He tilts his head down and sniffs. "I guess I'm getting used to it."

"When I was seven," Rose says, and they both turn to see her standing in the bedroom door. "My Uncle Paithoon, who weighed about a hundred and fifty kilos, sat on the board over the outhouse pit, and it broke under his weight. He went over backward, and we had to pull him out by his feet. I thought I would never smell anything like that again, but I was wrong."

"Go back to bed," Miaow says.

"I will, I am. Come in with me, Poke. As terrible as you smell, I need to talk to you."

"I can shower."

"I want to do this now. I need to do it now."

She turns, puts a hand on the doorframe to steady herself, and goes back in.

Miaow whispers, "Don't you *dare* close that door." Then she says, "You're a hero, even if you do stink. Edward will be so happy."

"I try to be useful," he says, and he goes into the bedroom.

Rose is already in bed, the covers pulled protectively up to her chin, even though the room isn't cold. "Sit on the clothes basket," she says. "It's plastic, and I can wash it tomorrow."

"I'll wash it."

"I know," she says as he sits. "I was just being nice. And put it a little farther away."

"Done." He backs it up, almost to the wall, and sits again, and they regard each other in silence. He's about to speak, but Rose holds up a hand.

"Today," she says, "I almost lost the baby."

He says, "I figured. I've been looking up your symptoms for weeks."

She turns her head aside a bit, but her eyes are fixed on his. "You didn't tell me you knew."

"I was afraid that—this sounds silly—that if I said it, it would become real."

She nods, clears her throat, but then she swallows. Without looking at him, she says, "I've lied to you."

"From how frightened you've been," he says, "I thought maybe you'd . . . umm, been through this before."

She says, "Twice." She clears her throat again. "I lost both babies."

"I'm so sorry."

"The fathers . . ." she says, and then she lets it trail off. After a moment of silence, he hears her swallow.

He says, "You were working, right? When you were pregnant those times, you were working."

Her eyes have changed. They're so much more distant she might as well have taken several steps back. "Is that a question? Yes, I was working."

"So—" Rafferty says, and he breaks off and raises one hand.

"You've got to let me get through this. See, the fact that you were working, what that means—to me anyway—is that those guys . . . well, they weren't with you."

"*With me?* I doubt they remembered my name."

"Well, I am," he says. "I'm with you."

She looks at him as though she's waiting for something.

"We're a *team*," he says. "We're the baby-keeping team. You and me."

Rose opens her mouth, but from the living room Miaow says, "What about me?"

"You're on it, too," Rafferty says. "You're our center of gravity; you're what Rose and I revolve around. We couldn't do it without you." He looks up to find her standing in the doorway, one hand still over her nose.

Rose says, "Oh." She looks at Miaow, and says, again, "Oh."

Miaow seizes the moment. "I ate your maraschino cherries."

"I'll get more," Rafferty says. "*Whatever* it takes, we'll do it. We'll bring this baby into the world, into this *team*, in a way that makes him feel welcome."

Miaow says, "Or her."

"So starting now," he says, "you want me to sleep out there so you can't hear me snore, or you want me in here?"

"You do snore," she says. "In here. But sometime we're going to have to talk about this. About that I never told you I had other men's children inside—"

"We will," he says. He finds himself sniffling, and for the first time in a little while he smells himself. He *reeks*. "When we've talked about everything that really matters. When Miaow is grown up and gone, and we're old and looking at each other and wondering where all time went and trying to find a subject we're not both sick of, we'll talk about this, okay?"

"That's a deal," she says. "I want a hug."

He opens his arms, just showing her all of it, all the sodden, filthy mess. "You're joking."

"No. We can buy new blankets. Come here and hug me."

He sits on the edge of the bed and puts an arm gingerly around her shoulders. She makes a choking sound, but when he looks at her, he sees that she's laughing.

"Miaow?" he says. "You want to get in on this?"

"It's okay," Miaow says in the center of the doorway. "I'll hug you from here."

Afterword

THIS STORY REALLY began with Lutanh, and for her I have to thank a very good friend, Bangkok resident Jerry Hopkins, rock journalist extraordinaire and author of thirty-six books, including worldwide bestselling biographies of Elvis Presley and Jim Morrison. Jerry made it possible for me to meet the person who inspired the character, and I don't know what the book would have been without her.

Not that this is literally her story. She and I talked three times, about ninety minutes at a time, in the bar where she worked, while I bought drinks for both of us and then tipped her for her time. She told me about her own childhood in Laos, and every night, other girls in the bar were drawn to the discussion and chimed in with pieces of their own stories, some of which got cemented into the mosaic that is Lutanh in the book. And much of it I simply made up as I went along. It's not meant as an anthropological study and I make no claims for its factual or sociological accuracy.

I had a vague idea when I started writing *Fools' River* that it might be fun to bring together three or four simultaneous stories and see whether I could tell them all in a very compressed span of time, perhaps forty-eight hours. I'd never done anything quite like that before, and I wasn't at all sure I could. As it turned out, things happened even more quickly than I'd anticipated, and it wound up being closer to thirty-six hours. There were times when I literally felt like I should be holding on to my hat.

Much of that energy came from good music. There was lots of

it this time around, including repeated listens to The Gin Blossoms, an upbeat band from the 1990s with a very downbeat history. Energy was also supplied by Tegan and Sarah, Rihanna, Alabama Shakes, the Allman Brothers, the immortal Little Feat, Chris Stapleton, Lyle Lovett, Ryan Adams, Paul Simon, Yeah Yeah Yeahs, Monsieur Perine (thanks, Peter!), The Fratellis, the *Hamilton* cast album, Pixies, Beth Hart, and many, many others.

Several people made substantial contributions to the book at various stages. Among them (in chronological order) are Dr. William Ledger, the Given Foundation Professor Emeritus of Obstetrics and Gynecology at Weill Cornel Medical College, for help with Rose's troubled pregnancy (all mistakes are obviously mine); beta reader of the gods Everett Kaser; editor *par excellence* Juliet Grames; copy editor to the stars Maureen Sugden; the ever-patient and all-knowing Rachel Kowal, who sees these doodles into actual book form; and publisher extraordinaire Bronwen Hruska. I'm blessed to work with everyone on the team Bronwen has assembled at Soho. This is my tenth Soho book, and I know just how fortunate I am.

And I also need to thank the real-life Fran Dependahl, who made a generous donation to a youth literacy organization to have a character named after her, Except for her remarkable self-possession, the actual Fran Dependahl is nothing like the character who bears her name.